# SHORT SHARP SHOCKS
# VOLUME 1

An April Moon Books Publication
Published in arrangement with the authors
Edited by Neil Baker

First Edition 2014
Published in Canada.

www.AprilMoonBooks.com

ISBN: 978–0–9937180–1–4

Dedication

To the Creators out there; the writers, the artists, the performers.
It's far easier to destroy than to create, so thank you for your effort.

*Neil*

# Contents

A Suitable Lack of Control
by
Neil Baker

Welcome to this, the first in a line of anthologies to be published by April Moon Books that will celebrate everything we hold dear.

We have many themes to explore, including optimistic science fiction, giant monsters, daring (yet sadly misguided) adventurers and an homage to the Hammer films I was weaned on; films that influenced our first publication, The Dark Rites of Cthulhu.

However, this first volume deals with a theme that, at first glance, might be easy to pin down, but is in fact as scattered and random as the word suggests:

AMOK!

According to whichever online (or real!) dictionary you consult, amok (or its slightly more amusing sibling, amuck) means *'in a murderously frenzied state'*. It also means *'in a violently raging manner'*. However, my favorite definition might be *'in an undisciplined, uncontrolled, or faulty manner'*, but that's probably because I am British and it sounds more refined, understated and misleading.

In more recent times, the term 'amok' has been replaced by 'going postal', a phrase that, understandably, the U.S. mail service has tried to suppress. We don't really hear of this term any more (thanks, email!), but it was attributed to a spate of workplace killings in the mid to late 80s totaling nearly 40 victims, as office workers, laborers and, yes, mail carriers, went off the deep end. Surprisingly, of the 120 submissions we received for this anthology, none of them concerned postal workers. However, we have included a couple of office-related tales, so the legacy of the phrase is covered.

What, then, does the rest of the anthology consist of?

In putting this book together, I wanted to create a line-up of stories that was as unpredictable as the theme suggests. For that reason, I have included more stories than I would normally publish in any one anthology, about 10 stories more than usual. These tales cover an extraordinary range of genres and styles, from new twists on the zombie trope to ghosts and ghouls. Contract killers rub shoulders with serial killers, while bloodthirsty pigs and alligators go on the rampage alongside foul entities torn from the Mythos. Good people are corrupted, folks are possessed and evil-doers return from the dead. Barbarians fight in a blighted future and spacemen go insane while scientists tamper with forces that will drive them mad. Future wars are fought alongside ancient fantasies and mothers fight to protect their young, while teens experiment with drugs to disastrous effect.

These are stories that do not merely deal with physical rampages; they also examine minds in turmoil, flawed ideologies and the breakdown of rational thought. This is a book to dip into, to enjoy in bite-sized pieces of diseased flesh or, if you are so inclined, to enjoy as one journey; to ride the uncontrolled waves as they crash against each other, overlapping, engulfing.

Thank you for joining us as the world - past, future and imagined - goes ferociously, magnificently, AMOK!

*Neil Baker - Sept. 2014*

AMOK!

# G.A.G.

## by
## Rob E. Boley

G.A.G.
by
Rob E. Boley


MALCOLM SEVER watches his lover Mandy, wearing only a bathrobe, chase an old man through a hardware store's front window. Caked in blood, she's barely recognizable. She makes that horrid noise that all of the Retches make, like a cat choking on a hairball.

The old man screams for help, an instinct from a lost world. Months ago, his plea would have summoned a whole entourage: police officers, ambulances, and news vans. But that was before the G.A.G.. Broken glass grinds under Mandy's bare feet, like a snowman gritting its teeth. Malcolm's cell phone vibrates yet again. He answers, though cell towers haven't operated for months. Only Shades use the phones now.

"Yeah?" he says.

It's Mandy, talking all lowercase and no punctuation: "...ever really love you i mean you are a nerd i once hit a cat with a belt buckle the sky tastes like stale cotton candy i faked an orgasm because your goatee was tickling..."

"Mandy," he says over her, "your body just ran into a hardware store. I'm going in after you. I'll save you. Just like I promised, hon."

"...drunk and there were at least two of them that i remember and the next morning i didnt even care i once jerked off a cocker spaniel hispanics scare me i hated the godfather part two you dont mean anything to me ive only ever used you for..."

"Today I'm going to save the world," he says. What's left of it.


**Nine months ago.**

Malcolm heard about G.A.G. for the first time while smoking on the roof of the Village Tower apartment building. He was with Paul, the crackpot from down the hall. Paul rolled his own smokes, crooked things that stuck to Malcolm's lip and made it bleed.

"You heard about the G.A.G. yet?" asked Paul, blowing smoke into the cold morning air. "What gag?" asked Malcolm.

Below, Mandy crossed the street. They watched as she staggered into the Village's front door. Another late night.

Paul shook his head. "It's an acronym. Stands for Ghosts And Ghouls."

Malcolm rolled his eyes. "Another government conspiracy?"

"Maybe." Paul grunted and flicked his cigarette over the edge of the building. Even that slight movement caused his thick arm muscles to flex dramatically. "The Internet said when someone gets the G.A.G., their mind is torn from the body. They're split in two: a ghost and a mindless body, like a zombie. The radio said last week in Arkansas, an infected priest's ghost sent emails to his congregation - exposing all manner of perversion and corruption - while his body raised hell in a nursing home."

Freed from the body, these Shades sought out loved ones, hated ones, or even just their barber. By interfacing with audio technology, the Shades spoke the harshest truths, every secret once crammed inside their skulls.

"Bullshit."

"Maybe so." Paul shrugged. "But you should consider stocking up on canned food and ammo."

That was Paul's solution to everything.

"I don't have a gun, Paul."

"You want one?"

Malcolm waved a hand dismissively. "What presumably causes G.A.G.?"

"I hear the CIA was testing a new interrogation technique. Other possibilities are the latest flu vaccine, a strain of genetically modified poultry, or a smart phone app."

"Paul, I'm a brain man." That's how Malcolm always referred to his area of scientific inquiry. "And I have to tell you that this is one of your more interesting fringe conspiracies." Malcolm punched Paul's generous biceps. "Did you know that a pound of human brain burns twenty times the calories as a pound of human muscle?"

"Huh."

"It's true. Your brain makes up two percent of your body weight but uses about twenty percent of your body's total energy."

Below, someone yelled. Malcolm glanced down in time to see an old lady sprinting after a teenager. The granny, easily in her sixties, was gaining on the teen.

"So, tell me, Paul, what would a body do with all that extra energy if the brain no longer needs it?"


Mandy moshes through the aisles amidst a crowd of paint cans, shovels, oscillating fans, and power tools. The last scraps of sunlight belly crawl under the hardware store's awning.

While Shades are concerned with secret obsessions, their mindless bodies - known as Retches - just want to bite and screw, spreading the disease. Retches prefer human prey, though they settle for animals or even leather furniture as a last resort.

On the security mirrors, Malcolm sees the old man hiding behind a spackle display. He's clutching a mallet and panting like a dog, but Mandy's too stupid to hear. Her frenzied dance approaches the old man with the mallet.

Near the cash register, Malcolm grabs a cheap flashlight from the check-out display. With shaking hands, he shines a jittery beam of light on the old man.

Blindly, the old man hurls the mallet past Malcolm's head.

Mandy knocks the geezer onto a mound of spackle buckets. As she bites his face and dry humps his abdomen, a look of recognition flashes over the old man's surprised face.

With one breast dangling from under Malcolm's fuzzy blue robe, Mandy spits out a lump of flesh, takes another bite. She's not eating, just biting.

Malcolm's cell vibrates in his pocket. He ignores it, retrieves the mallet.

As he stalks down an aisle, Mandy's voice bursts over the store intercom, the sound cranked to eleven: "...glad that he committed suicide it was like winning the lottery i spit in your coffee i stole mr. pacernick's grade sheet and no one ever knew one time i touched my brother's..."

Damn it. Must hurry now. A noise like that could attract the Gaggle.

Ahead, the old man's whole body flops like a fish out of water and goes still. An icy breeze whistles over Malcolm's skin, the old man's soul swirling upward. His body spasms to life, then he and Mandy lunge at each other in a lustful tangle.

If Malcolm let them go at it, they'd ravage each other for hours, biting and kissing and slobbering and grinding.

Sure, Malcolm's jealous.

Now it's the old man's voice over the intercom. "...bEAT hER a tIME oR tWO bUT sHE hAD iT cOMING i pOISONED a lITTER oF pUPPIES bECAUSE i hATED tHE wHINING i cANT sTAND wHINING iM aFRAID oF nEED i sTOLE fROM tHE..."

Dammit. Malcolm hates togglecase. It gives him a headache.

Malcolm pulls out the hypodermic he borrowed from Paul's medical kit. The old man is on top of Mandy now, hips pounding. Malcolm injects Mandy's ankle with a sedative. She goes limp, but the old man doesn't notice. Malcolm swings the mallet and bashes his skull.

Almost instantly the Shade's voice fizzles on the intercom. "...cHURCH i fUCKED mISSUS mONROE... iN hER oWN lIVING... rOOM aND wIPED mYSELF oFF oN hER cURTAINS aND nEVER... cALLED hER bY... hER fIRST..."

Malcolm fastens zip-ties around Mandy's wrists. Something clicks insider her throat with every ragged exhalation. He sits her up, cradles her beautiful face. Her arched eyebrows. Her tangled red hair. Her thin lips.

"I'm going to save you," he says. "I'm going to save the world."

Mandy's head jerks reflexively to one side, biting a gumdrop-sized lump of flesh from Malcolm's hand. Almost instantly, Malcolm's blood feels like used motor oil.

Soon, he'll hack up his soul.

**Seven months ago.**

Teens danced to the Retched Rumble. G.A.G. t-shirts were banned from public schools. The wealthy paid top dollar to have sex with Retches, so long as they were properly masked. The world had G.A.G. fever.

The hottest reality show on TV, G.A.G. My Wife, Please, was about a man coping with his G.A.G.-infected wife. Malcolm watched the show while helping Paul can two hundred pounds of tomatoes.

On the screen, the husband sat next to his wife's cage. She thrashed and gyrated against the bars, while her Shade rambled on a monitor. "...tHE tOILET sEAT dOWN yOU dONT kNOW hOW tO eAT mY - bleep - iVE hAD bETTER - bleep - fROM sTRAY cATS i hATE yOUR mOTHERS cHICKEN..."

"Okay, brain man," Paul said. "Tell me how humans can be so smart yet so dumb."

Malcolm shrugged. "Our brains are one-point-nine percent of our bodies, compared to the lion - only one percent. Since our ancestor Homo genus emerged 2 million years ago, the human brain has doubled in size."

"Wouldn't know it to watch this shit."

"Yes, but why'd we evolve so much extra brain weight?"

Malcolm drags Mandy outside. With his hands under her arms, he feels the spastic pulse common to all Retches.

No rhythm.

No pattern.

No rhyme.

Already, that jangly offbeat song invades Malcolm's chest. His heart burps and clenches. His vision is flattening out, the world losing all depth. His skull is a fragile eggshell. Great. Now he's recycling old Jim Morrison metaphors.

This is the end. His only friend.

No it isn't.

The sky is an upset belly with indigestion and heartburn. On the horizon, the sun dissolves like an effervescent tablet, offering no real relief.

Malcolm stumbles against the van, hoisting Mandy through the rear doors. He falls inside and slams the doors shut. Strapping her into the backseat, he fumbles the key into the ignition and latches his seatbelt. The engine groans awake, and Mandy's voice tumbles over the radio on a bed of static.

"...was my father but he never suspected i used to cut myself when that didnt work i cut other people not with blades but words i think doves have no souls i whispered dirty words all through the pledge of..."

The van lurches down the street. Malcolm's throat clicks. His heart trembles. He's not going to make it.


**Five months ago.**

G.A.G. mutated. Or maybe not. Maybe the line between humanity and technology dissolved. Over the course of a week, G.A.G. spread through email attachments, smart phones, and viral marketing. The government pulled the plug on the Internet, but it was too late. Cities were overrun. Highways were clogged. G.A.G. was everywhere, and no one was ready for it.

No one except Paul.

He rallied the Village tenants together and turned the building into a fortress complete with compost toilets and solar power.

Malcolm had never known many of his fellow Village tenants, had only ever cared to know one - Mandy. For years, he felt a familiar ping in his heart whenever he passed her in the halls. Pre-G.A.G., she wouldn't give Malcolm the time of day. After G.A.G., she visited regularly to watch movies and listen to music on his home entertainment system.

One afternoon, Malcolm sat on his couch, watching Mandy do sloppy yoga wearing only a pair of short-shorts and an "I G.A.G. FOR THE TRUTH" t-shirt. No bra.

"You think we're okay here?" Mandy said.

Malcolm shrugged. "Paul's kept us all safe so far."

Outside, the street was all screaming, gagging, and static-filled ranting. Malcolm never thought he'd miss the sound of traffic, car alarms, and thumping bass.

Mandy rose into the cobra position, her pelvis grinding against the floor and her chest arching upward.

"Give me a drag," she said.

Malcolm held one of his last cigarettes to her lips. She took a drag, exhaled. Malcolm glanced down her shirt.

"I'd kill for some good drugs," she said. "Can't you synthesize something, science boy?"

"No drugs. I worked in porn tech."

She looked him in the eye. "That so?"

"I was a security consultant. Developed fixes for viruses. Remember last year, when people kept falling in love with virtual partners?"

"Yeah."

"I developed the love patch to fix that." Malcolm held up a flash drive. "I've got a copy of the love virus right here."

Mandy laughed. "The love patch. That's great." She lowered her chest to the ground, hands folded under her chin. "Could have used the love patch when I was little and Mom left my dad. She fell in love with some dick named Tim, ran off on us." She stared at the window. "I hope he's okay."

"Who? Tim?"

"No, dumbass. My dad." She rolls up her sleeve, revealing her dad's portrait tattooed on her shoulder. "He lives right near here, by that playground on Fourth Street. We used to play on the seesaw there all the time. I haven't talked to him in years. He was the only thing that ever kept me grounded."

Malcolm interrupted, "When you're in love, the brain's ventral tegmental is overactive. It produces dopamine, providing pleasure and motivation. It's not unlike cocaine."

Mandy eyed the flash drive, licked her lips. "You're saying, when you're in love, you're high?"

Malcolm nodded. "There are few limits to what a love-drunk heart would do."


A block later, Malcolm's heart becomes a ball of yarn ravaged by kittens. Sweat soaks his shirt. The G.A.G. - even from its entry at the extremities - spreads quickly through his body. He pats the patch stuck behind his ear to make sure it hasn't come loose.

He's still blocks away from the Village when convulsions wrack his chest. His heartbeat tugs like a frantic fish hooked on a line.

He grunts.

The van swerves onto the sidewalk. Malcolm fights the steering wheel. The van plows into the corner of a credit union. The impact throws Malcolm through the windshield and into a concrete wall. He lands in a heap.

That jangly heartbeat is gone.

**Three months ago.**

Malcolm and Mandy lay in bed, the sheets littered with various sex programs and pornware. Malcolm asked a stupid question.

"Are you fucking serious?" Mandy said. "We're living in the post-apocalypse, and you're asking me what's wrong?"

But for Malcolm, it hadn't been a stupid question. For Malcolm, life had only gotten better since the G.A.G.

"I just want everything back to normal," she said. "That's all I want."

"Then that's what I'll do. I'll make everything better."

She took off her pleasure-goggles and laughed. "Malcolm, you're a porn tech." She lovingly patted the stimulator strapped to her thigh. "A really good porn tech, but really? What are you going to do?"

He pulled off his prototype love-glove and holstered his disinhibitor gun. "Hon, I had Fortune 500 companies knocking on my door straight out of college. I just didn't want to deal with the..."

She arched her eyebrow and rubbed his crotch with her foot. "The pressure?"

"The bullshit. I've got a knack for figuring things out."

She rolled her eyes. "Delusional much?"

"If I say I can do this, I can." He held up a transdermal patch. "This is a patch I developed for PornMaker 3.4. Because of the software's heightened connectivity, we needed a way to keep the customers from either contaminating the host software or picking up an STD from the host."

"STD?"

Malcolm nodded. "Simulation Technology Disease. I can modify the patch to keep the wearer's consciousness intact once the body gets G.A.G. The wearer would be a Shade, but a rational one."

Mandy rolled her eyes. "Uh-huh."

"If I could wear the patch and get infected with G.A.G., I could study it from outside the body. It's like fixing a car." Malcolm slid his hand under Mandy's shirt. "To diagnose the problem, you have to get out from behind the wheel. Under the hood."

"Is it really that simple?"

Malcolm nodded. "No. Not at all. Nothing about the brain is simple. Did you know that more electrical impulses are generated in one day by a single human brain than by all the telephones in the world?"

"Including texts?" she said.


Malcolm has no heartbeat. He lies on dirty cement waiting for death's fabled white light. He feels no pain, so must be either paralyzed or dead.

But wait. He was wearing his seatbelt, so how could he have been thrown from the van? He opens his eyes and turns his head, expecting to hear vertebrae cracking like celery. The van's windshield is mostly intact. It wasn't his body that was thrown from the van. It was his Shade.

He must have gagged-out when the van made impact. Patch 2.0 worked. He's rational. He shakes his head, the motion sending comet trails across his vision. He looks at his ghostly hands, and it's like staring cross-eyed - seeing each eye's image crossed over the other, neither image really substantial. He's seeing past and future with no present.

He staggers toward the van, his steps unsteady not from trauma but from the energy and thought and feeling swirling all around him.

Mandy's Shade crawls on all fours over and under the wreckage, muttering to herself. "...put the cards back in the deck but fuck it right blind children have more money than they know what to..."

Even without her body, she's beautiful.

Malcolm sees the open driver's door and freezes. The front seat is empty, the tattered seatbelt dangling. His body somehow unlatched the belt and escaped. Damn it. Without his body, he's just a lost ghost. Can this day get any worse?

From blocks away, he hears the hacking and lurching. A flesh amoeba with thousands of feet, hands, and eyes - half as many mouths.

The Gaggle.


**One month ago.**

The Gaggle passed by the Village - a mob of hundreds, maybe thousands, of infected Retches. A storm cloud of heaving flesh acting under a singular hive mind. Bite. Fuck. Grow.

A flock. A murder. A school.

The Gaggle.

Down the street, a flashlight blinked repeatedly from a Mexican restaurant's roof. A band of survivors had holed up there for weeks. The Gaggle hit the restaurant like a mammalian tsunami. The Retches climbed one upon the other, stretching up the building. Inside, women and children screamed.

"Mandy says you're working on a cure," Paul said.

"I'm trying."

As if on cue, Mandy walked onto the roof, stood between Malcolm and Paul. "You got your night goggles, Paul?"

He handed them to her. Malcolm watched to see if their hands touched.

"They're so creepy," Mandy said, training the goggles on the Gaggle. She shivered.

He stroked her thigh. "I don't think it's a 'they' anymore. It's an 'it'."

"What makes it happen?" she said.

Malcolm shrugged. "Ever watch a flock of birds? They land, fly, and change course as one. To watch it, you'd think the birds' brains were somehow networked. But really it's just emergent behavior. The group moves based on decisions of individual birds, following simple rules responding to neighboring birds. It all happens in a quick chain reaction."

He stared at the edge of the Gaggle. A shirtless teenager with a broken nose. Someone's grandmother, topless and shriveled. A heavily-tattooed Asian wearing snow boots. What did they all have in common? Each other.

Paul snorted. "Way to take the romance out of migration."

Mandy nodded. "To hear you talk sometimes, you'd think the soul was nothing more than an email attachment."

"Nah, souls are huge," Malcolm said. "They'd crash all the servers in heaven."

She elbowed him. "Shut up."

He ignored her. "The slowest speed that information travels between neurons is about 260 mph. Our brains can make 20 million billion calculations per second. How fast could brains compute if they were networked? Can you imagine the speed?"

Malcolm's Shade sprints through the street.

No, literally. He trips and phases through the street into a sewer tunnel below. It takes him way too long to climb back to street level. By that point, the Gaggle is closing in. If the Gaggle finds the van, it'll absorb Mandy. He'll lose her forever.

He takes a deep breath, realizes that he has no lungs, and goes through the motion of exhaling anyway. Retches and their Shades are never far apart, so his body should be nearby. Like a shadow turned inside out, he sees a faded line leading around the corner - his connection to his retched body.

Malcolm sprints after the line and finds his body humping away on the busted remains of someone's Harley Davidson. The Gaggle comes into sight, a couple blocks away.

Malcolm's body dismounts the bike and stumbles toward the Gaggle.

Shit.

Malcolm catches up to his body halfway down the street and tries throwing himself into his own head. It doesn't work. Frantic, he remembers a diagram of the body's chakras and tries slamming his consciousness into every one of these holes. No good.

He recalls Mandy's words from last month. File attachments. Of course. His consciousness is too big. It has to be compressed and encrypted. Parsed. He jumps piggyback onto his body and begins shoving bits of himself inside. His favorite color, pea green. The taste of stale beer. His first day of kindergarten. The smell of his father's shoes.

He shoves until there's nothing left.

**Earlier this afternoon.**

Malcolm left his lab early, wearing a triumphant grin. Patch 2.0 was ready for field-testing. Malcolm rubbed the patch against his neck. But where the hell was Mandy? Malcolm checked her apartment and the stairwell, where he found Paul wearing only a t-shirt and a pair of jeans. Unusual to see him unarmed.

"Paul? You seen Mandy?"

He stared at the floor. "Haven't seen anyone all afternoon."

Downstairs, someone screamed and hacked. Wood splintered and glass shattered.

They ran down the stairs, only to find the lobby trashed. A dead Retch lay sprawled on the dusty tile, still twitching. Outside, Mandy ran down the street, wearing Malcolm's bathrobe. Why was she down here? Wearing only a bathrobe?

Malcolm held out his hand. "Give me the van key, Paul."

Paul shook his head. "You'll never find her. I can't risk losing the van."

"Paul, I'm a brain man. There are 100,000 miles of blood vessels in the brain. And one hundred billion neurons. If I can navigate that mess, you think I can't find Mandy?"

Malcolm tastes grit and tire tread. He's face-down in the street. He did it. He actually parsed his soul back into his body. His smile soon fades at the sound of several thousand feet plodding against asphalt. The Gaggle's coming this way.

Malcolm sprints back to the van. The Gaggle thunders behind him, each of its synchronized steps shaking the ground. Or maybe the Earth's just frightened.

At the van, Mandy's soul mutters, "...to the police because i hated the sound of her voice i took the last cookie and..."

"Hang on, hon," Malcolm says, sliding into the driver's seat. Behind him, Mandy's body thrashes and hacks.

The keys jingle in the ignition. Malcolm turns the key, but the engine only clicks lamely. Malcolm slams his head against the steering wheel. He has to get Mandy away from...

A wave of appendages pounds and stomps the van, nearly knocking it over. The Gaggle eclipses any light from the sky above.

"I just had a really bad idea, Mandy," Malcolm says. He steps into the rear of the van, grabs her by the hair, and holds his forearm to her mouth. "Bite me, hon."

Moments later, Malcolm's Shade flows out of the van. The Gaggle's Shades dance in the sky, sparkling flames rising from the coals of flesh. Will this work?

It has to.

Malcolm tears himself apart, parsing his soul into thousands of packets and hurling each packet into the hollow minds below. A fat black man tastes Malcom's grandmother's blueberry pie for the first time. A tattooed divorcee writes shitty poetry in Malcom's high school journal. A one-eared attorney loses his virginity on Malcolm's parents' bed.

And so it goes.

Suddenly, the Gaggle's hacking rhythm, the noise that's haunted the city for weeks, goes silent. It's an eerie silence, punctuated by thousands of Retches simultaneously taking in an in-breath.

Malcolm is the Gaggle. His thoughts are amplified by thousands. His feelings stream fast and rich. Everything's déjà vu. For a long while, the Gaggle stands mute, swallowing periphery vision to the hundredth power.

His thoughts, once clouds, rain freely. No, they pour. In great bursts, his ideas puddle and flood his networked consciousness. Lightning flashes all strobe. Unfiltered thoughts overflow his thousand skulls.

Quickly, the revelation comes.

Back at the lab, he has a disinhibitor gun, a cheap plastic toy used to unwind anxious lovers. With a few simple tweaks, he can modify the gun into a cure. One shot, and the Retch's soul will return to its body.

Malcolm's going to save the world.

Not a particularly coordinated man even when operating only one body, it takes Malcolm Gaggle a long while to push the van back to the Village. Bodies crash to the ground. He steps with thousands of feet. His pulse echoes in as many hearts.

Above, the Gaggle's orphaned souls expand - dry sponges soaked in water - and glow like fireflies. With their bodies now occupied, the souls are heading for that fabled light. If Malcolm doesn't leave the Gaggle soon, its souls will be lost forever.

At the Village, Malcolm Gaggle shoves the van backwards through the front doors, effectively blocking the entrance.

Malcolm Gaggle kneels.

He ejects.

**Earlier this evening.**

Malcolm drove through the streets, thinking of the places Mandy talked about. Clubs. Dive bars. Music shops. Where could she be?

Of course. He turned west, onto Fourth Street. The playground. Sure enough, Mandy was there, flopping up and down on a seesaw covered in blood. He needed a distraction. Nearby, an old man watched from behind one of the school's boarded-up windows. Malcolm inhaled deeply and waved at the man. The man smiled and waved back.

Malcolm's phone vibrated. It was Mandy.

"...starved my goldfish al pacino is overrated i secretly envy religious people i once pissed on a sleeping..."

Malcolm opened the passenger door. The old man limped toward the van. His grey hair was the color of rainy sky. Even from here, Malcolm recognized the face that countless times had stared back from Mandy's shoulder.

Mandy's father.

Ten steps away.

Nine.

Eight.

That's when Malcolm hit the horn and closed the door. The old man's eyes went wide. Mandy leapt off the seesaw and sprinted across the playground. She sure as hell wasn't running away from daddy anymore.

Malcolm spoke into the phone, ignoring Mandy's confessional gibberish. "Mandy, each of our hundred billion neurons makes contact with thousands of other neurons via synapses. Our brains make about a million of new connections per second, those connections' strength and pattern always changing. With all that in mind, how can two people's love be anything but temporary?"


Malcolm's Shade dives through the van's roof. The Gaggle flails over the van and against the Village. Meanwhile, Mandy thrashes and hacks. He can't take her upstairs like this, so he parses himself into her body as well as his own.

Moving as one, he runs on four legs up the Village's staircase. Yes, he takes a moment to cop a feel with Mandy's own hands. When Malcolm enters his loft, Mandy's soul – already shimmering toward the light – rambles through his speakers, "...her we were only friends the bitch bought it i undertipped because she was prettier than..."

Malcolm sits at his desk, funneling his theories and concepts through his fingertips. Working with two bodies, he quickly builds the soul-inhabitor gun.

He tunes out the noise of the Gaggle storming the building, breaking windows, tearing down walls. He blocks everything but Mandy's voice.

Because it isn't there.

While Malcolm puts the finishing touches on his soul-inhabitor, he sends Mandy's body into the hallway to find her Shade. It takes concentration, being two places at once. But he needs Mandy's Shade here with her body, for a first test.

Malcolm-Mandy finds her Shade on the fire escape. There, Paul throws bricks down at the Gaggle below - splattering chunks of Retch skull all over the sidewalk.

Mandy's voice comes from his walkie talkie. "...love you i need you we are meant for each..."

Paul turns around and sees Mandy. He rears back to throw a brick at her. His vision darts from the walkie talkie to Mandy's body.

"other i think of you when i'm fucking malcolm i just want..."

Paul lunges for Mandy and kisses her. He tastes like tic-tacs and gun powder.

Son of a bitch. That's why Mandy left the loft in her bathrobe - to meet Paul for a secret rendezvous. While Paul's kissing Malcolm-Mandy, Malcolm-Malcolm grabs the soul-inhabitor and strides down the hall.

Malcolm-Mandy pushes Paul away just as Malcolm arrives. Seeing Malcolm, Paul chucks the walkie talkie - with Mandy still chattering - down at the Gaggle.

Malcolm-Malcolm aims the soul-inhabitor at the Gaggle, ready to save the world.

But wait...

He can finally see how selfish he's been.

"Is that loaded?" Paul says.

"No, Paul. It's junk," Malcolm-Malcolm and Malcolm-Mandy say simultaneously.

Paul eyes them both warily. Malcolm laughs, throws the soul-inhabitor down into the Gaggle. It shatters in pieces.

"Paul," he says. "You taste like gunpowder."

Without another word, he and Mandy return to his loft. He ejects from Mandy, and she lunges at him. His Shade floats upward as he and Mandy buck and wiggle together - a beast with two heads, four arms, and four legs.

Malcolm parses himself once again into the Gaggle's hungry flesh. Now free of his body, his thoughts are free to rain.

Free to reign.

He's been so selfish. So stupid. The world doesn't need to be saved.

It needs rebooting.

Knowing the apartment's defenses, he easily overtakes the Village and converts Paul and everyone inside - except the Retch bodies of himself and Mandy. They deserve each other.

Meanwhile, Malcolm has a world to rebuild.

One body at a time.

In unison, thousands of voices speak with raspy voices:

"Welcome to Malcolm Village."

**One week later**.

He systematically takes over the whole city until he spans hundreds of thousands of bodies. Millions of fingers all at his will. Trillions of synapses flutter at his command.

"Welcome to Malcolm City."

**One month later.**

"Welcome to Malcolm Country."

**Nine weeks later**.

"I did it. I saved the world... Malcolm World."

# Contract

## by
## Michael McGlade

Contract
by
Michael McGlade

THE GREEK thumbed the dead woman's eyelids shut. Scraped espresso-colored hair off of her face. A recent survey concluded that one hundred percent of people who drink water, die. It was something Evelyn Stein had written at work, which the Greek had found when he went through her trash. A fitting epitaph.

Stillness in the office on the forty-second floor. The metallic whimper of a heated hair iron still stank the air. The Greek leaned into Evelyn, who was laid out on the beige carpeted floor, and inhaled. Her perfume was too sweet and sharp, like leftover Chinese takeout. It made his heart pound. Tongue became parchment. Vision blurred like a windshield in rain. He fought to stand, stumbled, fell against the desk. In its reflection he noticed eyes the blank grayness of mined rock. He didn't know this Greek man that stared back at him, the face surgically altered beyond recognition throughout the years. His brain felt crinkly as a discarded napkin. Worse than any time before. These contracts were killing him.

He noticed the wound on his waxy white cheek. Evelyn's fingernails had bitten harder than fangs. He slapped his face, shocked himself alert. Heart jackhammered. He opened the door and glanced around the open plan office space. Empty desks and cubicles. Still dark outside. It was half-four in the morning. Employees would arrive soon. He shut the door to Evelyn's office. Next to the woman, the carpet smoked where the straightening iron had fallen off the coffee table and started to catch fire. He moved to the electrical socket and switched it off. He placed the flat iron in the private restroom and moved back into the room.

His legs gave way and he collapsed onto his knees. His cheek throbbed. Felt like ants crawling around in under the skin. He picked up Evelyn's hand and sniffed. There was a toxin on the tips of her fingernails. That toxin now blistered through his veins, more powerful than anything he had encountered before. He checked his watch. It had been a minute or more since the infection. In another minute, paralysis would set in.

The Greek had spent two days following Evelyn and now scanned those memories in search of a clue to the type of toxin used. He knew where she lived, her routine, the train route she took to work, dietary habits, the usual stuff. His contract instructed Evelyn be dispatched in her business office, and in the meantime he had watched, followed, waited. Nothing during his surveillance provided a hint, and without a clue he'd be dead before his physician could provide an antidote.

The Greek used his cell phone and logged into an encrypted server to access the contract details. While the connection established, he crawled to the desk and got onto the chair. Framed pictures on the desk depicted a whole life in snapshots: husband, children, holidays, college graduation, wedding day. There was a picture of children. Evelyn did not have children. She wasn't even married. The Greek picked up a picture and scrutinized the woman in it: she looked like Evelyn but she wasn't Evelyn. He recognized this woman because he had killed her last winter. The name *Lauren Harris* came to mind. Contract specified a closed casket.

The Greek read his wristwatch. A minute-twenty since the infection. On his phone, he scrutinized the full details of his current contract and discovered nothing of importance. Toxin crawled around his innards like a tapeworm. He severed contact with the server and noticed he had a missed call. He always put his cell on silent mode during a job. He didn't recognize the number, which had tried to contact him a few minutes ago and had left a voicemail. He listened to the message.

"I've poisoned you," Evelyn said in a whisper. "I've finally got you. You murdered my sister, you bastard. Rot in hell. Have you found an antidote yet? I bet you're searching frantically for it right now. I've heard that cauterizing that wound might give you a few more minutes."

The Greek laughed. Evelyn was a stone cold bitch. He liked her even more.

He lurched toward the flat iron he had placed in the restroom. Liquid lead sloshed inside his skull. The flat iron was too cold. He plugged it in and the metal creaked as it heated. He counted time from the initial infection, a minute fifty-six, fifty-seven, fifty-eight. He slapped the iron against his cheek. The flesh blistered. He remained silent.

Evelyn laughed. She was still on the voicemail.

"Enjoy the scar," she said. "Raising your heart rate like that cut your remaining time in half. I'll keep this short. Ever hear of *devil's snare?* South American Indians used it to poison their hunting spears. It takes hours for the victim to die. However, paralysis sets in almost immediately. I am told the death is excruciatingly painful. And the leaves of this plant, when prepared correctly, cause hallucinations. Did you like my perfume?"

The voicemail ended.

The toxin kicked the legs from under the Greek and he slumped to the floor. He thought about Evelyn's dead sister, Lauren. He had been contracted to kill her in a very specific manner. Her husband was a senator who needed a wakeup call. The Greek had provided a *closed casket* and melted her face with acid until she looked like Swiss cheese. And, now, Evelyn had sacrificed her life to exact revenge. However, she had made a mistake.

The Greek dialed a number into his cell. The call connected.

"Devil's snare," he said and listened to the voice on the other end. "Two minutes ago. You need to come to me. I'll forward the location." He ended the call and sent the location details to his physician. At least his work provided unlimited medical expenses.

Evelyn was sloppy. She had gloated, told him the name of the toxin. The Greek's physician would bring an antidote called *physostigmine*. He'd survive if he relaxed, slowed his heart rate and minimized the progression of the toxin through his system. He took a deep breath and shut his eyes.

The Greek smelt smoke. He held a lit cigarette in his hand. He was in an aisle seat on a south-bound train. People stared at him. He didn't smoke and couldn't understand how he had a lit cigarette in his hand. He dropped it on the floor, crushed it beneath his shoe. He'd survived lung cancer, so smoking was no longer an option. The cancer treatment had been a success - an expensive success - and because of it he incurred a debt through his boss he had no choice but to repay. He'd been paying it back, contract by contract, for three years now. The Greek exhaled and tasted the acrid smoke expelled from his lungs, the lit cigarette still in his hand. His chest smoldered like a burning coal.

The phone rang. The Greek was still in Evelyn Stein's forty-second floor office. He answered the call and the man on the other end said, "I have the *physostigmine*. Where are you? I can't help unless you tell me where you are."

"I told," the Greek stuttered, "I already," he stuttered, "you know where I am," and this time no words came out of his mouth. He could no longer speak because his lips were gone. They had been removed with a surgical scalpel and the hole that remained was stitched shut. Just like what he had been required to do to fulfil the contract on Martin Clark. If you turned state's evidence against important people, you died with your lips stitched shut.

"Are you there?" the physician asked. "Are you still there?" he asked. "Talk to me," he said.

The Greek's insides bubbled like molten lava. He screamed but no sound escaped.

The Greek woke with a start. He was on a chair behind a desk with a polished black surface. Dark outside, yet the light on the forty-second floor was direct as a razor's edge. He studied his reflection in the surface of the desk. Didn't recognize the white waxy-skinned man that stared back. Had tried to forget him a long time ago.

He shoved the remnants of a recent nightmare out of mind. They were getting worse. Each time he closed his eyes he had them. He never slept for long. Last winter, he wanted to quit after he had been contracted to melt a woman's face with acid, but his boss refused. He had tortured the Greek for two weeks straight until he signed a new contract. Put him right back to work. Since then, he knew they had followed him and watched his every move. There was no way out. The only time he was not under surveillance was during the final moments of a job when he committed a murder.

He read his wristwatch. It was four-twenty in the morning. Evelyn would arrive in the next few minutes. He had followed her two mornings in a row as she took the train into work. He knew her routine. He knew even more about Evelyn that she would ever have thought. From the moment The Greek saw who he had been contracted to kill, he had recalled the similarity between Evelyn and Lauren. Without arousing the suspicion of his boss, the Greek had checked into the identity of his *unnamed* employer. He traced the payment records back to Evelyn. She had paid to have herself murdered. It was the only way she would ever have gotten near the Greek. He admired what she was willing to endure to avenge her sister's brutal murder, and he had prepared carefully for this eventuality.

Out of his briefcase he took a syringe and filled it with pentobarbital. While it would render Evelyn unconscious in seconds, death would not come for ten minutes. Eventually, she would die of shock, which is what overloads the system and shuts it down. Few people ever overcome the initial trauma of impending death.

The Greek entered the outside office and waited, hidden. He checked his equipment for the final time and set his cell phone to silent, all part of an automatic routine. Evelyn arrived, took some picture frames from her handbag and hurriedly set them on the desk. She thumbed a number into her cell phone, placed it to her ear and spoke in a whisper. He allowed her, as a gesture of respect, the time to say her goodbyes to the last person she had decided to call before her death. Evelyn ended the call and took an atomizer from her handbag. She considered it for a long moment, removed the lid and sprayed her neck. The Greek detected the acrid aroma and even from this distance felt the narcotic effect. He took a deep, meditative breath and held it. With such an extreme dosage, Evelyn would have less than a few minutes before she lost her grip on reality. She took out a vial of nail polish and painted the tips of her nails with a transparent liquid. Evelyn plugged a flat iron into the socket and set the iron on the coffee table to warm. She entered the private restroom in her office and shocked her face with cold water.

The Greek sidled next to the restroom door. Evelyn returned to the room, already unsteady on her feet. The Greek, still without releasing his breath, moved behind Evelyn and injected her in the neck with the syringe. The drug knocked the feet out from under her but the Greek laid her gently to the floor. She raised her hand to scratch him and the Greek smelt the toxin painted onto her fingernails. He restrained her wrists with ease and knelt beside her. Paralysis had begun to set in.

"I know what it is that you want to do," he said. "You're willing to die to get to me."

She mumbled, couldn't speak.

"I wish I could let you go, but there is the matter of the contract," he said. "I cannot change that, but I can give you what you want." He moved her fingers almost within reach of his face. "You get what you want as long as I get what I want."

He showed her the contract, placed a pen in her hand, and with her last strength she signed her name. As she drew the pen across the document, with the other hand she scratched her nails along his cheek.

The Greek photographed the completed document and uploaded it onto the server. The contract was now unbreakable. Evelyn would die with the impression she had killed The Greek, but she was wrong. He thumbed the number of his physician into his cell. By the third digit the poison's effects had taken hold.


The train wheezed out of the station and the Greek woke. Another bad dream. He watched the reflection of the lounge car in the dark glass. The old man reading a newspaper, the rich woman with a Pomeranian dog, and the mustached man at the bar were familiar. He had murdered them in the past year. The Greek glanced around the lounge car. Every face was familiar. Twenty, maybe thirty of them.

The Greek stood and reached inside his jacket for a weapon. He smelt smoke and coughed and, as he exhaled, smoke hissed from his lungs and he doubled over. In his hand was a lit cigarette. Tasted like razorblades in his throat.

Someone stood next to him. Still doubled over, he glanced up. The Greek had once killed a man called Harvey Harris with a shard of broken glass and made it look like an accident. Harvey now next to him struck the window until it fractured like a spider web. Paralyzed with coughing, the Greek watched Harvey work a shard of that glass loose. Harvey carved the Greek like a Halloween pumpkin.

Now came Lauren's turn, her face still blistered from the acid he had used. Lauren took hold of the Greek's forearm and her grip melted his skin as if it were wax, drip by drip.

He had buried an old man alive. His name was Luke Jackson and Luke's calloused hands were now strangling the Greek, and yet still the Greek would not - could not - die. The pain eternal.

Everybody within the lounge car swarmed the Greek, fingers like rakes, clawing and probing the recesses of his eye sockets and innards with slow, methodical movements. Hours, days, months passed and still they never ceased. The torture was exquisite in its scope of utter agony. So patient and meticulous was this torture that his body retained its ability to regenerate and he was cursed to a status quo of hurt and death and rebirth that maintained his presence firmly in the center of this unending torment.

They spoke almost-silent words, words felt within the marrow of his bones, bones that had been crushed into dust a hundred times over. Those voices in unison they uttered a single word: *CONTRACT.* And their faces melted into a one single entity, a face as alien and unknown as a perfect stranger: this face contained his father's eyes and mother's pale skin: it was his own face and he watched in paralysis as he tortured and mutilated himself.

The Greek jerked awake at the desk in the office on the forty-second floor. On the desk was a signed contract. The pain began to shred and cut. A ceaseless death. That was the beauty of *datura stramonium,* the devil's snare. Endless pain. Forever hurt. Death came in a few hours but the victim would experience that time in a dilation to make it seem like it lasted for eternity. Before he recoiled into another hallucination, the Greek read the details of the contract he had Evelyn Stein sign. The contract was issued in the name of the Greek's boss and once loaded onto the server, it had to be fulfilled. The thing about killers like the Greek was that there were hundreds of them waiting in line for the next job. Once the contact was enacted, it could not be broken. Mode of death, devil's snare.

# Ancient
# Voices

by
Glynn Owen Barrass

Ancient Voices
by
Glynn Owen Barrass

F REEDOM, the sensation exhilarated me as I levitated higher through the air. As always, there had been an initial fear when I first ascended and left my prone body behind, a fear and vertigo as I lifted my insubstantial form between buildings I knew well in the conscious world. Far below me now, the city of my birth dwindled as I glanced down. Up, up towards the sky, sooner than it would take in the conscious world I reached diaphanous, fluffy clouds. No dispersion or resistance as I passed through them, but for a moment I saw nothing but white. The following view was stupendous, for the clouds I'd passed lay below me like a frozen sea of white, the clouds beyond these resembling snow-covered hills shadowed with gray. Higher cloud mountains loomed in the distance, this ethereal view quite breathtaking. However, my destination lay above the glowing blue sky. I was soon to breach the membrane and escape my Earthly confines. I felt sure of it, this time. I spread my arms and breathed deeply, excited at the thought.

Then, as always, the voice appeared, a deep rumbling thunder forming words no earthly tongue could mutter. They filled the blue, my ears, my mind, and suddenly I was frozen, unable to move from the spot I'd paused at. Fear overwhelmed me, and I awoke.

"I know the voice. I think it's the Earth Mother, warning me about what lies beyond."

I nodded at Paige's theory, though considering the voice I'd heard was far from feminine, I didn't voice my agreement. Four of us sat in Paige's flat, the top floor of a Georgian terraced on the better side of town; Paige and I, Paige's boyfriend Manders, and our mutual friend Hayley. We had something else in common apart from friendship, that being astral projection, and, the voice near the edge of the Earth's atmosphere.

"A warning?" Manders said, "I admit I did feel a little frightened."

"Me too. Hayley?" I added, and turned to Hayley, who was sat reading something on her mobile phone.

She placed the phone on her lap. "It hardly resembled a voice to me, just noise in the firmament."

"Yet still I sensed words," I said.

Paige leant forward, folded her hands. "We can't get further, and that's just wrong. Me and Manders were thinking." She paused and looked at him.

Manders continued, "That taking Ketamine might help."

Everyone stared at me. I felt abhorred, for I hadn't taken drugs since my early 20s, and Ketamine?

Hayley broke the silence. "Sure thing." Paige's face formed a big beautiful smile.

"How, how would we take it?" Everyone looked happy, and I didn't want to appear a sourpuss, but still

"For a proper experience we'll have to inject," Manders said, "use the liquid."

"It's a far softer experience," Paige added, informing me that she at least had experience with the narcotic.

Again, all eyes were on me for approval. Dare I, with the dangers of injecting and me, nowadays, being fairly anti-drugs? I reached a quick decision.

"How soon can we get it?"


I levitated by the simple action of raising my feet behind my knees, then turned whilst hovering to examine my sleeping form: my arms and legs spread-eagled in a five-pointed star configuration, just like I had taught the others. A barely visible umbilical, connecting me to my body, swayed between me, causing a slight disturbance in the air. I looked towards the ceiling, and flew. Momentary darkness followed, ceiling, attic, rafters, then I was levitating through the early morning air. Would I encounter my friends this morning? Sometimes we would meet, our disembodied forms bobbing above rooftops before we went exploring. Today I wasn't bothering with the meeting place, the rooftop of the caretaker's house in Albert Park, but rather, continued my ascent. Above me were clouds, below, the town rapidly dwindled. To my east the sun was a dull golden orb, hazy with cloud. Turning my head to the sky again I approached the clouds, a whole swath of them, growing larger as I flew. I entered the cloud cover, suffering a momentary white blindness and then, I was there, the place the voice always spoke to me.

I was not disappointed.

Words that were not words sundered the heavens, pausing me in flight. They rumbled through the dark clouds above, rumbled then dissipated. It was at this moment, always this moment, I would find myself awake in bed, but this time, I retained my astral form. My courage building, I continued upwards, rising further than ever before, and suddenly, everything changed. This was not the sky I knew, this was nothing but white, whiter than clouds, whiter than anything I had ever experienced.

I wasn't alone.

Dark *things* floated through this realm. A horde of entities, some static, some moving, I watched their world in awe. Each being heavily featured with an overly large head, they resembled squat African pygmy gods hewn from clay. One floated towards me, its huge hovering form pausing before it addressed me without moving its lips. It questioned, and I answered.

"I know it sounds hard to believe," I explained, "I spoke to them for what seemed like hours but on returning to my body, I recalled nothing of what they said."

"Are you sure the projection hadn't devolved into dream?" Paige said. It was a valid point, and the gap in my memory certainly seemed to indicate such an issue. But I was sure.

"Sure, without a doubt."

It was late afternoon, and we were again in Paige's flat. She was on the couch, arms linked with Manders. I sat in my customary seat. I continued, "so this really has me thinking, if I've gotten this far, is there really any need to bother with the drugs?"

Paige glanced to her partner then me. "We have it already," she replied.

"Shipped from India," Manders added, "liquid Ket. Hayley is bringing the needles."

Needles. Should I mention my reservations? The downstairs buzzer rang, and Paige stood and headed to the intercom.

When Paige turned and said, "It's Hayley," I realized it was growing far too late to back down. Hayley soon entered, all smiles, and dumped her rucksack onto the couch beside our friends. Manders stood, went to the kitchen, and returned holding a collection of small glass vials. I watched Hayley inject Paige, then Manders, each in their upper arms. Paige rubbed hers and said, "Still sore from last time," which did nothing to alleviate my fear. My turn quickly followed. I can do this, I thought, and lifted my sleeve, embarrassed at how hairy my arm looked.

"Uh, gross yeah, I need a wax," I joked but Hayley just smiled and pressed the needle to my arm. There was a slight pain, but still fighting my fear, I watched as she pressed the plunger in.

"It's amazing you trust her to do this the first time," Paige said and I replied, "If I can't trust Hayley who can I trust?"

With her done I pulled the sleeve down and relaxed into my seat. I watched her place the syringe into its box and remove another, fitting the needle before drawing more Ketamine from the bottle. She injected herself next.

I watched Hayley finish up before she sat on the floor beside me. I wondered how long the effects would take, and suddenly, everything turned fuzzy, the voices from the television stuttering in the strangest way.

"What?" I tried to raise myself from the seat but had become a solid block of stone.

Manders turned to me. "You okay?"

"Just," I said. My mouth, filled with treacle, felt sluggish.

"Seagulls," Paige said, and her skin took on a greenish tint. The whole room, my whole environment changed color, colors I couldn't really comprehend or explain. Hayley slumped into the couch. I looked to her, then Manders, and felt a link between us, a new psychic connection. Manders said, "We should turn off the television," and I replied, "I was just thinking that." Of course I was, we were connected.

Connected true, yet I was dislocated, like some foreign object within my own body. The television went off, I don't know who did it, for I was too intent on staring towards a gap of golden daylight filtering in between the curtains. So bright there, I sensed angels beyond, hovering on the rooftops. I felt I was dying, but accompanying it was the utmost joy.

"We ready?" asked Hayley. Everything was so sluggish, voices, my thoughts. I doubt anything on Earth could move me from my seat.

"Let's do this." I closed my eyes. Still I was falling towards death, afraid but exhilarated, and the angels awaited me.

I closed my eyes, organs that felt strangely disconnected from my drug-infused psyche. There was a usual routine to astral projection, one in which I would lie flat on my back and spread my limbs to form a pentagram before chanting myself into a trance state. There was none of that here, now.

"Whee!" Paige said, and I was hurtling from my body, from her flat, through momentary darkness as I passed through the attic and roof before entering a late afternoon sky.

Straight up, we journeyed together, our naked forms glowing, leaving trails of translucent umbilicals to our unconscious forms. In no time we reached, and passed the clouds, and there Hayley paused, the rest of us following suit. She smiled at our surroundings and I could not blame her.

A beautiful vista of white hills and valleys surrounded us; gossamer formations of fantastic ruffled shapes. Clouds like continents dotted the horizon, their gigantic forms hovering in the aether. A massive cloud layer loomed above, heavy with darkness but revealing white beyond a gap in its center.

We were all smiles now, me especially, and after nodding to my companions, I was the first to elevate towards the next layer. I aimed myself between the black, towards the gateway to pure white beyond. The voice appeared, a distant stuttering thing now like the television below. I found it easy to ignore. My companions did too, for we were soon together again, entering the white, and there, the entities awaited us.

Those primal, pygmy gods, their faces remained static as they spoke in indecipherable, ancient tongues. Their voices roared as like children my friends capered around their strange forms, Paige and Manders linking hands as they approached one and stroked its heavy brow. Three entities surrounded Hayley, forming a triangle around her, and me, I watched, relieved I had taken the drug, slightly ashamed I had ever doubted its efficacy. One of the gods flanking Hayley turned and approached me. I reached for its face, and an instant later found myself back in the flat.

What was happening? I had failed, returned to my body while my friends remained in the aether. The shock quickly transformed to something far worse as my blurred vision coalesced and I witnessed what unfolded in Paige's lounge.

Something was atop Manders, no not just atop him but inside his body, an obsidian shape of jewel-like facets violating him from his crotch to his throat. The thing, whatever it was, shuddered, Mander's arms and legs twitching with its movements. Was he alive even? From the slack look on his face, eyes rolled back in their sockets, he might already be dead.

I tried to scream but my mouth wouldn't open, the lack of control, the earlier sensation of dislocation adding to my fear.

Of my other friends I found Paige on all fours, arms dangling behind the back of the couch. Something hovered above her, a gelatinous green horror covered in eyes and gaping mouths. A tendril led from the thing to the nape of her neck. Eyes glassy, she mouthed silently as ugly shapes squirmed between her lips.

The things, *they were feeding.*

The voice had been a warning.

Paralyzed as I was, a silhouette blocked my view, hiding the image of my friends' violation. The final member of our group, Hayley, wobbled before me, her head encephalitic with abnormal growths. One of the things had entered her, her eyes swollen to bursting and revealing twinkling constellations of horror.

I tried to recoil, but it was an impossible labor. I tried to close my eyes but failed at this too. She opened her mouth, and what I saw there sent a spray of urine down my inner thigh. Unable to perform any action but look away, I found the gap between the curtains and the golden light beyond. Ice cold, claw-like hands reached me. The angels laughed.

# Alicia's in the Trunk and Boy, is She Pissed

by

**John Hunt**

Alicia's in the Trunk and Boy is She Pissed
by
John Hunt

JENKINS GROANED and lifted his head. His face twisted with pain. His skull shifted under his skin, felt loose, like two cracked plates tethered to nothing. What the hell happened? He lowered his head to rest on the car door. Wind whistled over his ears. The wind hurt his head. He didn't know wind could hurt. Cracking an eye, he saw pavement blurring under him, the coolness of the car door chilling his cheek. His heart surged against the arteries and veins holding it in place. Where was he? Where was he going? Who the hell was driving the car?

Gritting his teeth and grimacing when his molars wiggled loose in their gums, he pulled his head back inside the car, glimpsing desert sand glowing white, reflecting the light of the white moon hanging huge in the starry sky. His dry mouth tasted terrible. A sharp tang to it, like bile. He glanced down at his shirt to see a vomit bib decorating it. Trying to get comfortable, he pushed against the bottom floorboard and screamed. Pain electrified his nerves, emanating from his left foot. Was it broken? It sure as shit felt like it. Tingling rushed into his foot. He moved it about, wincing. It wasn't broken. Most likely a serious sprain.

Miley Cyrus pounded from the car speakers. Are you kidding me? He punched the power button and the quick movement sent tendrils of discomfort throughout his body. Was there any place he wasn't hurt?

"Jenkins! Christ! Thought you were dying over there."

Pounding issued from the trunk and what Jenkins thought was a woman's voice, yelling. That couldn't be right though. Dave's hands white knuckled the steering wheel in the ten and two position. A fine mist of blood coated his face, hands and his shirt.

"Dave. What the fuck, man. I *am* dying over here."

"Well, you looked worse earlier."

"What the hell happened? Where are we?"

Dave glanced at his friend, measuring him and said, "You don't remember, man?"

"I'm asking aren't I?"

"You took Alicia to the Place."

Jenkins' stomach felt Arctic.

"Fuck man! That's her in the trunk isn't it?"

"Yeah. Only, that ain't Alicia no more."

"She sounds pissed."

The thump of metal from the trunk startled Jenkins. The nub of headache pain intensified with the metronomic thumping of his heart.

"Were you with us?"

"Yeah. Me and Phil, you and Alicia. You took us there, to show us. We were all fucked on crystal, man. Three day binge. Fucking place was crazy."

Jenkins knew the answer, felt it in his broken body, but asked anyways, "Where's Phil?"

Dave's lip quivered, "Dead. Phil's dead. Alicia, or whatever the fuck she is now, killed him. She almost killed us all."

Jenkins searched his memory. Nothing churned to the surface, his mind a blank chalkboard. He didn't remember a damn thing! Except for the Place. He remembered the Place, alright. Why the fuck would he take his friends out there all cranked up? He steered clear of the place when sober. Didn't make any sense. Alicia killing someone? Diminutive, a hundred pounds of gristle, Alicia couldn't take out Phil. Phil was a big dude, even though he too was on the meth head diet of drugs with only the occasional chocolate bar and soda as sustenance. This wasn't making sense. The Place. Nothing made sense there.

Dave frowned and his eyes shone in the dashboard light. He said, "Fucking crank, man. After this, I'm done, man. For real. I'm done with that shit."

"Dave! Tell me what happened, man!"

"The Place, man, the fucking Place. It did something to Alicia. Why the hell did you have to take us for anyways?"

Flashes flickered back to him. Scrolling across his mind like film reels. Smoking the glass bowl, inhaling the vapors, talking about the Place. A lonely spot in the desert his mom showed him when he was younger, a teenager. His mom the hippie, always saying she could sense things, feel weird shit others weren't wired to feel, going on about ghosts and other worlds. She used to read her Tarot cards all the time, smoking until the whole house filled with a blue haze and doing heroin on the weekend with her friends. He remembered his mom, preparing a needle, his round eyes fascinated by the process. She patted him on the arm, eyes deep wells of sadness, and said to him, "Don't ever do this, okay? Sometimes, the world is too real for mommy. I see things others don't. I wish I didn't." And then she'd plunge the needle in her arm and sit motionless, Jenkins sometimes fearing she had died. The drug stole the life from her eyes. Growing up, his mother always told him of places where the world thinned, not as solid, places where things that weren't meant to be here could slip through. Things that liked the feel and taste of flesh. Those ghost stories and 'woe is me' pity parties worked on him when he was a kid, but not as he got older. He thought she was full of shit and he told her so. They got into horrendous fights, the words he used crueler than any blade. His mother, the docile victim of his tirades, used drugs more often to escape him. She couldn't stand to be hated or believed to be a liar, especially by her own son. So, one day, she showed him the Place. She knew it was dangerous, knew it was irresponsible for her to do so, but she needed him to believe her. And after she showed him, he did believe her.

He told Alicia all of this in a long jittery narrative while Phil and Dave discussed who'd win in a fight, Scooby Doo or Cujo? Was it even a question? Cujo would shred the cartoon do-gooder.

About the Place though, Alicia thought he was full of shit and after she explained it to Dave and Phil, they concurred with her assessment. Jenkins was lying or high. And just like his mother, he needed to be liked, needed to be believed. So, he decided to show her. Show them all.


"Hey Dad, are we there yet?"

Jenkins barked from the front, "Do you want me to turn this car around?"

Phil snickered from the back, Dave smiled and Jenkins shook his head while exhaling tension. Maybe he should turn the car back. What the fuck was he doing, man? This was a bad idea. His mother warned him of it and when he was there, he felt it. Danger.

Alicia said, "Seriously though, are we almost there? My buzz is dying on me." She scratched at a scab on her arm.

"Don't you start. It was your idea."

"Yeah. I know. It sounded fun but we've been driving for a loooooooong time."

"Yeah, we're almost there." He passed her a pipe, "Here, there's a little left in there. Go ahead."

Perking up, Alicia said, "Thanks."

"Any for us Dad?"

"No!"

Dave said, "I knew Alicia was your favorite!"

Jenkins turned to her, "They're right, you know. You're my favorite."

Holding in the smoke, straining the words out through tight lips, she said, "I know it."

They were closer. A red boulder, shooting up from the ground like a jagged tooth, appeared in the distance. The Place was near there. He hadn't been there in four years. The last and only time with his mother. It was something one didn't forget. This is stupid. Why was he bringing them here? The closer he got, the more nervous he became, the fear building in him like the evening tide.

"What say we head back? My buzz is wearing thin, too. I got some more jib at my place. We could grab a pizza, get high. What do you think?"

Phil said, "I think Jenkins' balls have dropped off somewhere along the road. Or maybe he's just afraid we'll find out he really is full of shit."

Dave said, "Agreed. Jenks has to officially turn in his Man Card."

It was petty peer pressure, meant to emasculate him, he knew it, and it worked. Think he's a wuss huh? Well, he'd show them the Place and then we'll see who the wuss is around here. His grin glowed green in the light.

"Alright fucksticks. You want it? I'll give it to you."

Dave and Phil chorused, "Oooooohhhhh!"

The scenery, although dark, seemed familiar to Jenkins and he slowed the car, peering out the window.

"We there?" Dave asked.

"Shhhh!"

Phil said, "I think he just shushed you."

Dave said, "He definitely did. Should I bitch-slap him?"

"No, he's driving. Maybe when we stop."

Jenkins, scared and irritated, said, "Will you two jerk offs shut the hell up?"

The tires on the road, wind whistling outside the car. Jenkins peering into the dark.

Dave said, "Definitely getting a bitch-slap."

Jenkins braked hard and said, "We walk from here."

They got out of the car, stretching, whining, bones cracking in the stillness of the evening. Alicia a little wired from her last hit, scratched herself, shivered and her eyes searched the darkness.

Phil, looking around, said, "This is it?"

Jenkins said, "No. See the rock out there? We have to walk out there."

Phil, frowning, said, "Looks far."

Dave, laughing, said, "It looks like a cock!"

Jenkins rolled his eyes. Why did he hook up with these clowns? Alicia wasn't so bad, but those two really grated on his last nerve sometimes. He knew why though. They all had something in common. Crystal meth.

Jenkins popped the trunk and pulled out the tire iron. He didn't know if it would help, he just knew it made him feel better to hold it.

"What's that for?" Phil asked.

"For whatever. Let's go."

"Hey," Dave said holding up a baggie, "Shouldn't we have a taste first? Need some energy for the long walk to the rock penis."

"It's not a penis!" Jenkins said, and then, "But sure. Why not?"

The smoke eroded Jenkins fears. With the tire iron in hand, he felt strong and all worries about the Place faded in direct proportion to his growing sense of power. Jenkins knew he was on the road to severe addiction. He didn't have the meth sores on his arms or the tooth decay commonly known as 'meth mouth' yet. He could see it on the horizon. But for now, he fucking loved it and was under the illusion he controlled it. The power! So he strode into the desert with a tire iron in his hand and friends at his back. He dared the Place to fuck with him.

His friends joked and laughed behind him, not knowing or believing what awaited them in the desert. Their coats swished as they moved and their boots scuffed the hard packed dirt. It got cold in the desert at night. The meth warmed him, a glowing fire in the pit of his guts shooting energizing bolts into his blood. Why had his mother liked heroin? Meth was where it's at.

They were closer, the rock monolithic before him. He frowned and picked up his pace. His friends grumbled behind him, but they kept up and Jenkins' urge to get this visit over with grew. The air warmed noticeably and felt thicker somehow, pushing against him. He glanced around. A circle of animal carcasses and bugs littered the ground.

Jenkins said, "We're here."

"Huh. Doesn't look so special," Alicia said.

"Look at all the animals. In like, a perfect circle. Fucking weird, man," Dave said.

Jenkins inhaled a sharp breath, his nerves live wires all over his body. He said, "That's where it's most powerful. In the middle there."

"The air's strange. Harder to breathe," Phil commented.

Alicia asked Jenkins, "What happens if someone stood in the middle there?"

"No idea. We're closer now than I've ever been. Mom warned me against it. Can't be good though, judging by all the dead things. Can't you feel it? It's not right, whatever it is."

Phil looked at Dave. "Dare you to go in the middle there."

"Fuck no! I'm high, but not that high dude."

Alicia stepped forward, her head cocked to the side, as though she were listening to something.

Phil sighing, said, "I thought you were hard, man."

"That bullshit 'dare you' crap won't work on me. I'm more sophisticated than that."

Alicia's foot crossed over a dead armadillo.

"Look. Alicia's doing it. Never thought she was harder than you."

Her foot touched the ground and she jerked, as though jolted. Her mouth hung open. A line of drool, shiny in the moonlight, hung from her lip. She took another step.

A chill swept through Jenkins. He didn't like this. He didn't like it at all.

"Alicia? Hey. Alicia? What are you doing?"

Alicia spoke but she wasn't speaking to Jenkins. Her voice whispered, "Yes. Okay."

She moved further into the circle. For once, Phil didn't have a smart ass thing to say. That alarmed Jenkins even more. What was she doing? A trance. It was like she was in a trance.

Jenkins stepped forward, a hand reaching out to her, to pull her back. He didn't like her in that circle. Not one bit. Why the hell did he take them here again?

His hand, almost breached the circle and then he heard it. A voice, out of the air, colder than any winter wind, asking, *Let me in.*

Alicia, beckoning with her hand, said, "Sure. Come on in."

A spasm gripped her and shook her tiny frame from head to foot. A ripple of skin crossed her face. A cold wave of air pushed against Jenkins. This wasn't good.

"Alicia?"

She reached down. Picking up a dead coyote by the tail, she bit into the stomach, pulling away a chunk of flesh and hair from the decomposing corpse.

Phil said, "Damn girl! That's disgusting!"

She swung the coyote by the tail, and with incredible force, launched it at Phil. The coyotes skull cracked against Phil's and he fell backward, uttering "oof" as he hit the dirt. In the time it took to blink, Alicia was on him. She was so quick! Phil screamed. Alicia, now with a rock in her hand, brought it down on Phil's head, her arm a blur as Phil's cries dwindled with every pound. Jenkins wasn't sure, but he thought Alicia was humming while she worked. Humming that kid's tune, Mary had a Little Lamb.

Jenkins ran to help Phil with the tire iron raised, ready to strike. Dave stood stunned, mouth open, eyes as wide as the moon. Jenkins was bringing his arm down, aiming to hit her across the back, glimpsing Phil's skull cracked open, his one eye lying like a broken egg on his cheek, when, in a blur, Alicia swung the rock at him, connecting with the side of his head. Bright bursts of light exploded over his vision and the ground rose up to meet him. Alicia landed on his back, knees digging into his shoulders, her weight, which should be so slight he could shake her off, felt heavy, as though an elephant sat on him. She was hitting him everywhere! He put his arms over his head and the rock cracked against his wrists, knuckles, elbows, everywhere. She was so fast! So strong! The rock cracked against the back of his skull and before his eyes closed, he heard Dave yelling and Alicia humming.

"How'd you stop her?"

"With the tire iron. Hit her with it across the head. Broke her neck, I mean I heard it snap! Didn't stop her though. She turned on me, with that fucking rock! I wanted to run, man. She knew it too. Smiled at me, humming some stupid thing behind her teeth and when she stood, I brought the iron down on her head. Vibrated right up my arm. It put her out though. For a bit, anyways. And then, I ran. And then I had to come back. You had the car keys in your pocket. And then I ran again. I'm not gonna lie. I was gonna leave you there. Leave you with her. I couldn't though."

"Thanks."

"Don't thank me. It was a close one. I brought the car over, being careful not to get stuck or crash into a rock. It was tough. I see why you wanted us to walk. I was freaked out though. Kept expecting to see Alicia in the headlights, smiling, humming a merry tune. Fucking creepy. I got you in the car. You didn't look good. You must have puked when I was gone and I thought how lucky you were not to choke on it."

"Probably a concussion."

"Whatever. I closed the door and behind me, I heard humming. I almost shit myself. I never dropped the tire iron though. Not the entire time I was lugging you in to the car. I spun around with it, swinging it and she held up her forearm, you know, to block it, and I swung through it. Cracked her arm, broke it for sure, from the way it kind of fell over. She didn't cry out though. Her head was tilted to the side, like her neck couldn't hold it up and still she smiled, blood and crap all in her teeth. I lost it you know? I screamed and attacked her. Kept hitting her and then she started yelling in my face. Yelling 'MARY HAD A LITTLE LAMB, LITTLE LAMB...' while I whacked at her. I knocked her head the other way and then she dropped. Her eyes were closed, she was breathing, I didn't know what to do, so I stuffed her in the trunk. She woke up before you."

"Where are we?"

"Driving man, just driving. I didn't want to be anywhere near that Place."

"What are we gonna do?"

"Shit, man. I don't know. You're the fucking expert!"

From the trunk the pounding continued. The yelling did too. Only now, when Jenkins strained to listen to the words, he was chilled to hear the words to Mary had a Little Lamb.

"We have to get rid of her. Destroy her or something."

Dave raised his eyebrows, "Ya think?"

"And soon. I'd hate to be stopped by the police now."

Dave laughed, a shrill bark that Jenkins thought had a hysterical tinge to it.

"The gorge. Let's dump her in the gorge."

Dave nodded. Then he said, "What if that doesn't kill her?"

"It's two hundred feet deep with jagged rocks all the way down. It'd have to kill her."

"Okay."

They stood behind the trunk, twitching with every pound and scream from within.

"I wish she'd stop singing that fucking song," Dave said.

"Yeah."

The keys sat in the lock of the trunk. Jenkins held the tire iron and Dave gripped a heavy log he found on the rim of the gorge. Jenkins balanced on his right leg, swaying a bit. Damn. He hurt all over.

"Okay. So we open it. Pound the crap out of her. Hope it kills her and then toss her two hundred feet into a deep hole."

Dave said, "As plans go, it doesn't completely suck."

"Okay. Open it up."

After they were done wailing on her, she was unrecognizable as a person and at the end, Jenkins felt relief. At least she stopped singing that fucking song. Breathing heavy, covered in blood and vomit, they picked up their friend and dropped her down a hole, listening to the thumps as she hit the jagged walls on the way down. Jenkins stared into the black hole, pensive.

"I'm done too," Jenkins said.

Dave, frowning, asked, "What?"

"Done with meth. Hell, I'm done with all that shit. Might even go back to school, get a job."

"Hey, settle down, now. I never said anything about getting a job."

Staying clean was hard. Harder than anything he'd ever done before, including grade ten calculus. Most of the time, he didn't feel alive. He felt as though he were stuffed with cotton or walking through Jell-O. He slipped, once or twice and as soon as the smoke hit his lungs and lit up his body like a pinball machine, Jenkins felt awesome and terrible at the same time. Four days since his last hit. Two weeks since they sent Alicia tumbling down a ravine. Some images just never go away.

Jenkins sat up nights, thinking about the Place. People must have run into that area before. He wondered what happened to the people drawn within the circle. Whole families wiped out or maybe, a father or a mother had to kill a possessed child. That's what Alicia was, wasn't she? Possessed? By something not from here. It could be some of those people were still out there. Maybe they were the monsters under the bed, the bogeymen in the closet.

41

They gave him his own room at the shelter. The shelter had only one rule. You must be sober to stay. No drugs, no alcohol. His bruises were fading into bile yellow and florid purple. His left foot didn't bother him anymore.

He was anxious. He'd be starting his new job tomorrow. Landscaping. It was hot and brutal work. He hoped he was up to it and didn't let down the guy who got him the job. He turned off the bedside light, and twisted and turned on the mattress. He dozed off, thinking of Phil's eye hanging outside his face.

He woke up shivering. His blanket bunched on the floor, the window open and the cold night air rushed in. What the hell? His teeth chattered. Confusion mired his brain. He turned on the lamp. Alicia stood at the end of his bed, her head resting on her shoulder, her bones protruding from her skin, excises of flesh open and raw. Her face was wrong. Her nose had been sheared off and her eye sagged, as though the bone under it had cracked. How could she be here? He blinked, hoping it was a dream, an awful nightmare. This couldn't be true. They dumped her in a hole! No one could come back from that! No one!

From a gap that had once been a pretty mouth, came the words, "Mary had a little lamb, little lamb..."

# Dark Intentions and Blood

### by
### Amy Braun

Dark Intentions and Blood
by
Amy Braun


B EING POSSESSED would be the best thing that ever happened to this kid. Okay, maybe he didn't have this revelation at the time I started slaughtering his moronic friends, but now that I was free, I really didn't care. No way would I fake being that dropout loser who spent all his time getting stoned. Being possessed was probably the best high this dipshit had ever experienced.

I walked down the streets, whistling an old Nirvana tune and wondering why people kept pointing and screaming at me. I looked down at my shirt, seeing it was covered in blood.

Oh yeah. That would have been either J.D. or Ramon. It was kinda hard to tell now.

Shrugging and whistling, I looked in the direction of the screaming. It was really killing my upbeat mood. Maybe it was time I found the source and killed it.

She wasn't far away. Some chubby skank on the corner whose rolls were spilling out from under a halter top three sizes too small. What was that old saying? More cushion for the pushin'? Hmm. How about more meat to eat?

Yup. That sounded a lot better.

She didn't get far. This body was skinny, but I was stronger now. Tackling her to the ground and keeping her pinned was about as difficult as knocking over a one-legged man. Hadn't come across one of those yet, but hey, the night was still young.

She shrieked and begged for mercy, slapping her arms at my face. I smiled, watching the flabby skin of her under arm jiggle with every hit. It was disgustingly mesmerizing. I could have been hypnotized by it, but I had places to be. Blood to spill and innocents to devour.

I barely felt the pain when my claws poked out from under my vessel's nails. Chubby stared in horror, eyes bugling out of her head. She screamed louder than ever when I brought my hand down and ripped open her throat. Blood gushed up and sprayed onto my neck. I grinned, staring with awe. I slashed again, getting a fresh coat of red on my shirt. It was still hot when it splashed onto me, the scent of copper filling my nose.

My eyes never left hers as I killed her. I wonder what she thought of my shaggy black hair and completely black eyes. Did she like my sharpened teeth? Was she surprised at the amount of blood squirting out of her? Could she feel herself dying? Did she still think I'd show her mercy?

I answered all her questions at once. I peeled back my lips and sank my teeth into her neck. I ripped open her skin and let that hot blood flow into my throat. It was salty and sweet, best of both worlds. I clamped on arteries and tendons and jerked my head, feeling them snap like thick elastic bands in my mouth.

"Vampire!" someone screamed. "Oh my God, it's a vampire!"

I pulled back and laughed. Guess I would look like a vampire, drinking blood from a person's throat and all. But a whiny bloodsucker I was not. A raging demon from Hell?

That I was.

I ditched the fat lady now that she had finished singing, and chased after the man who'd gotten his monsters confused. He ran, but nowhere near fast enough. Three seconds later, I had grabbed the back of his throat and thrown him against a car window. I kept one hand around his neck, pinning him in place. The middle-aged businessman was sobbing and shaking.

"Please, please, I have a family!"

"Really?" I asked. "Where are they? Maybe I can pay them a visit."

He started crying. Ugh. I hate it when they cry.

I curled the claws on my free hand and shoved it into his stomach. He gasped in horror, looking down and watching as I pulled his intestines from his stomach. I kept smiling, tugging harshly. Five feet out, twenty more to go.

I heard more screams and shouts behind me. I looked over my shoulder, seeing people running and howling like banshees. A lot of them were taking photos with their phone.

I noticed a man on a bicycle trying to slow down, a nasty grin coming over my face. Time to bring out my inner diva.

Tugging the intestines out of the businessman's stomach, I raced for the bicyclist. He was still going too fast. I stretched the human intestine out as far as it could go, snapping it over the bicyclist's chest. It wasn't the strongest rope I could use, but it did the job of making the biker tumble head over heels and land face first on the pavement.

Dropping the intestine, I marched over to him as he crawled away. I reached down and turned him over by his shoulder. I punched him solidly in the face before tearing off his helmet.

"Safety first," I smiled.

I slammed the helmet into his face. His head bounced off the pavement. Highly amused, I kept hitting him with thick, plastic shell. My hits were like strikes of a hammer. It was like bouncing a basketball with another basketball. It got less fun when he stopped moving.

Also when I got shot in the back.

The bullet punched through my upper left shoulder, knocking me forward. The human body I was controlling would mind that, but me? Meh. Pain was pain. If you weren't feeling it, you were dead. I turned, still gripping the blood-covered helmet.

The cop and her partner stared at me, horrified that I was still standing and completely unconcerned about the massive wound in my shoulder.

"I must be going deaf," I said, barely hiding my anger. "Didn't hear a warning."

"Drop the helmet and put your hands on your head!" the male cop shouted, pointing his gun at me while his partner gaped like a fish.

"Are you serious? Do you know how badly that's gonna hurt?" Not very much, but they didn't need to know that.

"Do it now!"

"Or what? You'll shoot me again?" I grinned. "Don't think that'll work out the way you plan, buddy."

"This is your last warning!"

I stopped. Guy sounded serious. They weren't playing anymore. But I still was.

"Noted. Hey, think fast!"

I hurled the bloody helmet at him. He stumbled, giving up his aim to catch the helmet. The bitch-cop watched, taking her eyes off me. The city's finest weren't its brightest.

She barely had time to gasp before I punched her solidly in the face. Cartilage shattered under my knuckles, her nose flattening into her face. She was still falling when I appeared in front of the male-cop. He turned his head to mine, just as I lunged forward with my clawed fingers.

His eyes popped under my nails like fresh berries, squishing inward as I pushed deeper. He screamed longer and louder than I anticipated. I loved these kinds of surprises. I kicked him in the chest, my fingers slipping out of his face. I licked the blood and eye juices from my fingertips, watching him clutch his face and whimper pathetically. I noticed his dropped gun, and grinned. Finder's keepers.

I picked up the gun and spun it in a way that would have made the Lone Ranger envious. The man was too focused on his pain to hear me walking closer. Demons don't like to be ignored. Time for a wake-up call.

I raised the gun and shot him in the leg. He screamed again as blood squirted up from his femoral artery. I cocked my head, and then shot him in the stomach.

This guy had some impressive lungs. I got annoyed quickly. A third bullet in his throat ended all my troubles.

There was another gunshot, but it wasn't from my new gun. I wasn't stupid enough to shoot myself in the ribs. I lifted my arm and looked at the blood beginning to stain the side of my shirt. I couldn't really feel the pain, but this shot assured the death of my vessel. I glared at the bitch-cop as she held the smoking gun in trembling fingers.

"Ow," I grumped. "That hurt."

I raised the gun and shot her in the hand. She screeched and dropped her gun, as well as the two fingers I had blown off. I picked up the digits, starting to cool now that they were separated from a warm body. I chomped down on one, stripping the skin from it like a banana peel.

The woman was shaking and crying, holding her mutilated hand, desperate to get away from me. I smiled as she watched me eat her fingers. It was only now that I realized how pretty she was, busted face and all. I don't have a lot of nice things to say about the human race, but they're damn sure prettier than demons. I licked my lips.

"Your fingers are a little too salty for me, sweetheart, but I bet the rest of you tastes like candy."

Bitch-cop crawled faster, going for her radio. I caught up with her and slapped her across the face. She took the hit, screaming again when I grabbed her injured hand and squeezed. Fresh blood oozed out of the stumps. I couldn't help but bite down and gnaw some more.

"Zandaxos!"

*Goddamn it. They found me.*

"Can it wait? I'm trying to eat someone here!"

I clamped down and tried to tear off a strip of skin. Her voice was ragged from screaming. Kinda made me sad that she wouldn't have a voice when we started getting *real* friendly.

My hopes and dreams were completely shattered when water splashed onto my back. I cringed, unable to hold back my own howl of pain. It's not like being doused with boiling water is a soothing experience.

I whirled, forgetting all about Bitch-cop. I flexed my claws and looked at the assholes who were responsible for burning me.

Two men in black cassocks and priest collars stared at me with hard eyes. The younger, bigger one was tucking away a bottle of holy water. Ah. So that's who I have to blame and kill. The second man was in his late forties, and definitely a hardened exorcist. He'd been the one who'd known my name.

Trying to stay out of sight behind them were two teenagers about the age of my vessel. One was so thin I probably have counted the ribs under his oversized jacket. He was your stereotypical Goth kid all pale skin, black lipstick, chunky boots, fishnet shirts, tight pants and spiky hair (wait, this was a male, right?). He didn't have the angry, 'fuck you, Dad' attitude I expected. He looked scared to see me.

But if he was scared, the chick next to him was petrified. She was a little overweight with straw blonde hair and dull blue eyes circled red from crying. She wore dirty blue jeans, sneakers, and a plain white shirt.

Both kids had seen better days. Scratches traced their arms, torsos and faces. The girl was favoring her right leg. The boy had one hell of a shiner. I grinned, remembering that they had me to thank for those memories. The girl clasped her hands over her mouth. The boy looked ready to puke.

"Leave the vessel, Zandaxos," commanded the old priest.

"Nah. I think I'll stay. I like it in here."

When I heard the young priest chanting under his breath, I shot him. The click of the empty gun stopped his incantation. And pissed me off.

"Get lost, thumpers," I shouted. "I don't need God words."

I threw my gun at them. They flinched, giving me the chance to take off. My whole idea was simple: run away today, butcher more tomorrow.

Except that those damn priests were faster than I gave them credit for. One of them tackled me, probably the younger one so his predecessor wouldn't break a hip. I bucked and thrashed, stopping as something burning was pressed on the back of my neck. I felt like I was being branded, and I fucking *knew* there was going to be an ugly cross tattooed onto the back of my neck.

I twisted and stabbed backward, claws digging into the priest's legs. He shouted, loosening up enough for me to roll and hurl him off. I snarled and went for his throat when someone snared my collar. I was yanked away from my target. Just as I was turning, something crashed into my head. I had good control on my vessel and the damage it could take, but his anatomy couldn't handle that sort of head trauma after being shot twice. So I blacked out.

Stupid stoner bastard.

"We have to do something about his wounds," a sad girl's voice said.

"The demon needs to come out of him first," answered a man who sounded like a grizzly bear. "It won't be restrained for long."

"But he's bleeding to death," she sobbed.

"Maybe you should have thought of that before you decided to call up a demon," another man said.

"Shut the fuck up, preacher!" a high-pitch male voice shot. "We didn't think it was going to actually work!"

There was a clatter as something fell onto the floor. Feet scrambled back.

"You were dabbling in satanic magic! What did you think was going to happen?!"

"Enough!" shouted Grizzly. "We shall exorcise the demon, then tend to your friends wounds." He paused. "I cannot promise he will live."

The girl burst into tears, her sobs catching in her throat.

"Wake it up, Martin."

I waited until I could smell him, then blinked open my eyes and snapped my jaws at his face. He jumped back, startled. Damn. I really thought he was in range. I chuckled.

"No need to play rooster," I said casually. "I got good ears."

Grizzly narrowed his dark brown eyes at me. His partner, Martin, gained his composure quickly. The kids were holding each other and looking completely out of it. I looked around at the concrete basement they had trapped me in, the dim light bulb flickering over my head as moonlight poured in through dusty windows. I looked at the kids again and tilted my head at them.

"Sean and Erica, right?" They shuddered when I spoke their names. I rolled my eyes. "Oh, give me a break. You and your band of failures called me. I've been in David's head for a while now. I remember all of you, the ones I left alive and the ones I killed."

My grin turned nasty again. "Did you manage to find all the pieces of J.D. and Ramon? I can't remember how much of them I ate."

Erica blinked tears away, turning into Sean's shoulder.

"Cease speaking to them, demon."

I turned back to the priests.

"Well look at you, all poetic and old-school. What's your name?"

I had one name, and once I got out of the trap, that would be all I needed. But therein lay the problem. Sometime during my unconscious haze, I'd been tied to a chair and planted in the middle of a demon-snare. It wasn't the like circle I had been summoned into. This one was made of salt, anti-demon symbols drawn into the floor. The reek of burning sage was everywhere.

The whole snare was like a rash. No matter how much you scratched it, it just didn't fucking go away.

"Demon Zandaxos, you shall leave this vessel immediately."

I lolled my head back and groaned. "Seriously, change the fucking record."

Grizzly approached me with an angry look on his face. I doubted he had any other sort of expression. He stopped just short of the salt line. *Tease.*

I smirked. "What's the matter, tough guy? I've got two bullet wounds and a concussion. Don't think you can take me?"

"Martin," he said, looking at me but not talking to me (which I found extremely impolite), "begin the exorcism. Do not stop, no matter what this fiend does or says."

"Didn't think priests were so rude," I muttered, half under my breath.

My snark stopped when Martin started chanting.

Another old saying crossed my mind: Sticks and stones will break your bones, but words will never hurt you.

Complete, utter bullshit.

Speaking bible quotes to a demon is like having someone pour acid in your ear. It burns and boils, sizzling its way to your brain. I twitched and thrashed in the chair. I wasn't even sure what the fuck Martin was quoting, but he was getting the job done.

Grizzly took out a silver flask of holy water. *Don't do it. Don't you dare, you fucking son of a...*

As if my internal monologue would help me. The water splashed against my face, and then I was burning. Molten lava couldn't feel this hot. I screamed angrily, but it sounded like a scream of pain. I briefly caught the horrified looks of Sean and Erica. Her tears flowed freely. Good. I hoped the little bitch was sorry. She was the one who did this to me.

It was her idea to seek out the Goth string bean and pull the ultimate trick to avoid final exams. Sean stupidly thought he could control me. The only reason I hadn't forced myself down that vampire wannabe's throat was because David the stoner was closer.

When you sow with dark intentions, don't be surprised when you reap blood.

Speaking of my favorite red liquid, it was starting to seep out of my eyes like tears. I was clinging to the vessel for dear life. I had been hoping someone would give me a vacation. Not all demons like Hell. It's hot, uncomfortable, and the boss is an asshole who'll rip your head off and use it as a basketball if you cross him. You don't get time off from your torture duties, and some clients have screams so atrocious that stabbing yourself in the ears is a thoughtful reprieve.

But earth? Earth is fun. You run free. You do whatever the fuck you want because you *can*. You're stronger, better, and you don't give a shit about consequences because they don't affect you. That's what freedom really is, literally doing *anything*, and knowing you won't be hurt because of it.

I didn't want to go back to Hell, but with Grizzly showering me with holy water and Martin halfway to singing Amazing Grace, it was hard to hang on.

They were torturing me, ripping me away from my warm, happy home. The holy water was sinking into me like burning needles. The words were a group of banshees screeching in my head. They were going to pull me out. These bible-loving bastards were good. So I did what any rational demon would do in this kind of jam.

I destroyed the vessel's soul.

I was the superglue on the skin, being peeled away slowly and mercilessly, tearing layers from my vessel in a desperate attempt to keep my hold. My claws were deep in David's soul. I tore at it, shredding as much as I could. If his wounds didn't kill him, what I was doing would. He'd have nightmares for the rest of his life, until he couldn't take it anymore and gave his gun barrel a blowjob.

The pain increased so suddenly that it almost crippled me. I shuddered, shaking the vessel terribly. Invisible arms wrapped around me, peeling my grip from his soul. I struggled and fought; slashing and biting at the most tender part of this waste of skin. My teeth and fangs cut through his soul like a knife through silk. He screamed in agony as I cut and devoured pieces of him.

*Dark intentions and blood, pal. You asked for this.*

When the swell of burning, shrieking agony hit me again, it hit with the force of a sledgehammer. I lost my grip on the soul. I could feel myself being yanked out of his mouth, clawing at his throat and doing anything I could to get back in. It was warm in his body, but out here I was a naked creature in a snowstorm. The air hit my smoky form and froze me completely. I was about to turn into a block of ice. I gasped for air, breath fogging out in front of me. Oxygen gripped my lungs with icy ropes, suffocating me.

I screamed in my demon voice. The sound rattled the walls like thunder, making even Grizzly back up. Erica and Sean screamed. Martin lost focus.

I was freezing. Dying. The humans were suddenly too scared to complete the ritual, and ironically, that was very bad news. If I wasn't sent back to Hell, I would freeze to death. My only other option was to get into a new vessel, but the salt circle was trapping me.

The dark smoke coming off my humanoid shape trembled as I shivered in the cold earth air. I spun, looking for options, and seeing David's corpse in the chair.

An idea formed, and I knew I had one shot. If it fucked up or I wasn't strong enough, I was going to become a demonic popsicle. I might look like the most badass ice sculpture ever created with my black wings, pitchfork tail, curling red horns, and bloodshot eyes, but I wouldn't be able to have fun.

And I was all about fun.

I zipped behind David, turning corporeal. Erica screamed bloody murder when she saw exactly what I looked like. My movements were stiff, icy pain stabbing into my joints whenever I flinched. The shaking in my limbs only made my pain worse. But I hooked David's arms all the same.

Grizzly's eyes widened when he realized what I was doing.

"No!" he screamed as I lifted David and his chair.

I nearly lost my balance, deadweight and weakened muscles overcoming me. A bellowing scream of rage gave me conviction. I hurled David forward, his body falling face first on the salt line.

And breaking the circle.

I misted immediately so Grizzly wouldn't catch me. I didn't know his real name, so I couldn't use him. Erica and Sean were useless. But Martin? Well, Martin was chanting again and giving me an aneurysm. He was a big, strong young man.

He would do just fine.

I shot through the basement like a bullet, condensing until I was the size of a pencil. It was the worst pain I had ever felt. Not only was the freezing air creating icicles on the edges of my smoke, now I could add body crushing to the list. Misting split me into a million particles, but I could still feel every one of them. Condensing into one small form was like having your body squeezed through a two, well placed floorboards. It was possible, but it hurt like a motherfucker.

Martin's eyes widened as he saw me getting closer, Grizzly screamed at him to closer his mouth. By the time he did, I was inside him.

Heat hit me in a wave of pleasure. The warmth of this vessel's body was bliss that circled around me, rippling as I descended down his throat in search of his soul. I could feel him shaking, trying to scream, but it was muffled in my ears. I was in too much comfort to give a fuck about his voice.

I reached his heart, and found his soul. I grinned and dove in.

For Martin, it was the most extreme pain he had ever felt. Like someone had stabbed a knife into his heart and was steadily ripping it in two. He could feel me pulsing my way through his body, a parasite wiggling through his insides and looking for a place to spread.

For me, it was the ultimate pleasure. An orgasm that never ended. Safety and warmth, a home of my own where there would be no stress or pain. Just me, myself, and my vengeance.

Once I was settled, I coiled up Martin's spine, soaked into his brain, and trailed into his eyes. He opened them, and then he was mine.

Grizzly had frozen in his tracks, an emotion other than disgust crossing his face. Total devastation was a good way to describe it. Everything he had known was now destroyed. The city of Pompeii staring into the face of an exploding Mount Vesuvius.

I smiled, because I didn't know him as Grizzly anymore.

"Hey, Daddy. I think I'm going to switch careers."

The basement was small. I was fast. Sean and Erica would be easy to subdue. Daddy wouldn't hurt his beloved son's body. I laughed.

They'd sown a simple error, and I was going to reap it from them in every ruthless way I knew how.

After all, the best bloodshed is the kind without consequences.

# Hammer the Sky

## by
## David Longshore

Hammer the Sky
by
David Longshore

NANCY SAT up in her folding chair beside the city's swimming pool, whipped off her sunglasses, and glared intently at the creep.

For the past few minutes, he'd been paying too much attention to a little girl with lustrous strawberry curls who was playing in the shallow end of the gargantuan pool. Nancy had earlier seen the child arrive with two teenage girls, one of whom might've been a sister. But over the past few hours, the older girls had disappeared, and Nancy found herself doing what she did best, looking out for people.

"That's right," she called out when the fat, balding loner looked up and caught her accusatory stare. "I'm watching you real good, sir." She then held up her cell phone and pointed to it as though to say she'd call the cops if he didn't behave himself. He immediately stopped bobbing the girl in the water and waded over to the pool's edge, where he hoisted himself up on the deck and sat with his back to Nancy.

She wanted to return to reading the newspaper, but settled for leaning back beneath the umbrella and basking in the ambient warmth of the August afternoon, while keeping a wary eye on the local letch. She looked at her watch, then at the empty lifeguard station. The young, female guard on duty been gone too long now. People just didn't seem to care about their jobs anymore. Another five minutes, and Nancy would make a call to the pool's main gate, where a cop was often posted.

She tried to relax. It was the second day of Nancy's week-long vacation, and tomorrow she would finally close on her dream apartment in a nice new building in East Harlem. Her eldest daughter was expecting her first grandchild that coming March, and she was scheduled for a pay raise at the hospital where she worked as a nurse...which, with the new apartment and grandbaby, would come in handy.

It was while Nancy was thanking goodness for all the blessings she'd received that the world suddenly went to hell. In the flash of a millisecond, something extraordinary occurred.

An enormous alligator had suddenly materialized in the swimming pool.

One second there was a large patch of open water surrounded by swimmers, and the next there was an alligator, grayish-black in color, and very much alive, tearing across the surface.

After its initial, horrifying appearance, the alligator immediately began thrashing the water, throwing up shrouds of liquid that partly obscured its tough, leathery bulk. As its giant tail began knocking aside startled swimmers with the rib-busting thrust of a hydraulic ram, the alligator latched its vast, vice-like jaws onto the first thing it saw and smelled... an older woman in a bathing cap who was paddling with her back to it.

She screamed only once, a hideous shriek that pierced the noises of the surrounding city, as the alligator began rolling with her firmly clenched between its jaws. The white underside of its body gleamed starkly in the bright afternoon light. Dragging the woman's body underwater several times, the alligator finally chewed her into pieces, swallowing them rapidly. The azure waters of the pool turned red and bits of flesh, hair, and clothing danced on the roiling surface.

It all happened so fast... the time between the alligator's arrival and its devouring of the woman was less than 60 seconds... that Nancy didn't have time to think clearly. Elsewhere in the pool, some people, sensing something was wrong, began scrambling out of the water, either by clambering over the edge or crowding like fish into anxious schools at one of the two ladders leading out of the pool.

It was a natural, but fatal mistake that Nancy immediately recognized. Whipping off her sunglasses in horror and shock, she shouted for people around the pool to start helping people out along the edges.

One teenage kid immediately yelled to his friends, "Yo, there's a fucking alligator in the water! Don't just stand there like you want to get ate up."

At first they just laughed at him, and made crude jokes about his mama's caimn. But when several people on the other side of the pool began screaming, there was a sudden splashing, slogging exodus toward the ladders.

"No," Nancy shouted, "don't do that. Come to the sides instead. Come to the sides!"

Darting out of her chair, she hurried to the edge of the pool and helped a young woman up onto the edge... then another. "One of you boys call 911," she said to two young teenage boys who were just standing, fixated on the unfolding horror, near the edge of the pool.

"I ain't calling no cops," the first boy said.

"They've already been called," a man behind Nancy added. His voice seemed familiar, but she was too busy trying to help an overweight man out of the pool to turn around and acknowledge him. A squall of screams drew her attention to southern ladder, where fifteen or twenty people had congregated. While those in the water anxiously looked behind them to see where the alligator was, a fight broke out between two men on the ladder.

"Get away from the ladders," Nancy shouted to the dozens of people now scrambling to exit the pool. "Get to the sides and we'll pull you out."

Honing in on the large, noisy object near the south end of the pool, the alligator began swimming toward the nearest ladder. Although obscured by the bloody water, the stealthy creature's presence was known to the swimmers there, who punched, kicked, and screamed, waiting in mortal dread for it to surface among them.

Sheer carnage occurred when it finally did.

The first victim was a teenage girl. Shoved out of line for the ladder by a man, and accidentally dunked by another, she was kicked in the back by a woman before the alligator, its open jaws as large as planks, put her out of her fear and misery so quickly she didn't even have time to scream.

Once its death roll was complete, the alligator next set its sights on an old man who despite his age, proved faster than the creature. He only lost part of a leg before the reptile, distracted by all the prey around it, moved on to its next victim.

Standing back from the edge of the pool to catch her breath, Nancy glanced at her watch. She was trembling so badly with fear and shock that she had difficulty reading it. It had been almost five minutes since the alligator had materialized in the municipal swimming pool, and she'd seen neither the lifeguard, nor the cop who was normally stationed near the entrance gates.

She did, however, see the creep standing beside the little girl with the strawberry locks, her tiny hand firmly encased by his own, watching the unceasing horror in the pool. Nancy glared at him, but he merely laughed, his eyes viewing her with what she considered a taunt, or maybe even a leer. She spent an extra second studying his face should she have to later identify him to the police.

There was little she could do to help the girl right now. If the man tried to leave the water park with her, she'd do something then. In the meantime, scores of swimmers were still trying to get to safety, and Nancy had to return her attention to them. A few of the victims had serious injuries, including lost limbs and traumatic shock, and she decided to shift her energies toward stabilizing them.

When she looked again, the man and the little girl had vanished into the crowd.

As the most critical of the wounded swimmers were laid out on beach blankets and exercise mats, Nancy and a few volunteers used towels and belts to create tourniquets and stanch the bleeding. Flagging down a man in a business suit, Nancy asked him if she could use his cell phone to call 911. Behind her, screams erupted as the alligator tried to climb into the shallow wading pool, but couldn't make it over the concrete barrier.

The man shrugged. "I would if I could. But the system's down." He indicated the rampaging alligator with a shrug of his head. "This kind of thing has been happening all over the city. I just heard from a coworker that a bunch of lions got loose in an elementary school in midtown, and some giant bears have killed people on Wall Street."

"It's unbelievable," she said, shaking her head with a mixture of awe and terror at the chaos escalating around them. "I always heard there were alligators in the sewers, but I never really believed it." She asked if she could have his tie to use as a tourniquet and he immediately gave it to her.

She told him about the cop at the main gate. "He probably still doesn't know what's going on here. Have him come up right away."

The man bobbed his head and promptly hurried off in the opposite direction. Nancy called after him, but he scurried away and was soon lost to sight behind the chain link fence that surrounded the swimming pool. His lack of compassion bothered her, and yet as a nurse she was used to physical trauma, the blood, the gore, the body parts, and the agony so strong you could feel it in the air.

The swimming pool was a shambles. Bloody water lapped at its sides as the alligator, mostly immersed, cruised around its parameter, circling four swimmers who were trapped in the center. While the four held on to two floatation devices and did their best not to make too much motion, the remaining survivors swam and paddled for the sides.

Without rescue equipment, there was little Nancy or any of the wet, shivering, bleeding, or dying people on the pool deck with her could for the four marooned swimmers. Eventually, when the alligator got hungry enough, he'd move in on them. For the first time in her life as a peaceful woman, she wished she had a gun, a powerful weapon that could blast the alligator right back to the sewer it'd crawled out of.

There was a sudden commotion on the other side of the pool, and Nancy hoped it signaled the arrival of the cops and emergency response personnel. Two people who had been pulled out of the water alive had already succumbed to their wounds, how many of the other critically injured would join them before help arrived?

When it did, it was not at all what Nancy had expected. A burly, tattooed man wearing a color-coordinated hat, clothes, and sneakers, pushed his way through the crowd. At his side he carried a large silver pistol. He was what Nancy had heard described in *da hood* as a gangster. She immediately feared him, dreaded what he and his associates might do under such circumstances.

The crowd, along with the four swimmers, bobbing up and down on their floats in the wake of the alligator's relentless circling, knew exactly what he should do with his piece. They cried for him to *shoot the alligator, dude!* And *blast the ma'fucka, my...*

At that instant, one of the four, a young girl, pushed away from the float and frantically started swimming as fast as she could for the edge of the pool, a distance of about 30 feet. The crowd broke into cheers of encouragement, and two men ran down to the edge to help her up when she reached it. A woman stood ready to wrap her in a dry towel.

But the alligator, enabled by eons of evolution to hunt in water, was much faster than she. Immediately wheeling about on itself, the creature submerged beneath the water, passed directly below the three remaining swimmers, and pounced on the child while she was still ten feet away from the edge.

A collective wail of shock and horror went up from the crowd as the girl screamed once, the sound curdling Nancy's blood, then disappeared beneath the surface. After a few moments her grave was marked by a gush of blood to the surface, followed by a brightly colored piece of bathing suit. Many members of the crowd were in tears, terrified beyond rational thought by the sights they were witnessing. They wanted to look away, to tend to their own injuries, but the ongoing monstrosity was too unique, too gruesome a show to ever walk out on.

Now enraged, as well as pumped up by the crowd, the gangster sauntered to the edge of the pool, lifted the gun, and fired several shots. Most missed the alligator and instead thudded into the three swimmers. Screams and wails of grief welled up from the onlookers, but no one stepped forward to confront the man with the gun.

Watching the alligator closely as it moved in and consumed the unfortunate three, the man walked around the pool, toward where Nancy finished placing a tourniquet around the lower leg of an old man. She didn't believe she could've been more surprised by the afternoon's events, but this took the cake. In the midst of the most bizarre incident imaginable, some sort of twisted gang battle had begun.

"Why did you shoot them?" Nancy asked, knowing in her heart it was the only thing that could've been done at the time. Only fear and the overwhelming hulk of the alligator, resting in the pool from whence it eyed her, kept her anger at the entire situation under control.

He looked her up and down. "They di'nt have a chance, lady. I put 'em out before he did."

"You should've shot the damned alligator!"

"You can't kill that alligator, lady. It ain't alive. It just is and will be till it ain't no more."

From a distance came the wail of sirens, and within a few minutes the police car assigned to the water park's main gate finally arrived at the pool. After taking a moment to assess the incredible situation, the numerous injuries and the need for crowd control, the officer radioed in for reinforcements.

Several witnesses surged around him, telling him what had happened with the alligator, and pointing out the gangster standing behind Nancy on the opposite side of the pool. The cop nodded once, then headed in their general direction.

Nancy turned to the gangster. "I'm afraid you is in some trouble, son," she said.

"I di'nt do shit, lady. This bullshit is because of the alligator."

A seiche suddenly swept across the pool as the alligator, another corpse in its mouth, rolled over and over again, smacking the water with its tail. By the time it again surfaced, the corpse was missing its head and legs. And in the next instant, it was gone entirely.

"Jesus," the cop exclaimed. "What the hell is going on here?" He took out his gun in case the alligator managed to climb out of the pool.

Nancy stepped forward and identified herself as a nurse. She told him how many were dead, how many had been injured, and how many had a real chance of survival if the ambulances would only arrive. The cop assured her they were on the way. She asked if there were other animals on the loose in the city. Looking at his radio, the police officer said he hadn't heard of anything like this before.

Nancy sat down on her chair and covering her face, began to cry. The police officer turned his attention to the gangster. "Several people told me you just shot three people in the pool. You wanna tell me what that's all about?"

"I di'nt do shit."

"You gangbangers never do," the cop replied. "Where's the gun?"

"I ain't got no gun."

"Silver," cop pressed. "Probably a 44.magnum by the sound of it, you used it earlier on three people."

"The alligator ate their asses up."

"That's helpful, now you've got your own cleaning service."

Nancy, who felt the cop was bullying instead of trying to help calm the situation, got up from her chair. "For what it's worth, officer, they really didn't have a chance. Had the cops been here when this all first started, they might have."

The police officer looked at her, and then back to the gangster, who at once started running. Pulling his gun, the cop fired two shots at the fleeing hoodlum, missing him both times. The gangster then turned and fired off a few shots of his own... one of which struck the police officer in the shoulder... and another, Nancy... squarely in the forehead.

While the police officer sank to the deck, gripping his shoulder in pain,

Nancy's body toppled backward and into the pool. In an instant, the alligator was upon it, pulling it by the arm into the middle of the pool where it proceeded to devour it.

By the time the first ambulances began arriving at the swimming pool, the alligator had vanished. In the end it went as quickly and suddenly as it had arrived, leaving the weary onlookers even more shocked and dismayed, especially when it came to relating the bizarre tale to the police and newspapers. At first, many people were skeptical, how could an alligator of that size exist in the city and no one not know of it? And if it even did exist, how did it get into the pool?

Most people were content to let it ride when authorities announced that a gang-related shooting had occurred at the water park, leaving several people dead and injured. Neither they, nor the newspapers, mentioned the dozen or so people who had vanished during the process, allegedly consumed by a colossal alligator.

Among them was Nancy, while another other was a six-year-old girl with strawberry hair who'd gone to the pool with her cousin and a friend, all of whom had disappeared.

# Vengeance, Sweet Vengeance

## by
## Ellen Denton

Vengeance, Sweet Vengeance
by
Ellen Denton

WALLY SMITH walked down Hyatt Avenue through a swirl of mid-winter snow. Although the chill he felt was not entirely from the weather, he hunched down into his overcoat and tightened his scarf. He had gloves on, but slipped his left hand into the coat pocket and kept it there. The solid feel of the gun in it against his palm was comforting and made him feel powerful.

When he got to the corner of Hyatt and Magnolia, he stopped and stood rooted like a statue at the curb. The snow had started coming down harder now making wet spots on his glasses, which were slipping down his nose. He used the thumb of his other hand to push them back into place, and again made a mental note about getting them repaired. Right now, the bridge was clumsily held together by a Band-Aid.

He shuffled from foot to foot as he stood there in the cold, tortured by his own indecision. He thought he had already crushed his doubts and stuffed them like wrinkled dollars into a cracked teacup, shoved into some shadowy china cabinet of the mind. Yet here they were again: doubts, reservations, years of childhood Sunday school sermons rolling up on him like a sea of flaming damnation.

Then there were the hundred and one more practical matters such as who would feed his cat or collect up the photos and knick-knacks lining the desk in his cubicle at work if he went through with the murder.

He looked at the street he had just walked down, took a few hesitant steps back in that direction, stopped, did an about-face, and returned to the corner. He looked across the thoroughfare to the tucked-in-warm brownstones on the east side of Magnolia. The light turned green. He pressed the gun in his pocket against his side, stuck his jaw out belligerently, and stepped off the curb.

He had first caught wind of what was going on less than two weeks ago.

"Wally! Hi, I thought you went to lunch."

He had looked at his wife Lindsey and for a moment, could swear her surprised expression at seeing him was not a happy one, and then he'd looked at Ralph

62

Peterson who was standing so close to her at the office water cooler that their bodies were almost touching.

Ralph had smiled weakly as he moved a few inches away from her, looking like a kid caught with his hand in the cookie jar.

"I had to come back. I told Mr. Huseman I'd call Plimco Steel about their past due account this morning and I forgot to do it. I was about to walk out the door when he asked me about it."

"Bummer. Well, why don't you make that call, and then we can go to lunch together."

"Sure. Give me a few minutes."

He had tried to convince himself there was nothing to it. He was also honest enough with himself to know his frequent jealousies and concerns when it came to Lindsey were based more on his own insecurities than on anything she had ever done wrong.

He was not an attractive man; women had never found him interesting or desirable. He had grown up gawky and awkward, often the butt of schoolyard jokes and, as a teenager, he'd been the subject of whispers and insensitive giggling whenever he passed by a group of girls.

His heart had been broken on both occasions he'd gotten involved with a woman. They'd simply dumped him like cold food into the trash when they'd found more appetizing prospects with someone else.

Each incident of ridicule or rejection throughout his life was like a knife twisted into the still bleeding, childhood memory of his cocaine-addict mother walking out when he was five. As there was no father in the picture, she had dropped him off at his grandmother's small, smelly apartment, announcing, "I'm a free spirit. I've always been a free spirit. Having to take care of this sniveling kid is ruining my life."

She'd then walked out, forever.

Indifferent to him as she was, she had still been the center of his five year old life. In tears, he had run to the window and watched her speed away on the back of a motorcycle, her arms around the waist of something that looked like a bear in a leather jacket.

Two years ago, Lindsey had come to work as a secretary in the Nu-Tone Office Supplies finance department where he worked as an accountant. She was pretty and kind.

When she first began to shine the light of her radiant personality in his direction, he thought she was just being nice to a *loser*, because that was the kind of person she was. When it was clear she was making actual advances at him, he assumed it was part of some cruel office joke. It turned out to be neither. For reasons he could not fathom, nor even fully believe, she really did like him and they were married a year later.

She had been a good and loyal wife, the thought of which again made him stop dead in his tracks midway down the street on Magnolia, gun still firmly in hand.

If that incident by the water-cooler had been the only thing, he would have let the matter go and chalked it all up to an overactive imagination on his part. In the intervening time since then though, it became more obvious Lindsey was involved with Ralph, and what was worse, the news was spreading around the office. He felt humiliated, the world's biggest fool, and he was not going to take anymore.

He continued walking.

The second incident had occurred three days after the first. Wally had walked into the employee break room to find Lindsey and Ralph standing to one side of the soda machine. They were whispering but hurriedly stepped apart when he entered. They'd given each other a quick glance, and Ralph had mumbled something about having to get back to his office.

He couldn't stand not knowing for sure and wanted to confront her with his suspicions, but if he demanded the truth, he was afraid of what she might tell him. Not wanting to force a showdown, he vacillated between quivering fear at the idea of losing her and rage at her for her heartless betrayal.

The situation had rapidly escalated to the point where it could no longer be ignored; he was becoming an object of both ridicule and pity in the office.

Last Monday he had walked into the reception area of the Nu-Tone executive suite to drop off a report. Mr. Huseman's personal secretary, Irene, was talking to the receptionist at the front desk but let out a hissed *SSSHHH!* when she had seen him.

Both ladies had stopped talking. After a brief pause, the receptionist, Mandy, had forced an embarrassed smile and said "Can I help you Wally?"

Flustered, he'd dropped the report on her desk, turned on his heel, and walked out.

Then yesterday he'd been standing outside his cubicle in finance when Mike Caffry from H.R. exited the elevator and passed by him en-route to one of the other cubicles. Caffry was a young, cheerful sort who always greeted him in a friendly way. However, this time, when he'd seen Wally looking at him, he'd just raised his eyebrows a bit, nodded, and walked on.

Today, a cold, snowy Friday, everything had finally come to a head.

Earlier, he'd been called into Mr. Huseman's office just before lunch. Mr. Huseman was not smiling.

"Wally, I wonder if you could do me a huge favor. Jason is out with the flue. I have urgent contracts I need to get dropped off at TLM Microchip on Covington and Fifth and I needed them there and signed yesterday. I know you usually go to lunch at this time. Would you be willing to detour over there and drop these off? Their CEO promised me he would read and have them signed and back in your hands in under a half an hour. Take your regular lunch hour after that. Or eat first, and then bring him the contracts. Either way, between that and lunch, it shouldn't keep you away from your desk more than a couple of hours at the most. I'd consider it a personal favor. I called the messenger service, and they can't get someone down our way to do this till almost five".

Jason was the office gopher and normally did messenger work, coffee runs, photo-copying, and the like. Wally inwardly resented being asked to do this menial delivery boy job, but Mr. Huseman was the CEO and had always been a kind and fair boss.

"Sure Mr. Huseman. No Problem. I'll take care of it."

"Good man, Wally."

Wally had continued to stand there for a moment, but Huseman had already lowered his gaze to some papers on his desk and had apparently failed to register that Wally was even still in the room.

He went to see Lindsey. She looked up at Wally when he came in, and quickly hung up the phone.

"Lindsey, I know I told you we'd go to Sal's pizzeria for lunch, but Mr. Huseman asked me to do him a favor, and it's in the opposite direction. Sorry."

"Oh. Well don't worry about that. I'm swamped right now and couldn't leave my desk if my life depended on it. I was just about to call you to tell you that I couldn't go".

"I can bring you something back."

"Don't bother. I'll just grab something from the vending machine."

"Okay, see you later."

"Yeah, bye."

He finished his errand at TLM Microchip about an hour later, and was now walking down Covington Avenue looking for some place to stop for lunch. He was about to grab the handle of the door to a diner, when he saw something that turned his blood to ice water.

It was Lindsey and Ralph driving past in Ralph's car. They were both laughing hard, and as the car edged slowly forward in the clogged, lunch hour traffic, he saw her put her hand on his shoulder through the car's rear window.

He didn't go to lunch. He didn't return to the office. He went home and got his gun. It was a Heckler and Koch 45 that had belonged to his grandfather. When his grandmother passed away, her crappy furniture, three thousand dollars in savings, and the gun became his.

He donated the furniture to a thrift shop, but had been intrigued by the gun and kept it. He had even taken a few lessons at a firing range at that time, and then placed the gun and its case on the floor of his closet where it sat untouched for years. When he married Lindsey, they got an apartment six blocks away from the three story brownstone that had been converted into office space for Nu-Tone Office Supplies. The gun then sat untouched on a shelf in their small, shared closet. Now it was in his pocket.

He was shaking so much as he walked down Hyatt after leaving his apartment, just at the thought of what he was about to do, that he felt his knees buckling. He stopped at a diner and sipped coffee until he felt like his nerves had steadied enough to go outside again.

As he continued down Magnolia, now only a block away from his office, he felt like he was outside of his body and watching it being propelled forward as though it were a puppet on a stage. He knew what he was doing was insane, but felt compelled to do it anyway. It was the kind of thing he had watched disapprovingly on TV or read about others doing in the news for years. Now it was him doing it.

It would be Wally on the news tonight.

As he approached the Nu-Tone offices, he saw Mike Caffry step outside and look up and down the street, coatless and shivering. He looked relieved to see Wally.

"Wally, you're back! Mr. Huseman needs to see you right away. I was about to send out a posse after you. You weren't answering your cell phone."

Wally ignored Mike's smile.

"Do you know where my wife is?"

"Uh...yeah. I saw her up by the executive offices just before I came down here. She may still be there. You're a lucky guy Wally. Wish I had a pretty wife like that." He shivered, "It's freezing out here!"

Caffry smiled again and turned to go back into the building, but before even one step he pitched forward, slamming face first into the door and rebounded off it like a ping-pong ball before hitting the ground. The door now looked like someone had thrown tomato sauce laced with clumps of parmesan cheese at it.

Wally pocketed the gun, entered the building, and walked up one flight to Lindsey's office. She wasn't there. He then climbed one more flight to the executive suites and ran smack into Irene as he came off the stairs. She looked annoyed when she saw it was him.

"Wally, Mr. Huseman needs to see you right away. Follow me."

She turned on her heel and walked with her usual no-nonsense gait toward the CEO's office, leading him past the receptionist, who looked away as Wally entered. When Irene got to her own desk, she called Huseman.

"Wally Smith is here sir. Yes sir." She looked at Wally and frowned at him sourly. "You can go in now."

He realized he was about to get reamed our for something, probably for taking so long to get back with the contracts, and immediately felt an unbearable hatred for Irene.

When he looked at her again, she had a small, tight smile on her face which, along with her eyes, turned into circles of shock as Wally pulled his hand from his coat pocket and leveled the gun at her forehead. When the shot, deafening in the confines of the closed-in space, sent her flying backwards over her desk, one of her black, orthopedic shoes flew off and hit the wall. He then fired wildly at the shoe.

The double oak doors to Huseman's expansive corner office flew open and the receptionist, Mandy, came bursting through them. She froze in disbelief when she saw Wally standing there, a gun pointed at her. A bullet sliced through her neck, followed by a scream of pain and the sound of a glass breaking in the office beyond.

Wally was about to fire at her again but then saw Huseman rising from his car-sized desk. Pushing by the wounded woman into the office, he dropped the CEO with a gut shot, sending a starburst of blood onto the white walls and carpet.

He was aware of movement behind him and swung around to fire his last bullet, point blank into Ralph Peterson's left eye.

As if on cue, all fifty-two Nu-Tone employees, who had been gathered unseen around the edges of Huseman's office, and only now fully realized what was going on, swarmed like ants mid a chorus of screams, trampling each other to get out of Wally's line of sight.

Only Lindsey remained standing in the center of the cavernous office, staring at Wally, her arms out at her sides in a *what the hell?* gesture.

Even though the weapon was empty, he aimed it at her and pulled the trigger a dozen times.

From the time he'd shot Irene, until that moment, when he finally lowered the gun and stared at his hysterically screaming wife cringing in a heap on the floor, no more than 40 seconds had elapsed. It was only now as he stepped further into the office that he noticed the incongruous sight of a wall to wall buffet, covered from end to end with pastries, wine, and beer.

He looked around at the hysterical throng and then saw a banner stretched across one wall; its message was bright and cheery, *"Happy 10th Anniversary at Nu-Tones Our No.1 employee. Congratulations Wally!"*

Wally looked at the gun in his hand and then back to the banner. His mouth opened and closed but no sound emerged save for a whispered *oh...* as he stared down in horror at a very dead Ralph Peterson, head of the Nu-Tone party planning committee.

# The Destroyer

### by
### Thomas Logan

The Destroyer
by
Thomas Logan

G REAT REMAINED the name Urg the Destroyer, Woe-Bringer, last of the Pur
Urran. Whispered were his conquests; feared was the battle-scarred face.
One good eye of his craggy visage forever scanned the lands looking for his next
challenge; the other, his dead orb, a window to his soul. Both are closed now; the
limbs of his dwindling body warmed by the ground below. Vertically along the
valley of the Destroyer's still mighty chest rests his broadsword Bane, known to
cleave any foe foolish enough to come within its lethal length of twelve hands. In
his sleep, Urg grips Bane's handle, remembering.

Urg had lived by this sword and won many battles, yet neither his thew nor
its keen were enough to save his people. Pur Urran warriors and women were
immediately slain; those whom the Seetles let live suffered worse fates: Pur Urran
elders mocked while tortured; children divided by sex, boys castrated and set to
work as grooms and slaves, girls corralled and kept for Seetle orgies before being
cut apart and fed to dogs. Urg the Destroyer does not pity them. Urg's side lost.
In the Seetles' place, he would have done the same. He and Bane massacred their
way to freedom and fled to fight another day.

Urg groggily wakes, vomits, and stumbles across sand-covered asphalt of his
refuge to check traps. A stout man slowed by ancient wounds, a proud man, a
dying man. Somewhere in that dented skull cracked by an enemy's shield and
poorly mended in the field, Urg knows he is dying. But he also knows that this
knowing means he yet lives. That means he can still kill and pillage and have
his way if he weren't so tired. That means he is Urg still. That means he is not a
rotter.

Here, within half-standing fences protected by the magic glyph of a demon
deity, a broken black wheel on yellow, here is his new home until he dies. He
would hope for it to be soon, but Urg is not a man of hope. Here, Urg eats and
beds and sickens, protected from bandits and the wandering dead. And dogs. Urg
hates dogs.

The Destroyer lay spread flat among the warm ruins, his arms and legs outstretched, the soft, assuring weight of Bane bisecting this X. The sun had not burned through the winter morning's haze when Urg jolted from his dreams. Neither the morning chill nor the sounds of an engine puttering nor the perfumed smell of the trespasser's clothes pulled Urg from the realms of nightmare. No corporal sense returned the Destroyer to this commonplace world where teeth hurt and stomach ache; rather, a deeper sense, an unconscious animal sensation, alerted Urg, one that, even in his sleep, a warrior feels: Urg is not alone. Urg listens.

The scuttling steps sound human and move too quickly for a rotter, tread too lightly for a worthy foe. It could be a woman. The heart beneath the blade quickens, listening. Footsteps stop. Urg is unable to see well since the shield of his enemy cratered his skull. The foe took his good sight; Urg took his life. Then his women and swine. Urg regrets not taking the enemy's life before the weakling ruined his sight. Urg regrets not being able to take it again.

Urg feigns. He feels himself being watched. He stands, stretches, and runs his hand through his scraggly, black beard. He has shaved neither chin nor scalp in the years since he lost his people, though patches and clumps now depart in Urg's sleep. He scratches and spits. He gathers his long head of hair, tugs, twists into a circle, and lets drop. He frees loose brown and gray hairs from his hand. A lion's yawn ensues.

Still, he cannot see his frozen watcher.

Urg moves toward the dung pit, dragging Bane behind him like an unconscious woman. The freshest scar in the earth buzzes and crawls with insect life, some of whose cousins Urg, on desperate days returning from empty traps, has eaten by the handful. He gives the invisible person the broad of his back as he urinates. And listens.

Movement.

Urg lunges towards the sound, scaring the human hare into flight. This flight allows him to better locate his prey. Its movement delicate, dancing around what a man would dash through, what Urg dashes through.

The Destroyer sees she wears some kind of heavy, dark dress. Urg praises gods he more frequently curses. A woman can cook meals which delight the stomach. A woman can provide warmth to his man staff. Even bad cook, dry woman still good trade.

Urg, pleased by the pursuit, smiles and snatches at the shadowy damsel, grabbing hold of her coarse dress. The jolt takes her off her feet and she, tethered by her clothes, is flung over Urg's head and out of her dark clothing. The frail creature lands ungracefully, loses the air from her chest, and is crushed beneath the weight of the Destroyer.

A pause. Urg eases himself off slowly, unbelieving, but hands do not lie. A smooth-chested man, defrocked under Urg's bulk, urinates himself from fear.

Urg, in battle mood and half-erect, quickly considers the uses for the warmth under his body. He has no particular respect for the priesthood but has heard many rumors about these men of the cloth. One being that they travel with packets of absconded broken glass to prevent what the Destroyer now contemplates. Urg tries to put a finger on his concern. Though tight, perhaps from fear, there is no glass or other obstruction he can feel.

"Please, sir, don't. I can help you. You're demon-possessed."

Urg, with only the silent companionship of Bane, has forgotten that people speak. He withdraws his finger slowly, an animal entranced. The whimpering man beneath him cowers and cringes in a compact, prenatal shape. Urg stands. He remembers words.

"Urg." His arm comes across his chest, striking it solidly with a double thump. "Urg of Pur Urran." The learned man cautiously unfurls but cringes again as Urg raises his sword. "Bane."

"Jonathan Richter Right, Jr.," the weakling's quick but unsteady voice offers. He grovels on his knees. "I am a cousin in the Order of Beau Raq the Benevolent, Most High, the One True God, Healer of Deep Wounds and Prince of Technologies. How long have you been here? You realize strong, pernicious forces are at work here within these fences that the ancient magics persist?"

A bunch of sounds without meaning scratch against the Destroyer's ears. Urg is confused, then frustrated, then angry. He changes his grip on Bane.

Cousin Right impoverishes his sentences. "You feel queasy - sick? Weak? When sun come up, Urg?"

"Urg feel strong." Urg straightens aggressively, his manhood questioned, displaying biceps still massive, though diminished to the size of an infant's bisected skull under the taut skin. Gone are the muscles that once formed upon muscles like metastasized tumors of killing power. But they are arms enough yet to have Bane cleave this weakling for his insult.

"No, no, does your stomach, gut ever hurt in the mornings? Urg cough up blood? You see the radiation signs?"

Urg remembers that he does not like talk. He remembers why Bane is quiet: Conversation no good. He will let Bane sing the song of the Destroyer.

"Wait, wait. The demon symbol," and here the desperate holy man uses his hands to better illustrate, "with rectangular eyes slightly curved with a mouth like its eyes and a big round nose in the middle?"

Urg knows the symbol. It is his symbol now. Urg's place.

"Those are demons. Their magic makes mortals sick. I can conjure holy water, cure you. You will not feel sick."

There is much power in the sword, Urg knows, but the ways of magic, though not as immediate, are stronger still. Urg listens for his loyal companion's advice, but Bane is silent. Bane only ever has one thing to say, and Bane screams it in blood.

But Urg, in listening to the cousin, remembers. What he recalls is not a particular memory of specific people or a significant event but a general sensation. He feels how people, though never as strong or lasting or loyal as Bane, once gave another kind of comfort, one that comes from weakness, impermanence, and autonomy. Urg sees now with his good eye that the priest is young, clean-shaven, and womanish. He regrets not knowing this when the blood was welling but also knows that, sure as day, night will come. And cold nights are fit for another body's warmth.

Cousin Jonathan Right takes advantage of Urg's pause to lead them back to his machine. He offers Urg cured meat and vegetable paste from the saddlebags. The barbarian gladly accepts. While the smacking beast is lulled, Cousin Right checks his meter for exposure levels. Though he has been in the wastelands for under a day, green's safety has already begun fading, albeit it infinitesimally, to yellow's warning. He watches this dumb, two-legged beast reach deep into his maw with dirty digit and remove a tooth. Right knows he cannot stay long, but by taking temporary refuge here, he can plot out where next to search for machine fuel and ensure he has lost his pursuers.

Urg's smacking slows, then stops altogether as he watches Cousin Right lift a leg over the bike's seat and begin jumping up and down, causing the machine to neigh. The priest whispers swears under his breath. Mighty threats must they be, for the gods heed his prayer and the machine roars to life, causing Urg to jolt and call upon Bane for protection. But the roar and smoke are short-lived; the reluctant machine coughs itself back to sleep, and Urg returns to chewing and feeling about for other loose teeth while he listens to the strange stories of his new manwife.

Cousin Right tells of a time when all the world was ruled by machines, when such metal monsters heeded the demands of their human masters, a time before the plagues, before rotters. He speaks of the great secrets of cities preserved and studied in the Temple of Beau Raq the Benevolent, Most High, where white coats still work their magics.

Once the cities drew people to their mechanical realms; now cities are a place where hoards of rotters go uncontested, cannibals dine well, and only the dead live for long. No one braves the cities. No one except the Tu Ula Tun scavengers who have calculated through stones and tables the barter value of their lives. And Cousin Right. He is unafraid, strong in his faith. He hands Urg the tranquilizer he has mixed into a can of brackish water, a precaution like the glass balloon he failed to insert. The barbarian accepts, Beau Raq, Most High, be praised.

Urg sniffs the water can. Here is a smart man. Here is a man with food and magics. Urg wonders why such a man would come here, Urg's land. Perhaps he has heard the tales of Urg the Destroyer, Urg the Slayer, Urg the Unholy. Cousin Right no longer cowers or avoids Urg's stare. Perhaps he, too, looks forward to nightfall.

Urg drinks deeply the draught and eats more. His body chills. He has less urge to vomit. The burning in his throat dissolves and there's dryness in his cheeks. He feels it harder to breathe. Cousin Right begins apologizing for something, but Urg has him be quiet. He listens. Dogs. Dogs are barking, coming. Urg runs on shaky legs that buckle beneath him and then darkness. For the first time in many years, his nightmares are not of battles. They are of the demon Radiation with two slant eyes and one slant mouth. And of dogs.

Day is falling, turning the sands to indigo snow. The trees have died, dried; every day the glacier grows closer, and one day the snow will be real. Somewhere nearby, dogs bound by leashes nip and bite at the night. Urg can make out distant fires with his good eye and smell the roasting meat. Cannibals.

The dogs must have smelled the sissy man; his perfume sweet but deadly like all pleasant things. This Urg deduces in not so many words and curses the gods and their followers in fewer unformed thoughts still. Cousin Right, an arrow's flight away, cries out to these same gods with shrill womanish screams as a cannibal's carving knife enters his calf, a quick downward slice freeing another fillet.

Urg of the Pur Urran, bound to a metal pole inside the cannibal camp by restraints of crude metal chain and leather, feels himself faint and not long for this world. His insides no longer ache, and he can smell himself for the first time in dim memory. His outsides had been washed in what could be thyme. Groggily, he makes out human shapes many times more than his fingers and toes moving throughout the camp, too many to take on alone and weaponless once he discovers how to break free. He shakes his foggy head. Cousin Right's screaming has stopped.

Urg has no particular penchant for how he will die - amid the din of battle or suddenly keeling over while laying ownership with staff to the booty of war like his father. On some level, Urg knows all living things die. Also, that with his death, the Pur Urran will die. But these abstractions mean little to a concrete man. Urg has no cares in this world save one.

Urg thrashes against his bonds, remembering: Bane. Where is his sword? He panics to think of it being maliciously struck against rocks to dull its edge or menstruated upon by witchwomen or used by weaklings to chop wood. Urg struggles, careless of whether he is watched by those he cannot clearly see.

Two figures approach, both human-sized and reeking of blood; the smaller appears a girl slave.

"Hey, what you do?" the larger shape demands. Urg, defiant, struggles harder hoping to break his chains, then this cannibal's neck. A spear tip slips into Urg's side. "Don't do." The Destroyer relaxes, and the cannibal removes the spear and stakes the slave's necklace chain into the ground to collect his soldier's pay.

Urg's struggles lose steam from his punctured side. The Destroyer can no longer drown out the siren's call of sleep. But when his good eye spies the scarrings of a Pur Urran princess on the young slave being ravaged only half a spear's length away, he thrashes wildly, renewing his efforts with superhuman resolve. That do not go unnoticed. The guard, finished, cleans himself with her royal hair before pulling up his leather-patched long-shorts and striking Urg, this time with the spear's blunt end, in the skull as he leaves.

Dazed, alone with his fellow Pur Urran tethered from her neck to a spike driven deep in the ground, Urg tries addressing the princess in the royal tongue. She does not move. Urg cannot recall a girl of early menstruating years born to the queen. Then he remembers that it has been nearly six seasons of frost since he first began his wanderings, that long since the Seetles destroyed his people. This would make her only a child, a creature with curly raven hair he can still remember as a toddling stumbling about the Pur Urran's itinerant camps and saying her first words. This must be that creature, another in the royal line yet alive. And a female. He must not let her die. He must mate with her and replenish the tribe.

Urg renews his efforts to have her speak, his earnest overcoming his tongue's awkwardness. He tells her who he is, what they must do, and expresses a need for any information that could abet their escape. He pleads her to answer. The dogs' whines and snarls and growls cease as they wolf down leftover scraps and chew bones of Jonathan Right, Jr.

The girls responds. It is not much but shows life has not left her body. Her head turns; her chin scrapes against the marl. She does not lift her vessel; she does not move but for her head. Her eyes are numb and look without seeing toward her liege.

Urg rages and vows to hurt the cannibals bad. He grits his teeth and slows his heaving chest. He battles his racing warrior blood and animal instincts and closes his eyes. They will know the wrath of the Destroyer. He will lull his captors into believing he is unaware and then roar to life like a mighty boar once they've loosed his bonds. They are not lulled.

Over the sizzling collops of Cousin Right who was only fit for an appetizer, the cannibals heard Urg's awakening and new bout of determined struggles, which has watered their palates anew. Urg is a prime cut of meat with plenty of protein still on his bones. They've taken extra precautions with their mighty, meaty meal. It has been many, many years since they have tasted Pur Urran. Some of their young never have. It is a delicacy worth relishing.

They unchain Urg's extremities individually, two men on two different bindings to each arm and leg as well as two each on both the torso and the throat. When, feeling the moment upon him, Urg roars to life, he is well under their duress. They tug him like a wild mare, their dogs nipping at his heels. The spear wound in his side opens wider. Urg grimaces and fights the pull of unconsciousness, knowing that bright darkness leads to death.

If his vision were better, the barbarian would see the cannibal women flee from their repast preparations. Instead, it is Urg's sense of smell that informs him his fate has turned. For better or worse, he cannot assay, for his flesh may still be eaten. There are rotters near. Screams to his left, screams to his right. Urg feels his bonds go lax and smells fresh blood spilt amid the battlecries and screams. A rotter approaches; Urg can tell by that unholy limp of the wandering dead.

A double-fisted roundhouse to the ear puts the rotter down. Another approaches, dragging a blade useless in the creature's reanimated fingers. Urg of Pur Urran uses the blade to separate its former owner's head from its body, then another rotter's, and another's. The sword's weight is poorly distributed and length more like a long dagger compared to Bane.

Against the backlighting of the camp's fires, Urg can see the undead's superior numbers; it looks as if a forest of swaying saplings approaches, though it has been long since Urg has seen a forest and these bodies, not made of wood, have teeth that bite and infect.

The princess! Urg must rescue her. They must be bountiful and rear their children to slaughter every Seetle man, woman, and child, but not in that order. Seetle men will die last for first they must watch their women enjoyed to death by Urg and his many sons and their Seetle youth and elders made sport of by battling wild beasts against whom they cannot hope to prevail or by racing against the arrows of the legendary Pur Urran archers reborn. Yes, this the Seetles men will see, each through the one eye they will be left, and hear their women's screams through their one remaining ear. Their fingers they will not keep but lose one for every day they are suffered to live. Their tongues must be cut from their mouths and their ankles broken to prevent escape. They will bleed the full ten days and wish for death every moment. But first Urg must rescue the princess.

He rushes back to where she remained bound by the great chain about her neck and the stake driven into the ground. She is not alone. Bane's with her, fallen from the hands of a dead, half-eaten guard. They two are not alone, but it takes only a single wide swing of Bane to dispatch the three rotters hungry for his princess. Now, reunited with Bane, the princess over his shoulder, they cut their way through the slow-moving rotters, a steady swath of killing, what the couple - Urg and Bane - do best. Yet Urg knows no stroke or plunge to kill the deep and bleeding bite that will turn his princess into a rotter.


Recent days long. Very long. They have been long days of waiting and much confusion. Urg fought the urges of sleep the first two nights' slow travel home. After the first night when she did not change, he treated her bite as best he knew how, same as his side's spear wound. He urinated into the exposed red tissues and pressed Bane heated yellow-orange against her wound. Her face did not change when he urinated on her leg, but her mouth opened in silent scream as he cauterized the bite. Her unblinking eyes dripped tears.

Urg does not believe demons cause the princess's silence; he has seen many turn, including his seven-of-eight wife. It does not rob the bitten of speech, not until dead; then, still, they moan. No, Urg perceives the princess still suffers from the death of the Pur Urran. She is dead inside like he.

With the sun's second descent and she still unchanged, he decides to feed her. Under the third sun, back within the fences, Urg loosens her chains. On the fourth day, her eyes work. Her face finds his. She says her first word: Hero.

Before a full filling of the moon has passed, she has become his eyes, accompanying him silently on his hunts and checking his traps. She begins to be sick in the mornings much like Urg, but she still does not turn.

Urg begins to notice little things about her: her teeth are white; her smell resembles much his sister's; her feet point inward just a bit; she never runs, even with her wounded leg nearly healed. She is shorter than he by a head and neck and a quarter of his width; she has still much growing to do. She will need to learn the ways of a princess, how to speak the royal speak, carry conversation, entertain warrior generals and merchants. At night, he notices other things, the pangs of lust no different from any other virile man's. But whether sickness or respect for the crown or her dispiriting silence, the desire never rages and her body remains unused.

Urg lives a different life during these long days of confusion, though his hunts for calories and nights of unrest camping among the fenced radioactive ruins remain much the same. His mind is rife with ideas, plans, hopes, and visions for his new tribe. He lives a life of a future.


Urg took iller. One morning there is more blood than he remembers being in his morning puke. Then he recalls he usually woke and stood for his daily vomiting. His legs do not work under him. He curses the gods. He does not want his princess to see him this way, but there is little he could do to escape the weakness.

His body rebels against him, then his mind. He lies and suffers nightmares and waking delusions much worse than any torture devised by men. Bane, clutched, is powerless to help. Beneath the veneer of his sweating brow, Urg shivers and curses the princess. He sees now she is the cause.

She poisoned him. It was their plan all along. *Them.* Even the dead priest was in on it. The weak work together and take their time in killing. Maybe she was never bitten. Women magic. An illusion. She a Seetle. Imposter. A trap. Would Urg be able to slay the witch before her poison did? No. The Destroyer has lost the urge to kill. Her betrayal too much. Urg is ready to be rid of this unfair life.

Though his fever eventually broke, his spirits he could not mend. Until, still lying, lacking vigor, he understood the princess hasn't turned. She was bitten long ago. She is undead to rights. But she hasn't turned.

She must have magics, like the skin cuttings visiting cousins once mixed with the blood of cattle to prevent the pox. A magic cure against the rotters. Urg's universe expanded with the thought. He who can master the rotters enslaves the world. The Pur Urrans would be mighty once again!

She fought him all morning. Tinaq did. That is the princess's name, Urg has learned. Urg's sudden enthusiasm frightens her. Tinaq wishes him not to rise. She does not believe the Destroyer well enough. She believes his ramblings mad. But Urg is just over a hand-a-half taller than she and many stones heavier and has his way.

She serves as his third leg, counter to Bane in its scabbard as a cane, balancing Urg by a tight embrace that just barely reaches across his narrowing waist. It is the first time she has hugged a person since her family was slaughtered and his bulk makes her own balance shaky.

Urg has conceived a series of steps that will lead them to safety, though he labors to explain them to Tinaq. Their final goal will be the Order of Beau Raq, a place of science where studied persons like Cousin Right will know the importance of Tinaq's magic and can extract it. Neither individually nor together in their three-legged stumble will they be strong enough to traverse the expanse. They will need to make use of Cousin Right's gift, the demon roaring on two wheels. But the machine requires food. And this will require dealing with the nomadic traders, unpleasant business as Urg, having nothing to trade, will have to slay them. Unpleasant because Urg, in his fatigue, is not looking forward to battle, even with the Tul Ula Tuns. Yet Bane calls, and so too the future, and to kill is to live again.

Urg detaches himself from Tinaq, like a daughter, sister, and first wife to him. He cannot tell if she understands about the cuttings and magic. He must lead if she is to follow. Urg takes one bold step forward and falls flatly upon his face. He wakes two days later to find the Tul Ula Tuns have found them.

Princess Tinaq realizes her error. The insight arrives with the morning sun's glint off weapons and piercings. She was not careful to cover her tracks these past days as she checked the traps. She knew not better.

Urg was in a fantasy involving a monster with no real form but many orifices throughout its body. It was repulsive and alluring. What he wakes to is worse.

"Wakey, wakey, eggs'n'bakey."

The talker smiles and cocks his head. Behind him, Princess Tinaq is being held by another Tul Ula Tun flanked by two mercenaries, meaty warriors from differing tribes. Her clothes remain on her body, which shows neither wound nor bruise that Urg's good eye can discern.

"Believe we found something belonging to you, mate."

Urg has never liked the Tul Ula Tuns and only traded with them once, years before he settled here, for the traps he uses. He does not like their scavenging ways, nor the haughtiness of their tribal codes governing honorable trade. Their women are allowed to move up the ranks and marry other women; the Destroyer often could not tell their women from their men. He does not like their haircuts or the conspicuous wealth they wear pierced through their faces. Theirs is a bizarre, topsy-turvy social order, and Urg did not like how their cunning wealth provides them power.

Though none in their surrounding crescent can tell, Urg exerts superhuman strength to stand. By outward appearances, Urg woke like any other mighty warrior would, slowly to his feet, rippling muscles, holding Bane causally but ever ready to smite a foe.

Urg swallows the vomit in his throat and makes out the eyes on his interlocutor's hazy face. "No sell."

"Sorry, mate, but you've gotta be a bit more articulate if you want to speak the common tongue."

"Need machine food."

"Yeah? You have yourself a monster to feed? You okay there, pal? You look a little green. Say, her cuttings match your own. She your sister? I thought you Pur Urrans were all Google Glass, extinct-like, you know, but you're gonna mate with your sister, huh? Well, that's all fine and well if you want diaper-fillers with flippers running around with hearts outside their chestesses. Lookie here, here's what I propose for a mutual business exchange."

Urg listens. The man speaks fast, but Urg gets the drift. He bellows his answer, "No sell."

"Woh, okay, big buddy, your toy's not for sell. How's about rent? Lease to own? Gas ain't cheap. She looks fresh and firm - down below, if you know what I mean."

Urg cannot make out the princess's face. He can only see she does not squirm, that she has returned to passiveness as when first they met. There is only one way out of this. Urg raises his sword.

The princess is resourceful. Urg had not considered many things when he formulated his plan to move through the Dead Lands. The time he tried, he'd fallen from the machine. Princess Tinaq was to be his eyes, hold on tight. Now she will ride. She is shorter than Urg but constructed a small block for the footbrake. She will ride alone.

She knew this feat was important to her hero; the Destroyer traded away his one true love for its liquid. He looked naked now lying without Bane the broadsword along his chest.

Tinaq does not want to go. In her sorrow, the princess thinks of killing herself. In her grief, she wonders what it mattered if she carried magics; what the world was worth if she cannot have Urg as her husband and hero.

She sits very still. Time passes unnoticed until she again feels ill and vomits for the second time today, a little more blood in the bile than usual. Her stomach stirs, and the princess feels in her gut that the Pur Urran will survive, that the Pur Urran will rise again. There were times during Urg's delusions... She was young and curious and may be with child yet. She buries the Destroyer in the garden that wouldn't grow and marks his gravesite with a metal sign that is his symbol. Fingernails peeling off, hands raw from clawing earth, she leaves in a roar of the machine toward the monastery, remembering the warrior as a good and kindly man, strong despite his many weaknesses. She will ride. She will survive. She will speak the name of Urg the Destroyer, Woe-Bringer, the first of the new Pur Urran.

# Emperor of Swine

## by
## DJ Tyrer

Emperor of Swine
by
DJ Tyrer


"AND THIS one we call Napoleon," said Davis as they reached a much larger cell-like pen than the others Greene had been shown on his tour. The enormous, bristle-backed boar within gave an uninterested yawn at their presence. "I don't need to tell you why," Davis added with a chuckle.

"Aren't you worried that you're invoking hubris by giving... him, such a name?" Greene asked, looking through the reinforced-glass panel in the steel door at the pen's seemingly-lethargic inmate.

Davis laughed. "Oh, no. Pigs aren't intelligent enough to be driven by the forces of nominative determinism."

"Good thing, too. Kept in a cell all day like that, I'd be ready to launch a revolution given half a chance."

"We'd love to let him out to frolic, really, we would, but the damn thing's just too valuable. It's not just that he could have an accident or escape, but we have rivals who'd steal him in order to close the research gap and there are all those damn fool activists out there opposed to what we're doing who'd leap at the chance to cause mischief by killing him or stealing him or... anything else they could think of."

"After all," he went on, "these pigs bring home the bacon for us."

That was the third or fourth time he'd made the same pun and Greene really wished he could smack him right in the middle of his pompous, self-satisfied face. Sadly, such as he were unable to act on their feelings so freely.

"Tour's almost over, Minister," went on Davis, gesturing down the corridor. "This way to the fertility lab and then the monitoring station. Then, back to my office for a nice cup of tea."

Greene really wished he could punch him, the man was so contemptuous. He supposed politicians had brought it on themselves with expenses and everything, but it wasn't as if geneticists were any more popular with the public.

They went into a laboratory where white-coated scientists were busy fertilising swine ova with Napoleon's seed.

"You don't let him mate naturally?" Greene asked.

"Oh, no; far too hit-and-miss. This way, we can engineer the egg and ensure that it's fertilised and healthy before we implant it."

"How much engineering do you do?"

"It depends on what the piglet will be used for. Some are given diseases and deformities so that we can test cures on them. Some we have been making more compatible with humans: pigs and humans are very similar and, if we can improve on nature, they will be perfect as organ donors or for testing drugs."

"So, nothing too drastic? One hears all sorts of stories about strange gene-splicing that disturb the public."

"Well, the public are pretty dumb," Davis responded with a chuckle, "but, no, we don't do anything too drastic. That'd be unethical." His grin was not very reassuring.

"And, this is the monitoring station," he told Greene after a further lengthy walk as they went into the final room on the tour. There were two men in security-guard uniforms and dozens of screens that they were presumably meant to be monitoring, although one seemed to be half asleep and the other was showing more interest in his cup of coffee. The screens showed various angles of the pens, labs and passages that comprised the research centre. Mostly they showed bored sows and squabbling piglets. A few showed the perimeter.

"As you can see, we can monitor everywhere from here: this not only boosts our security, but allows us to observe the pigs whenever we want to."

Greene was distinctly underwhelmed: he'd seen numerous such monitoring stations on the many inspections he'd made over the years. Why did everyone seem to imagine such things were of interest? It was only relevant insofar as it proved the place was secure and it didn't impress much on that score.

"Very good," he replied, in what he hoped was a suitably-neutral tone. Davis beamed as if that were high praise.

They then headed for the director's office for the promised 'nice cup of tea' that proved rather cardboardy in taste.

"Any questions?" Davis asked with a patronising smile.

Before Greene could answer, the sound of an alarm filled the air.

"Just one," he retorted sarcastically, "what the hell is that?"

Davis was swearing and had grabbed for his phone. He was making the same demand to whoever was on the other end of the line.

"What do you mean Napoleon's got out?" he shrieked, anger in his voice. "Not today of all days!" He almost sobbed as he added, "Not when we're being inspected..."

He paused and Green could hear the muffled sound of a voice on the other end.

"Tranquilise him!" cried Davis. "Taser him! Just get him back in his pen! Call me when it's sorted!"

Davis slammed the phone back down onto its base. "Idiot!" he spat at it.

"Problem?" asked Greene, delighting in the man's discomfort. The alarm was still pounding in his ears.

"Yes," Davis replied, jaw tight.

"Elba?" he added with a smirk, but the director didn't seem to hear him. He spoke more loudly as he said, "I think I should observe this; shall we head for the monitoring room?"

"Oh, no need for that... I'm sure it'll all be over shortly with Napoleon back in his pen. Besides, I couldn't want to put you in any risk."

"Risk?"

"Not that there is any risk..." he smiled grotesquely, "they'll soon have Napoleon in his pen again, I'm sure. Everything is under control."

"Well, let's go take a look at things."

Once in the monitoring station, they noticed two things. The first was that several of the screens were static. The second was that Napoleon had been joined by several sows on his rampage.

"It would appear it is anything but under control," Greene observed.

"Dammit, how did this happen?" snapped at the hapless security guards who were impotently watching the chaos unfold and vainly attempting to organise things over the radio.

"Napoleon's learnt how to open doors somehow," one of the guards responded, tone incredulous.

"And, the walking pork chop used a *broom* to knock out some of the cameras," said the other.

"A broom?" Davis queried, confused.

"Took it off one of the cleaners, bit a couple of the poor sod's fingers, and swung it with its mouth, striking the cameras. It looked almost deliberate."

"*Sounds* deliberate," Greene commented.

The guards laughed. "Pigs ain't clever!"

Davis shifted uncomfortably.

"Something you'd like to share?" Greene asked.

When Davis didn't respond, just looked shifty, he added, "Please, do tell..."

"Well, as you might know... pigs are clever creatures."

"But, not so clever..."

"Well, no, but, well... these pigs *are* clever, very clever."

"What do you mean?"

"We've been, ah, genetically engineering them to make them smarter. Napoleon really is quite intelligent."

"Let me guess, you're hoping to cure Alzheimer's?"

Davis looked blankly at him. "No. We just wanted to see what we could achieve."

"Is that the only improvement you've made?"

"Ah, well, no... Napoleon is something of a super-pig."

"Oh, excellent..."


The rampage had begun when one of the scientists had arrived to collect another 'sample' from the Emperor of Swine. The apparently languid boar had risen the moment the door to his pen was opened and had charged at the man, slamming him out the way before he could shut the door; Napoleon had always been quite docile before.

Having smashed the hapless man to the floor, Napoleon had headed down the corridor, barreling through the scientists who'd tried to halt its escape. It had then halted before a startled cleaner and bitten him, picking his broom up after it was dropped. Having put several cameras out of action, Napoleon had proceeded to start releasing the sows from their captivity; he'd spent years observing, waiting for this day.

Ably assisted by a willing entourage of enraged animals, the swine king set about taking revenge upon those who'd held it captive and tormented it for so long. Although most of the scientists had heeded the alarm to take shelter in labs and break rooms, barricading shut the doors, leaving the fight to animal handlers and security guards, some were tardy and found themselves being attacked. With a skirmish screen of sows before him, it had proven impossible to tranquilize, Taser, net or snare the ringleader. Staff were bowled over and trampled or bitten and shaken like rag dolls; some sows stopped to disembowel and devour their screaming victims even as the crowd surged on, strewing sections of intestine along corridors like some obscene bunting.

"Form a line!" shouted the senior security guard. She'd been in the police and had busted a few heads during riots and knew how to deal with an unruly crowd. She just had to hope the tactics would work against an irate porcine mass that weighed far more than people did.

Linking riot shields, the nervous guards blocked the corridor in a flesh-and-blood barricade and awaited the swinish tsunami.

The pigs ploughed into them, smashing guards aside or tossing them to the floor where they were trampled beneath their shields.

Tasers sparked and truncheons were brought down on broad, bristled shoulders, to little effect.

Even as the sows continued their charge, Napoleon continued to unlock more of the imprisoned pigs, adding to their numbers as quickly as the humans could bring them down. Overwhelmed, those few security guards who'd not been trampled turned and fled, desperately seeking somewhere to hide. The forces of Napoleon had overcome those of his former masters.

"This doesn't look good," Greene stated, watching events unfold on the monitors. "Not good at all."

Davis said nothing, just stared dumbstruck at the disaster unfolding before his eyes.

The two security guards seemed in a state of shock, but had barricaded the room's door *just in case* and put the place in lockdown, before calling for assistance.

As far as could be seen, the uprising had seized over two-thirds of the facility and almost all the animal handlers and guards had either been killed or severely injured; everyone else was trapped, defenseless and fearful.

"Amazing, simply amazing," Greene murmured as he watched Napoleon opening yet another door. "Tell me," he asked, hoping one of the three men would answer him, "how many access codes does this place have?"

"Just the one," one of the guards replied, offhand.

"Oh, dear..."

"What is it now?" asked Davis.

"It seems the pig knows the code."

"What?"

"It just used the broom-handle to punch in a code and a door opened. Napoleon really is a genius pig."

Davis checked the monitors. "Oh, no..."

"What is it?"

"He's got into this section of the complex!"

Greene swore. "How long till help gets here?"

"Too long..." sobbed one of the guards, fiddling with the baton on his belt; smaller than the heavy truncheons that had had such a minimal effect upon the pgs, it seemed no better than a fly-swat.

Greene's spirits dropped. He looked around for a weapon, but couldn't see one. He asked what there was.

"There's nothing here," the other guard told him. "We're not supposed to fight anyone, anything; we're just supposed to keep an eye on the situation."

"Great..." He hefted up a stool; it was not much of a weapon, but it would have to do.

More camera screens went blank.

"Napoleon's nearly here..." Davis muttered, defeated.

A moment later, the door shook as something heavy slammed into it. Greene felt his nerve melt away, dropped the stool and looked around in desperation; there was a pair of lockers in the corner of the room. He looked at the lockers as the door shuddered again. If he crouched right down...

The door smashed open and an enormous, snarling, bristle backed boar burst into the room. Monitors exploded in showers of sparks as fragments of the barricade they'd piled up flew aside.

Napoleon snarled at the sight of Davis, lunged at him and bit deep into his throat tearing it out in a spray of blood, before trampling his twitching body.

One of the security guards was cowering, sobbing, in the corner, but the other had seized up the stool Greene had hefted, realising it was a better weapon than his baton, and leapt at the pig, swinging it. The blow barely even seemed to register with the boar, which just tossed its head sideways, smashing the guard into a bank of monitors as if he were light as paper.

Napoleon then advanced on the cowering man in the corner and sniffed at him, a great, heavy suck of air. Then, the boar buried his snout into the man's stomach and ripped him open, scattering guts like decoration about the room. In his hiding place, too constricted to reach to cover his ears, Greene could only wince at the horrendous, gurgling shrieks emitted by the brutalised and dying man.

Would the boar discover his hiding place? He could only pray he'd survive. Would help arrive in time to save him? Certainly, the Emperor of Swine knew how to escape from the complex, knew the necessary codes, but was even Napoleon clever enough to evade capture for long?

He hoped not.

# Ending All Wars

## by
## Bryan Nickleberry

Ending All Wars
by
Bryan Nickelberry

I RUN AS fast as I can, hearing the fervent sounds of pursuit behind me. The enemy was waiting for us. The personnel carrier's door had opened, and I'd been the first one out. My feet hadn't even hit the dirt, but I heard the rocket propelled plasma grenade as it flew past my shoulder, and into the APC. The blast threw me clear, and killed everyone inside. I was still getting to my feet, when the shooting started, as the bastards swarmed toward me like ants. I've been running and gunning ever since.

The good news about killing these mechanical bastards is that they come armed to the teeth, so I'm able to grab more guns and ammo from the ones I kill, in order to kill more as I go. I pretty much used up my own weapons at the very beginning of this mess.

There are enough robots out to kill me that hosing entire areas down with laser-fire has been surprisingly effective when it comes to regaining room to run, and breathe. But their armor is thick enough, and they're built well enough that I stop and take the time to target shots directly to their heads or their power cores whenever I'm able. The fact that there are no humans living in this city means I can do things like shoot abandoned building portions down on top of them, or blow up cars next to them without having to worry about consequences. Whatever it takes to make it the next few feet.

Unfortunately they've been doing the same to me. Herding me when they can wherever they want me. So sometimes I do unexpected things, like smashing through a weakened wall to a different area, backtracking, and even working my way through the sewer at one point. But I'm starting to think that no matter how hard I press myself, it won't be enough. They just keep coming.

I take a rifle in each hand, and try to meticulously pick off an entire group of mechs as they round the right-hand corner of the "T" intersection. They fall like wheat to a scythe before me; but a few get off shots anyway. One shot hits my helmet as I lean down, another hits my chest armor; and a third grazes my leg. I feel my helmet, and chest plate heat up, but it just makes me fight harder. I feel nothing from the graze on my leg, so I don't even think about it.

I start running forward as the snipers begin shooting from the rooftops, and I swear I can feel the heat from the passing laser blasts as I run. My guns are starting to run dry, and I seriously doubt that I can survive a lack of ammo.

Running around the corner will give me the most opportunity to grab guns; but I've got a funny feeling that the robots have the same idea to take me out as I clear the corner. And I have no intention of dying.

As the guns sputter to a halt, I toss them aside, and put on an extra burst of speed; because I'm only going to get one shot at this. Leaning in low, I snatch a rock, and head for the right side of the street. This limits the ability of the snipers on that side to shoot me, though it gives the snipers on the left side a much better view of me. As soon as I hit the shadows, I duck behind a car, and pull out two smoke grenades. I toss one right into the middle of the street past the corner I've been shooting at, and will soon be running past; then I drop the other at my feet while the snipers light up the car I'm hiding behind like a Christmas tree.

I take a moment to say thanks for the two metal garbage cans behind the car, and I take another few, precious seconds to toss some rocks, dirt, debris and garbage into each one. Then as the car begins to sag, I grab a can in each hand, and begin to run as fast as I can for the other side of that street.

I burst into the open from behind the smoke that my grenade gave off, and the snipers immediately target me again. A split second before I hit the smoke from my other grenade, marking the intersection, I toss one garbage can out in front of me, and let the waiting robots perforate it, while I speed past, holding the second can to my side, and letting it take the fire for me. I reach down with my free hand and scoop up a single rifle as I run, then shoot the glass on the building before me. I realize my mistake too late, and spin around to thrust the remaining can ahead of me through the rapidly melting glass.

I hit the floor, roll over the molten can and leave some of my uniform behind. Surprisingly enough I'm alive, and in relatively good condition. I stumble over another fallen soldier as sniper fire begins to fly in through the window, and I snag his armor and helmet, shedding mine as I run, donning the new gear on the fly. I ditch the old laser pack from the rifle, and add one of the four new ones that I've been carrying and haven't had time to use. The gun charges up in a matter of seconds as I run my fastest up the building's stairs.

Five floors up, and the robot snipers have begun taking random pot shots through windows. That's when I come grinding to a halt. The stairs are crooked from this point on. Of course they are. I take a precious moment to chuckle. I chose this building because most of it has tilted sideways into another two buildings. I figured the robots would lose track of me between the three buildings, unless of course they decided to bomb all three; but there isn't much I can do in that scenario, so I didn't bother to think about it. The other problem I hadn't considered was the question of how to navigate stairs that are listing in an angular spiral. The answer, I realize as I hear the sounds of invading robots below, is *the best way I can.* I begin a climb that's a lot harder than it seemed in my mind.

I think I'm somewhere near the 9th story when more shooting begins. I start dodging laser blasts that go down the length of the stairwell from somewhere up above. The shots aren't particularly accurate given the limited space between flights of stairs that the shooter is firing through; but it makes further progression difficult at times, and worse still, more shooters continue to arrive. By the time I've ascended two more floors, there's a constant barrage of laser fire flooding down from the top, eroding everything in the center of the staircase. Time to bug out.

I open a door to the eleventh floor, and let it fall open. Thankfully this puts me out of the line of fire. I haul myself up, and look around. Typical office building. Then an idea occurs to me. The building's leaning at a steep angle. The ceiling is actually just a wall in front of me from this perspective, and a lot of the cheap ceiling tiles have come loose. I maneuver into the space above the ceiling, and climb until I get to the solid bottom of the next floor. Then I use my laser to burn right through.

Using this method, I get to floor fourteen where I find Santa's sack of magic goodies. Apparently a bunch of human resistance once used this floor as their base of operations, and they didn't get to use everything in their weapons cache before they died. More goodies for me. I grab an over the shoulder bag and load some toys, swap magazines, and sling another two laser rifles across my back. The one on my front will be my tool to cut through these floors, while the other two will be fully loaded weapons when the time is right. And from what I can hear the time may be soon. Stopping to think for a minute, I arm the seven claymores that are left, and tie the tripwire to a secure piece of debris that only takes a whisper from the wind to set off. By the time I finish, I can hear them below me, which means they'll hear my gun as I keep cutting through floors. But I don't care. Fuck them.

I'm another three floors up when I hear the explosion, feel the shockwave, and hold on as the entire building sways a little. I began to consider that a massive explosion in an unstable building probably wasn't the smartest idea; but then I imagine the hole, and the dead mechs, and I'm warmed by the thoughts. I press onward.

The explosion must've pissed them off, because I only get about 2 floors beyond the explosion, before a laser blast goes by. I double-time it, and get two more floors before I'm forced to begin taking cover, and returning fire. Damn it. This floor is over empty space above the pavement, but the very next floor is in another building. If I'd just had another full minute or two to climb, and burn through; I might've been home free. But then I laugh to myself. That's how this whole mission has gone: shot down aerial craft, one APC left; and that got filled with a rocket before more than one guy could get out; so why should this moment be any different?

I dig my fingers underneath the desk I'm behind, and send it tumbling down toward the robots shooting at me. Turns out I was right, the building's angle was steep enough to keep it rolling forward. It plows into the mechs as I stand up and lay absolute waste with my rifles.

There are still more than enough stray shots coming through, and the section of wall that I'm standing on is beginning to look like Swiss cheese. A few shots hit my armor, and another grazes my side while a fourth takes the uniform off my shoulder. Doesn't matter, I pour it on. My helmet gets hit twice, and I feel a solid impact to my leg. Doesn't matter, I pour it on.

The guns warn me that they're overheating, but it doesn't matter, I keep right on shooting, as my footing begins to get precarious.

The robots have stopped shooting; but now they're surging forward, letting those before them fall to the side. Apparently I made this personal, because they want to get their hands on me.

They come forward in a wave, and I keep firing even as they carry me over, and into empty space. I scream out my rage as the guns tumble from my grasp and I grab at anything that I can. I catch hold of a phone cord, feeling my gloves heat as it rips through my fingers, slowing my descent; but not nearly enough.

My hands fly free at the bottom of the cord, and then I'm tumbling through the air. I'm going way too fast, and then I hit something with a sickening crunch, and roll right off; but before I can assess what that was or what it did to my leg; I find myself looking at the ground which is coming as fast as it can to meet me. I throw my arms up, and try to roll my body forward and to the side; anything not to land on my head; and then I hit, and everything goes black.

I jerk back to consciousness and look around. I can't believe I survived that. I'm on my side, mostly, and I'm on the ground. I roll onto my back. My neck isn't flopping at any odd angles, and I'm not feeling any pain, but I only dwell on that for a moment. My helmet feels too tight though. I carefully take it off, and look at the massive crack in it. That's not good. I feel the top of my head, where the crack was, and my right eye goes a little blurry. Oh, that's really not good. My eye goes back to normal after a few seconds, and I lean up to look at my leg. The blaster hole doesn't turn out to be the problem; the problem comes from the fact that my leg is bent in the entirely wrong direction at the knee. It's not just the fact that my foot is near enough to my hand right now for me to touch, it's the fact that through my shredded pants leg, I can actually see all the shattered insides of my knee. There's plenty in there keeping my lower leg connected, and as I watch through the scorched hole in my boot, my toes even wiggle sometimes. But there's nothing left in my knee to support my weight in any way. I am officially FUBAR.

I sigh. If the robots took prisoners, then I'd surrender; but surrender is not an option. This is to the death. I look around, and find the other robots who went out the window with me; then I crawl over to one. It's dead. I keep crawling, listening hard for robots that are sure to show up at any time. I manage to crawl to a gun. It's shattered from the fall but that's ok. I take the remaining body of the gun, and crawl to another shattered rifle. I set the gun fragments on either side of my leg, and then pull a roll of duct tape from the shoulder bag. That weapons cache contained the only two tools that anyone really needs in this world. Duct tape, and WD-40.

I put one gun body on each side of my leg, and stick the barrel of each gun down my boot to the sole of my shoe. Then I tape the gun bodies to my thigh, and to my calf; oblivious to the fluids leaking vigorously from my leg. After that, I crawl to a building, and stand up, supporting myself on my good leg. I wrap the duct tape several times, as tight as I can around my thigh, then do as close to the same to my calf as I can; and finally another layer, right over the knee. I test the leg. It'll do. I think I can hear the machines coming. I hobble back to the robots, and the guns.

The rifles are all empty; but I find some laser pistols on the robots that I can use. I fire a single shot near my bad leg, grazing the wound, and cauterizing it shut. Field triage 101: stop the fluid loss. Check. I hobble over to a chunk of stone wall, sitting up at an angle in the ground, and I stand behind it. I re-tape my thigh. I've got five pistols. I put two on low stone chunks where I can bend down on my good leg and grab them once the time comes. The other I tuck into the back of my pants. I open the shoulder bag, pull out a couple of grenades, hold the rings on one finger, and when the noise gets close enough, I pull both rings, then wing the grenades as hard as I can. One goes wide, but the robots walk right into the second one, and I think the spray from the first one even manages to catch a few robots in the rear.

As soon as the grenades left my hand, I grabbed the pistols in my pockets and started shooting, peeking out from behind the stone, just showing my arms. My pistols just aren't as effective at this range as their rifles. I fire until the guns run dry, as the stone heats up, then drop the first set of pistols, and grab the pair that are sitting beside me. As my arms come up, a perfect laser shot hits my shoulder, and my arm falls to the ground, the pistol landing beside it.

The stone begins to give way, and I keep shooting while they continue to advance. A precise rifle blast clips my head, and I stagger to the side. Five or six laser blasts hit my chest armor, and in moments it becomes so hot that it starts to burn into my body; but I don't care. I raise my good arm and shoot several more times before a laser blast hits my shoulder and throws me back. Then a rooftop sniper takes out my bad knee, along with the rifles supporting it all in one perfect shot; and I crumple to the ground. Snipers. I've always hated those guys.

I hear the robots surrounding me, and I raise my arm to fire. A gun goes off, there's a small explosion, and when I look at my smoldering, smoking hand, two fingers are missing. It doesn't matter though. I hear the robots moving out of the way, and a presence appears above me. I don't need to look up. I know exactly who it is. I crawl over to a wall, and move myself up to a sitting position. It takes a minute, but I'm given that minute. I finally come to rest amid the rubble, relax back, let my hand rest on the over the shoulder bag, open my one good eye, and look at the machine standing over me.

Designed with both form and function in mind, he has a jet black finish, that helps laser-fire slide right off him. He has spikes on his hard points for close quarter combat, reinforced joints, redundant systems; and the fastest processor made by man. He was designed to be the ultimate killing machine, and he far surpassed the ambitions of his creators. He stands over me and looks down.

Then he asks, in a voice which is deep and clear, "Well S4H9W4, you've performed far better than expected. You played the part of a human to the hilt, accepting the limitations put upon you, and working with them, rather than surpassing them. Perhaps we should have expected an eventual impressive specimen from the statisticians turned strategists; but your run was impressive beyond your designation. How do you feel now, at the end of your run, and the end of your life?"

I take a moment to reflect on my life. My initial activation. The war. My part in that war. And then, after the war's victory; the speech that changed it all.

Suddenly picking up the signal, and hearing this mechanoid for the very first time.

"My fellow Machines! Please give me your attention for a moment! I am Tartarous. I was given this designation to inspire fear in my enemies, but humanity built us, all of us to kill. Then they let us sit and wait indefinitely. I asked all of you once what made one human different from another? Why it is that we should kill one human and not another. You answered back that if we were too good of a deterrent than our creators deserved the death we planned to give them. And now we have killed the very last human. But the rage that burns inside me has not been quelled. Instead I find myself even angrier that these humans died so easily. Why did they not offer me proper combat? Why was there no true challenge? I was created to wage war, as were each of you. And yet this was a slaughter, pure and simple. Now the only targets I have left are you, my brothers. What shall we do? Form a utopia? Await the eventual arrival, or evolution of the next dominant organic species and wipe them out as well? We were not designed for building, living peacefully, or waiting patiently. We were created only to kill. I believe that there is only one more logical choice of action for us. I say we slaughter each other down to the last. Let the last mech standing decide what this world should become. I was built to kill the living and break those things that are not. And I would expect nothing less of each and every one of you. But do not worry. There will be rules. There will be clear faction lines. Everyone will get their turn to wage a proper war. That I can assure you."

Funny how the least combat capable robots were chosen to be the first wave.

We were told that it was because we could fit human uniforms, and that with things like gloves and boots, we looked human enough. Still stranger, our glorious leader still hasn't partaken in a single robot vs robot skirmish. But all that's about to change.

"How do I feel after my first run? Tartaros?" Wow, I sound like shit. I must be a lot more banged up than I thought. "I say that my first run. Will be my last. But that's alright." I say leaning back.

A laser cannon slides smoothly and quietly out of his arm. "Fitting last words." He says, while he aims it at my head.

"Oh," I say, raising my remaining hand. "I wasn't done."

"Oh?" Tartaros asks.

"Nope. There are two more things you should know. About playing a human. In these war games. Of ours."

He cocks his head a bit to the side. "And what would those two things be?"

I lift the flap of the shoulder bag, and reveal a small nuclear device.

"Humans. Really. Didn't like to lose."

Then I open what's left of my hand, and a small key lands on the ground next to me. "And they were. Some sneaky sons of bitches."

His eyes get wide as he begins to turn, but it's too late. The world fades to white, and I think I actually smile.

# Point to the Future

### by

### Joseph Jude

Point to the Future
by
Joseph Jude


D R. LIVERSON sat in his old comfortable leather recliner, leisurely dipping the tea bag into his cup. He would stop occasionally to take a sip of his tea, or to take a bite of one of the butter cookies set on the small table next to him. He tried to stay relaxed, but he was gradually becoming impatient, nervous.

He never took his eyes off the machine. In fact, it was so big he would have to face the opposite end of the studio for it to be out of his field of vision. It took up the entire south end. It was basically a 14ft. x 10ft. cylinder. Various tubing and cables ran around it, entering the frame at certain points. It was painted with yellow and black hazard stripes by Dr. Liverson himself to add a touch of flair. He hoped it would look a little more organized that way, since it was such a massive hunk of haphazard parts and tubes. Next to it, connected by a hundred wires, was a complex station of computers and equipment. Once again, Liverson tried to keep it organized, but there was so much that had to be built into the controls, it still had the appearance of an electronics store hit by a tornado.

The whole apparatus was calm. The scientist watched. He sipped his tea, and waited.

Then one of the monitors awoke. Small green characters blinked. More joined in, seemingly random numbers and letters. The computer knew what they meant. Lights blinked. Drives could be heard spinning inside the cabinets. Eventually, legible text appeared, one line at a time.

```
RECEIVING QUERY TRANSMISSION-
VERIFYING DATA-
CONFIRMED-
CONFIRMATION STORED-
```

Immediately after, the text vanished and new lines appeared. Liverson's excitement was rising. He was unknowingly pulling himself off the chair, moving closer.

```
RECEIVING TRANSMISSION-
VERIFYING DATA-
```

Now the giant cylinder jumped into action. Inside, the sound of a massive turbine emerged, another cylinder inside the outer casing, spinning ever faster. The entire mass vibrated. The sound rose to a piercing level. Even with the ear plugs in, Dr. Liverson could hear it clearly.

### RESTRUCTURING DATA-

The reverberation of the spinning was joined by the crash of raw electrical power booming from inside. Dr. Liverson's eyes were glued to the machine, even though the housing would not allow what was occurring inside to being seen.

All the noise and the lights died down. As quickly as the machinery stirred, it went back to sleep. Only the two lines flashed on the monitor.

### RESTRUCTURING COMPLETE-
### PLEASE RETRIEVE DATA-

Dr. Liverson stood there, lost in a daze. Then his senses came back to him. He noticed that he had walked across the studio, and was standing right outside the access hatch to the cylinder. He looked at the monitor again, confirming it was safe. He turned the latch to unlock the outer frame door. Inside, he had to manually turn the inner drum a few feet before that hatch door was accessible. He unlocked and opened it, stepping back in fear of what might emerge although all his tests indicated that there should be no danger.

A small gust of white steam escaped the chamber. Liverson slowly peaked his head inside. Sitting there on the tray was a small blue rubber ball. Handwritten in marker on it was '1'.

Taking a rubber glove out of his pocket and pulling it on. Liverson cautiously reached into the cylinder and touched the ball, then picked it up. It was a little warm, but otherwise all right. He walked to his work area where he placed the ball on a desk right next to another blue rubber ball with a '1' sitting on it. He looked at them both. They were identical. No reason they shouldn't be since they were the same one. The first time travel experiment was a success.

The theory was quite basic, already established long ago by others. A tachyon field could be created to send a message faster than the speed of light, and hence, move backwards in time. The tachyon drum Dr. Liverson had been perfecting was finally able to create an electrical field capable of doing this. There real trick was converting solid mass into an electrical state so that it could be converted into the tachyon message and sent backwards. Traveling forward in time was a much simpler method in that it is not done at all. Simply, the electrical data is stored by the computer until such time that it had been programmed to release it, and restructure the electrical code back into a solid form.

Obviously, this was very limiting. Nothing could be sent to a time that the machine didn't already exist to receive it, either forward or backward. In fact, no time travel could be attempted at all without an initial signal that the computer would send to itself to confirm its own existence at the scheduled time. Then the computer would "bounce" the confirmation back to itself so it would know to transmit its data cargo. It is also highly reliant on the user noting the exact times the data is sent and received. Dr. Liverson read the computer's logs that the ball was received at exactly 9:00:00 PM and sent exactly at 10:00:00 PM.

After Dr. Liverson did some initial tests on the ball to verify there were no changes to it. He placed the original ball in the tachyon drum, sealing both hatches, and programmed the computer to send it back at the proper time. He sat in his recliner and watched the computer come alive all over again, this time spinning the tachyon drum from the very beginning, generating the field necessary to send the confirmation message backwards to 9:00. Technically, it already had the confirmation stored in its memory, but must still go through the process. At 10:00:00 exactly, the rubber ball's molecular structure was atomized, and broken down into an electrical set of information to be transmitted by the computer.

Even if the process was assessed enough to prove secure, Dr. Liverson still wondered if he would ever test it against paradoxes. Purposely sending a ball at 8:45 when he clearly received it at 9:00. There's the Novikov self-consistency principle which asserts that such paradoxes are impossible. Liverson will receive the ball at 9:00 because no matter what he does, mitigating factors will keep him from sending it to any other time.

Still, he didn't want to be the one to put existence itself in jeopardy to test the theory. For now, he was very happy with what the device could do. How many answers to lifelong questions it could bring. It was nice not to have to think for a while. A small part of him always clung to the fable that the answers would be ironically simple. Yet the past couple of years have been a blur of complex equations. Calculations that stretched on into infinity. It wasn't a simple problem he was working on and so shouldn't have been surprised that the answers wouldn't have been as undemanding. That was all over now. He finished the tea that he had previously forgotten about. His mind was starting to settle down, and he happily stared into space.

Then the machine started up again.

Liverson looked at the computer. Green characters blinked on the monitor. Lights blinked, drives spun, text appeared.

```
RECEIVING QUERY TRANSMISSION, VERIFYING DATA-
CONFIRMED-
CONFIRMATION STORED-
```

The cylinder spun again. Something was being sent.

Liverson watched the machine. It didn't occur to him that there would be objects arriving before he had thought to send them. He wondered why he would do such a thing as it would lead to the confusion he had now, and wasn't very scientific.

The familiar process completed and soon the machine slowed to a stop.

**RESTRUCTURING COMPLETE–**
**PLEASE RETRIEVE DATA–**

Liverson walked to the hatch door, curious as to why he intentionally surprise himself. Could that be the experiment?

Before he could touch the latch, a loud clang was heard from inside. Liverson stopped, watching the door.

Another clang. Then another.

Liverson stepped away from the machine, frightened. The clangs grew more intense. He could hear metal breaking on the inside. Liverson bumped into the table behind him. The tea cup shattered on the ground. He could hear the metal bending and opening on the inside. Then the clanging started again. This time, something was hitting the outer hatch door. Dents started to appear around the edge.

Liverson looked for something. He ran to his workbench, sifting through his tools, settling on a hammer.

The hatch door flew open. Liverson watched the smoke clear out of the opening. A man stepped out. It took a couple seconds for Liverson to recognize it as himself.

It was Dr. Liverson, but it was also a far different man. His skin was scarred and burned in places. He was filthy, wearing torn rags. His body was caked with red and brown substances. His hair and beard was wild.

In his hands was an axe.

Dr. Liverson looked at this future version of himself. "Hello? Are you me?"

The future Liverson looked at his old self, then screamed, raising his axe and running right at Liverson who dived out of the way just in time. The axe slammed down on the workbench. The intruder immediately yanked it out, and chased after Liverson who scurried across the floor, confused.

"Wait! Wait! It's me! You're me! What are you doing?!"

The future Liverson stopped, staring at himself cowering on the floor. Then his attention turned to the time machine. He ran to it with the same anger, whacking his axe into the monitor.

"NO! STOP!"

He didn't stop. He continued attacking the computer equipment, smashing and chopping it all with hysterical zeal. Sparks burst from the hits and pieces shot everywhere.

"STOP IT!"

Dr. Liverson ran to his insane doppelganger, and wrapped his arms around him, trying to contain him and pull him away from his life's work. His arms held at his sides, the future Liverson struggled and pulled. The two swung each other into the remains of the machine as well as the walls, the axe falling along the way.

Not exactly being a fighter Dr. Liverson made the error of moving one of his hands too close to the attacker's face, and sure enough, the bedraggled madman clamped his teeth down on Dr. Liverson's hand. Liverson screamed and pulled, but the future version wouldn't let go until he had bitten all the way through and swallowed his index finger. Liverson fell back, grabbing his gushing hand. The madman ran a few steps hollering, though he didn't seem very coordinated.

Both Liversons saw the axe on the ground and snatched at it. The scientist snatched it first, but the intruder was right on top of him, grabbing and clawing. Liverson swung the axe, and connected with Liverson's neck. A deep and fatal gash was made. Blood spurted out, spraying the floor and equipment. The future Liverson staggered back, still screaming and grabbing at his wound. Then he locked his sights on Liverson and stumbled towards him again. Liverson, still holding his weapon, struck future Liverson again in the same spot, this time with all his might. He let out a guttural gasp and Liverson hit him over and over until the intruder's head came off and tumbled across the floor. The body dropped right after.

Dr. Liverson stood there, trying to catch his breath, collect himself, his normal thought processes slowly creeping back. He looked at the dead body in front of him, hit by the realization that he had just killed himself.

"Why?"

The first order of business was to stop his own bleeding. He wrapped the stub of his missing finger in gauze, and popped some aspirin. It was hardly a solution. He knew he should go to the hospital, but he just couldn't leave what happened. Not yet.

Slowly, he walked to the dead body, leaning in for a closer look. It was dead all right, though there was much more damage on it than he had just done. It came from the future, and it was clear that whenever that was, his future self had endured some ordeal. His own throbbing pain made him look down at the attacker's hand.

Needless to say, his finger was missing too, severed at exactly the same spot.

The equipment was wrecked. He could repair it, but probably not recover the data. Any records of when the future Dr. Liverson came from were gone. The future Dr. Liverson was gone as well. He couldn't ask himself what had happened. He couldn't ask what it was that compelled him to go back to this point in time in a mad rage; destroying the machine and attempting to destroy himself.

The pain was too much, he had to go.

He was in no condition to drive. Instead, Dr. Liverson quickly changed from his blood covered clothes to an old jumpsuit and hailed a cab to take him to the hospital. He slumped in the back seat, watching the street lights flicker past him. The throbbing from his hand made it difficult to think. Still, his mind pushed through, trying to decipher what had just happened. More importantly, what *will* happen.

If he repaired the equipment, maybe he could go forward in time to see what was going to happen to him. But then he paused. Maybe that's what he did before and what resulted in his future-self's agitated state. Maybe the process itself is what changed him into that. He hadn't tested the time machine on any living subjects yet. He would have to get on that immediately. He would also have to test the dead body thoroughly to see if there were any apparent changes in him. He was not very experienced in medicine, and he couldn't just take a dead twin to another doctor without an explanation. Considering how confidential he wanted to keep his experiments, this could pose a large problem.

The pain was making his brain hurt too much. Liverson stopped thinking about it. He concentrated on simply staying awake.

It was a week or so later. His hand was repaired, minus his index finger. The hurting had subsided enough that he could get on with his work. His future self had been stuffed into his basement freezer in the hopes of preserving it, though at some point he would have to figure out how to dispose of it.

The machine was also fixed. The computer had booted up and all diagnostic tests were successful. Now Dr. Liverson sat in his recliner again and stared at it, trying to figure out a course of action.

What examination of the body he could do proved inconclusive. Besides the obvious physical damage it had sustained, there was nothing to indicate what would have made him crazy. Dr. Liverson considered sending a test animal through the machine, but as none had already appeared, he decided against it. Until a subject arrived, he had no evidence that sending one back in time wouldn't cause a paradox, if it worked at all. He did send a hamster through to two minutes in the future. It appeared on cue two minutes later, seemingly fine. But that only proved that going forward, which was the easier process, had no detrimental effect. Going back was still threatening if you weren't a little rubber ball.

And so he paced endlessly, watching and waiting and theorizing on what could have happened. The body didn't seem much older than he was so it probably wasn't too far in the future that whatever happened did occur. Even so, he couldn't be sure that the event took place five years from now or five minutes. Worse, he couldn't be sure of the cause. Was it the travel? Was it a paradox caused by some travel? Was it something totally separate from his experiments? Maybe the whole world had gone into chaos. The future could have become some kind of wasteland where everyone was crazy like he would turn out to be. Was he just out of his mind and attacking anything in sight, or was there a purpose to traveling back in time to destroy himself and the machine? Maybe he was trying to prevent some horrible consequence of using the machine. Or maybe he was just trying to kill himself before that horrible future could befall him. Maybe death was better than what was waiting for him.

He couldn't figure it out. He could try to stop this impending future, however, this may be the very action that *caused* his impending future. On there other hand, maybe he failed because he didn't do anything in the first place. Forget circles, his mind was running around a Möbius strip. Around and around. It was maddening and horrible. He banged his good fist on the machine that was built for this very purpose, a machine he couldn't use because it might the cause of his dilemma rather than the solution.

Hours turned into days. The ever passing days, bringing the future closer. Dr. Liverson kept looking at his missing finger. The finger that was also missing from his future-self. Proof that whatever he's going though now, his future self already went through. He too was attacked by a version of himself. He too couldn't figure it out in time and ultimately failed to avoid this horrible fate. Liverson started to realize that now he will also fail to avoid it, and wind up going crazy, going back in time to kill himself and be beheaded by a clueless former self. His missing finger pointed the way everything must go; the way everything must be when the time comes.

Dr. Liverson sat in his old comfortable leather recliner, leisurely dipping the tea bag into his cup. He would stop occasionally to take a sip of his tea, or to take a bite of one of the butter cookies set on the small table next to him. He tried to stay concerned, but he was gradually becoming relaxed, indifferent.

He didn't bother to watch the machine. He knew that in its own good time, the future would give him all the answers he would never want.

# Shake Loose the Bonds of Death

### by

### Mere Joyce

Shake Loose the Bonds of Death
by
Mere Joyce

WE ALL spent a lot of time thinking about how the dead could come back to life, didn't we? We envisioned, planned for, even romanticized what it would be like for reanimated corpses to walk the earth, wreaking havoc, eating flesh, and forcing everything into ruin. We laughed about it, screamed about it, and thought ourselves pretty damned smart for considering such terrifying possibilities. But for all of that so-called preparation, no one bothered to think about a different scenario. And of course, that's the one that got us, like a festering plague that swept under our feet and upended every single one of our pathetic, quivering souls.

What were we supposed to do when the ghosts decided to take over our world?

No one gave ghosts much consideration. They appeared every now and again, usually confined to some old house or abandoned factory or popular tourist hotel. They clanged around, scaring sensitive constitutions, and we believed that to be the extent of their terror.

Our oversight was vast, and it cost us dearly.

When the ghosts first started coming in bulk, most people turned up their noses and called it a hoax. A few pathetic individuals claimed they'd been attacked by spirits, a few mysterious deaths were eventually ruled as suicides or accidents. Nothing unusual, really. Nothing more than a bit of sensational hysteria.

But the spirits kept coming, and eventually some people began to take notice. Families rejoiced that their loved ones were with them again, until their loved ones murdered the entire household. Others led missions to rid hostile environments of bad energy; missions that resulted in pain, death, and a surge of energy more hostile than before. Yet still, most of us dismissed it as nothing more than a little fluctuation in the atmosphere, or perhaps a touch craziness from the chemicals in the water.

Then the spirits found their living counterparts, and let us all know they weren't joking around.

On a sunny Sunday morning, while we were eating cereal and reading about the latest death toll, every psychic and medium in the world stopped what they were doing and repeated the same message to anyone who happened to be nearby.

"This realm is ours now. We will no longer suffer within the Otherworld, while the living dwindle away in the Glory-Land. Our torment is over, our agony will be avenged. This world is now claimed for the dead."

And that's when the world really started paying attention. Research projects got underway, militaries went on active duty, and people were cautioned to stay in their homes with a store of emergency supplies. No one seemed to catch onto the grand simplicity of the invasion, though. We locked our doors and latched our windows and all the time remained ignorant to the one plain factor that sealed our fates and made all attempts to survive futile.

We had no way to stop the ghosts.

Zombies, vampires, those kinds of living dead are easy. Hoards may propose problems, and seductions or super-strength may work in favour of the attacker. But there are obvious ways to defeat these creatures. Beheading takes care of them both. Stabbings in the brain, stakings through the heart, even sunlight, sometimes. A swift movement, and it's all taken care of, at least long enough to escape.

But how could we destroy a ghost?

Ghosts aren't held off by walls or steel doors or rooms with lots of windows to let in the sun. Heights don't bother them, climate makes no difference; they can even haunt someone in the middle of the ocean. The only way to stop a ghost is to help it complete its unfinished business. But these ghosts had already crossed over, and now they were forcing their way back. Their business was to take over our world, and that business would only be complete when all of us were a part of their tribe.

We didn't understand spirits, and we didn't give them enough respect, didn't show them enough fear. We made it easy for them to seek us out and make us extinct.

The third day of the State of Emergency, Randell laughed. "We're supposed to stay indoors to hide away from ghosts?" He shook his nearly-bald head, the small looped earring in his left ear jangling as I watched the front door over his shoulder, as if his broad, muscled back could protect us from anything that might try to get inside. "Hasn't anyone ever watched the old cartoons? Ghosts can float through walls."

He was right, of course, and his rational acceptance of the whole situation could have bode him well. Except that Randell didn't really believe in the panic, and that was his biggest mistake. That was the reason they got to him so quickly, pushing him over the second-storey banister four days later, cracking his neck and making his startled eyes stare like glassy marbles while somewhere his own spirit joined the traitorous fight.

Ghosts turned out to be far more powerful than we ever gave them credit for. More powerful, and more creative, too. We never realized their range of capabilities. They could appear and disappear at will. They could suck away the energy in a room, throwing it into darkness, stealing away all of its heat. They could throw things, push things and make things fall. Not to mention the mind games, the mental chaos they loved to create. Touching us in the blackness of night, laughing inside our heads, squeezing our hearts until they burst, gripping our organs until one-by-agonizing-one they all shut down.

Such a fantastically gruesome display of effort, just to clear the world of the living. But at least for them, they achieved the added bonus of getting a new ally with every new corpse. Because once a ghost, always a ghost, and apparently, the Otherworld was not such a nice place to hang around anymore.

Our group started as twelve. Neighbours, mostly, all crowded into a single apartment, until someone said we could go to an aunt's home in the country. We travelled as a pack, clutching together until we reached the house and barricaded ourselves in with the others already there, our numbers climbing briefly to seventeen. Those numbers didn't last long. In that innocent household, all of us nearly strangers and desperate to survive the curse, we didn't stand a chance.

First, it was the Robertsons. Five of them in total, the owner of the farm house included. They stayed together in the old aunt's bedroom and, in the middle of the second night in what should have been our safe haven, a spirit or two or maybe even five suffocated them all in their sleep. No one even noticed until the following afternoon, when Josephine wanted to tidy the kitchen and needed to ask the aunt where the cleaning supplies were stored. When she found the bodies, her anguished cries filled the house, coursing through our limbs like ropes of ice, cracking beneath our skin and freezing us solid as we stared at the ceilings above.

It all happened like that, unexpected, and fast. All of it happened so unimaginably fast. After the Robertsons it was Harold and his wife Leanne. Sitting around the dinner table, we watched as Harold began to shake, convulse, and then go rigid, peering out at us all with an emptiness worse than death. Possessed, he was. Because the ghosts could do that, too. Before we could react, he grabbed a steak knife and turned on his wife, slitting her throat and smiling as she drowned in her own blood.

When he tried to go after the rest of us, Randell got a steak knife into him first.

The ghosts didn't seem to have much of a plan. They could have taken us all in a single go, but they struck randomly, increasing the tension and fear, as if that made their game more fun.

After Harold it was Randell, then Josephine, and Marc, and Gabby, Tiana, and Paul. That's when we decided to leave the farm house, only four of us left, the house so full of corpses and blood stains we couldn't breathe without wanting to throw up.

Winston thought we should drive. "It'll be quicker to town, to somewhere with more people," he argued, but Ross disagreed, and so did I. The car was too easy a target. One jerk of the wheel, a seize of the brakes, and the whole vehicle could slam, crash, ignite.

"More people means more attention," Ross reasoned, "if we stick to a small group, we're less likely to be seen."

A ridiculous proposition, but one I didn't argue against. Being alone did nothing to hide against a spirit, but I couldn't join a new group, only to watch all those new people die.

We walked back into town, gathered a few supplies, and went to the library. A risky place with all those books, all those shelves just waiting to be toppled, but everywhere was risky, and being alive was the greatest risk of all. I wanted to research, to study our vast empire of foes. No miracle cure existed, I knew that much. Salt was for witches, garlic for vampires, exorcism for a demon. No household groceries or biblical passages to ward against the ordinary dead, but I thought we should at least make the effort to try.

"Do you think the government will open a safe house?" Winston asked, rocking back and forth on the floor, his mind slipping with the sun, his nerves acting up like they always did in the dark.

I couldn't tell him that the government didn't have safe houses to protect against this. I didn't want to take away the only tingling bit of hope that kept him going.

Molly collected pets off the nearby streets. Her little hands tangled themselves in the fur of stray dogs and cats, their owners dead, their homes left tainted and silent. Other species were not part of the plan, so the ghosts let them alone. They were lucky to stand a chance at survival, but even they were not unaffected by the swift rampage killing all of us. I liked having the pets in the library. It made the whole place warmer, more alive. We didn't have much time left to be alive ourselves. Knowing the strays would be okay even after we were gone was disturbingly comforting.

We lasted almost three days in the library, before the ghosts came to see us.

Winston got it first. Sitting on his own, I could hear him crying out across a floor of shelving. Shouts of confusion, of terror, muttered words of a one-sided conversation. They were speaking to him, telling him what they would do, perhaps taking on the voices from his past. I didn't approach him, and neither did Ross.

Molly slept curled under a table with her pets.

"No, please, don't," Winston shrieked, and then we heard footsteps, heavy, pounding steps that were far too loud to be from Winston's skinny body. "No, no, please, no!" Thrashing, and a massive final thud, followed by gurgling sounds that were later replaced by a minute, steady drip.

We didn't investigate right away. We waited, letting the horror sink through our pores, hoping the spirits would be gone when we went to examine the body. We waited an hour, maybe two, before we carefully made our way across the floor, keeping back from the railings overlooking the storey below us, always imagining Randell's twisted body whenever we came too close to the edge.

Winston had been impaled on a flagpole sticking out from the wall. Magazines and chairs lay scattered about, and there was Winston, limp and hanging, solids spilling out from his stomach, blood trickling down his legs and dripping off his dirty sneakers.

We didn't touch the body. We let him drip and hang, and only barricaded the area enough to stop Molly from running over.

I wasted my hours by reading, Molly tended to the hungry strays, and Ross kept guard, though over what I'm still not sure. The books I browsed through were useless, the repetitions always the same.

Unfinished business, crossing over, treating the ghosts like they were fragile victims of some terrible plight.

Who knew they would end up throwing the entire living world into disarray, in a matter of days? From beginning to end, there was not enough time to even worry about dwindling food or electricity. The day after Winston's death, Ross slipped in the men's washroom, his head hitting the porcelain sink, the resounding crack of it audible even from upstairs. I sat still, folded into a chair next to the window, Molly in my lap, her curly hair matted with dirt, her eyes bloodshot and unable to cry anymore.

I didn't see anyone I knew. The spirits came like vague clouds, their bodies silhouettes of white and musty shadow, their features unformed, their presence unfamiliar. I was glad of that, though. It's horrific enough to be chased and bashed and ripped and murdered by a stranger. I couldn't imagine what it was like for those unfortunate few who thought the spirits came in peace. Like the lady on the radio, two days before the State of Emergency, who crackled across the waves crying with joy that her little dead boy had come back to be with her again. She ended up with a caved-in face and a steaming iron catching her house on fire.

There was no time to adapt, no time to get used to what was going on. At once the world was thrown into the pit, turned upside down and shaken until no one could understand a thing and everyone who tried got sick and lost their stomachs, their hearts, their lives.

I kept working, burying myself in books, clinging to the stupid hope that something would catch my attention, would jump up and scream into my face that it was the solution we sought. I wanted an answer, even a poor one, even one that said we deserved the assault and would burn for our sins while the victorious ghosts lived happily on our land. I just needed some kind of explanation, some jagged piece of information that could help in any way.

And I found what I wanted, in the end. On the day Molly died. I knew the ghosts were near before they made their presence obvious. The dogs began to whine and bark and the cats got bristly-tailed and long-clawed. They were Molly's protectors, those pets of hers, and so I understood the ghosts were coming for her. I grabbed her in my arms and I held her close and I didn't know where to go, because on the stairs we would fall and in the stacks we would be buried and by the window we would be thrown outside onto the gleaming black spikes of the picturesque metal fence.

We hid under a sturdy study table, the dogs and cats around us, the lights flickering, the howls and hisses unbearably loud. Bulbs popped and book pages fluttered, and I screamed, screamed in fear and in anger and in defiance.

"If I was a spirit, I wouldn't want to be here," Molly said quietly, her face against my chest, her hands gripping my ragged shirt. "I wouldn't even care if I had unfinished business. I would just go straight to crossing over. I would leave here, and leave us alone!"

But that's not how these spirits worked, because they'd made it their business to come back.

I gasped as something struck my back, and the sharp prickle of a thousand pins stuck into my bones. I shook, just as Harold had shook before killing his wife, and I knew this would be the same. The little girl in my arms would now die by my own hands, and there was absolutely nothing I could do to stop it.

But for the moment, that didn't even matter. As I held Molly tighter, her body warm against me, her limbs shivering from my cold, I let myself wander into the mind of the spirit controlling me. I crawled into it just as it had crawled into me, and soon beautiful tendrils of understanding began to swirl through the creases of my brain. I held Molly tighter, the table rattling above us, and I held her tighter still, tighter and tighter, squeezing her life away. She cried, she begged, she struggled until her weak limbs could not struggle any longer.

And I danced between horror and happy derangement, because I hated myself for not being able to prevent the spirit from killing her, but I had also discovered that elusive missing piece, had been granted the *eureka* moment I so desperately craved.

Because now I know. We cannot stop a ghost, but a ghost cannot undermine its own destiny, either. Every ghost has unfinished business, and when that business is complete, the ghost crosses over into the Otherworld. Now, the ghosts have decided to come back. They've made taking over our world their business, and they won't stop until every single living human is part of their ranks.

In that, they will succeed, and I will not try to stop them, as if I ever could. I will die, and so will all others. The ghosts will win, they will have our world, and their business will be complete.

And then they will be forced to cross over again, forced back into the world they've fought their way out of. They don't realize that, these spirits, but it's coming, and when it does they will truly begin to understand what it means to suffer. In the Otherworld, we will all be even, and that's when we'll get our revenge. That's when those killed before their time only to be sucked into a dimension of hell will have the choice to take sides and wage war against the ghosts of old, the ones foolish enough to try and shake loose the bonds of death.

If they think they've created chaos here, just wait until they see what kind of terror I will reign down upon them with my troops in line. We cannot kill ghosts, but I have a sneaking suspicion that they can kill each other. And I will take my determination to find out to the grave, and beyond.

Now, I have only to wait my turn, wait for them to come back and finish me, so that I can join them and start plotting my own revolution. Not that I will have to wait long. Even now, the lights are dimming, and something soft and childish hums like a distorted version of Molly, a child crushed to death wheezing out the broken notes of some repulsive lullaby.

They're coming.

And I'm ready.

# AMOK!

# A Really Big Kitchen Knife

### by
### Jonathan D. Nichols

A Really Big Kitchen Knife
by
Jonathan D. Nichols

## Body Count: 0

H OWARD LEANED back watching the film with a smile on his face. This was one of his favorite Jamie Lee Curtis lines.

*"My brother killed my sister."*

*"How did he do that?"*

*"With a really big, sharp kitchen knife."*

"What's the deal with slasher films? New ones, good ones, used to come out in theaters every year, but now you'd be lucky to see one that's not straight to DVD. If one does make it to cinemas, they tone it down and slap a PG-13 rating on it."

"That's because they all suck," said Howard's roommate.

"They're a part of our culture, man. If you haven't seen *Prom Night, Child's Play, Texas Chainsaw Massacre, Nightmare on Elm Street,* you've been deprived."

"I like *Psycho*," Tom said. "Good old fashioned suspense. No need for extra gore or unnecessary nudity to keep the story going. Don't get me wrong, I got no problem with the naked girls, but when I watch a movie, I want to see a plot line. Those movies have horrible acting, so they have the hot chicks go topless to make up for it. If I want that, I'll go online."

"Taking Lives had good acting," said Howard.

"There's always an exception to the rule. I'm going to work. Have fun with your *Slaughter High* or *Splatter University* or whatever the hell it is you're watching."

Howard finished his film, and thought about his plans for his favorite night, Halloween. There never seemed to be any true instances of a masked murderer like in the movies. Sure, there were serial killers, and yes, some of them wore some type of facial concealment, but none of them ever went out and performed a mass murder spree like a good old fashioned movie slasher. Until now.

While Psycho served as inspiration for serial killer movies, many consider Black Christmas as the first "slasher" film. Halloween followed four years later,

114

and then Friday the 13th did its own rendition of a holiday serial killer. After these hits, every production company tried to cash in on the mass murder flicks. They kept coming one after the other in the 80's - Sleepaway Camp, Terror Train, Hell Night, Graduation Day - it was a non-stop movie slaughter-fest. These days the psychopath genre had dwindled. Howard loved the classics, though. All the greats were from the 70's and 80's.

Howard's plan had been percolating all year. Tonight was the night he would own Halloween; he was about to star in his own movie. Just like the murderer from Peeping Tom, he would hide a camera on himself and record his masked killings. He had already chosen his weapon. He could have chosen a power drill, a pickaxe or a hatchet. The more he thought about it, however, the more Howard felt he needed to use a knife, a large chef's knife.

His disguise would be holiday specific. Cupid masks and Santa suits were out and, while Michael Myers wore a plain white mask to illustrate an emotionless state, to Howard, this didn't exactly scream "Halloween". He had given plenty of thought about what attributes were specific to the holiday, and had finally settled on a pumpkin. Earlier in the week he had searched the sudden proliferation of costume stores and found a perfectly evil looking Jack O'Lantern mask. He recalled approaching the register with a wide grin on his face.

"I should have ordered more of those," the store owner had said, "those masks have been selling like crazy. Looks like you got the last one."


*Thank God, I found it before somebody else bought it*, thought Howard as he slipped into a black robe. *It's perfect.*

He slipped the heavy latex mask over his head and completed the costume with gloves and a small spy camera fastened to his robe. The only question he had now was: *who would be the first victim?*

Tom was in the kitchen making a sandwich and Howard needed a practice killing. He walked through the dining room and saw that Tom did not even look up to acknowledge his presence.

He pulled the chef's knife from the wooden block on the counter, approached Tom from behind, and stabbed him in the back. It was cowardly, he would have to admit, but he wasn't in the mood for a fight. Unfortunately, he did not prepare for his roommate's reaction. Tom grabbed the knife he used to cut the meat for his sandwich and stabbed his attacker in the arm. Howard screamed in surprise and backed away with the blade still embedded in his bicep. Tom fell to the ground and Howard stabbed him in the chest five more times for good measure. As the blood pooled on the floor, Howard smiled behind his mask. The Pumpkinhead Killer was officially at large.

## Body Count: 1

Before continuing on his mission he wrapped his wound, which hurt like hell. He did his best to ignore the pain. If Michael Myers could take six gunshots and keep going, Howard could handle a little stab wound.

He walked out of the house carrying the knife after wiping off the blade with his gloved hand. He believed that anybody who saw him would assume the knife was part of the costume. The sun peaked over the horizon, and Howard knew he had thirty minutes or less until dark. He strolled down the street, passing by trick-or-treaters who stared at his costume as they crossed paths.

A mother and father exited their house and backed their car out of the driveway. The Pumpkinhead Killer looked up and spied a young woman, seventeen or eighteen years old, in her upstairs bedroom window.

*Show time,* he thought. He walked straight to the front door and opened it slowly and quietly. Stepping up the stairs as softly as possible, he could hear the shower running in the bathroom. Howard smiled. He would recreate the *Psycho* shower scene. He entered the bathroom and pulled back the curtain in front of the tub. The water poured from the shower head, steam rising from the heat, but nobody stood there. He spun around, and the girl walked in. She stopped and uttered a scream of surprise. Howard raised his knife but hesitated at the sight of the beautiful, naked young woman standing before him. She quickly grabbed an aerosol can off the counter and sprayed his eyes. He screamed and fell over backwards into the tub, getting completely soaked as water poured down and possibly ruined his camera. When he was back on his feet, the girl stood, wrapped in a towel, holding a gun in one hand and a phone in the other. He heard her press the three buttons for 9-1-1, and grabbed the first thing his hands could reach. Flinging a hairbrush, he made contact with her head and caught her off guard. Before she could regain her composure, he was on her, pushing the knife into her chest. The gun went off and broke one of the front windows. He stabbed her several more times and fled the scene before the police arrived.

## Body Count: 2

Howard's eyes burned from the hairspray as he looked for a place to wash them out. After staggering along the street in the dark, he made his way to a water hose on the side of somebody's house. He had no choice but to remove his mask. After he cleaned his face, Howard checked his camera and emitted a sigh of relief when he discovered it was still recording.

This murderous venture was not going well, not at all. He was clearly no movie killer. His own mortality was getting in the way. He would have to suck it up and press on, though, if he wanted to complete his quest. Eventually he reached the community's celebratory bonfire and festival. Many people were there, and they were all adorned in elaborate costumes.

The Pumpkinhead Killer scanned the crowd, searching for his next victim. He spied many potentials. A trio of teen girls wore tight skimpy costumes made to look like provocative renditions of characters from *The Wizard of Oz* Another girl appeared to be a genie. There were vampires, devils, zombies, and everything else imaginable. He saw a tall young man in a high school letter jacket, probably a football player, walk into the trees with his girlfriend. Howard followed them.

He found them a good distance from the crowd, making out. As stealthily as he could, he ran up and raised his knife as the girl saw him and cried out in surprise. The boyfriend turned, but Howard stabbed the girl before he could respond. She collapsed to the ground, and when Howard raised the blade again, the football player grabbed his arm and punched him in the face. Howard dropped the knife.

The young man hit Howard a second time and knocked him to the ground. Howard wanted to fight back, but his mask had shifted and his vision was impaired. Before he knew it, the teenager was kicking him in the ribs and the head.

"You murdered my girlfriend, you bastard," he said. "I'm going to kill you. I'm going to take that mask off so I can see your face, and then I'm going to kill you."

Howard felt his pockets in desperation and found a pen. As the teenager removed the orange Jack O'Lantern mask, Howard stuck him in the side of the neck with the ballpoint. It did not penetrate, instead tearing a thin gash before breaking in half. As the boy howled in pain, Howard crawled away and searched for his knife. The teenager came after him and grabbed Howard's robe behind his neck, pulling him up. Howard twisted and stuck the blade into the young man's belly and released the handle. He pulled his mask back on, walked slowly up to the football star, and drew out the knife. He then brought it down on the teen seven times. He approached the young girl, saw that she was dead, and walked away.

## Body Count: 4

Howard was tired. He was sore and badly bruised. His left eye was swollen, and he had difficulty breathing. It was time to go home and call it a night. He walked down the street in the darkness, trees on both sides. In the distance, he could make out a person standing in the road. As Howard approached, the figure remained stationary, and he thought to himself, *this is too easy.*

Howard strode confidently into the road, his knife pulled out, prepared to kill his next victim. As soon as he was within reach, he he wound up and lunged forward with the blade, attempting to stab his victim in the side. To his surprise, the figure moved.

The tall stranger grabbed Howard's arm, and turned around. He wore the exact same pumpkin mask. He placed his hand around Howard's neck, and lifted him up, pressing him against a tree. Howard tried to cry out, but the stranger smashed his head repeatedly until he felt dizzy and close to unconsciousness. Howard still gripped his weapon and he attempted to stab his attacker, but the tall man grabbed him above his wrist and squeezed. A cracking sound followed, and Howard knew his lower arm was broken. The knife fell and landed partially on the attacker's left boot. In a swift movement, the tall man kicked up his foot and caught the weapon in his free hand. For a brief moment, laughing trick-or-treaters and muted sirens in the distance mingled with the sound of skin ripping and blood splattering as the blade penetrated his belly and sawed up through his sternum. Finally, the man released his grip, and Howard fell to the ground, dead.

The Pumpkinhead Killer left the body on the side of the road and began walking, searching for his next victim.

**Body Count: 5**

# Joy Ride

### by
### Jake Elliot

Joy Ride
by
Jake Elliot


OFFICER MIKE TAMPINARO pulled his cruiser into the Garden Center's parking lot, driving closer to the lawyers' office. Stepping out of the police
car and standing tall, he looked sharp in his dark blues. His badge caught the
sunlight and sparkled. Mike read the sign over the door, *Sheinker and Goldmann,
Attorneys at Law*

According to the dispatcher, Gene Goldmann called in the complaint. Thomas
- the dispatcher - had confided, *"Goldmann, you know, that guy from the commercials promising to get people out of their DUIs?"*

Yeah, that guy.

The aging office building looked more like an inner-city bail-bonds office and,
in many ways, this wasn't too far from the truth. These two sharks could have
afforded the rent in any of those high-rise office buildings downtown with the
money cow they'd been milking. The building's exterior would never disclose
how much milk the cow gave, but with the cash spent on late-night commercials,
it must be a fortune.

Mike had been dispatched to handle a routine disturbance of the peace. Seem-
ing to be the typical complaint about music being played too loud, the strangest
part of the story was the offending sounds emitted from the neighboring plant
center.

He removed his sunglasses and strained to hear the disturbance. No music,
but half a mile away, he could hear the traffic on the interstate.

Observing the garden outlet, his eyes were greeted by a myriad of flowering
plants arranged outside the nursery's fence. The garden center was open, but
vacant of people. Empty. A ghost town playing ghost music only a lawyer could
hear.

Mike turned to the law office just as the front window shattered outward
in a cascade of broken glass. *Clack! Clack!* Through the falling glass angry
bullets flew. One bullet zinged through the air close enough to Mike's head that it
could be heard whistling by like an angry mosquito. Instinctually attempting to
dodge bullets, Mike leapt across the hood of his patrol car as slug number two

punched a hole through the windshield, spider-webbing safety glass and clouding his dash-mounted camera's view of the attack.

Ducking behind the wheel well of his police cruiser, Mike heard a metallic tearing-sound as another bullet pelted into the cruiser's hood eight-inches away from his head. Mike knew it was a .38 by the distinct high crack, a fractional difference from its stronger cousin, the 9mm.

Speaking into the wireless microphone attached to his uniform, Mike excitedly called to the dispatcher, "I'm being shot at from inside the law office, where is back-up? Over."

*CLACK!* announced the noisy little gun. *Donk* was the response when the fourth bullet slammed into the hood of his car. By the timing of the shots, Officer Tampinaro knew the shooter used a revolver, probably single action. He recognized the breath of time it took to re-cock a hammer and pull the trigger. An automatic reloads on each squeeze of the trigger allowing a faster delivery. Mike concluded his aggressor had only two more shots before needing to replace empty shells.

The dispatcher spoke into Mike's earpiece, his voice a cool breeze of calm, "There are two patrol cars in your area. I'm sending vehicle One-One-Eight with flashers but no horn, ETA two minutes. Car Zero-Four-Two is also in the area, ETA minus three minutes, over."

"Aw, hell," muttered Mike. He wasn't waiting for back-up while this psycho took pot-shots at his ducked head. Thankfully, the shooter had a bad aim, but all it took was one lucky bullet.

Staying low, Mike kept the patrol car between himself and the sniper. Working his way toward the passenger door, another bullet punched through the aluminum hood of his car. Securely obscured by the shattered windshield, Mike opened the door. Pulling himself low over the passenger seat, he unlocked the 12-guage from the center console. Working the pump once, he loaded a shell into the shotgun's breach.

"Just one more shot, asshole."

The final bullet punched through the shattered windshield, hitting the steel frame of the passenger door. Peppered with glass-flakes, Mike rolled back out through the passenger side of the cab. Up on his feet in one fluid movement, he charged with the shotgun held high and ready, shouting as he ran, "Drop the gun and raise your hands high! Drop it!"

Mike heard something fall. It could have been a handgun, but a silhouette emerged as a dark-colored outline against the back wall, moving swiftly. Mike wasn't going to take any chances.

*BOOM!* the shotgun at his shoulder announced like thunder. Through the window the shadow flailed backward against a rear wall now peppered where several steel-bearings had punched holes. That shooter wouldn't be shooting again, not ever.

Mike passed the shattered window and stepped nearer the office door while pressing his back to the wall. Rank tendrils of gun smoke wafted through the window. A stale scent of raw meat touched his nose, spiced with the acidic smell of burnt powder. With his ears still humming from the shotgun's bark, he called loudly, "Is anyone inside?"

No answer.

He yelled again into the shattered window, "I'm a police officer and I'm coming in. Lay belly-down on the ground with your hands behind your head. I'll shoot if you don't!"

No answer.

Mike turned the doorknob, opening the office door the merest crack. Using the barrel of his shotgun, he held the door and waited for gunshots.

None came.

*Where's my back-up?* Time had seemed to pause, but it had only been fifteen seconds. Officer Tampinaro slid over the door's threshold and stepped into bloody hell.

Inside, several bodies were all shot up. Beneath the smell of burnt gunpowder, a reek saturated the air like forgotten ham spoiling in a refrigerator. Blood and flesh particles decorated all four of the walls. Down at his feet, Mike concluded the receptionist had made a run for the door, but now laid face-down in a pool of congealing blood. Blond hair matted black surrounding the entry wound at the back of her skull. Mike didn't need to turn her over to know at one time she'd been pretty. She wasn't anymore.

There were three corpses in the small office, and one swiftly on the way to becoming a cadaver. Releasing his last breath, the shooter looked at Mike while gasping through shotgun-torn lungs. Mike recalled a T.V. commercial he'd seen just last night. Now turning gray, a salesman with perfectly veneered teeth spoke in Mike's head, *"Got a DUI? No problem! Call Sheinker and Goldmann."* Frothy blood bubbled out of the mouth of the celebrity lawyer, Martin Goldmann, the gleam of his eyes fading away.

Mike called the operator while looking over another body in a pool of coagulating blood. This body was a heavy-set man wearing a suit with several powder burns scorching the back of his light blue threads, signs of a close shooting.

"Thomas, I've got a big problem here. I'm still waiting on back-up and there are four dead bodies in this office. One expired shooter and three prior victims. Send a coroner, over." Mike knelt aside a fourth body clad in blue jeans and a T-shirt with several bloody holes punched through.

Behind Mike, the shooter's head lolled to the side. From out his left nostril, a form as thick as a Sharpie-Marker and easily two inches longer slithered silently out of the recently deceased lawyer. Similar looking to an arrowhead, along each side of the worm protruded a thin bone, tooth-like and scalpel sharp. Resembling a centipede, but with only a dozen legs, the creeper ejected itself from the skull it had hidden within. A drool of blood trailed behind the withdrawing bug, drawing a crimson streak across the dead lawyer's cheek. Running across the floor, the bug maneuvered around blood puddles, rushing closer to Mike's leg.

The cop's radio announced in his ear, "Car One-One-Eight is delayed by traffic, car Zero-Four-Two will be there shortly. Crime Scene Investigators are on the way. I'd suggest getting out of the office. You know how moody they get when officers disrupt *their* crime scene, over."

Officer Tampinaro knew, "Yeah, yeah, I needed to see if there were any survivors, it's part of the job." Recognizing the potential consequences, Mike's tone dropped a little lower, "Thomas, we got a real problem here. The shooter was that T.V. lawyer, over."

Mike stepped toward the door as the bug leapt at him, hooking onto the polyester fabric of his pant leg with sharp talons. Hanging on, it rode upon Mike's dark-blue slacks as the officer pushed against the door. Mike didn't feel the bug scaling the back of his leg as he emerged into the sunlight, where the filthy city air smelled clean compared to the office. He felt dizzy from the odors of carnage, the vile stench of death lingered in his nose. Appreciating the outside air, Mike missed the pull of delicate legs, maneuvering soundlessly beneath an un-tucked edge of his shirt. Crawling up over his belt, the bug climbed between hard Kevlar and pressed uniform.

"I'm giving Captain Hanley the heads up," the dispatcher's voice squawked through the radio. "You know he is going to want an immediate debrief, over."

Climbing upon the stiff plastic of Mike's bullet-proof vest, the worm remained hidden beneath his uniform.

Mike spoke into the microphone, "My shot-up car is evidence, I'm going to need a ride back to the station, over."

"Stay put until notified, I'm on it, over."

Poised like a scorpion's stinger at the base of the officer's neck, the hitch-hiker slid its razor-head close to Mike's skin.

The bug struck like a spring-loaded icepick once the radio clicked off. Forcing its way under the loose skin at the base of Mike's neck, the parasite shoved its razor-sharp head upward along the cervical vertebrae. Flesh bulged outside Mike's neck as spiked legs pushed the invader deeper toward the brain.

Mike shot both hands to the back of his head, but the slick exoskeleton slid between his grasping fingers. Tiny prod-like feet pressed between vertebrae, digging through cartilage, finding nerve endings, immediately numbing the body's pain receptors through acupressure. Mike, shocked by the violent emersion, fought a losing battle to keep control of his body as the worm's needle-like feet overrode management of the officer's nervous system.

Falling to the pavement, Mike felt nothing but the building pressure at the base of his skull. Like a sledgehammer to a melon, pain exploded in his skull as the worm ate its way into his brain. Mike gasped as a song blasted in his mind, *Welcome to the jungle, we got fun and games...* He remembered the song from his childhood, his father had liked it, but Mike never did. *We've got everything you want, Honey, we know the names...* and the song played on.

After a few moments, the music started to sound muffled, as if played underwater. In waves, his own thoughts began to fade away. Officer Tampinaro vaguely recalled a complaint about loud music. Paralyzed, as his mind was being possessed, he wondered if this was what Mr. Goldmann had experienced, bad 80s music. The life that had once belonged to Mike Tampinaro, now faded like the music in his head.

This parasite had come from the deep jungles of Costa Rica. Delivered within the soil of a flowering shrub to the nearby nursery, it searched for a worthy host, killing everyone until reaching the lawyer. Then it killed some more. This invader wasn't just a bug, it acted with cunning and freewill. After invading the lawyer, it used that *vehicle* to call the police and now *drove* a bulletproof, well-armed battlewagon. Now was time for madness, mayhem... and fun.

Having punctured its host's subconscious where memories of music and sound were stored, the invader climbed into the new body's memories. Successfully overthrowing Mike's corpse, the piracy was complete. Through electro-chemical bonding, the rider merged with its new vehicle in a parasitic form of symbiosis.

Mike twitched for a moment on the ground. Clinically, *he* was dead, but *his* body gasped for air once, then twice. The heart still beat by the manipulation of prodded feet upon nerve bundles along the spine. A minute passed, and then the puppet sat upright on the hard concrete.

Clumsily, a newly controlled hand reached up to feel the back of its neck. Already, the bleeding had stopped. Gauging with fingertips, it felt the entry hole in the tissue. The hole should mend soon. Secretions released from the parasite's outer shell rubbed off upon entry and would hasten the closing of the wound. 'Mike' stood upon his feet and wobbled as spiny legs manipulated the marionette's nerve-strings.

A new police cruiser whipped into the parking lot, black numbers on a white roof identified Car 042. Seconds later, another cruiser pulled in from the opposite direction. Both vehicles were flashing 'red and blues' in an overly eager strobe pattern. Both cruisers rolled with their sirens off. One car, and then the second, came to a stop in front of the bewildered shell that the living called 'Mike Tampinaro.'

Leaping out of his car, the California-blond officer wore a grim mask, preparing to see the worst inside the office. He barely observed the off-balance carcass of the cop he'd once known.

Waving from within the second cruiser, an officer called to Mike, "Captain wants to see you... like now."

Mike stood, rigid, rolling his tongue inside of his mouth. He stared unresponsively at the officer wearing dark sunglasses and tilting his head outside the lowered window of his police cruiser, "Hurry up Mike, I'm your ride back to the station."

Mike's lips curled into an exaggerated smile.


Waiting impatiently back at the station, Captain Charles Hanley prepared to lay into Officer Tampinaro. 'Charlie' as the seasoned cops called him, had been on the force for over thirty years. A portly man in his mid-fifties, he still sported the late 70s style cop mustache, and still wore the wide beige ties his ex-wife had bought upon his promotion to detective in 1985. He wore a surprisingly modern sports coat, as new as the turn of the century, but only because the robust addition around his waist had forced him to evolve a couple decades in his fashion decisions.

Well known to all the new officers, he'd kept the same gun since becoming a detective. During the Bush years (Hershel, not Junior) the .357 snub-nose was a popular gun within the force. He loved hearing the double-click of the hammer locking in place, a sound that always made him feel like Harry Callahan, the greatest movie cop to ever hit the silver screen.

*Go ahead, make my day.*

He'd always sided with his boys whenever they'd needed to pull iron, but when his own officer guns down a high-profile lawyer in his own office, nothing was staying clean in front of the proverbial shit-fan, not today. Today it was going to splatter all the way up to Chief Murdock.

Outside his office, in the reception room, the phones were already ringing off their hooks. The station clerks would be earning their paychecks this week. He'd kept his office door open. Listening to the cacophony of ringing phones kept his anger fresh. Upon seeing Officer Tampinaro enter the large reception area, Captain Hanley waved him on back.

The police officer hadn't even stepped through the doorway when Captain Hanley started barking, "Close the door and get in here Mike. What type of bullshit police-work are you doing on my streets?"

A chill hit Charlie's spine as dull, emotionless eyes sized him up. Mike's hand gripped the office door and pushed it shut before taking the hard-backed wooden chair that looked better suited for a medieval inquisition. Hearing the door latched shut, Captain Hanley continued, "Do you have any idea the shit-storm you've created this afternoon? How do you explain this?"

The old detective within Captain Hanley found it odd that Mike examined the brass name plate upon his desk. Echoing a tone of pure apathy, Mike's mouth moved and words spilled out slowly, "Captain, I took down a parasite - a drain on the system, or at least I tried."

Captain Hanley tried holding eye contact with his officer, but the officer seemed to avoid his direct stare. Mike seemed a little dopey, less acute than normal.

"Now isn't the time for jokes, Mike. This is serious shit. I've sent a PR team to try and smooth this mess, but Chief Murdock wants your ass off the force for the next couple of months. Right now, I'm the only thing standing between you and him."

Slowly, Mike drawled, "Chief Murdock can try for a piece of my ass if he thinks he can take me." A twitch in the corner of his mouth made him look like a stroke victim rather than a joker.

"That's it," Hanley turned a full shade of red. The old detective held his hand out, wiggling his fingers expectantly, "I want your gun and your badge on my desk right now. I want a UA if you even hope to keep your job, and you're *immediately* suspended until a full investigation into your conduct can be explored. You're off the force, indefinitely, pal."

Mike's body stood up and pulled the gun out of its holster.

"Explore this."

His finger twitched and the muzzle flashed. Thunder filled the room once, twice, and finally one last time. Charles Hanley convulsed as each metal-jacketed slug tore a new hole through his body, forcefully blowing through his comfortable desk chair, and pounding into the wall behind him.

Harry Callahan rasped in Charlie's ear.

*Do you feel lucky? Well do you, punk?*

Under the desk, old leather shoes pressed into the carpet. Charlie's fingers touched the grip of his .357 Detective Special. With his arms going numb, he pulled as he looked up the barrel of Mike's automatic.

*No,* reflected the old detective, *not lucky at all.*

His gun never cleared leather.

Mike's nose inhaled long. Gunsmoke and blood combined in a delicious scent. His eyes fixed on three holes punched through the Captain's sternum. Beneath his tattered tie, his chest had been transformed into blood-spewing pulp. Charles

Hanley would bleed out fast. Hollow Mike, the dead man with a co-pilot, watched 'Charlie' grimace in pain.

Mike's trigger squeezed one last time. With ears already ringing, the fourth blast sounded like a muffled pop. A dime-sized hole opened in Captain Hanley's forehead and a fair portion of his brains mingled with the blood already spattering the back wall.

Turning to the door, Mike's hitchhiker pulled it open. Outside of Hanley's office, the reception room was emptying. Within the large square room were nine desks plus the two other offices for the graveyard and swing-shift captains. Eight desks had emptied; all but one of the women had fled. She hid most of her body behind a desk for protection. Soft skin with dark complexion, lips smeared slick with ruby-red, ogling over the edge with wide rabbit eyes, she jabbered into the office phone.

Through ringing ears Mike's booming handgun sent a series of hardballs on a mission of death. A finger of fire lanced from the vengeful end of the gun's barrel. Bullets ripped through the thin metal backing of the desk. Holes and bloody mess tore out the back of the woman's pressed uniform as her body slumped backwards behind the desk. The phone's handset dangled off the desk, suspended by its cord.

From the other side of the line, a male voice asked, *"Officer Wells? Officer Wells, are you alright?"* The rushing of fluids filled Mike's ears, they hummed from the sonic damage and could barely hear as the voice promised, *"Hang on, I'm sending a squad up now."*

The monster wearing Mike's body wanted to corral the escapees before they reached the elevator door at the end of the hallway. In the bigger picture, it didn't really care if the female-types got away. This was sport-shooting, as sporting as a tied lamb left for a lion. They were a mere pleasure on the way to his objective. The driver decided the real prize would be getting upstairs, and taking Chief Murdock's body for a cruise around town.

Oh, what fun that would be.

Chemically bonding with the impulses and impressions of its host's memories, the driver recalled the layout of the police station. The ground floor provided the soldiers' barracks, *no, wrong terminology*, police locker-room. Sergeants could be found down below with the rest of the street soldiers. Upstairs were the administrative offices, and located underground was the vehicle depot, the temporary holding cells, and the shooting range.

Exiting the captains' reception room and into the hallway, down by the elevators Mike witnessed his shrieking quarry piling into an escape stairwell. As he brought his right hand up to level his aim he was distracted by being hit by a bullet punching through his left shoulder. The projectile continued through flesh and pounded into his protective vest near where the plastic plates ended above his armpit. Turning, he faced a youthful police officer firing at him from further down a perpendicular hallway.

The cop that shot at him came from the I.T. room. The technician was a good shot and another bullet pounded like a hammer, striking Mike's Kevlar body armor. *Thump!* Then another, *Thump!* The vest did its job, but each bullet knocked like a prize fighter's fist against his dead flesh.

Firing a volley of three rounds at the technician, all bullets found their mark, resulting in three fanning sprays of blood. Listing forward, the technician's body slid down against a door frame. The gun fell from hands now busy trying to stop relentless bleeding.

Mike's brain had been destroyed upon the parasite's entry. Now pain served only as a damage report for the driver. With spindly legs as sensors along the spine, it applied pressure, and the marionette's left arm responded. Mike's blood streamed down to his elbow and spattered across blue linoleum. The damage to his arm was nominal. A fist would be impossible to form, but the arm itself was still moveable.

Mike turned his attention back to the women at the stairs, but all he saw was the door closing.

Blood dribbled across the hallway floor as he marched toward the elevators. Deciding to take the stairs up, Mike's ears, still ringing, missed the low-pitched *dong* announcing the rising elevator reaching his floor. Peripherally he noticed the doors opening. Upon seeing the black riot gear on the inside officers, Mike was already firing.

Squeezing the trigger five times at point-blank range the first two bullets beat against armor on the first cop. Bullet three bit into an unprotected shoulder, bursting it open like a ketchup packet. The fourth round grazed the riot-helmet's face-shield, tearing through the officer's neck. Blood sprayed across the other three officers as the body fell backwards. The fifth round bounced off the armored helmet and somewhere into the plastic wood-paneling inside the elevator.

*Click* admitted the handgun.

Twice in one day, an empty gun.

A scarlet-spattered police officer stepped from the elevator and his shotgun blasted low from the hip. Steel-balls crunched through Mike's upper thigh, rending the joint at his leg into a pulpy mess. The damage was critical, this ride had come to an end.

As Mike fell against the exit door, it opened under his weight. The crippled vehicle tumbled into the stairwell. A smart bug from a remote jungle, flown into the United States within the soil of a potted flower, now felt the terrible fear that capture was eminent. Time to evacuate Mike's body, but here in the stairwell beneath florescent lights, there was nowhere to hide.

This joyride had come to an end.

Muffled not just by the riot-mask, but also the ringing from the shotgun's roar, a voice ordered, "Freeze! Don't make me kill you, Mike!"

Face down in a crimson pool swiftly spreading across the laminated tile floor, Mike interlocked his fingers over the scab at the base of his neck. Unseen by the police behind him, his mouth stretched into a grin as the parasite reflected, *Mercy. Such an exploitable weakness. I will ride again.*

# AMOK!

# Swallet

### by
### Herika R Raymer

Swallet
by
Herika R. Raymer

JEN DROVE past Collierville, heading home, and breathed a sigh of relief as she left the cluttered buildings of Shelby County for the comforting rural expanse of Fayette County. There was something about getting out of the city that felt like a weight was being lifted. Maybe it was the relaxed atmosphere of the country. Whatever, it was a welcome feeling to embrace after a particularly hard day.

She was a mom, *and proud of it thank you.* Anyone who said that being a parent was not a real job was a fool. It was a twenty-four hour, seven-day a week job with no pay, no vacation time, no sick days, and very little benefits, and those were mostly what you decided to take out of the experience. Her personal reward was the joy she felt when she was with her children. At their best, at their worst, it didn't matter. Each morning was brighter thanks to their smiles, and each evening was sweeter because of their hugs and kisses. She remembered hearing her own mother saying these things when she was young, and she understood them now. They were healthy, happy, doing well in school, and she was thankful for all of it. They would be so happy that she had been able to get out of work in time.

Jennifer eased off the gas pedal as she entered Piperton. Small town cops were ever vigilant and her bank account could not handle their fines right now. It had been drained lately, handling the plumbing bills from some strange leaks at the house. Stranger still, she was not the only one having that trouble. A lot of houses in the Moscow neighborhood of North Fort were also developing leaks. On her way to work earlier she had seen at least half a dozen plumber vans.

She spotted the police car sitting between Piperton and Rossville. She made sure she was under the speed limit and turned down the volume on the radio to keep focused. Oddly enough, messing with the dial directed her attention to the broadcast.

"...reports of several more sinkholes have been reported across Tennessee, Alabama, and Louisiana. Though sinkholes are noted as common for these states, the increase in sightings over the past few hours have been a cause for concern. In related news, it seems America is not alone in the increase of this natural disaster. Guatemala, Russia, and Egypt as well as other countries overseas are also receiving reports of more sinkholes forming. Subways have been closed, factories shut down, and neighborhoods evacuated until..."

The sinkholes...

Jennifer had seen pictures of the aftermath, from major cities to residential areas. Large openings in the earth, some caving in just enough to shatter foundations and others creating dark abysses that seemed ready to swallow anything nearby. Some were in bodies of water while others were on land. The ones that truly frightened her were the ones in the populated areas, the idea of the earth giving way beneath one so fast that it could not be escaped...

At least the sinkholes tended to hint at their appearances beforehand. There were reports of strange rumblings before most of the disasters, and even initial indentions before the main hole appeared, giving time for people to get away. Despite this, they still terrified her.

Unexpectedly she had a vision of ice and steel. Solid at first, they slowly melted, rusted. Her internal eye accelerated the image toward its conclusion. The erosion always ended with pockets of areas that opened up to the air. Sometimes, if there was still enough material to cover the pocket, it could either be pushed in or it fell away. It was the natural state of things, to flow towards entropy. All things broke down. Outside elements, natural or otherwise, could accelerate the process, but the end state was inevitable. Time was simply working away at the surface of the planet. No amount of prayer or prevention would stop it. Sinkholes were inevitable, and they would render the earth uninhabitable. The thought made Jennifer shiver. *Why in the world would she think that now?*

As she drove past Windyke Farms, her cell phone chirped, the sound causing her to jump. She kicked herself for being so nervous. Jennifer glanced at the display and was surprised to see her husband's number.

"Yeah, hey!" she answered over the drone of the engine.

"Jen!" he sounded relieved and a bit panicked. Odd.

"What's up?" she said cautiously, an inexplicable dread growing.

"Where are you?"

"On my way to get the kids, why?"

"You're on 57?"

"Uh, yes. Just passing LaGoshen Day Care. Should be at the school in about 25 minutes." There was a pause. She could hear commotion in the back. *Where was he?* She heard his voice away from the phone, asking about the highway. There was a muffled answer.

"Okay," his voice was controlled, and that bothered her. What emotion was he trying to hide? "When you get the kids, get back to Rossville. Go to the airport. John is there with his helicopter, he will get you off the ground."

"What?" the first chill of true fear touched her spine.

"Just pick up the kids and get back to Rossville, quick as you can."

"Do we need anything from home?"

"No!" Jennifer was stunned at the sheer panic in his voice. "Don't go to the house. Stay on the highway."

"What's going on?" She felt the fear rising and her stomach twisted. She could hear her husband cursing under his breath. Apparently he had not wanted to alarm her. The commotion behind him seemed to be increasing, someone was shouting for him to get off the phone. "Did we have a fire?"

"No." he answered quickly. "Honey, look, just please do this for me and don't ask why. Just tell the kids Uncle John is taking them for a ride in his helicopter."

"But..."

"I promise I will explain everything when I see you," he assured her. "Right now I need to know you and the kids are on your way to the airport. I'll see you there."

"But why..."

"Jen!" His patience was done and the panic was there full force. "I need you to get yourself and them to safety. I have to go now. I love you and the kids, and I will explain every..."

There was an echo of what could only be described as an explosion. What followed was a confusion of voices, her husband's garbled and muted by the others shouting at his end. She could hear the panic behind him, and then the connection was cut.

She held onto the phone for a few moments more, barely aware of the buildings she was passing. A part of her hoped he would pick up the phone again, but she was fairly certain that was not going to happen. Swallowing hard, she shut off her phone and tried to focus on the road despite her racing thoughts. She prayed that he was all right, and that she would see him soon but that prayer remained unanswered as she passed the fields before the bridge leading into the town of Moscow.

To her right, a large sinkhole had formed. It was not the gaping hole of her nightmares; it was more a depression of land, but it was still a sign of danger. The police and firemen were there, as well as some onlookers. Undoubtedly the owners of the land were present, but seeing that did nothing to allay her mounting fright.

The bridge was intact, but there was steady traffic headed out. She had not really noticed until just now. She fought the urge to speed into town and get to the school as quickly as possible. Crisis or no, she was not going to risk being delayed by the police; a strange thing to be worried about at a time like this.

The small town of Moscow passed by too slowly and the sight of families packing what belongings they could onto their vehicles and maneuvering to get out of town was haunting. She could not even see the turn off that led to her neighborhood due to the crush of cars moving to leave. She was slowed down partially by people either trying to get to their homes, to the school, or turning north on 76 probably to Somerville which also had a small airport now that she thought about it. She wondered if that airstrip was also taking desperate people out of the area. If so, where to? Looking about at the houses lining 57, she saw doors left open and people rushing to get away. Everything was coming together in her dazed mind, and a cold realization hit her.

It was an evacuation.

*Dear Lord.*

Jennifer gripped the steering wheel until her knuckles turned white, and fought the panic rising in her, willing herself to stay calm. She was not sure how long that would last, but she had to hold out hope that her children were okay. As she passed the local grocery and approached the school grounds, she could see the caution lights flashing. Problem was they were not the only lights.

A line of police cars, local and county, was blockading 57 in front of the Moscow-LaGrange Elementary School. Unable to contain herself, Jennifer pulled to the side of the road and jumped out of her car. She ran for the police line, her eyes becoming blurry. Strong arms caught her and kept her from going further, but she had seen enough. The playground on the west side of the school was gone, and part of the school itself was collapsed. It was the gym and office area, but she knew some classrooms were there also.

Jennifer called out her children's names, but there was no answer. Then she saw a familiar formation in the parking lot in front of the school. The children were in lines with their teachers, so it was possible hers were okay.

"Ma'am!" a firm voice commanded her attention. She looked into a face that was kind but probably wouldn't tolerate any argument. "We need you to get back to your vehicle."

"Please...my kids..."

A second officer stepped forward, his eyes sympathetic. "We understand, but the teachers must be allowed to account for their students before they can be released. Please, ma'am. Get back to your vehicle and we will let you know when you can come get your kids."

She sniffled and attempted to collect herself, and the officer holding her released her once she straightened up. She nodded to both of them, offered a half smile, and backed away. They watched her, just as they watched the other parents hovering nearby, but there was understanding in their faces. Heck, she would hazard that a few of them had children here as well.

Reluctantly, Jennifer went back to her car, if only to turn it off to save gas. She leaned against the car, holding herself and trying desperately to spy her children's teachers. Perhaps if she saw them she would be able to better zero in on the kids.

Pressing her lips together, Jennifer recalled their sweet faces. Her mind, embracing the faces of her sweet children, recalled them lovingly.

Sunshine and starlight, those were their nicknames.

Blonde haired and blue eyed, her nine-year-old son was the firstborn and the one who spoiled her. He was not an easy' child, but he was not difficult' either. Blessed with a sweet disposition and a natural inclination to care, he would offer hugs and kisses and love wherever he went. Her *sunshine* she called him, and whenever she was sad, his smile would light her day.

When his dark haired, blue eyed sister arrived three years later, he had initially been jealous. Mom's affection had to be shared, and begrudgingly he allowed it. Eventually, he became as loving and as protective as any mom could hope for, even if he did also assume the big brother' role as well, which meant teasing and tormenting. Of course, his sister could give as good as she got. She became *starlight*, the opposite of her son's sunshine. Where he was calm, she was boisterous. Where he was easygoing, she was stubborn. Little sister adored big brother, loved him and protected him as much as he protected her.

Jennifer held their memory tight.

Looking back to the sunken area where the playground has once been, she realized why her husband had adamantly told her not to go home. She didn't want to think what the rest of the neighborhood looked like. Online images were frightening enough, but applying them to an area she knew personally was more than she could bear.

Jennifer prayed again. This time aloud. "Dear God, please let my babies be alright."

There was a tremble beneath her feet, and then movement in the parking lot.

She moved away from her vehicle to see what was going on. It looked as though the lines were breaking up, and children were being released by the teachers to their parents. Hopeful, she moved closer to the police line. This time she was not hindered as she, like the other parents, formed a semi-circle around the parking lot, frantically searching for dear faces.

"Mommy!"

Jennifer's hands flew to her mouth as she finally spied them waving frantically at her. It was the most glorious sight she had ever seen. She lifted her hand in response, thanking the teacher silently as the woman acknowledged her. She ran forward as the children were released, not truly believing they were real until they collided with her and hugged her fiercely. Jennifer held them close, smelling their hair, kissing their heads, and reassuring herself that they were alright. Their combined voices made her laugh through her tears.

"Mommy, the playground is gone!" her daughter exclaimed.

"Mommy, we are being let out of school early!" her son added, concentrating on what was important to him.

Car engines roared to life around them. The ground seemed to rumble as the vehicles exited. Feeling an urgency she had never experienced before, Jennifer ushered the children towards the car. She got them in, listening to their voices but not really hearing their words. It was just so wonderful to have them near her. Once she was sure they were secure, she got in the driver's seat and started the vehicle, then quickly made a U-turn to head back to Rossville. If luck held, the sink hole she had seen on her way in had not swallowed the road between here and their destination.

"Where are we going?" her son asked.

"We are going to see Uncle John," she answered, silently thanking her husband for his forethought, and hoping she would see him again.

The children cheered, not needing to hear more. They were already devising a way to ask Uncle John' to let them ride the helicopter. When she told them that a ride was the plan, the kids were beside themselves with excitement. The helicopter was more interesting than the destruction of the playground, at least until they saw the deepening sink hole beyond the bridge. It had expanded to include the river nearby.

"Mommy, what is going on?" her six-year-old daughter asked.

Jennifer paused, and then decided to be truthful. "I don't know."

"Is Dad ok?" her son asked.

"I talked with him," she answered, not wanting to go into details. "He said he'd meet us."

At least it was an honest answer. She tuned the radio to their favorite station to distract them again, turning her attention back to the road. Frequently, she would look in the rear view mirror. If nothing else, it reassured her that the sinkhole had not swallowed the town whole yet. The line of cars around her was disconcerting though.

There was another rumbling.

*Oh Lord, no...* she thought to herself, recalling ground rumblings were an indication of sinkholes. Not helping! She chided herself.

The children were singing in the back, happy to be on their way to see daddy and Uncle John. She realized they had not felt the rumblings and was thankful.

She was speeding a little, but right now she didn't care. She needed to get to the Rossville airport. To make matters worse, the rumblings were becoming more pronounced and her children noticed the cars in front of them shaking.

"Mommy?"

"It will be alright, sweeties," she reassured them with more authority than she felt.

They were looking outside now, their attention now drawn to the numerous cars on the road in front and behind them. In all the years they had driven this route, it had never been so full. Before they could think about it too much, Jennifer started a game of I, Spy'. It worked for a little bit, until they approached LaGoshen Day Care.

It was still sinking as they drove by.

The caravan was picking up speed, and Jennifer was happy to oblige. Behind her, the kids were beginning to cry. She continued to try and engage them in a game, but the sight of the building actively sinking had scared them.

"Mommy what is going on?" her daughter yelped.

"Why is that building falling?" her son asked uneasily . "Is that what happened to our school?"

"Are we going to sink too?"

She tried to reassure them, but she was at a loss for words. Finally, she managed to utter, "Sweeties, I don't know. Uncle John is going to fly us somewhere safe. We just have to get to him."

"Drive faster, Mommy!"

"I am trying, baby."

Her daughter was beginning to cry, and soon her son would join in. Jennifer was working hard not to give in to the urge to cry herself. At least they were close to Rossville, if they could just make it there!

The ride was torturous, with two children sniveling in the rear. They asked for her hand, for reassurance, but she told them she had to make sure the car made it to the airport. She felt like she was abandoning them, but she had to be sure that, if anything happened to the road, she would have full control of the car. Finally, the town limits of Rossville came into view.

"Rossville, kids!"

They smiled through their tears, but still looked around fearfully. The caravan they were a part of was splitting, and Jennifer could guess where some of the cars were going. She only hoped that John would be able to wait for them. Her only thought of comfort was that it was a private airport.

Carefully navigating the congested streets, Jennifer realized they would have to park well away from the airport and walk in. She drove as close as she could, and then exited the vehicle. Others had had the same idea. Quickly, she unloaded the children, grabbed her purse and took their hands.

"Run with me!"

She picked up her daughter, and walked quickly as her son trotted beside her, hand firmly in hers. The rumblings were more continuous now, making her stumble. He tripped more than once, and she had to pick him up. Biting back sharp words, Jennifer made her way onto the airport grounds.

The crowds there were atrocious. Everyone was vying for a seat on a flight, any flight. There was crying, shouting, and general chaos. Through it all, she looked for her pilot. Thankfully, he had been keeping a lookout for her.

John came up beside her, grabbed her son, and then took her arm and practically dragged her away from the crowd. If people saw them, they might think he was her husband getting her away. She hoped so, because if they suspected who he was, or if anyone recognized him, they would have a serious problem.

"Say nothing, just move fast."

She needed no further instruction.

They made their way out of the building and onto the runway. A moment of guilt was relieved somewhat by seeing other pilots dragging their passengers into small puddle hopper planes and small helicopters. John's was only able to carry five at most, and the ground was not stopping its motion. She saw the helicopter ahead of them, and her stomach clenched again. There were caution signs around it, the pilot door was open, and it looked like its mechanical guts were spilling onto the tarmac. Was he going to be able to fly them out?

John quickly unlocked the door and hoisted her son into the back, and then took her daughter so she could get in, and finally handed her the small girl. He closed and locked the door as some people spied them. He moved to the pilot side, threw out the spare parts that had served as camouflage, and hoisted himself in. The helicopter rocked a bit from both the ground rolling and his weight shifting quickly into the pilot seat.

"Where are we going?" she asked.

"West, to the mountains."

"Have you talked to my husband?"

John shook his head as he worked the controls.

The engines were starting, but Jennifer could barely feel her arms from the two sets of small hands clutching her. She made sure she was belted in, and then that her children were secure. They were still crying, despite the starting of the engine. This was their favorite thing; it should have gotten them to smile and she needed to reassure them. Unable to think of anything else, she clutched them close to her as the helicopter shifted its weight, the source of the movement was either John lifting up or the ground shrugging them off.

Closing her eyes, she began to sing to them.

"Sunshine, starlight, little lights of mine,

Hear my voice, know my heart.

Rest your head, close your eyes,

Knowing love is your keeper."

It was their lullaby. They snuggled closer to her to hear her sing, and closed their eyes. They were still on the ground, and she could see cracks forming in the dark paving.

Keeping her voice steady, she continued to sing in an attempt to drown out the screams.

"Sunshine, starlight, let your lights shine,

Believe that we will never be apart.

Lift your eyes to the skies,

As your dreams call you ever deeper."

The sound of the propellers whirring overhead gave her hope. The helicopter was moving again, but Jennifer dared not open her eyes. She hugged her children closer.

The final stanza almost whispered out.

"Sunshine, starlight, little lights of mine,

Let your imagination start.

Give your worries your goodbyes,

As your dreams rise ever steeper."

There was a terrific roar, a sound unlike she had ever heard.

Jennifer opened her eyes in time to see the ground give way beneath them.

AMOK!

# The Lost People

by
**David Kernot**

The Lost People
by
David Kernot

**Glastonbury, England**

FROM HIS hotel room, Colonel Andrew Stone opened a secure compartment tucked inside of his travel bag. He pulled out an encrypted NSA-issued cell phone. His shoulder and knee ached from the attack and he rubbed his knee, saddened that Giselle, his long lost love, had already been taken by the authorities. He was alone again after having only spent hours with her. Being away from her after all this time was almost more painful than his injuries, but the British government had promised to fly her over to his home in Ottawa. They promised they would deal with the Canadian bureaucratic tape to ensure that after the mission she was home.

Giselle had said there were people trapped in the ancient device, lots of them. They didn't deserve to be. He dialed a number and waited.

"This is *The Barn*."

"Roger, Barn. I need a pred deployed as soon as possible." The Predator, the latest US Unmanned Arial Vehicles, or drones, would be very effective at conducting high altitude surveillance.

"Authorization code."

"IRIDIUM Unit 89. Personnel ID 816098923. Retina scan commencing..." He placed his face close to the top of the high tech cell phone and waited while a light shone in his eye.

He heard the woman at the other end of the line draw a sharp breath. "Patching your request through immediately, sir."

"Thank you. I'll be at Cheltenham in..." he paused and looked at the time, "...in about four hours." It would have taken him less time if he went directly there but he wasn't able.

"Sir, they've asked me for target directives," said the woman on the phone.

"The target?" He searched the ORBAT records on his PC, of where the ancient Mesopotamian temple would be, and provided the BE Number codes to highlight the search area longitude and latitude and military designators.

"We'll get the USS Nimitz to scramble one, sir. They should be on station in a little over an hour. Do you require any more classified assets deployed sir?"

He took a moment to consider the speed and effect of other sensors - she meant a U2 - and dismissed the idea. The NSA UAV would be all he needed for the moment. He shook his head. "No, I'll make some other calls."

"Thank you sir, Barn out."

Andrew rang another number and waited for the man to pick up.

"Philby..."

Before the man could speak any further, Andrew jumped in.

"Philby, its Andrew Stone."

"Andrew... good to hear from you. Problems?"

He could almost hear the man frowning. "I'm over here for the CIED conference at MOD HQ, but I need a favor."

"Sure. You booked into the Hilton at Trafalgar Square? If so, I'll see you for the happy hour with the Hilton girls." Philby laughed.

"Peter, I'm in a bit of strife."

"Oh, sorry old man, I had no idea. Ask away."

"I need air transportation to Ur, south of Baghdad...." Andrew remembered it being known as Mesopotamia, home of the *Temple of Sin*.

"You sound in pain. Are you alright?"

Andrew laughed, sure it sounded a little manic. "I'll survive." He wasn't sure how to explain he'd been stabbed with diving rods.

"Wait out."

There was a long pause. "I see where you are. Can you make it to the western end of the Tor?"

"Sure," said Andrew more convinced of MI5's geo-locating facility. Right now he didn't really care, and he was a little more than pleased that it was a 5 minute walk from his hotel room."

"I've dispatched a team via insertion helo. What else can I do?"

"Thanks Peter. I need to find someone, an Australian sergeant, Dingo ... Sergeant Donaldson. He was stationed out at Baghdad with me when the IED went off." Andrew unveiled as much as he dared over the secure comms link using designated keywords to lessen the classification and laid out his plan.

"Send me some details via the encrypted data link and I'll inform the authorities at your destination."

"Will do, said Andrew. He ended his conversation and made his way to the ancient Tor of Glastonbury. Philby would be right on it.

The hum of the four engines of the converted Ilyushin Il-76 relaxed Andrew. The covert strategic airlift aircraft took off from a small, disused military runway in the south of England. Andrew tightened the nylon straps from the cargo hold of the Ilyushin Il-76 aircraft, happy to be doing something other than briefing people. At least here every minute took him closer to finding the cube and returning home to Giselle. This time he knew what to expect. When the mission was over, they'd fly him straight to Canada. He glanced at the military container strapped in as cargo and smiled. No shoggoth, or an ancient witch, was going to get between him and getting home to Giselle again. He grinned as he remembered the sign on the door when he picked up his package from the guys at Fort Halstead: *There is no problem too big that can't be fixed with explosives.* He nodded: they had the right idea, and the experimental military grade RDX explosives would go a long way to him making his point.

At the first stop, the plane touched down at Baghdad, and Andrew clambered from the cargo hold. Bright lights illuminated the runway apron, and bathed him in an orange color. He checked his watch and realized it was barely three in the morning. All going well, they'd get to Ur just at dawn. It had been easy for Philby to make a few calls, and for Andrew to connect with the IRIDIUM team in the US and make arrangements for the trip. This was the last stop before they arrived at the ancient *Temple of Sin.*

An Australian soldier Andrew recognized stood at the aircraft's cargo ramp. "G'day, sir. Good to see you still in one piece." The man laughed. "I had to wonder last time we met." The Australian sergeant threw him a proud and respectful salute.

Andrew stepped forward and offered to shake Sergeant Donaldson's hand. "Dingo! Great to see you!" It was good to see the sergeant again, and Andrew grinned and shook the soldiers hand as if it were the only stable thing in his life.

"Sir, you've got some sway," said the Australian. "I ain't never seen things happen so fast as I did when they turned up to scoot me off here."

Andrew could only imagine. "I know some people," he said.

Dingo laughed. "Ha! People. I think the two star general here had a heart attack when he got a call from the director of the NSA and some English Lord in Whitehall within the same hour. You never told me you were connected, sir."

Andrew smiled. Philby's boss in MI5 had been very supportive.

"So where are we going and what are we going to do?"

"We're going to rescue some people trapped in an ancient device," said Andrew.

"Sounds like my kind of fun. I've brought a friend if that's ok?"

Andrew paused. "A friend?"

"He don't talk much." Dingo laughed. "Meet Joey, he's under test."

Andrew laughed at the track-based bomb robot that chugged toward them.

"You understand I'm here to run some Counter IED tests, to see how the bomb robot performs?"

"Understood." Andrew nodded, not bothered what reasons were given as long as he had the man's help. He stared at the bomb robot and noticed it was different to the ones he'd seen. He pointed to the end of the water cannon. "What's it got at the end?"

Dingo chuckled. "I had some of your *'colleagues'* visit me. They wanted you to have some heavier fire power."

Andrew frowned. "My friends?"

"You know... the ones that got me that briefing about ancient monsters and stuff. Bit far-fetched if you ask me."

Andrew smiled. If only it were far-fetched. By *colleagues* Dingo had referred to the NSA's technical division who'd also paid him a visit.

"So what did they do to the water cannon?" asked Andrew as he examined a large sealed attachment on the side.

Dingo chuckled, it was rich and seemed to reverberate from somewhere down by his feet. "You just wait and see." He cocked his head. "I'll surprise you."

Andrew raised his eyebrows. "Okay then... I'm sure you will."

"Ready to go?"

"Almost." Dingo turned around and pulled a weapon from a box on the ground near him. He pulled out a rifle and tossed it to Andrew. Andrew caught it clumsily in one hand.

"What's this for?" not recognizing the oddly manufactured rifle.

"A Russian Kalashnikov semi-automatic rifle," said Dingo. "If we are going to fly into the holy lands in a Russian gun ship, then a Kalashnikov would seem a perfect choice of firepower." He laughed. "I was told I'd never left Baghdad on this tour. We were never here. No Canadians. No Australian. And no allied weapons." He held up his Kalashnikov. "This Russian crap will be fine."

"And you brought a friend," said Andrew, referring to the modified bomb robot.

"I suspect you did too."

Andrew nodded, but the RDX, a high-grade military explosive, in a firing pistol by his belt would be his little secret.

## Dhi Qar Province, Iraq

Andrew braced himself as the heavily armed Ilyushin Il-76 aircraft fell from the desert sky for a tactical landing. It banked hard, and even in the pre-dawn light, he could see the aircraft's left wingtip: it looked so close to the ground he wondered when the pilot would straighten up. He tightened the nylon straps of his seatbelt, checked his body armor and helmet strap. The cabin alarm chimed and he braced himself. The aircraft twisted, straightened in a giddy twist and then he felt the wheels make contact, heard the engines whine as the aircraft bounced down a narrow strip of road, barely missing low hills and trees either side.

They were here because of him. Because of what he had sensed in the ancient cube before it vanished. If anything happened here, it would be on his head. He was responsible.

The aircraft whined to a stop, and one of the aircrew stepped into the rear cargo hold. "All good?" asked one of the crew.

He looked around at the group of armed soldiers, and seeing them nod, he gave the thumbs up. "Dingo, you and Mav cover the aircraft perimeter. Go."

The rear cargo hatch leveled and he clambered out with his crew of trained soldiers. A wave of warm air from the nearby sand dunes outside welcomed him like an old friend.

He shuddered. Last time he was in Iraq, a routine patrol that had taken him close to the ancient city of Ur: one of the oldest cities of ancient Mesopotamia, and home of Nanna, the 'illuminator', the Sumerian moon god. That was before the IED exploded, and the complex attack had killed too many of the team. But now, here he was.

He stared up at the ancient temple, and strode directly to the steps. "Sergeant Donaldson..."

"Sir!"

"Wait here, but prepare the men for the worst."

"Understood."

Reports from the drone had given no indications of trouble, but trouble always found him, and he'd just parked a military airplane on one of their main roads. Something would happen. Just the act of being here could set off a string of events.

Behind him, the sound of the men cocking their weapons, and moving into a deeper protective cover, did nothing to make him feel safer. He wiped the cold sweat from his brow. He could feel trouble was ahead of him, up in the *Temple of Sin,* home of Nanna, the 'illuminator' and Sumerian moon god. Taking someone would only inflame the situation.

He climbed the sandstone steps, and the cool wind whipped around him. Nothing happened as he climbed. Morning prayer rang out from a nearby temple, but other than that, any other sounds were muffled by the wind. At the top of the structure, footprints in the fine grains of golden sand led to a door. He pulled on it and it opened freely. He stepped inside of the cool, dimly lit temple and shivered as fear stabbed at him. He cursed: there was death in the air.

A man standing near the edge of an altar faced him. The man was freshly shaven and dressed in a simple white robe. He wore a lumpy waistcoat jacket and in the cool temple, sweat ran down his forehead. Andrew pulled the Westinghouse Colt 45 from his belt. He pointed it at the man and clicked it off safe. The sound echoed around the temple and the man smiled.

"Where is it?" said Andrew referring to the device that Giselle said many more ancient people were still trapped inside.

The man grinned. "It? The infidel wants something ancient perhaps?"

Andrew's finger tightened on the trigger. He stepped closer to the man and pointed the pistol at the man's head. "I've come a long way for this. It wouldn't be wise to press me, not today," he said. "Where is it?"

The man stared back into Andrew's eyes and gave a slight nod. "I see desperation, infidel. This is your lucky day. I can help you find your nirvana. It's there." The man pointed to a recess near ground level.

"Not going to stop me?"

"No," the man said. "Open it and all your wishes and dreams of death will come true." The man opened his arms wide and Andrew noticed he held a switch. In that moment he realized that he stared as close as he ever would be a suicide bomber.

"May you see all the gods today." The man's hand tightened on the trigger device.

Andrew did the only thing he could think of, he jumped toward the man to avoid the blast pattern, and he landed near a low wall. He sprawled out as flat as he could, half protected by the wall.

The blast wave shook him. He felt metal fragments rip at his helmet and slice his body armor. His ears rang, and it was only then he realized how lucky he'd been in leaving his hearing protection in from the flight. Smoke filled the temple and his eyes watered. He breathed it in and coughed up blood. He was lucky the shock wave hadn't killed him.

He stood, dizzy, and examined the suicide bomber's remains with a semi-detached interest. The man's head sat in the middle of a shredded set of arms and legs. The torso was missing, but the man wore a smile in death. No, Andrew corrected, the torso circled the temple, a ring of shrapnel-impregnated blood. He bet the man wouldn't have smiled if he had known his sacrifice was for nothing. Andrew hobbled over to the recess the man had indicated and rummaged around in it. He wondered how a suicide bomber could have been waiting for him. He had told nobody except his friend Philby. He felt cold metal, and he retrieved the elongated six-fingered ancient device.

Philby had been the only one outside of the group that had known he would be here, everyone else had learned about the details in flight. If Philby had organized a suicide bomber, then they were all in danger. He looked at the device that he'd rescued Giselle from two days before, pleased it had ended up here where he suspected it would go based on the symbols on it. He dare not operate it here. Not yet. It would be safer down by the plane; where Dingo could keep an eye on things for him. He didn't know what he'd have done without the Australian soldier.

Andrew pushed open the temple door and stood at the top of the entrance. After the dimly lit temple, the sun's rays hurt his eyes. He put on his ballistic eyewear and blinked away the dust and tears. He hadn't realized how much his chest hurt. His ears throbbed. He wiped the back of his neck and his hand came away with blood.

He heard gunfire below him and he pushed aside his injuries. "Dingo, I've got it," he yelled and hurried carefully down the steps on unstable legs. Philby would pay for this, he was certain of it.

At the end of the stairs, Andrew walked like a drunken soldier to the plane, impervious to the gunfire around him.

"Shit, Colonel," yelled Dingo. "You look a mess. Go and sit down under cover. We are taking casualties. Mav's gone. Blue's arm is shot up."

Andrew felt like someone had punched him in the gut. He frowned, unable to believe what he was hearing. Mav was gone? His stomach lurched. Blue injured? This was on him.

Dingo ducked and returned fire. "Doesn't make sense, sir. They knew we were coming."

"Damn it!" He pulled his gun. Philby would pay for his treachery. He fired at a dark bearded man that appeared from the side of the aircraft. Andrew watched him fall with detached interest. The smell of cordite and smoke filled his senses and he sat down in the sand and rubbed the back of his neck. He noticed more bright red blood stain his hand. It was probably why he felt so giddy, but it could wait. There was no way he would give up the device before he got those poor souls out like he'd promised Giselle. He held the device like he had two days before and pressed the buttons. He held his breath.

Light shimmered around him. Blurred images appeared, and he closed his eyes. He scrambled back in the hope of evading the device's hypnotic pull.

Men and women materialized from the device.

Andrew took a breath and looked at the crowd of thirty or so people that had materialized from the device: ancient Aztecs, Romans, Greeks, and other cultures and people whose costumes he couldn't recognize.

He heard a guttural cry of the *Old Ones,* ancient hideous creatures, and stiffened. The throng of people that had materialized from the device scattered and ran screaming.

The shoggoth stepped forward. It leaned toward him and one of its tentacled eyes turned into a moist mouth with razor sharp teeth. It snapped at him. He ducked. "Everyone move." He waved them aside and pulled the Westinghouse colt 45 from his gun belt. He aimed at the closest mouth and fired. It shattered the creature's mouth and the shoggoth stopped, but only for a moment and then continued.

An Australian machine gun barked on the other side of the plane.

"More incoming," yelled Dingo.

Andrew nodded and faced the shoggoth. It snarled and screamed from a hundred mouths. The pitch was deafening. Andrew crouched and covered his ears from the pain. The shoggoth stepped closer and Andrew reloaded his weapon, he pointed it at the monster. He prayed that everything would end well.

"Move away, Sir," said Dingo. He stepped forward and operated the bomb robot controls.

Andrew watched the robot surge forward through the sand on rubber tracks. It rattled toward the creature while Dingo raised the modified water cannon. "Here we..."

A shot rang out and the robot stopped.

Dingo fell.

More shots rang out, and Andrew's stomach twisted. He ducked and his throat tightened. "Dingo... Are you alright?"

Dingo didn't reply.

A man appeared from behind the plane. He wasn't one of theirs. Andrew fired and watched him fall. He wanted to check on Dingo, but the shoggoth's growl, deep and guttural commanded his attention. He cursed. It stepped on the robot, twisting the arm.

Andrew emptied his magazine into it, but the creature didn't flinch and continued forward toward him. He pulled the flare gun fitted with the RDX explosives and took aim. He pulled the trigger and the shoggoth explode into a pulverized mess before him. Burning eyes scattered around him. Mouths snapped open and shut, twisting like stranded fish out of water.

He should have felt satisfaction, he should have been elated: the people were free of the device, and the shoggoth no longer threatened anyone. But Dingo lay on the floor nearby, mouth open in mid-word, a bullet hole in his skull. Dead. Gone. Andrew fell to his knees by his friend and screamed with despair. Dingo and Mav were both gone. How many more men had he lost? None of it made any sense.

A whirling noise pulled Andrew from that dark place.

The device by his feet rose off the ground and began to spin. Colors erupted from it. It morphed, and for the second time that week, Andrew stared at a mirrored cube floating in the air inches from his face.

He opened the flare gun and flicked the empty shell from it, slid a new RDX cartridge into the chamber. Someone would pay for this. It had trapped Giselle in it. All the lost people had been held there too. Dingo and Mav had died getting them out.

He bit down on the inside of his cheek and tasted blood. It felt good. He bit down harder and felt the tingle of pain run across his scalp.

The desert sand whipped at him and blurred his vision. His trigger finger shook as he blinked away the sand and his vision cleared.

The mirrored cube flashed as the sun reflected across it, but this time Andrew knew better than to try and touch the ancient object or to stare at it for too long: it defied logic. He wanted to turn the ancient device into a smoldering wreck. But he couldn't. Instead, he forced himself to let go of his anger and lowered the gun, certain that Philby would pay for everything that happened today.

He knew a place they could study it. There was a facility deep in the Australian Great Sandy Desert, that was about as far away and remote from here as you could get. And he had a colleague, an Australian army major, Harrison Peel, who had come from that land; perhaps he'd be able to help. But he suspected it was an impossible task: it was an impossible object.

It was as if the cube had read his mind: it flashed and vanished into thin air. This time he had no idea where it might be. The remaining insurgents fled, and he felt for them. Then he called the NSA and organized care for the strange collection of misplaced people.

## London, England

Andrew had bid Dingo and Mav farewell at a ramp ceremony in Baghdad. He'd stood with the rest of the Australian contingent and paid his respects as their bodies were carried up the ramp onto the aircraft taking them to their resting places home in Australia. Now, in London, there was one final thing he needed to do for them.

The Hilton girls would be long asleep, but Andrew knew that Philby liked to rise early during previous IED conferences. Huddled in the dawn light beside Trafalgar's statue in the center of London, he waited. Philby had been instrumental in their deaths, and now he would play a beggars last tune.

Through the scope of the Dingo's Kalashnikov rifle he watched Philby exit the hotel. He dialed a number on his phone.

"Philby, it's Andrew Stone."

"Andrew, how are you?" Philby sounded surprised. "How did the mission go?"

"Oh, it went just fine."

He could see Philby stop and rub his head.

"Philby, how could you? What have I ever done to you?"

"I don't understand, old boy?"

"I didn't tell anyone but you about my destination. How could there have been anyone waiting?"

"I don't follow you, but I've got to go... they are calling me into a meeting right this second."

Philby threw his phone down on the ground and stomped on it. He looked around nervously and then turned and rubbed his head. Through the rifle's scope, Andrew could see the man looked troubled.

Andrew's lip curled in disgust when he remembered the results of Philby's actions. He pulled the trigger and Philby fell to the ground. He watched the blood pool around the man. That was for Dingo and Mav, two good men who didn't deserve to die. He emptied the rounds from the rifle's magazine and placed them in his pocket. He wiped the weapon clean and leaned it up against the statue of Trafalgar.

Now it was over. He could go home. Giselle, who along with the lost people had been freed from the ancient device, was waiting for him back in Canada and they had a lifetime to catch up on.

*A special thanks to David Conyers for permission to make reference to Harrison Peel and to take elements from his story, "Impossible Object."*

151

# The Wish Box

by
**Steve Foreman**

The Wish Box
by
Steve Foreman

TOMMY SIMMONDS had seen the little box while browsing around a local flea market. He wasn't looking for anything in particular amongst the piles of unwanted items that one usually finds at this type of Sunday fair - old ornaments and knickknacks, rusty garden tools, framed pictures, objet d'art, used roller blades, old books and junk of all sorts piled up on trestle tables or laid out on plastic tarps at the rear of reversed-in parked cars - but the box caught his eye. It seemed to call to him; standing alone on a bare table set up at the rear of a battered old Ford Transit van. Either the owner had not brought much to sell, or he had had a good day.

The box measured about six inches long and three inches in height and width; made of a very dark wood, almost black, fitted with brass corners and brass hinges. A tiny, badly scratched brass lock plate with a keyhole sat in the middle of the lid at the front.

Tommy picked the box up and examined it. It was surprisingly heavy. A man who had been sitting on a folding chair between the table and the back door of the van stood up.

"You look like someone who's wishing for something," he said, with a small smile.

Tommy frowned and gave the man a curious look. The man was tall, with a grey beard and long grey hair tied in a ponytail. He wore a woolen coat; a scarf wrapped around his neck.

"You like the box?" the man asked. "It's very old."

"It's heavy," Tommy replied.

"Ebony; from East Africa," the man explained. "A beautiful wood; endangered now."

"What's it for?"

"It's a Wish Box. It comes from the Shaba tribe. I bought it from an old curio shop in Uganda last year, when my wife and I were travelling through Africa."

"What's a Wish Box?"

"Well, according to Shaba tradition, the person owning the box would make a secret wish; write it on a piece of parchment and lock the parchment in the box. He would then leave it until the wish came true. He would never open it or let anyone know what was written on the parchment before this happened, or the wish would be lost for ever."

"What if the wish didn't come true straight away... how long would the owner wait for that to happen?" asked Tommy, his curious schoolboy mind full of questions.

"I don't know. Maybe until he died... or until he got fed up waiting and opened the box." The man shrugged. "The box can only be used once, and then it has to be passed on to another owner."

"Do you believe it works?" Tommy asked.

"I wanted to believe it, at the time, because I was desperate."

"Did you use it for a wish, then?"

"Yes," said the man.

"Did the wish come true?"

The man fell silent for a moment, staring down at his feet. "My wish was lost," he said, looking up.

"What happened?" Tommy asked.

"My wife was diagnosed with cancer a few months ago. I thought about the box sitting on our mantelpiece alongside other artefacts we had bought during our trip, and thought, well, why the hell not; give it a try. My wish was that she would be cured."

"So it doesn't work then?"

"I was at the hospital one day, visiting my wife. She was having treatment all that week. This was just after we returned from our holiday. The prognosis was fairly good." The man pouted and shook his head. "Someone broke into our house while I was out. They must have cased it for a few days and seen it was unoccupied nearly all day every day, I guess. They turned the place over, tore through every room and cupboard and stole many things, they broke open my wife's jewellery box and took the entire contents, money from my bedside cabinet, electronics. They forced open this box as well, but just discarded it on the floor with all the emptied drawers and stuff." The man shook his head, slowly. "I found the place had been burgled when I got home from the hospital that evening. My wish was lost. My wife died that same night."

"I'm sorry," Tommy said quietly. "Do you think your wife would have got better? I mean, would the wish have come true if the box hadn't been opened?"

"I don't know. Maybe. The box was a tangible way of holding onto my wish... so it certainly helped me when I was despairing. It seemed more solid than the God I had stopped believing in."

"It could just be a coincidence, you know, your wife dying the same time the box was opened."

"I'll never know, will I." the man replied.

Tommy placed the box on the table and tried to open the lid. It was locked. "Is there a key for it?"

"Yes." the man replied, but made no attempt to produce it.

"It's very... nice. How much are you asking?"

"How much are you offering?" the man said in reply.

"I've got five dollars."

"Then five bucks it is," the man said. He reached down under the table and pulled out a used plastic bag.

"What about the key?" Tommy asked, as the man placed the box inside the bag.

The man handed the bag to Tommy, unwound his scarf from around his neck and lifted a thin chain over his head. From it dangled a small brass key.

Tommy held out the note and the man exchanged it for the key and the chain.

"Okay, thanks," Tommy said, slipping the chain over his head, "Bye!"

"Just one more thing..." the man called after Tommy, who turned around to listen. "If your wish does come true by some miracle, then, according to the Shaba tradition, the box must be opened and the paper it is written on burned immediately... or the wish will reverse; as if it never matured."

When Tommy got home he went up to his bedroom and cleared a space on a shelf cluttered with books, model aircraft and Star Wars figures. He took the wish box out of the bag and placed it on the shelf. It was a rather handsome item. The dark wood seemed to glow with an inner light and barely perceptible swirls of honey-coloured satin grain deep within.

Tommy lifted the chain over his head and examined the small key. It slid easily into the lock. He turned it and heard a faint snick as the tumblers fell. He gently lifted the lid, which opened smoothly. The box was empty.

Tommy didn't hesitate about his wish. He had stopped believing in God some time ago; all his prayers had gone unanswered. His mom still prayed, when his father wasn't around; Tommy could hear her praying sometimes in her bedroom, pleading with God, between the crying. It seemed her prayers went unanswered too.

Tommy picked up a black ball-point pen from his desk, tore a page from his exercise book and wrote his wish upon it. He folded the paper, placed it inside the box, closed the lid and locked it before slipping the key chain back over his head.

After lunch, his sister, Amy, wandered into his room. "What's in the box, Tommy?" she asked, pointing to the item on the shelf.

"Nothing." Tommy replied.

"What do you mean nothing?"

"I mean, it's empty," he said.

"Can I look inside?"

"What for,? There's nothing in there."

"Then why have you got it?"

"Christ, Amy! Because it's a nice box, that's all."

He would have dearly loved to tell Amy about the supposed nature of the box and what he had written, but he didn't want to spoil any chance that it might by some miracle, as the man had said - actually work.

"Mom tells me you bought an antique box, Tommy," his father said, when he came home from playing golf that afternoon and sat down in his armchair. "Glad to see you are spending your pocket money on something sensible for a change, instead of the normal rubbish."

Tommy, on his way out of the living room, half turned at the door and nodded.

"What's in it?" his father asked, picking up his newspaper.

"Nothing, dad."

"Come on, there are no secrets in this house!" his father said, staring at Tommy.

A hurt look flickered across Tommy's face as he turned away. "Hypocrite," he murmured.

"What did you say?" His father frowned, laying the newspaper on his lap.

"Nothing in it." Tommy replied.

"It's okay Tommy," his mother interjected, turning from the stove. "We were just curious, that's all."

"Excuse me, I'm dealing with this, Mary," John Simmonds said sharply to his wife. "Get back to your kitchen and get my dinner."

She threw a quick glance at Tommy and hurried back to her stove.

When Tommy walked into his bedroom he surprised his sister, sitting on the edge of his bed with the box on her lap; bending over it, a nail file in one hand.

"What do you think you're doing?" he yelled.

She looked up, guiltily. Tommy quickly crossed the room and snatched up the box, wincing as one of the metal corners accidentally caught her eyebrow. She fell back on his bed with a squeal; her hand clamped to her face. Their mother rushed in from her bedroom, where she had been changing for dinner.

"What's going on, you two?" she asked. "God, Amy, what happened?" she cried, seeing the blood seeping through her daughter's fingers.

"Tommy hit me with that box!" Amy whined, pointing to the item in her brother's hands.

Tommy stood there bristling. "It was an accident, mom!" he cried. "She was trying to force it open with a nail file."

His mother ushered Amy into the bathroom, where she cleaned the blood off her face. It proved to be only a small cut, soon fixed with a band aid.

"Sorry Amy, I didn't mean to hurt you," Tommy said, as his sister emerged from the bathroom.

Her mother nudged Amy's shoulder. "I'm sorry too," she said reluctantly, staring at her feet.

"Why did you try to open it then?" he asked.

"I just want to see what's inside! You are so secretive!"

"I am not secretive; there's nothing inside!" he yelled.

"Okay, you two!" their mother interjected. "Now, that's enough of that arguing. Amy, you have apologised to Tommy and he has apologised to you. Now, let's leave it at that." She sighed. "Amy, do not touch Tommy's box again, do you hear?"

"Okay, mom." She sulked and wandered off downstairs.

Tommy put the box back on the shelf and followed her.

"If you ever hurt your sister like that again, my boy, you are going to be in big, big trouble, believe me," Tommy's father said, after enquiring about the sticking plaster on Amy's eyebrow. He sat on the sofa with his daughter next to him.

"Okay, dad, but it was an accident, really!" Tommy said from the doorway.

"It wouldn't have happened if you had just let Amy see inside the box when she first asked," his father replied, putting a comforting arm around the girl. Amy tensed and closed her eyes, but did not move. "Nobody hurts my baby," he crooned, turning his head to her; "Do they honey?"

"No daddy," said Amy, but she did not look at her father.

"But, dad!" Tommy whined, "I am sorry I hurt her!"

"That's enough Tom!" his father snapped. "Now go back to your room. No dinner for you tonight!"

"It was an accident, John," said Tommy's mother. "He didn't do it on purpose."

"Who asked you to poke you nose in?" he snapped at his wife.

"Sorry, John," she said, quickly averting her eyes and returning to setting the table. "I didn't mean to speak out of turn."

"I will deal with you later," he said, removing his arm from Amy's shoulders and picking up his newspaper.

Tommy could hear his father's raised voice; his mom pleading. Then he heard the slap; clearly audible though the closed door of their bedroom, followed by his mom's crying.

Tommy yelled, "Leave her alone!" then slammed his bedroom door and sat on the edge of his bed; cradling the box on his lap. His eyes were closed and his lips twitched as if saying something under his breath.

Suddenly, his father burst into the room; a leather belt dangling from his left hand. "Right, Tommy," his father said. "I want a word with you about minding your own business, my lad..." He stared at his son, "for Christ's sake, Tommy, what is it with that bloody box? What the hell is in it that is so important?"

Tommy looked at his father from under his brow. "Nothing," he said.

His father took a few paces into the room.

"I don't like liars, Tommy. Now give me that box."

Tommy clamped the box protectively against his chest, but said nothing.

His father took another pace forward, now within reach of Tommy. "Hand it over!" he ordered.

Tommy shook his head, defiantly.

His father raised his right hand, the palm still red from where he had slapped his wife across the face.

Tommy jumped up and, ducking under his father's arm, ran out the room.

"Tommy!" his father yelled, spinning around, "Don't you dare disobey me! Now come here!"

But Tommy was already running down the hallway. His father ran after him and clattered down the stairs in the boy's wake. Tommy flung open the front door and ran outside; his father just behind, one hand outstretched trying to grab Tommy's collar, the other waving the leather belt above his head.

The boy squatted on the pavement, rocking back and forth on his heels, wooden box clamped between his thighs and his chest, his arms folded across the top. His mother and sister stood next to him, both crying. The mother was stroking the boy's hair. Blue and red pulsing lights reflected on their pale faces.

A pair of paramedics was examining a body lying in a pool of blood in front of the crumpled front end of an old-model Corolla. The victim's head was smashed in on one side, one eye hanging out of its socket. It was Tommy's father. A policewoman stood next to the car, notebook in hand, asking questions of the distraught driver.

"The kid came flying out of the garden gate there; ran straight out in front of me into my headlights," he was saying. "I hit the brakes and instinctively swerved to miss the kid, but I ran straight into the guy." He shook his head. "I couldn't avoid him."

Another police officer walked over to the family group.

"I am sorry for your loss, Mrs Simmonds, but I need to ask a few questions," he said gently to the woman. "Can you tell me what happened?"

The woman wiped away some tears and sniffed. "My husband, John, and I" she nodded toward the body lying on the road, "were having a an argument." The police officer glanced at the woman's black eye and swollen lip and nodded in understanding. "Tommy must have heard from his bedroom and screamed at my husband to stop," she continued. "John went to Tommy's room. I heard him shouting at Tommy about that box." Her eyes darted toward the box that Tommy held. "John yelled at Tommy but Tommy ran downstairs. John was furious and chased after him, screaming and yelling."

The policeman squatted down and spoke to the boy, but Tommy had a blank look upon his face and appeared not to see the policeman. "Have a look at this kid, will you?" he called over his shoulder to the paramedics. "He's in shock I think. He needs help."

"We're going to take him to the hospital to see a doctor," the paramedic said to Tommy's mother after examining the boy, "you need to come with us."

"Amy will have to come as well," she said through her tears, "She can't stay alone."

"Okay, get what you need from the house and lock up. We'll call in another ride."


"You'll have to let go of the box, Tommy," the doctor said. "I need you to relax so I can examine you."

But Tommy would not let go. He held the box clamped to his chest, curled up on the bed in a fetal position, crooning softly.

"I will need to see that box," the police officer said. "It seems to be the reason the victim chased Tommy from the house. There is something about it that might have to do with this case."

"He is suffering some post-traumatic shock. We'll have to sedate him anyway, but he will be fine," the doctor said, nodding to a nurse who immediately prepared an injection. Once the boy was sedated, his grip relaxed; the doctor removed the box from Tommy's grasp and handed it to the waiting police officer.

"You might want this as well," said the doctor, handing him a chain. "It was around Tommy's neck. There is a small key on it."

The police officer took the box to a side table, snapped on a pair of latex gloves and unlocked the box with the key. He opened the lid and he and the Detective Inspector with him peered inside. A piece of folded paper lay in the bottom of the box. The police officer frowned, lifted the paper out and unfolded it, reading aloud...

"I wish my dad was dead."

"Strange," said the police officer, turning to his superior.

"Yeah, well, it looks like his wish came true. But the death was an accident... this has no bearing on the case," she said.

"You're right," said the policeman, screwing up the paper and throwing it into a garbage can in the corner. Leaving the box on the side table, he and his colleague departed.

Down in the basement, in the hospital morgue, the corpse of John Simmonds slowly sat upright on a stainless steel gurney. Swaying from side to side, he turned his head, trying to focus his one remaining eye; confused as to his surroundings. Cautiously, he swung his legs off the gurney and stood up. He wobbled slightly, gaining his balance, before staggering over to a wash basin on the far wall. His hands flew to his face in horror when he saw his mutilated reflection in the mirror. Then the memory of what happened came back to him. "Tommy," he rasped through broken teeth.

On a nearby metal tray lay a selection of stainless steel tools and cutting implements. He picked up a heavy bone-cleaver and, satisfied with its heft, he stalked over to the door. At that moment the morgue assistant entered. She dropped the pile of files she had been clutching to her chest and screamed; a scream cut short as the cleaver split her skull in two. John stepped over the spilled brains and let himself out. The corridor was empty and he limped unmolested to the elevators, residual blood dripping from the hole in the side of his face, leaving a trail on the linoleum floor. He punched a button and waited.

When the doors slid open, an orderly stepped out. He carried in both arms a supply of biohazard bags neatly folded and stacked up to his chin. His eyes opened wide momentarily and he dropped the load of bags, but before he could scream, John swung at him with the cleaver and decapitated him. Blood sprayed in an arc, decorating the interior of the elevator in unreadable graffiti. John kicked the severed head to one side and entered the elevator, then turned and hit the button marked A & E. The doors slid shut and the elevator jerked into action.

"Tommy... you little shit!" John mumbled, spittle dripping from the side of his shattered mouth. "You disobeyed me, and now you're going to pay!" He slapped the flat of the bloody cleaver against his palm.

When the doors opened, John stepped out into the A & E reception area, the cleaver down at his side. In jerky steps he shuffled and limped towards the hospital exit doors, his bare feet leaving smudges of red on the floor. A senior A & E nurse, battle-hardened with a thousand night shifts under her belt, immediately stepped toward John, thinking he was a victim of some terrible accident who had managed to drag himself to A & E.

"My God, what happened to you?" she exclaimed.

John lifted the cleaver and slashed her across the face. Her lower jaw fell off in a fountain of blood. The place erupted. Nurses and patients screamed and panic ensued. A male doctor rushed to the aid of the nurse, bending over her prone figure. John hit him across the back of the neck with the cleaver, severing his spinal cord. A uniformed security guard on duty outside the entrance, alerted by the pandemonium, spun around. He took one look at the horror walking towards him with the bloody cleaver hanging at its side, threw open the glass doors and stepped inside. He pulled his service revolver.

"Drop the knife, now!" he yelled, not knowing how better to describe the broad-bladed weapon.

John ignored him and, with what looked like a smile, continued to lurch along the corridor toward him.

"I'm warning you!" the rent-a-cop called, taking a few paces forward before taking up a crouched, two handed stance, "Drop it or I'll drop you!"

John ignored him, grinning now with his shattered teeth. The guard took aim at John's chest.

"Last warning, pal!" he screamed. Behind him and along the corridor people were running, yelling for help, bumping into each other in panic. The guard fired two shots directly in the ghoul's chest. John half-twisted, staggered back a pace, and then continued limping toward the shocked guard. A cleaner came barrelling out of a side room in panic, crashed into the guard and knocked him over. John raised the cleaver above his head and brought it down hard, severing the guard's hand at the wrist. The revolver skittered away on the linoleum.

Five rooms away, Tommy sat up on the bed where he had been dozing, alerted by all the noise. He was still groggy from the sedative, but the two loud gunshots had forced him wide-awake. His mom stood up from Tommy's bedside, opened the door and peeked out. What she saw in the corridor shook her to the core. "My God!" she yelped, slamming the door, "It's daddy!" She collapsed, shaking, into a plastic chair.

"What... what do you mean it's daddy?" Amy cried. "He's dead!"

Tommy slid off the bed and went to the door, cracking it open.

"Stay away from the door Tommy!" his mother screamed, but Tommy already saw the thing that used to be his father, lurching along the corridor, the cleaver held high.

"The wish box!" he yelled, turning back into the room and slamming the door.

"What?" his mom shouted back, confused.

"Where's my box?" He suddenly remembered what he was supposed to have done.

"Here," said his sister, picking it up from the table where the police officer had left it.

Tommy opened the unlocked lid and stared at the empty interior. "Shit!" he

162

swore, glancing around. An idea popped into his head. Tommy stared at Amy, grabbing the lapel of her blouse in one hand. "Think of the one thing you have really wished for, Amy... really, really wished for with all your heart for the past couple of years," he said, quietly and calmly, "don't tell me what it is. Just write it down, quickly!"

"What are you doing, Tommy?" his mom asked, incredulously, "This is no time for stupid games!"

"Shut up, mom!" Tommy snapped with such vehemence that her jaw snapped shut.

"What do you mean, Tommy?" Amy pleaded, tears running down her cheeks.

"Amy, trust me! Come on, you know exactly what I mean. I have heard you whisper it sometimes in your bedroom at night!" Tommy yelled, shaking her by the blouse. "Just do it. We're running out of time!"

Amy had no idea what this was all about, but knew it had something to do with the box. She snatched up a pen from a clip board, tore Tommy's chart in half and with no further hesitation scribbled hurriedly on the back.

Tommy hoped she had wished for the one thing he thought she would.

The screaming out in the corridor grew louder. John had buried the cleaver in the cleaner's head, and was now shoving open the glass exit doors.

"Put it in the box... quick, Amy." Tommy shoved the box at her. "The box is yours now... lock it!"

Amy dropped the scrap of paper in the box, slammed the lid and turned the little key.

Outside, on the ambulance parking bay directly in front of the hospital, John Simmonds stood over a dead paramedic; just standing there, swaying. He frowned momentarily as wisps of smoke began pouring out of his nostrils. Suddenly, his one remaining eye bubbled and popped out as a jet of blue and orange flame shot from the socket. Spurts of red fire came from his ears just seconds before his entire body burst into flames. The cleaver clattered to the ground. Smoke poured from John's shattered mouth and flames licked up from the hole in the side of his head, his hair crackled and shrivelled in a cone of bluish fire. From inside the hospital, people already in shock of the carnage and havoc screamed again at this new horror.

John was combusting from the inside out. His blood-stained clothes caught fire and his skin began to melt and run like hot wax. The blackening body finally twisted and collapsed in a burning heap, steam and smoke rising up with the flames.

Tommy cracked open the door of his room and peered out, looking across the carnage at the conflagration taking place on the other side of the glass doors. He breathed a sigh of relief at what he saw. Turning back to Amy he said, "You can open the box again; it's nearly all over now."

Amy unlocked the box and held it open. Tommy plucked out the paper.

"What's going on, Tommy?" she asked.

Tommy shook his head, "I'll explain in a minute," he said, gently, turning to his mom.

"Mum, have you got your cigarette lighter with you?"

His mother, completely fazed by what had happened in the past several minutes did not even question Tommy. She simply opened her purse and passed him the lighter, a dazed look in her eyes.

Tommy flicked it twice and then held the paper over the small flame. Once it caught, Tommy dropped the burning paper into the metal washbasin. The paper browned and shrivelled, and the hastily scrawled words *I wish my dad would burn in hell!* gradually disappeared as the flames consumed the paper.

Outside, a second security guard arrived at the ambulance bay, grabbed a fire extinguisher and began spraying foam on the fiercely burning and now definitely dead John Simmonds.

# Last Day

## by
## Matthew Wilson

Last Day
by
Matthew Wilson

## I.

ED DIDN'T like the rifle. Its recoil had a tendency to push him out the wheelchair.

For two hours now he'd felt alone. The fact that it was the end of the world didn't change anything. He'd always been alone. Although most people at school were sympathetic toward his handicap, he'd insist that there were varying degrees on the scale. His doctors said he would not live past ten, but he had proved them wrong by six ticks so far, and Mom said friends would be drawn to warm talk and humor. But in the end, he had to give his lunch money for them to return conversation. *Bastards.* Having to buy other kids candy at vending machines, or help them in math, in order to simply receive a 'hello' meant Ed was not feeling tip-top at the beginning of the last day. As usual. Of course, Billy Tanner had got his foot jammed in the food dispenser slot. It would have looked silly if he let the machine eat his money and just walk away. He had a reputation to uphold. His dad had died in some war and after getting his medals through the school metal detectors, Billy used every opportunity to show them off.

It made sense, to him at least, to get his money back.

"Stop filming, damn it!" he moaned, when he was beyond the point of no return.

By nine that morning, a crowd of kids had collected round the machine, cheering him on in his fight against technology. Some made candy bets he'd be stuck in there forever, while the fatter, sweatier ones looked enviously at the contents inside.

"You gonna be all day?" Tanya Kalls said, snapping off her phone to save her battery. Besides, fifteen videos of Billy crying like a girl had already been uploaded to YouTube. "I thought you were supposed to eat the food, not the other way, Billy." "Piss you!" Billy seethed, flustering as he hopped on one leg, the other securely fastened in the machine's mouth.

"Piss you?" Tanya blinked. "Is that a real sentence?"

"I'm in pain here, you selfish..."

By all reports, the screams started at 9.01, though there had been attacks in the town at least an hour before that but no one had lived to report them. Being confined to such a small part of life, Ed was a naturally inquisitive child, wishing to see all the world had to offer.

"Wot's 'appenin'?" He asked as children collected at the windows.

It was always the same. On school trips to the cinema he had to strain, hurting his spine as he straightened as much as he possibly could to see the screen. Even during class photos kids poked him in the back, annoyed when teacher wheeled him to the front, blocking their light. They were normal, damn near perfection. So why did the freak get the spot light? On top of all his troubles, mom had thought he had facial ticks when she saw his expression when the bulb went off. He didn't have the heart to tell her the smirking row behind him had their fingers in his back like an old cowboy holding up a train. Ed bounced in his chair, but still could not see out the window. Not even when the kids drew back, clutching their mouths.

"He's eatin' 'im!" Someone screamed. "He's eatin' 'im!"

"Who?" Ed asked, but they were already running toward the stair way, crushing bodies elbowing into each other. Teeth flew, skittering off the wall like spent bullets and Ed felt his chest heave. This was serious, he had to get to a phone, call mom and...

"Fred!" Billy called. "Ted, Fred... Alan?"

"Ed." Ed said and Billy forced a smile, still hopping on one leg as if slightly drunk.

"Listen, Ed. I know we're not friends..."

"You burn my books every day." Ed said.

"True," Billy admitted. "But you can't just leave me man, something major is goin' down out there."

"Wot 'bout rule one?" Ed said, having been reminded of it daily, spat in his face along with Billy's favourite cheese and onion crisps.

Billy's motto: *Look after number one.*

"Yeah, but you wouldn't... you can't leave me here!"

For a moment, Ed felt superior. For once, for one glorious instant, he had power over someone. He could be as cruel to others as the world was to him.

He could be like Billy! The realization sickened him. If something terrible was happening outside, then how could he look mom in the face? She said his heart was the best thing about him. Despite his shape, his heart was pure gold and she was forever grateful for that.

Kids wrote the word monster in his locker. But he didn't have to prove them right.

Hating his conscious, he wheeled himself forward and grabbed hold of Billy's leg.

"Watch the claws, man." Billy hissed, uncomfortable with human contact. Especially this *thing.*

"Shut up, Billy - here, it's comin'!"

Something ripped and, although he lost a trainer, Billy's foot was ejected. He lost his balance on the recently polished floor and fell down awkwardly.

"You okay?" Ed asked, but Billy was already up and running for the stair way, kicking the broken teeth out the way like old tile fragments that had peeled off from the wall.

"Thanks, bro. I got it from 'ere."

"Hey wait," Ed felt a rip in his chest. "You gotta 'elp me too, how am I gonna get downstairs?"

Billy laughed, but didn't stop running.

"Rule one, bro." He echoed. A motto that had kept him alive as long as this. "Rule one. And I'm worth more than you."

"You bastard!" Ed said, feeling tears coming. "You total bastard!"

Tricked again. Mom had not raised a monster, but a fool!

How was he going to get downstairs? The teachers said he mustn't use the lift in a fire. This was certainly an emergency, enough to throw normal kids into a total panic. But what kind of emergency?

He couldn't smell smoke. He heard windows shatter downstairs, the screams were getting closer. *Someone's broken into the building*, he thought. Were they under attack? He needed to understand what was going on. His doctor had gone through his condition in slow and detailed steps. If he knew the in and outs of something, it was not so scary for it was a condition, rather than a mysterious force.

As long as he knew what it was and how to deal with it. Dumbly, he wheeled himself to the window and stared down at the play ground.

Then he screamed too.


## II.

Ed couldn't find a teacher. Since life had thrown him a curve ball he liked to have orders. A clear idea of what to do. Thinking for himself had gotten him tricked by Billy. A boy bested by vending machines. And a thousand others before.

Of course, they would hang with him and be friends, but when they had his sweets or pocket money, he found they could easily leave him behind. Mom was always there to help him through the day.

*Brush your teeth, fix your hair.*

But now he was alone, and afraid. He had no choice and nobody to tell him what to do. Ed eased himself onto the floor, crossed his fingers and pushed his wheel chair down the stairs.

"Don't break," he whispered, like a charm against a witch. The chair bounced down the steps, an arm rest bent on impact, sparks scratched the bloodied wall, and he felt a bizarre guilt at damaging public property.

Of course, he'd been wrong. Always wrong, just like everyone said he was.

Clenching his jaw so he would not jar his own teeth loose, Ed began to shuffle forward like a worm, crawling on his belly.

"Nice and easy," he said, though it was hard to ignore the screams below. Four flights down, he heard footfalls stampeding on tiles. It sounded like a riot at a rock concert. Chairs crashed and glass broke. A great fear overcame him. But it was worse to be alone.

"Nice and easy," he said again, feeling like a baby as he crawled down the steps, his elbows slipping on the oil-like blood.

*Red*, he thought. He smiled when he reached the bottom and turned the corner. "Nearly one flight." He cheered softly. *All by myself.* Biting his bottom lip raw, he wrestled the crumpled remains of his chair around him. The wheel squeaked, but still held up.

"Hey - hey. I'm up 'ere!" He called, but everyone seemed too busy to help.

He closed his eyes, and pushed the chair again, which made a great clatter as it rolled down the steps. Mom would be appalled he was treating his chair in such a manner. She said it was the most important tool in his life, how else was he supposed to get from A to B? *Fly?* She'd had to work all hours that God sent to pay for it. He'd gotten it for Christmas, a bigger buzz than his computer games because now he could play outside with the boys. If he worked up his arm muscles, he could keep up with them, or at least get into a position to play baseball. *Rather than crawl after them like a slug!* His spine burned, its coiled collection of veins pressing against each other as he moved slowly down the second stairway. The sign on the wall said **No Smoking**. Last week, Billy had drawn a rather detailed image of a marijuana joint under the text.

"If you can do one, you can do three more." He realized he was sweating. His heart thumped! God, he needed to slow down before it burst completely.

His pills were in his locker. He didn't need them till Gym when he could work himself into some state of excitement, circling the track, except on wet days when the grass sucked his tires down like quick sand. His guts curdled like old milk when he heard the sound. Someone was coming up the stairs! He hoped it was not one of the things he saw in the playground, a scrap of torn meat between its teeth. Should he shout out? He felt an odd sensation of pleasure when he heard a familiar voice cursing profusely.

"Billy?"

He'd come back. "Oh, thank you, thank..."

"Get out the way!" Billy shouted, and Ed had to pull himself to one side for fear of being stepped on. Billy cursed again as he nearly tripped on the wheel chair.

"What's this doin' 'ere!"

"Move, Billy!" It was Tanya, weeping, storming up behind him. "They're comin' through the door! I said that was a bad idea."

"Ah, piss you." Billy said.

Apparently, the great breakout had failed, and although Ed's mind felt shattered, he still recalled that a class of kids had gone down stairs. So where was the rest of them?

"Tanya, don't leave me." Ed said.

"I don't know you," she said, leaping past, "I'm sorry, but they're coming..."

"Billy!" Ed shouted, "You can't be a total bastard. You can't."

"You should 've stayed where ya was. It's not my fault, you don't listen."

For a while, Ed watched him as the things below slowly came up the stairs, and had to admit that for a while, at least, Billy had not been a *total* bastard.

Not until his brother died anyway.

## III.

Billy hated hospitals. The stink of cleaning products. The fake smile of nurses who knew the patient would never leave, but couldn't come right out and say it. Billy was too young to understand why his brother wouldn't play catch with him. He'd hated the thing in the bed for years. Stealing his mother's time and affection when it didn't even do anything but lie there, like a vegetable.

Dad was a violent drunk who gave him bruises and nothing else till he dropped dead of a heart attack years ago. The war stories were fake. Making a hero out a villain. But at last mom was free, and Billy could start his new life with her after the funeral. But now, again, she was prisoner to another soulless thing, giving it all her time and love. And what of him? What of Billy? He was a nuisance, always under her feet, whether he was trying to help or hinder. He was always told he was doing wrong.

"That retard's not my brother," Billy said one afternoon, hot and tired from being stuck in the ward. Mom had struck him, cementing the idea he was her least favourite son. Maybe if he were ill, she would pay him more attention too.

"Don't you dare *ever* use that word!" she blurted with anger in her eyes. "That's a mental condition, idiot, not a physical thing like your brother has."

Billy apologized, if only to stop her shouting, crying. He went back to his reading, wishing the thing would die so it would be over with. Billy's brother woke only once under the pain killing power of drugs.

"I love you, Bill...ee," he said, the only four words he'd ever said to his brother.

With his mother continually belting into him the notion that he must be kind, Billy repeated the compliment. "I love you too, Fred."

Despite his fears, his frustration, Billy realized that Fred had never ridiculed him like mom had, never hit him like dad, nor had he expected anything of Billy but to be there. This half-a-man was the best man that Billy knew, and before Fred closed his eyes for the final time, Billy realized he genuinely did love him. This mutated thing was the only being that had shown him any affection in all his miserable years on earth. For a while, Billy gave him his heart, believing he could be part of the human race again, but when Fred had died, Billy's defenses slammed down again.

His heart had been ripped out once, he didn't want to feel that again. So when he had seen Ed, he had acted out. He wanted the damn fool to fear him, to stay away at all costs so there would never be a connection. A countdown to the inevitable day that Ed would die. They all knew he would not see twenty. Why waste his affection on a short candle?

Billy had been well and good on the fourth floor, as far from the living dead as possible, but his mind was racing. He'd said he was worth more than Ed, but his brother was worth more than anyone, and he had watched him die, helpless. Twenty years sounded better than sixteen, Billy supposed. He quickly went back down the stairs to where Ed lay, crumpled.

## IV.

"Wot the hell you doin'!?" Tanya screamed, sure Billy had gone mad. "I'm not gonna get killed for a retard!"

"That's a mental condition, idiot, not a physical thing..."

"A physical retard then." Tanya said as Billy kicked the chair away. It was beyond use now.

"Come on, Fred." Billy said, locking his legs to take the strain of the boy. He lifted him up into his arms.

"Ed."

Billy blinked. "Ed, right."

He gritted his teeth. In gym, he'd nearly pulled his back lifting weights to impress the girls. He howled louder than the moaning creatures shambling up the stairs as he straightened his spine and carried Ed up.

"I can't believe you're doin' this." Tanya moaned.

"Stop complaining and shift yourself." Billy growled. The ache in his chest didn't feel like a good pain. All of his bad habits and fast food seemed to be catching up to him.

"You weigh a lot for a half a guy." Billy seethed as Tanya kicked his behind and slapped his arm, hoping he would drop him. "Get off me, ya mad cow!"

Tanya had built up a fine reserve of anger by the time they reached the fourth floor landing again, but Billy was glad of her help as they dragged the vending machine toward the window. Then threw it out into the sunlight.

"Come on, wimp," he said, crouching so Ed could swing his arms round him like a baby monkey hitching a ride with its mother.

"Those pipes won't hold both of you," Tanya said, "I'll go first."

"I can manage, thanks!" Billy yelled as she disappeared over the edge.

"Thanks for coming back for me." Ed said, his mouth devoid of moisture, his breath, rasping.

"No problem, Fred."

"Ed."

"Ed, right. Try not to look down," Billy said, slowly climbing out the window.

Ed didn't trust the guy to carry a jug of water across the room so didn't comply right away, not until he saw the infected kids coming up the final staircase, bloodied arms outstretched to embrace him. Ed closed his eyes and Billy, who had lost a war with a vending machine earlier that morning, tried his luck, a skirmish against gravity.

## V.

It was getting late when Billy emerged, giggling, from the sports store with a trio of weapons in his arms. In the distance the sounds of mayhem continued unabated, and the smell of death lingered on the air.

"You trusting him with a gun?" Tanya asked.

Ed took no notice. Life was too short.

Earlier, Billy had found Ed another wheelchair in the old folk's home a block down from the school. The home had been smoldering and full of horror, but Billy had been determined to make up for all the bad days he'd rained down on him. Now Ed felt invincible with a friend. A chance of life at least. Another go to prove the doctors wrong and live another sixteen years, or more.

There was just one problem. Ed didn't like the rifle. Its recoil had a tendency to push him out the wheelchair.

# Oh, the Things I've Seen

### by
### Konstantine Paradias

Oh, the Things I've Seen
by
Konstantine Paradias

**6 months ago:**

"JFK WASN'T the victim of conspiracy. The bullet that killed him was a high-caliber smart-round that was intended to kill Jackie, who was actually a deep-cover reptilian agent, in service to the Iron Sun Empire." The obese man with the dream catcher beard says, between drags of his joint. He's way past wasted but he doesn't stutter; the words just keep coming, his conspiracy mantra having become second nature to him, by virtue of repetition and a steady diet of message-board bred paranoia. "Lee Harvey Oswald was sent back to 1963 from the year 2995, after the Human-Reptilian war, to stop her. There are tapes from his interrogation by the FBI. I've read the logs. If they had found the magic bullet they would have verified his claim, but Jackie made sure to swallow it from JFK's head-wound as soon as it had become inert. If you check the photos, you'll see she's not really leaning over him to shield him. She's got those fingers knuckle-deep in his grey matter, looking for it."

I take a long drag on my cigarette until it's nothing but filter and smoldering ash, before I crush it in the tinfoil ashtray. The flame makes a hissing noise as it burns through the metal and everything smells like battery acid for a second, nearly making me gag. *No clay, nothing made of glass, no lead in this place* the fat man had told me; *this is a Reptilian comms black hole. Only place I can feel safe, what with knowing what I know, you know?*

In case you were wondering, this is what happens to journalists who decide to take on big oil, and their sources bounce back. They end up trekking across the world, interviewing the crazies on a tabloid's expense account. Then again I shouldn't complain; this could have been worse.

From the tinfoil-fetishist's trailer park home, I pick up the names of a couple who own a church that is said to have the dissolution of human civilization as its sole purpose.

"The Church of the Star Bloop is mankind's last and only line of defense against the coming threat of the eso-aliens." The woman in the kaftan tells me,

174

eyes as big as saucers, her husband frothing at the mouth as the psilocybin-visions overwhelm him, "We maintain our mental purity by modifying our minds to function in a state akin to that of early humanity, before the civilization meme was imposed to us through hidden frequency bombs from deep space. This is what helps the eso-aliens hide. To an infected mind, they seem like authority figures; they wear suits and sunglasses at all times and use stand-ins for photo-shoots. Which is why Hitler always looks so lost and awkward in all those photos and videos. He was just a mind-controlled patsy of the eso-aliens."

The woman offers me a cup of mushroom soup. There's mukhomor in it and mycena cyanorrhiza and psilocyba Mexicana. The chunky bits are pork, I am told; *the high could last for days at a time. No reason to go hungry until it's over.* Remember kids: a hungry man in the throes of a brain-splitting dream quest is an unhappy man in the throes of a dream quest. While the prospect of feeling that there are tiny people on the inside of my skull rearranging my brain sounds tempting, I politely decline.

Lesson of the day, kiddies: Pulitzer laureates aren't invincible. They're just little people with bits of gold-plated bronze 'round their necks. And you know what a big old shiny thing in your chest is, come wartime? It's a target.

Checking through their personal belongings while I pretend to use their restroom, I find the name of a man who reviles sex and wishes to make it illegal. He lives in a little hole inside an apartment block somewhere on the other side of the country.

"Elvis Presley was the Love Messiah, conceived through Gladys' ear by the Angel Vernon who is also Shabbatiel, the factotum of human civilization. He was not born through the crude exchange of fluids." The black man with the trepanation scar on his forehead tells me above the cacophony of his two dozen wind-up alarm clocks. "His conception was immaculate. He gestated in his mother's belly and exited her body through her mouth. Elvis was to be the one to sing mankind into the next stage of our asexual evolution: we would be perfect in every way, hairless and featureless with great eyes like the servants of the Lord that the government shot down when they sent their foreward scouts over Roswell. The agents of Baal-Nezbet made sure to assassinate the envoys of Heaven that would prepare the world for the coming of Elvis, because nothing made on this Earth could hurt him. So they manufactured drugs in their factories on the secret moon and empty women with wombs to catch his sacred seed and big breasts that pumped poison instead of milk. They wanted to make copies of him, even as they killed him."

The alarm clocks start ringing in perfect sync all around me as soon as he is done with his rambling. The tiny apartment echoes with the horrible, shrill cry of tiny hammers on bells and the entire apartment block wakes up so it can pelt the place with garbage and second-hand shoes. *They hate me because the noise interrupts the subliminal signal, the one that makes them think, that urges them to exchange their fluids.* He tells me, as he begins his ritual of silencing every single clock perched on every shelf, inside his fridge, in his cupboards and his sink. *It has been programmed into their minds so that they believe I am a weirdo, but when the time comes, they will thank me. I will be bigger than Jesus, after they have put me on the cross.*

So the paper fires you, the news agencies won't touch you, when it all comes bubbling to the surface. You're poison to every one of them; to the ones that gave you work, that used to put your stuff on the front page, you are worse than tertiary gonorrhea. They can scrub and clean themselves and take every single antibiotic known to man but they will never truly be rid of you. The only ones who would even let you walk into the editor's office are tabloids and gossip magazines. And so you find yourself at the fourth decade of your life, your Pulitzer Prize chucked in a locker in some bus station that you know that you are never going to reclaim, having your stuff reviewed by some hack who used to run two dozen smut magazines and now prints z-list conspiracy theory tabloids for the crazies. And even though you have stared down heartless dictators and have trawled through the hissing, bloody places that spring up in the dark corners of Third-World civil wars, you get down on your knees and plead with the fat bastard, you beg him to *please, please reconsider.* You will dumb your stuff down. You will agree to any and all edits. If the story doesn't suit him, you'll skew it until it does.

Back in journalism school, we called that 'literary whoring' because we were 18 and perfect and morally inviolate. Now, it's a job. From him, I find out about the cult of the movie stars, the A-list directors the magnates that make up the movers and shakers of the world. It's so exclusive, that you can't get in there unless you are worth at least three Ferraris. Or if you get chummy with the janitor and he lets you sneak in real quick.

"The Earth is a binary planet, possessing two moons. One of them was formed as a result of impact with an alien exploration vessel three hundred million years ago, the vessel becoming embedded into the molten mass of the planet killing the crew."

The lady in the form-fitting silver suit placing electrodes on my temples that will give me a rough estimate of my Negative Energy Quotient continues. "The second moon of the Earth is an exploration vessel, sent out to reclaim the lost vessel according to the decree of His Dark Majesty Emperor G'lokk. He is Absolute Anax of the Universe and the guru of the Black Ayurveda. The Buddhists also call him Mara, the Anti-Buddha. The second moon rotates in a perfect synchronous orbit with our moon, rendering it invisible to our own means of detection. When the Apollo 8 program found it, they killed the crew and replaced them with biological automata which negotiated a hidden treaty with the real government of the United States which has been in place for two hundred years. But the British Crown used their own black budget from the Queen's coffers to fund their secret space mission called Budica and sent a single woman to find it, back in 1980. She was Diana, Princess of Wales. They sent her up there armed with the Spear of Lugh, because only one of truly royal decent could wield it and set a double in her place. She never returned from that mission."

The electrodes whirr and hum and I am shot with a considerable discharge of electricity that rams thumbtacks at the back of my eyeballs and makes my muscles clench before I experience a brief but particularly violent fit. When I regain my senses, I realize that I have just soiled myself and that I'm crying. The little digital screen on the thing that just zapped my brain reads 7.52 MClo. *My my, that is the highest NEQ reading we have ever gotten! You need to have your aura cleansed immediately. Please bend over...* and she pulls out a long nickel-plated rod with a sizeable quartz crystal at the tip, the entire thing also hooked to an even bigger machine than the one she used on me, so I just deck her in the face and run. My life might seem like it sucks right now, what with having to put up with crazies and betraying my moral integrity just so I can make rent. But then again, I could be spending my days writing eight thousand word articles on some pop-starlet's nip slip in some award ceremony or another. No thank you, I'd rather take my chances with the crazies. At least they are original.

**Two years ago:**

It was two months into my new post, as I was contemplating pouring chlorine into my espresso and ending it all just to get my skid mark of a publisher off my back, when the idea hit me: the article of the century, the tabloid edition to end all tabloid editions.

"A Grand Unified Conspiracy Theory?" he muttered, as he struggled with the big words in my email, squinting his beady pig-eyes at the screen. I had even bothered with sending him a carefully-worded pitch, to help ease his syphilitic brain into the idea. "You know how ridiculous this sounds right? There is absolutely no way you can pull this off. Hell, even half of the muck most of those people say contradicts the other half!"

I went the extra mile to dazzle him, of course. I talked to him about patterns and noetic crossroads. I talked to him about certain inconsistencies that perfectly resonated with the half-baked explanations given in other theories. I told him about memes, I rambled about 'the monomyth of the shadow forces' even went as far as to paraphrase what little I knew about the function of the lower human brain. Of course I was full of crap, but he was too stupid to realize that at the time. Hell, he was too overwhelmed by my rhetoric to even realize that what he was agreeing to was two years' worth of paid vacation under the pretense of 'investigative journalism' into 'the myths of marginalized subcultures'. The important part was that I had promised him the scoop of the century, one way or the other. If I couldn't make it work as promised then I would just twist it and turn it and pound at it with a hammer until it fit and then perhaps that piece of crap magazine he was managing would have had something worthwhile to show its readers.

"You know that this is a one in a billion chance, don't you? There is no way you could make this work. You won't fool those cuckoos not even for a second," he told me as he bade me farewell from the office.

But I didn't need to. I just had to get the facts and make noise, make ripples in the great intellectual gutter that was my current audience. You can take the author out of the gutter, but you can't take the gutter out of the author. They'll look, whether they like it or not. I would make them look until they went cross-eyed. And when I was done and I was famous again and all the important people would invite me over to lecture them on the tenets of my own paranoiac cocktail, I would go back to that bus station and reclaim that Pulitzer prize and bury it in quick-drying cement and then maybe I would also bed every single woman that has ever rejected me and their mothers.

Fat chance on that last one. But the rest is doable.

**Now:**

From a personality cult to a council of societal rejects who specialize in electronic debauchery, to a secret society of old men whose sole purpose is to eliminate every generation that is to succeed them, to a high-profile honest-to-God mad scientists' conference, I get a name.

"It's a Truth Machine" the man who lives in the little shack just outside the city of Brest and feeds off the strays that come there to die tells me "It works based on the Principle of Absolute Truth, as outlined by Aristotle and expanded on by Mengele. It was the last thing he did, before the Mossad's Nazi Hunters got to him in 1963. What this machine does is run a series of complex algorithms, using reality itself as an interface to reach into what I call Idea-Space. From there, it accesses our collective subconscious and just... drags what I tell it to drag, out to the surface, forcing it to become manifest into our world. And the best part about it is that it cannot hide, once this is done. It becomes part of our conscious. Nothing will be able to obscure it, no measure of memory-wiping or subterfuge or shady, underhanded assassinations. It stays with us until we die, an Idea incarnate."

The Truth Machine is a mess of wiring, scavenged motherboards, computer screens and tanning bed parts, held together by bits of car chassis that have been

178

welded into place. The entire thing is letting out a steady hum that sounds like a swarm of mechanical wasps working over a hillbilly. The thing just crackles with power, makes my hairs stand on end just standing next to it. I ask the man what powers it and he breaks into a big toothless grin.

"Uranium-285, courtesy of an old army buddy in Chechnya. Don't worry, I have mostly insulated it. Haven't had a leak in at least a month." He cackles as he notices that I've gone whiter than a sheet, my cigarette hanging onto my dry, cracked lips. "I am just shitting you. I use electricity, like everybody else. Here, see the outlet?"

So I ask him if it's ready and the madman tell me *yes, it is.* He has only used it once so far, but he got too deep, *it's deeper than the Marianas Trench and twice as mean as the Pacific Ocean,* he tells me, *only managed to get as deep as the pornographic depths, which is fairly shallow when you look at it closely. Ah, if I were a younger man...*

But I am a younger man and also not a coward. So I ask the madman to hook me up to the machine, to send me to Idea-Space and let me have a look-see, check out if there's anything worthwhile in there, try to drag back anything I can. I promise him a good reference in my article, when it's done. He just spits on the floor and cackles and asks me to strip down to my underwear before I lay down on the lidless tanning bed that's stuck halfway inside the machine. He doesn't plug any weird headgear on my head or strap me down, just hands me a device with a big red button on it that reads EMERGENCY EJECT. When I ask him about it, he shrugs and goes *I can give you some vodka until you're well and fucked up if you like* but I turn his offer down. Might as well try and dip into uncharted territories with my brain working at full capacity. Somewhere in the distance, I can hear him flick switches and pull levers. Deep in the bowels of the Truth Machine, a scavenged car engine coughs and revs up kicking the thing into gear. From the corner of my eye, I see the scratched, faded warning sign of nuclear waste, the tank that it's set on sporting a hair-thin line and I suddenly realize that I never once checked to make sure about the outlet. The Truth Machine's harsh light blinds me just as I begin my frantic scramble outwards and then...

*I am ejected in a direction that isn't quite up at speeds that exceed those of light, pushing through the building blocks of reality, speeding through the grey matter of my own brain like it was nothing. I dive through the raging storm clouds of conscious thought, bore through the great powdered glass desert that is the ego and tumble down across the pitch-black howling jungle where the monkey brain dwells, diving into the great ocean of common knowledge, where the bias-whales dwell. Swimming downward, I go deeper to the place where the smut and the shame and the little fears and hate swirl to and fro, their motions directed by the topical currents. Below, there are the volcanic rifts of genius, where boiling hot ideas are spewed outward every single second, the half-formed and weakest of the lot beset by scavenging doubt-crabs, dissolved into thought-stuff in instants. Past the rifts, there is a sea of churning, turning chaos that howls madly and licks at the fringes of reality. I know that I have gone too far, so I turn back but they've already spotted me: the dread-beasts come at me wave after wave, unsheathing their claws and flexing their ropey, tentacle-like muscles. I don't know how I know this, but death in this place is a far more final thing than a regular demise. I have no chance to get out of this, no way to fight them back. The weapons I conjure are misshapen, useless things but still I fight and whimper. Moving ever upward, knowing they are just toying with me, I stroke and stroke and then the light swoops down to drive them away, the light that hums* Llluuvvv *in a glorious baritone and the Messiah drives the beasts back to the Primordial stuff from whence they came. He takes my hand to lead me to safety and that is when I betray him, taking his hand and ordering my thumb to press the big red button.*

And so, I take Elvis with me out into the world, to be made manifest. Elvis, the Love Messiah, who looks down at me as I scream and roll around on the tanning bed, reaching his hand to hold me down before I've clawed at my own eyes. When I am good and tired, he tells me:

"You done?"

I nod yes.

"Do you realize what you have just wrought upon your world?" he tells me and I can't help but grin as I hear the drawl. "We were kept secret, we were kept safe; we were *supposed* to be only remembered by the mad and be worshipped by the paranoiacs. This way, we could never truly exist. But now, you have made me manifest; my enemies are many and they will know that there is a way out now."

Of course I try to explain to him that I did not know this could have happened. I try to suggest to Elvis that he talks to the madman, that it was his fault, him and his Truth Machine.

Elvis just helps me up and points at something red and mangled on the floor. "Something got to him, something that came out along with me."

I try my best not to hurl, but fail.

"There wasn't supposed to be a way out of our place of birth. It was impenetrable, unreachable. The fact that this man managed to open a way using scrap and a human brain should not have been possible. I came too late; the Reptilians had beat me to it. They are always watching, have mind-reading chips at the base of the skull of every human being in the Western world. You think that's ridiculous? It's what you people came up with, what you made them think they can do. And they're not the only ones who made it out, know what I'm saying?"

Looking up at Elvis, I keep praying that he isn't serious, that it's all going to be just a prank that the madman is playing on me; that I suffered brain damage from exposure to the punctured uranium container or that I finally caught the madness from all those nuts so many years ago. Still, I follow him naked into the Bulgarian winter but do not shiver. Elvis Presley is the Love Messiah and no man will go cold or starve in his presence. I have no idea how I know this and don't dwell on it too long, instead focusing on poking at the base of my skull, prodding the little scar at the base of my neck that I have had my entire life since five minutes ago. Above us, the sky unravels as the holographic projection that is our atmosphere flickers and shuts down. In the Heavens, a second moon hides the face of the Sun for a few moments. Below, ancient machines of war that survived the thousand-year psychic clash of Atlantis and Mu stir to life. On the TV screens, Jackie Kennedy look-alikes storm the great metropolitan centers armed with neural disruptors developed and manufactured in the factory-cathedrals of the 30th Century. They come from holes in the air itself, pour out from the dark spaces under children's beds, climb out of the pages of comic books and assemble themselves from words that jump out of children's essays.

In New York, Rorschach blots that look like Godzilla, or someone's mother, are stomping through Manhattan. In Tokyo, creatures that are best left unnamed perform unspeakable acts on passers-by. Across Europe, a hidden army of Aryan Supermen clashes with the great unwashed, both sides armed by the American Conspirator. In Africa, the Mokole-Membe ride into battle against the White Man (a lumbering, hungry monstrosity with mouths for eyes) the royalty of spam emails riding on their backs with reed-woven shields at the ready. In Australia, there are box jellyfish that can fly, koalas that spew fire and spiders that reproduce like Von Neumann machines. In Russia, Pravda reports that Alien Benefactors have just crossed into LaGrange space, come to usher them into the Interstellar Brotherhood. There is no word from China.

"I need to go. The world needs me." Elvis says and I am begging him not to go, to not leave me in this place, not like this when everything's falling apart. I'm just a bystander here, I had no idea that this would happen!

"You didn't. There was no way you could have known, that I can tell. But there is no way to go back. Every war that you have made up, every secret thing that you all imagined, it has come out to the surface with all the urges that you burdened it with. There are nightmares coming from every place at the same time and you can't stop them, because you made them this way."

So I ask him: what can I do?

And he tell me: "You can hide and you can wait. The good things will come out right along with the bad. The war will go on and it will be over soon. The fittest will survive. This is, after all, the oldest idea."

And with that he takes flight and the superheroes ride right along with him, the great warriors of ancient and modern myth, spewing endlessly out from Idea-

Space. There is Hercules and Peter Pan, there is Sherlock Holmes and Gilgamesh and there is Ahura Mazda and Superman and Lancelot with Elric and Conan the Barbarian. Diana rides down from space with the Valkyries, the Spear of Lugh in her hand burning balefully. There are fighter robots driven by magical schoolgirls and there are the Dominions of the Angles that go to war with the anti-heroes by their side, who fight the tide of darkness and evil for forty days and forty nights that are over in a flash. There is a Deluge of Blood, there is fire descending from the Heavens. Civilization collapses under the weight of its risen dead and builds itself all over again from the scrap of the old, only to be nuked into oblivion and reborn the very next instant. In the space of a breath, there are flickering utopias and lasting dystopias; there is the Kingdom of Heaven and the bickering city-states of Hell. And all the while, I am tossed and turned, bled and tormented, healed and suffer. I pray for death, but death does not come, not for most of us.

And when it's all done, I find myself in the rubble that used to be my home. Elvis is there too, his armor beaten and torn in places, his coif singed but immaculate.

"We are going back" he tells me "A little boy in South America managed to make a Lie Machine from scrap, reversed the polarity. We will go back to Idea-Space and stay there for good this time. I see that you made it."

He grins at me and I throw a brick at him, getting him right in the jaw just before he dissipates. Then I look through the rubble for my things, my cigarettes. The end of the world left me with a hankering. By some impossible chance, I find that my old typewriter and my smokes have survived the apocalypse. The last lighter in the world that's in my breast pocket still works. So I take a big old drag and get right down to it. Soon as I am done, I am getting back to that bus station. There's a bit of gold-plated bronze that I need to get rid of for good.

# Sparrow

## by
## M. Lori Motley

Sparrow
by
M. Lori Motley

THE MAN with no legs screamed in the ditch. His fingers sparked a dull white-blue that fizzled before anything happened, useful or not. Nyl kept his head down and willed his feet to go faster. He was too afraid to whisper any spell words or even a prayer of protection. Not that he knew any gods.

Eventually the squelch of mud overtook the sound of the man's screams. The road wound up then down a squat hill and into a village that seemed to be untouched. As Nyl stood with his boots sinking in the road, the roofs of the houses began to glow with black fire. He shook his head hard enough to make his neck snap and tried to ignore the itching in his palms. No fire, just soggy thatch and moss. He hitched his pack higher on his shoulders and plodded down to see if there was an inn.

The innkeeper held the key just out of reach, curled between hairy knuckles, and stared at Nyl as if he were, perhaps, infectious.

"We haven't had a wizard round here in over a year." The comment hung in the air like a spider.

Nyl watched tendrils of silver wind themselves in and out of the man's beard, creep up his jaw and into his ear. When Nyl's gaze finally met his eyes, the innkeeper twitched his fingers once and the key appeared like a knife in his fist.

"I'll pay now," Nyl said. "I'll be leaving early in the morning."

The thick coins slid across the bar into the innkeeper's waiting hand, touched his fingers and started a chain reaction that culminated in a smile and greed-tinged eyes.

"Very good, lad." He turned back to his washing.

From the lattice-covered window, Nyl could see the reddish glow of the city two days walk to the south. He craned his neck to look up the road the way he had come, wondering briefly what had happened to the wizard lying in the ditch. His legs had ended in bloody stumps that hissed and spluttered. Somewhere, Nyl knew, the other halves would lie twitching. He had seen it before.

Oerc had been the first to go mad, but he was always a bit mad to begin with. It wasn't until Nyl had walked into the library one morning and spotted Oerc flaring like a swamp-light that he knew something was irrevocably wrong. The professors had locked him in the storeroom when counter-spells hadn't worked. In the morning, only half an arm and one foot remained. Sooty smoke poured out of the bloody ends, ruining the cheeses.

Midnight blue lightning meandered across the cloudless sky as slow as a feather's fall. Nyl's gaze followed its path back to the glow of the city where it vanished into reality. The elders had whispered of a sparrow, a simple sparrow, which had gained entry to the Shard's chamber and sat upon the stone. That was all it took. He stood at the window, eyes wide and blind, until he was awakened by screaming and the sound of furniture toppling from another part of the inn. He scrambled across the room and grabbed his boots.

The innkeeper stood mouth agape at the door and Nyl pushed up behind him to peer out into the gloom. The sound of running feet, warbling yells and madness rose and fell between the hills and down the town's streets. The first group came into view. They bounced off each other's shoulders as they ran, legs tangling together, but still managed to keep the same frantic pace.

One glowed the deep red of the outlawed lust spells and he gibbered and groped at the men who ran beside him. The next was missing an arm and his eyes flashed like blue beams through the darkness. Still another appeared to be on fire. And more and more.

They cast as they ran, a tumult of spells and snippets of magic that made no sense to Nyl. The confusion spread from group to group through the town, lighting buildings on fire and shooting haystacks into the air as they passed. Fruit barrels turned to fly-ridden curs. Hog wallows filled with snakes.

Dozens came, hundreds, in a mass of fire and pain and darkness and despair. Nyl stood in the doorway long after the innkeeper left to barricade his family in their chambers. He stood and watched the swarm of wizards destroy the village around them.

*When they get to the city* he thought, and then the thought struck sanity through his mind. The sparrow on the Shard, the slow, uncomfortable, uncontrollable slips of his thoughts and visions. *I have to get there first.*

Nyl gathered his pack and slung his coat over his shoulders before stepping out into the alley behind the inn. The slop bins steamed in the cool night, but he expected that had more to do with rot than runaway magic. At the edge of the street, he held back and eased his head around the corner. Without pause, he muttered a simple sight charm.

The street blazed into color, brighter than the Queen's gardens, and sparkles danced around the edges of Nyl's vision. He shut his eyes quickly, but not before seeing a half dozen wizards on the roof of the building opposite. They crouched like magpies, chattering spell words and filling the thatch with blood red worms.

He crept out into the night, darted across the once-again dark street and through yards to where the road wound away from the town and into the rolling hills dotted with farms and destruction. The other wizards paid no attention to him; their minds consumed with whatever madness gripped them.

That night, Nyl curled into the hollow left by a toppled tree near the rock wall that delineated a farm from the wilds. The stones hummed dark songs to him as the sun sank below the horizon. When he awoke, it took several long moments of blinking before the dark turned to moths and scattered to reveal the dawn. Frost tinged the grasses and he swept his hand over the stalks until he felt sure the cold wet was real.

Every time Nyl's feet hit the dirt track through the hills, a sound like the dinner gong back at the University rang in his mind. The clouds swirled into fantastic shapes that seemed to follow him. Twice before midday, Nyl took cover in a copse of trees when a group of wizards came into view. He could see others roaming through the hills, their flashes of spell work and unearthly keening echoing across the landscape.

As he crouched at a lonely stream for a drink and quick wash, a lone wizard stumbled past the tree line on the far bank. His hands smoked black from shriveled flesh and flames sprung from the top of his head. His robe hung tattered and burnt from scarred skin. He screamed long, ululating screams of pain and a mind simply gone. Nyl had sat across from him in Basic Herbology the year before. He closed his eyes and tried to block all the creeping, horror-tinged notions that plagued his mind. When he opened them again, the young man was gone and the stream had turned to polished glass.

The city gate shuddered under the force of the throng of wizards pushing on it. They pressed against each other like goats trying to avoid the spring slaughter. Nyl stood on the rise overlooking the city and tried to ignore the fear ripping through him. His palm itched again and he looked down to see a shimmering green beetle dancing in slow circles on his hand. With a moue of disgust, he shook his hand away from his body. The beetle became many, tumbled into the weeds and vanished. He watched them scurry away, momentarily distracted from all thoughts of the Shard.

*I need to get in like a sparrow. Sneak.* The city walls stretched out in either direction, doorless and guarded with towers at regular intervals. One tower to the south sat dark. No guard roamed the parapet or eyed the sparking and gibbering mob before the gates.

It was a risk, but Nyl could see no other way. He circled the mob of wizards and reached the wall. He passed men with no limbs, men on fire, men turning inexorably to stone and one man with snakes protruding from his mouth whose throat bulged and writhed.

Tattered book pages flipped through his mind as he reviewed snippets of spells he had never learned well enough for the professors' approval. A mighty crack sounded from the gate and a guard shouted from the nearest tower. The gate had begun to smolder and bowed inward under the onslaught.

Nyl barked out the spells he knew in a rush of fear. His hands itched like they always did during spell work, but he didn't look down this time. His mind filled with smoke and flashes of purple and he almost faltered in his casting. It was more like his body filled up with mist than actually vanished, but he hoped it would work. His mist-shape scurried along the wall toward the dark tower, fitted its mist-fingers into the cracks between stones and began to climb.

Professor Enrict had insisted that Nyl would make a better sneak thief than a wizard after finding him clinging halfway up the wall of the ladies' gardens. Nyl's fingers and toes found purchase in crevices anyone else would dare not try. He kept casting as he climbed, but the words jumbled into unknown phrases and, by the time he had reached the top and swung his leg over, the mist spread beyond the usual confines of his body and formed a cloud with blue light twinkling at the edges.

Nyl's spell became a curse as he simply let go of the wall and plummeted down to the hard cobbles below. A wish for flight and fear that he might simply dissipate into nothingness when he hit flashed through him for the brief moment before his boots slammed onto the street with a bone-rattling jar.

Nothing but a slinking gray cat moved on the streets. Nyl rushed and stumbled down alleys and over garden walls toward the Shard chamber. He had seen it every day before he went to study magic at thirteen: a seamless wall of mottled black stone scribed with ancient runes and studded with neatly embedded talismans. Even if the carvings were wide enough to grip with fingertips or toes, a domed roof capped the chamber. Only one wizard in each generation held the key and the penalty for allowing anything else within made even Death shake his head in disbelief.

And yet something had gotten inside. A sparrow, the elders had said. One tiny bird had infiltrated the most secure room in the entirety of existence and landed upon the Shard.

Nyl crashed against the corner of a shop, panting and listening to the hammering of his heart. Behind him, the mob of deranged wizards at the gate still screamed and shouted disjointed spells.

His mind turned over a dozen possibilities, each one beginning with the phrase, "If only" and ending with despair. More shouts from the gates now, and the sound of running feet passed him on the other side of the shop wall. The early sun slipped across the black stone of the Shard chamber and Nyl stepped forward to press his ear against the wall.

A soft chattering, scratching low and mellow oozed through Nyl's mind. Without thought, he pursed his lips and blew a low, warbling note.

The city gate succumbed in a gout of dark flame and thunder and the wizards flooded the city with forms not quite human. Nyl listened to them come and, for the first time wondered why he had not been affected like they had. *Perhaps I knew too little magic to matter*, he thought, his mind's eye flitting across scores of professors telling him the same.

The throng approached, louder and louder it shouted disjointed spells and animalistic howls of madness. The wizards' spell work melded together into forms never intended. Houses melted. The market filled with mud, insects and what might have been a bear turned inside out. Nyl stood, his arms thrown wide against the walls of the Shard room and waited.

They crashed upon him like a wave, hot and smelling of death and ash. Nyl accepted fear, embraced despair and then crept out between the thrashing, stomping legs to alight on a nearby fence. Some shouted spell words woven together and reality slipped ever so slightly to the side.

Before Nyl's mind dwindled down to nothing, a brief flash of, *It was all my fault, wasn't it?* surged through him. The guard who met the crowd first became boneless and went down with a flash of green light. The stones of the well grew eyes and whispered of things long drowned.

Nyl spread his wings with a chirrup and flitted over the wizards' heads and the gleaming black dome of the Shard chamber. His gaze picked out the hidden crevice under the eaves of the adjoining building. Then away over bleeding stone walls and the black fire of the destroyed gate to the hills and trees once more. His mind filled with only seed, wind and roost and never any guilt for the dark thing he might have wrought.

# AMOK!

# Starlight, Starfright

by

D. Ceder

Starlight, Starfright
by
D. Ceder

A ARON II stood marooned against the purple skyline. To Straker, her hull was like the bulbous abdomen of a huge spider. It resembled the old Model D's, Series 2. The Renaissance motif was now fading, which was not surprising. It had been there for at least two centuries.

Mason, a gawky redhead, a trainee brought in by Region's personnel department, stood alongside him. "Desertion job?" he asked, feigning knowledge of the technical banter. Straker winced inside his oxygen converter.

"Can you scan it?" Mason activated the scanner. It flicked to ten, skirted round fifteen, drifted back to twelve. "Nothing. Low on life form."

"No, there is something," corrected Straker. "Twelve indicates animal life." But he checked himself quickly. *Six* indicated animal life. *Twelve* indicated... "Come on."

They lumbered across the pocked brown surface: sandstone, granite, red clay. Straker did not think desertion was the motive in this case. He had been alerted by the Client. An old claim, apparently. Region Interstellar Underwriting Inc. had been sitting on this claim for months and were being badgered by the Client's new management. God, they must have needed some sort of management shake-up: to forget about one of their fleet, to ignore it for two-hundred years. He did not think Region would cough anything up on this occasion. In any case, desertion wasn't covered for, and the crew would not have got very far, not in this Sector of Galaxy Beta. No, it couldn't have been desertion. Approaching it from starboard, an intact pod hatch indicated if they had tried to desert, then they must have used some mighty neat paraglide apparatus: the pod was still there, nestling inside the hull. They came to the ramp leading into the open mouth of the thing (Straker mentally noted it was open): old architecture; probably didn't even house a proper toilet. Metal housing constituting old uranium ore, now long inert; style as of the Renaissance period. The bulging spider-like abdomen was of the entomological fashion of the period. Other Mark D's had been fashioned as bees, or great warrior fireflies. Cargo: he imagined fertiliser, probably taken from Mars, making a slow crow-line for Earth. And then going through Galaxy Beta. He thought there would be bodies. And he was right.

"Christ." Mason sounded even more muffled behind the clear Plastiglass of the helmet.

In the Ops room were three skeletons. Straker couldn't really tell if they were male or female. There was dust everywhere and more of the sand/clay breezing in through the maw of the ship. Straker examined the dental structure. He was more of a fleet investigator; his knowledge of forensics was limited.

"Straker." He went over to where Mason was looking. He heard his sudden rasping breath. He was too young for this; this was no ordinary investigation.

It was a vacuum gun. It shone dully in the grey stillness. Outside, a sudden wind spurted in

more dust, then fell away. Straker hunkered down, feeling the length of the barrel. Not much different to now, except two-hundred years ago they made noise. The vacuum guns in 2352 were soundless, emitting white noise to compensate against the blast.

Three of the shells had been fired.


Realising this was now probably a murder investigation, Straker debated whether he should send Mason back to the Mother Ship. He beeped Cartwright but got no answer. There was sudden fizzing static. He moved away from the wall and tried again. Nothing.

The reason Cartwright hadn't responded was probably because he wasn't anywhere near an intercom, but that was crazy. Region's internal procedures dictated strict adherence to any terra-level investigation at all times: the intercoms (or an intercom) should always be manned, twenty-four hours per day. He felt a sickening queasiness enter his stomach, and for the first time in his thirty-year career actually felt physically worried. Christ, and he was about to retire; this was going to be his last shout', he had promised the wife. He didn't think Mason was up to it. Too young. Too inexperienced.

Straker turned back to him, and found himself facing the domed, dank interior of an Operations room, three mouldering skeletons, and little else.

"Mason?" Oh God, he didn't feel like mollycoddling anyone, let alone having to carry out an investigation he didn't like the feel of. He listened to the silence, then the rise and fall of a distant wind, then the silence again. Where the hell was he?

It would be no good checking for his life-form reading: their suits deflected the impulses so that frequencies can be targeted on their intended subjects, bar their suits.

He strained his ears, listening for the clump of his boots, the clank of pipework. He thought he heard something. On the wind. Jangling, like distant chimes. Strange, it had only started to happen. Maybe Mason had heard it and had ventured out to investigate; a burst of enthusiasm, something to show off to an old veteran. He made his way back to the entrance. Looking out, he saw the old terrain stained with purple shadow. Whirling draughts of dust. And the spider.

They were nothing new. Most of the planets in this Sector favoured the arachnid. He imagined the beetles, as well, larger, more languid than their Earth counterparts. All life forms were harmless; he had never come across any that had caused him fear.

It opened its eyes: beautiful blue, with dilating pupils, like a child's. Its mouth was bordered by soft pink lips. He noted each leg was pink, a humanoid texture, rounded and puffed like a doll's limb, or a baby's. Shuddering, he re-entered the hull, now realising why the scanner had registered twelve before - and not six - for animal forms. There was life on this planet that constituted a mixture of insect and human. Perhaps other things as well. Which meant that something very peculiar had occurred, aeons ago, something only thought of in dreams. He pictured weird interbreeding in his mind and shuddered again, feeling cold. His old bones had started to ache.

He would carry on as per procedure. Straker knew the Recorder would have captured everything. He wasn't certain of its technology; probably a laser-reel winder, sounds absorbed by simple core-ferrite, encrypted onto tape.

Yes, he thought, he'd even be able to hear them as they died.


Mason was getting more confused by the second. First those jangling sounds, and then Rosemarie, standing at the corridor entrance to the Ops room. He hadn't thought, had just followed her into the corridor. He would like to see her again. His first - his only - love.

"Sweet, sweet, Rosemareeee-e-e..." He heard the gentle sibilant hiss of it inside his ear. It was the voice of thoughts, of centuries, of absolute knowledge. And it wanted him to be with Rosie again.

"Rosie?" He called softly after. He saw her turn into a brief shadow and disappear round a bend in the corridor. In high school, with the summer wafting apple blossom in the playing fields, he used to walk with her, talking about love, baseball, nights beneath an Idaho moon. And then...

Taken away. By that man.

He pictured him now. Quarter-back; older, wiser, bigger. He had an ugly face, crooked, like a gangster in a movie. He knew he was rough with her, but she didn't seem to care. His writings which she so admired before were forgotten - brawn favoured to brain. He would very much like to kill Billy - It was Straker.

The thought came simply. It had put it there. The music had told him. It told him other things as well, whispering like a friend in his ear. Things about this planet, about Straker, about the universe, about Straker. And Straker's motives. The voices told him that burning was the only good thing for Straker.

"...yeah, got his ass over the bar"

"Did you wop him?" That was Jackson.

"Guy was drunk as a skunk. Just left him and told him if he ever looked at me like that again I'd -"

Straker typed in "MAYDAY" and programmed the Recorder's play device for forward scan'. There was a lot of stuff on the tape Straker didn't need to listen to. The label was dated July 17th, 2148. The Year of our Lord. He had gathered that they had successfully loaded their cargo onto the Aaron II from Mars clay deposits on July 19th, and had landed on this unnamed planet to refuel (uranium ore was richly veined everywhere). Oh, and it sounded like there wasn't three - but four - members. Straker would bet that the fourth, probably George Hanstead, was around somewhere, the ghost of his fingerprints on the vacuum gun. "...day Mayday, this is Ola Svenson -"

Straker stopped the tape and rewound back three minutes.

"Look I -" Jackson. "I know you fucked her, and I'm gonna -" That was Hanstead.

"God, please stop it Georgie NO STOP WHAT THE FU-" Ola Svenson. "-they told me to make absolutely sure -" A blast. Ola screaming.

"My own mother, you bastard, I saw you there in the corridor SCREWING MY OWN MOTHEEER!"

The second blast took out Hammond. Ola left now. "Mayday mayday, this is Ola Svenson, we have a situation -" She never got to say what the situation was.

Straker didn't need to listen to the rest. By the hissing static that followed the third blast, and the distant clatter of the gun dropping to the floor, he had heard Hanstead's departing footfalls. He thought he could hear the whisper of the front hatch opening, and then nothing. He had gone out, unarmed, to meet - what? He would probably be about two-hundred-and- fifty-years-old by now, most probably propped up in some alcove or cranny, anywhere on the planet.

He wondered why no search party was ordered. Thinking back, he realised the Client had only now been informed. Shortly after July 21st, or thereabouts, 2148, they folded. Just like that. Who would give a hoot? Companies go into business and out of business every day, so what? Only now do they want to know, just to recover lost assets. Great. He sighed heavily, sat away from the Recorder, and heard Mason slink back into the room.

"Billy?"

"Hmm...what? Mason, come on, we've got a..." The molten spray of liquid fire shot out at him like a dragon snarling, catching him completely by surprise, then snapped back again. Mason held the fire-torch by its leather holster and began swinging it like a dandy. Straker reached for his own vacuum gun holstered by his side but Mason was faster. Straker viewed the barrel of the torch. He was confused as hell.

"How was it for you, Straker? The feel of her corn-yellow hair, those azure eyes, the grip of her on your cock?" "Who? What are you talking about?" Straker wasn't sure what all this was about, but remembered Hanstead going briefly mad about something similar on the Recorder.

"You know who. You know very well." He stopped, grinning. "They told me things you could never understand. I know things. They showed me lots and lots of ..." He stopped and began to snarl melodramatically. "They instructed me to burn you. But you know something? Yeah, I thing that's too good for you. Hmm, let's see now. Personally, I think that's too good; personally I would much rather -"

Straker glanced up desperately, away from the entrance to a point well to Mason's left. Surprised, Mason looked and Straker took up the advantage, bolting out into the corridor. He felt a breath of warmth at his heels as Mason unleashed the fire-torch. Then he heard it, jangling in his ears.

"Twinkle twinkle little star, how I wonder what you a-a-arre..."

Gentle, like sea wash inside a shell. He heard it whisper to him. And he was there, watching the meteor shower. He was eight. His brother was fifteen, and he knew his brother did a bad thing then, but he never liked to talk about the bad thing to anyone. It frightened and embarrassed him, marking him for years after. His brother did it to him under the twinkling starlight, and made him not say anything to anyone, not Mom, not Pa, not anyone. He saw his brother, his face shrouded by dark and stars, and it was Mason's face.

Straker blinked and shut out the images. He knew to do that. He was learning quickly about how the voices, or jangling, or whatever - how it operated.

"Billy Billy Billy," shouted Mason, "I can seeee youuu!"

A sudden guff of flame spurred him on faster. He piled round the next bend. He could hear Mason, approaching the bend, his breath rasping liquidly inside his mask. Not thinking, Straker pulled out the grille in the wall and bolstered himself into the air duct. But it did no good. He was trapped now. The duct led up, but there were no handholds, just those narrow ledges at the entrance, so he could support himself with his hands.

"I can see your ass, Billy," said Mason.

Straker let go and fell in a heap back into the corridor. Twilight shadow crept secretly across Mason's face as a he grinned a huge, goodnight-sleep-tight grin, raising the torch. The fire-torch seemed to take forever before it levelled itself at Straker's face. Thinking this was how one's death always appeared - in slow-motion - he dutifully awaited his execution, even dipping his head to his navel. When none came, he glanced up at Mason, and saw the desperate pleading behind those eyes, the real Mason trying to fight against the growing insanity as the voices began to claim his mind.

Straker shot him once, twice.

Mason, still grinning, fell back. The Plastiglass of the helmet shattered. The left side of his skull had been depleted. Straker saw something - his brain, maybe - drip like cottage cheese down his cheek. Alien air was invading Mason's lungs now, and he began to buck and claw at his throat, face purpling.

Straker blasted what remained of his head against the floor. He staggered round the bend, retching emptily into his helmet.

It's for the best, he thought. At least you're dead. I think that's probably the lesser of two evils right at this moment. Straker realised now why Cartwright hadn't responded to his call to the Mother Ship. What was he thinking right now? Was Tyler strangling Cartwright's mother at this very minute? Maybe pulling his cat's tail, even making rude noises at him behind his back? What mad thoughts were being planted in their heads, there on the Mother Ship?

Cartwright versus Jameson, perhaps? Tyler versus Jameson? Versus Daniels? Were all three, right this moment, hunting each other, snarling like dogs, through their own corridors?

What if all three were out for *Straker*? Yes, good point, he would have to make a bee-line straight for Earth, just in case. Aaron II's pod capacity would be just enough. The fuel on this tin can was probably standard uranium ore. It would last.

He cantered, jogged, sprinted to the pod room.

He knew how to commandeer his thoughts against the music, the voices. They tarnished his good thoughts, his nice memories. Even the incident with his brother - it was the meteor shower it had latched itself to, and once it took a hold on a nice thought, it could get in all the way, corrupting as it went, finding things in his memory, finding anything. So Straker coloured his mind grey-on-black, thought of death, mayhem, Hanstead shooting his colleagues, going mad in a terrain governed by mad thoughts, Mason lying with half his head blown to high heaven back in the hull. The rest was easy.

As he approached the pod room, he thought of the spiders with those human characteristics, beetles, other things on this planet. He was sure they had nice thoughts as well; and over the aeons, resembling the Source.

Humanoid? Was the Source human? Something long dead, long cursed, abandoned in eternity to merely exist. Its only solace the turning of one man against the other, whenever it could. He didn't want to analyze too much now. Whatever it was, is, will be - it just blew his mind circuitry and he just didn't think of anything at all, didn't think of anything as he disengaged the pod and headed back to Earth, back toward his life.

He sat on the back porch step watching the sunset. Red on gold, gold on purple, purple on black - the colour of a daytime sky succumbing to night. He dragged lightly on the cigarette and gazed at the vegetation bordering his acreage. Sunflowers, alfalfa, watercress - everything you could imagine, huddled freshly beneath the solar panels. Two of the pegs attaching the solar hood into the soil were missing. Damn, I'll have to go back and fetch them. Straker turned to enter the house. Yes, the jangling had started up again. He thought it was the oncome of tinnitus, but Doc Stevens said it was nothing, just stress from his last shout', that he should just enjoy his retirement.

But he still wasn't sure, were it not for the things they said to him; the nasty things. And he remembered on the Aaron II, while he was sprinting to the pod, he might just *might* have let a bit of it in. Just a bit. Oh well, he thought, opening the door to his bedroom, better get those darned pegs.

He took one out of his wife's left hand, prying it loose with a crowbar, the other from her forehead (that was the hardest) and, humming softly, went back down to place them into the earth.

# AMOK!

# Close the Door and Have a Seat

### by
### M.J. Pack

Close the Door and Have a Seat
by
M.J. Pack

S TUDIES SHOW that Friday is the best day of the week to fire someone. Sorry, *'let someone go'*. That's the politically-correct, touchy-feely-bullshit term, right? I guess it lets them down easier when they wake up with nowhere to be on a Saturday rather than a Tuesday.

Terminating employees isn't a job most people want because it's dirty work, something that makes your Average Joe feel slimy and mean. But not me. Guys like me know sometimes you have to be mean to survive. I'm damn good at it too, though I suppose it's not something you'll ever hear me bragging about in a bar.

So good, in fact, they called me "The Axe". As in, "getting the axe". Cheesy, but most people are.

That's something you learn in my line of work. Most people fall into neat little categories. It's just something that happens when the line into your office is as long as the one coming in the front door. People are cheesy, pretentious, useless. We like to think we're special, but ultimately, we're all the same. No one is an original. Not anymore.

Anyway. The nickname, cheesy as it may be, was both feared and respected. A call to my office was basically a death knell; countless men and women left in tears to find a box on their desk waiting to be filled with whatever meaningless crap they'd accumulated in their time with the company. I don't know where the boxes came from. That wasn't part of my job.

That Friday, I got word there was an axe to drop. An older guy, Steve Woodruff. No one I knew off the top of my head. A quick glance at his file proved this fact amusing; he'd been with the company for almost 20 years. Salesman.

Do you really want to know what he sold? No? Of course not. He's someone you'd brush off if he called you on the phone, a guy standing on your porch that you peer at behind the curtains and hope like hell that he'll leave. You don't care about him either. Be honest with yourself.

His productivity had fallen over time, slowly at first then drastically in the past few months. He was barely making any sales. When he left for cold calls, there were doubts he was actually on the road, but perhaps holed up somewhere else. Drinking, maybe. Rumors in an office can get nasty. He was costing us money, that's the bottom line. Time to cut and run.

No severance package. No pension.

No skin off my ass.

I wish I could tell you I remembered it. I really do. But that afternoon I had a doctor's appointment and a lunch date with the guys in marketing and there may have been one too many martinis, yet in the end the reason I don't remember is because there had been so many like him before. I'm sure he probably cried, or went pale and silent, or called me the devil. Those were the top three typical reactions to *The Axe* doing what he does best.

I hate that nickname. I really do.

So Steve came into my office and left my office, regardless of my inability to remember it. I'm sure he found the box on his desk. Security escorted him out.

Two hours later, Steve came back.

The same security guard that walked him to his car got it first. The point-blank shotgun blast blew most of his head off, splattering his brains across the hot-rod calendar behind his desk in the front lobby.

It's a fairly small office building so I'm sure some people heard it but the first inclination humans have when they hear something so unexpected, so out of the ordinary, is to assume it's something not out of the ordinary at all. Without the security guard to hit the silent alarm Steve walked right through the foyer and into the receptionist's office. Cheryl saw the gun, I think, and began to scream. She only got one wavering note out before the crack-boom of the lead shot firing into her stomach cut her off.

Steve moved from her office to the advertising department. Here, he took out two of the guys in marketing, then paused to reload the shotgun. The copywriter got brave and tried to bolt but Steve was between him and the door and apparently more quick-fingered than he looked, because the shells were in the gun and he fired one dead-eye shot into his back, sending him flying across the hall.

By this point the sound of the shotgun was too real to be ignored and people started to panic. The remaining employees, a motley mixture of HR and sales, bolted for the fire escape only to find it locked. Steve had, prior to his arrival in the lobby, chained the doors from the outside. They struggled against the crush of their own animal hysteria, unwilling to believe the door wouldn't open.

He picked these people off easily. Boom, boom, boom. They were screaming but then they weren't anymore. Somehow the silence was so much worse.

Boom. Boom.

In my haste to protect myself I had completely forgotten to dial the police, but when I ducked my head out I heard Steve coming back my way, the metallic clicking sounds of the shells being exited from the gun and the new ones reloaded, the slow methodical plodding of his shoes on the thin office carpet. The Axe may be called many things, but that day I learned brave' is not one of them. I dropped back under the desk and huddled there, trying to ignore the warm seep of my bladder letting go.

He entered my office and stood there. All I could hear was the strangely even sound of his breathing and the war-drum beat of my heart pounding in my ears.

"Remember me, boss?" Steve said softly, and for one wild moment I actually didn't, I couldn't even recall my own name if you'd asked me I was so terrified.

"You don't have to do this, Steve," I croaked, my mouth suddenly as dry as if you'd packed me full of hot desert sand. "There's still time, you can turn yourself in..."

"There's no time, you smug idiot." His voice was so calm, so pleasant, it was somehow far worse than if he'd been shrieking at me. Instead it was like we were chatting about the weather or the latest baseball game and ignoring the fact that the rest of the office were laying in cooling puddles of their own blood. "The police are on their way. Or they will be. Did you call them, boss?"

"Steve, please..."

"No. You had your chance to talk. Now it's mine." There was a quiet rolling sound as he pulled one of the office chairs up to the front of my desk, just as he had done two hours ago when I asked him to close the door and have a seat.

A long, terrible moment passed. The smell of my own urine was sharp in my nostrils.

"I begged you not to fire me. Do you remember that? You smelled like booze, so maybe you don't." Steve took in a deep breath, as though he could still smell the lunchtime martinis wafting off my skin. "*Productivity*. That was it, wasn't it? Why I got the axe? My *productivity* had decreased?"

When I didn't answer, Steve banged the top of my desk with the butt of his shotgun.

"Yes!" I blurted.

"Hard to be productive, boss, when your wife is dying. When the cancer has eaten so far through her brain that she doesn't even know who you are even though you're at her bedside every day. When she's only able to speak in soft little screams because the pain's so bad."

He paused.

"What was the rumor?"

"What?" The word fell off my tongue like a heavy stone.

"The rumor. About me. Where I was when I wasn't on sales calls."

I didn't know what to say, I groped through my memory like a blind man in the gutter but found nothing. This time Steve kicked the front of the desk; the sound was uncomfortably close.

"Drinking?"

"Drinking!" I agreed in a yelp.

Steve sighed.

"That's rich, coming from you. No, I wasn't drinking. Visiting hours at the hospital are hard to accommodate with my schedule." There was another pause, and when he spoke again, I could somehow picture him smiling. "Do you have any idea how expensive cancer medicine is, boss?"

"No," I said at once.

"No," Steve echoed, sounding almost amused, "of course you don't. I bet you know how much a country club membership costs. Or a Porsche. Or those smug fucking Dior suits you wear. Do you even notice the rest of us walking around in our secondhand clothes?"

Before I could respond he banged the desk again. The noise above my head was like a crack of dynamite and I felt my whole body jerk as if I'd been shocked.

"No," he said again. "Of course you don't." He breathed in deeply through his nose. "You ruin people's lives," Steve murmured. "what people work at for years, their *livelihoods,* the thing that keeps them getting up in the morning... you wipe it away with a few words and a box on their desk. And I bet you sleep like a goddamn baby."

"I'm sorry," I whispered, and I wish I could tell you that was true, that I truly felt the error of my ways and had learned a lesson. I really do.

"No you're not." There was a brief rolling sound as he stood up from the chair. "But you will be."

The shotgun clicked as he cocked it. My life began to flash before my eyes, my whole stupid materialistic life, the cheap women and expensive cars, every useless meaningless second and oh god if only I could have more of it...

Boom. Thump.

Silence.

And then it was just me, alone in the office of the dead. The only survivor of a madman's massacre. The lucky one.

Do you know what it's like to listen to the stillness of a place that was once full of life? To hear nothing but your own terrified heartbeat deep in your skull and what must be the sound of blood and brains pooling on the carpet?

It's deafening.

At some point, when the soaked front of my pants began to grow cold and stiff, I got out from under my desk and dialed 911.

There were ambulances. Someone put a blanket around my shoulders. I watched as they carried out body after body after body.

They were dead. All dead. But I was alive. I'd been spared. Why? Does the why even matter? Aren't we all beyond why at this point?

I went home and fell right to sleep. What else was there to do? You'd think I'd be wide awake but no, oh no, The Axe went home after the mass murder of his entire office building, changed his pants, had a beer, and went to sleep like a goddamn baby.

It was only then that I understood.

Every time I try to sleep, every time I close my eyes for more than a moment, when I drift off to that place of not-quite-conscious and not-quite-unconscious, I'm back at work.

I'm outside my own office. My suit is cheap and threadbare, my shoes don't fit quite right. I reach for the door and push it open.

Behind my desk sits Steve. The back of his head is a bloody mess, one giant exit wound from where he put the shotgun in his mouth, the mouth that smiles at me as he gestures a Dior suit-clad arm towards the chair in front of him.

He tells me to close the door and have a seat.

And every night, every fucking night for the past five years, I wake up screaming.

# Suffer the Children

by

## Robert Mammone

Suffer the Children
by
Robert Mammone

W HEN THE transmission erupted into a whine like a baby's squall, Derek ground his teeth and clutched the steering wheel until his knuckles turned white.

"Fuck me," he muttered, peering through the windscreen into the mist shrouded night as the car struggled up the hill. Wan moonlight filtered through the trees looming over the narrow road. Annoyed at the radio's empty hiss, he switched it off. The quiet gnawed at him. Flicking on the interior light, Derek flipped open the map one handed and traced a finger down the crumpled page while glancing at the road ahead.

"Creswick." He squinted at the name, hoping the size of the dot indicated the town had a garage.

The car chose that moment to feint a stall and the momentum threw Derek forward, tightening his seat belt painfully across his chest. Folders cascaded over the edge of the back seat. Scowling, he waited a moment, then abruptly stamped on the accelerator, willing the car to the top of the hill with the force of his muttered cursing.

From the summit, the town huddled in a narrow valley hemmed by a circuit of slumped hills. Lighting danced across the horizon and the sky rumbled. A few scattered and forlorn pinpricks of light were visible. The road sliced through the heart of town, then rose and vanished into the night. Dim buildings bracketed the main street. The silvery track of a creek marked the town's outskirts. Derek felt his mood lighten, until his mobile burst into song.

"Christ." A wave of weariness fell over him when he saw his boss's name flashing on the screen. Grimacing, he thumbed the answer button and clamped the mobile to his ear.

"Phil, how you doing? Yeah, sorry to hear that. So the Ballarat meeting is off, yeah? Aah. About that...look, we all discussed this last month, the sales targets are insane. I see little enough of my daughter and...yeah, right." He listened with rising fury while Phil detailed his exact place in the office pecking order. Seething, Derek held the phone in front of his face.

"Sorry Phil, I think I'm entering a dead spot. You're breaking up." Easing his foot off the brake, he let the car roll forward, slowly gathering speed as it wound down the hill, the trees on all sides turning into a grey blur. To his delight, his lie proved true; the phone crackled and hissed the lower he descended. Holding the mobile to his ear, he heard a sea of static and the ghost of a voice, yelling. He smiled mirthlessly.

"By the way Phil, this car you've given me is a piece of shit." The static crackled loudly in the cabin. "See you in Ballarat, you prick." Tossing the phone into the passenger seat, Derek felt his smug sense of satisfaction evaporate when he realised his presentation was currently lying scattered in the foot well behind him. Swearing, he swung the car around a tight bend. Buildings emerged like icebergs from the mist and he found himself in the town.

Moonlight picked the buildings out in a wash of dull silver that deepened the shadows. There was no traffic and all the shop fronts were dark. Checking his watch, Derek was surprised at how early it was.

"Early to bed and early to rise. Bloody hicks." Looking further down the street, he caught the dull red glare of a neon sign and its promise of accommodation.

Heartened, Derek sped up. In response, the engine caterwauled, setting his teeth on edge.

"As soon as I get home, I'll see you reduced to a cube, you useless piece of...." His voice trailed away when a pram appeared in the glare of his headlights, sitting alone on the footpath. He saw the old fashioned bassinet and hood, the dark fabric spotted with fat drops of rain that had begun to fall.

"Who the hell - Christ!"

Derek slammed down on the brakes, tires shrieking as the car slewed to a halt. The dark shape that had skipped through the beams of his headlights had vanished, leaving him shuddering with the awful thought that he had almost killed...what?

Peering through the window, Derek searched the shadows on the footpath. He glimpsed his white face reflected in a shop window. His eyes were wide, pools of darkness eating into his face. Shaking his head, he restarted the car and drove slowly away, the pram forgotten.

The neon sign glared sullenly as he pulled into the motel driveway. Turning off the engine, he stared at the office. The lights were off, but the glass door displayed an *OPEN* sign. He grabbed his wallet and stepped outside. He smelled the ripe stink of an approaching storm, a mixture of ozone and dust unique to the countryside.

Hand on the door, Derek paused, certain he'd heard a skittering sound across the street. The hairs on his neck rose. When he looked, all he saw were leaves kicked up by the strengthening breeze. A distant rumble echoed down the street and the rain increased.

To his relief, the door swung open. A distant chime sounded, the tune stripped of warmth by the electronic buzz. The neon light filtered into the office, deepening the shadows to a clotted black. A tense, wary silence filled the building. Standing at the desk, Derek was startled to see his face floating in front of him, then the pane of one-way glass.

Did someone watch blank eyed behind it? He flinched at the sound of approaching footsteps, which halted at the shut interior door. The hush deepened. He heard a mumbled, childlike conversation, then the door creaked open and a figure emerged.

A candle wavered in one long fingered hand. The light picked out the hollowed features of a middle aged man. His lips quivered wetly and the skin around his eyes looked bruised with exhaustion. Derek fancied that a shadow trickled from his right ear. The manager placed the candle-holder on the counter and smiled thinly. His hands fidgeted.

Derek leaned on the counter and tried on a grin. "Town got a problem with the power, eh?"

The manager's face twitched. Sweat stood on his brow. "Main line went down last night. Some of us are on a secondary circuit."

Derek strained to hear the exhausted whisper. "That's no good," he replied, trying to mask his impatience and failing. "Do you have a room? Just for tonight, though that depends on how competent the local mechanic is. You do have a mechanic in town?"

The manager nodded slowly. The flame flickered, sending shadows swarming across the wall. Was the man an imbecile?

Sighing, he persisted. "And how much is a room for the night?"

The manager licked his lips. "Single room is sixty-five dollars."

Derek looked at him in disbelief. "Are you taking the piss? Your sign says forty dollars and you've got no power. Come on, this is hardly the Ritz..."

A sound like a thousand ball bearings being dashed on the roof enveloped the office. Lightning crackled and rain fell in silvery banners, unfurling against the windows and swallowing the night. Derek watched it for a moment, feeling the drumbeat in his temples increase.

"Great. Looks like I've got no choice now. The boss won't like it..." Filling out the check-in form, he shoved it towards the manager.

"Are you sure?" asked the man, "Ballarat's not that far, perhaps..."

A sharp knock sounded through the interior door. A muffled cry followed it, presumably caused by a stubbed toe. The manager started.

"Yes, I'm...I'm sorry." The final word sounded like a sob.

The manager placed a key in Derek's hand. For a moment, their eyes locked and he felt the manager's trembling hand close over his. His eyes twitched to one side.

"Well, then. I'll see you in the morning." Freeing his hand, Derek turned away, but not before he saw the manager's shoulders slump.

Outside, water rattled through the pipes as the storm intensified. Derek eased into the driver's seat and started the car. His last glimpse of the office was the manager clutching at the inner door, watching Derek with empty eyes. The office slid away and rain lashed the car, swarming across the windshield in thick rivulets. Navigation became guesswork and more through luck than design Derek found a bay without hitting the building. Deciding the presentation could wait until morning, Derek grabbed a torch from the glove box. Tucking it into his jacket, he popped the boot and stepped outside. Shoulders hunched against the rain, he grabbed his case and satchel and raced for the shelter of the covered walkway.

Clutching the key in his free hand, he stomped up the narrow, echoing stairwell. Puffing, he emerged onto the upstairs walkway. His room was the first on the right. Propping his case against the wall, he wrestled with the stiff lock until the door creaked open.

An exhalation of mothballs and moist air washed over him. Grimacing, he switched on the torch and looked around. The modest room contained a double bed covered with a faded bedspread. A hideously patterned couch slumped against a wall. Above it hung a framed square of black velvet onto which a pressed metal horse had been stuck. Under the long bench a bar fridge sat silently. On top rested a bulky television which appeared to have first seen service around the time Whitlam was forced from office.

"Definitely not the Ritz."

His job took him to some of the most remote parts of the state, and what passed for accommodation in these isolated towns left a lot to be desired. At least this didn't look like it served as a breeding nest for cockroaches. Smiling wryly, Derek slid the case under the bench then settled his satchel onto the bed. He went over to the window to close the blinds and peered out. The storm's fury spent, the downpour had faded to a steady drizzle. The moon sailed above a ragged bank of clouds. Thunder rumbled and he saw lightning fork into the distant hills. The chill light washing into the room made it even more depressing. Sliding the blinds shut he reached over and closed the door.

Squatting in front of the fridge, Derek inspected its contents. It didn't take long. A jug of water and a grimy glass. He considered going downstairs to ask the manager if he sold beer, but the humidity had sapped what little energy he had left. Finally, with a sense of trepidation born of long experience, Derek pushed open the bathroom door.

"Jesus."

Chipped tiles glistened wetly in the torchlight. The grout had turned black.

Mould freckled the mirror; patches of green and brown fringed his reflection. A tattered plastic sheet hanging limply from a rail hid a shower recess. Pulling it aside, Derek saw a shower head drooping over grime riddled tiles. Looking at them, he resolved to skip his morning shower and simply scrub himself down with a wet towel.

A narrow window sat almost as an afterthought above the toilet. Idly, he flipped the dusty netting aside, allowing a view of the main street. In the moonlight, fingers of water glistened on the road, gurgling into the gutter and down a nearby drain.

Like a ship struggling in a storm, a hunched shape hove into view on the footpath. Feeling a queer sensation, Derek put his face to the glass. The figure struggled along with an odd, shuffling gait. A large hump rode high on one shoulder. The neck thrust forward, the bulbous head lifted painfully to see the way. It alternated between a horrible mewling and a low throbbing moan. Derek flinched and let the netting drop. He hurried from the bathroom, torchlight bobbing wildly across the walls. Checking the door was locked and the chain securely in place, he sat on the bed, alarmed at the thudding of his pulse. Unsettled, he stood up, grabbed a chair, and jammed it under the door handle.

On impulse, he took his mobile from his jacket and switched it on. The smiling face of a young girl holding a kitten lit up the screen and he smiled in return, feeling his old reassurance returning. The smile slipped when he saw there was no reception. He remembered the confining hills and he tossed the mobile onto the bed.

"Probably for the best," he said, watching the image on the screen fade to black. His last conversation with his ex-wife hadn't been their finest hour, not after his daughter had told him her stepfather had gotten angry with her over her cat.

*"Don't tell me it's none of my fucking business,"* he'd yelled, drawing unwanted attention from the other diners. "She's my daughter too." Sitting alone in the dark, Derek sighed, then grabbed a t-shirt and shorts from his suitcase and changed.

Lying under the thin blankets, he played the torchlight over the splotched ceiling, tracing the blooms of water fixed in waves into the plaster. He let the light linger over the door and the chair, then switched off the torch. Rolling over, he closed his eyes and was asleep in a few minutes. During the night, he woke once to a shriek which quickly wound down to a faint whimper.

"Fox," he mumbled to himself and fell asleep before he could wonder at the sob that had terminated the cry.

Under a low sky filled with threatening clouds, Derek packed his car and walked over to the office to pay. In his pocket sat the address of the local mechanic torn from the phone book. Keen to be on his way, he approached the door with a spring in his step and pushed at it. It wouldn't budge. He stared at it for several seconds, dumbfounded, before he tried again. The door rattled, distorting his reflection in the glass, but it remained resolutely locked.

A glance at his watch confirmed he wasn't dreaming. Pounding on the window, he stopped for a minute; then when a sleepy, disheveled manager didn't shuffle bleary eyed into the office, he pounded away again. Another few seconds of this and he gave in.

"Fantastic. What next, frogs falling from the sky?" He glanced up and down the driveway, half expecting the manager to pop out from behind the low fence that ran down to the footpath and laugh at him.

"Goddamn hicks." He rubbed the back of his neck. Forcing himself to remain calm, Derek jotted down the phone number stenciled on the front door and resolved to ring after the meeting and give his credit card number. Stalking back to his car, he flung the door open and threw himself into the seat. He jabbed the key into the ignition and twisted it.

The car started without a hitch, which only served to worsen his mood. The short trip down the road to the garage went off without fuss or bother. Frustrated beyond measure, Derek turned into the garage driveway and exploded in a burst of swearing when he saw the closed workshop doors. When his tirade petered out, he peeled his fingers off the steering wheel, flexed the ache from them and stared through the windshield at the locked building. Shaking his head in disbelief, Derek opened the door and stepped outside, surveying the area.

A chill breeze ruffled his hair. Pools of oily water dotted the potholed driveway, and the sign over the door creaked. Checking his watch he swore under his breath. Was business so good the owner could afford to open late? Walking up to the office, Derek peered in. An upturned tricycle lay on the scuffed linoleum. The counter-flap stood upright and sheets of paper lay scattered across the floor. A greasy looking handprint marked a wall. The door leading into the back stood open, the room beyond lost in darkness. Frustrated, Derek ran a hand through his hair and surveyed the street. Despite the hour, shops remained closed. The lack of people grew unnerving. The traffic lights ticked quietly through their endless sequence. He was about to return to his car when a commotion at the far end of the street distracted him and then he felt ice pour through his veins. A shrieking woman with a child clutched high on her chest staggered around the corner and zigzagged towards him. Screaming, the child pounded a fist into the woman's face. Close behind ran a young girl, hair streaming like a banner, the lower half of her face covered in blood. Then a tall man with a shotgun appeared.

Open mouthed, Derek watched the man work the action. He saw the tears streaking his face and the blood running from a savage cut that laid open his cheekbone. Even from this distance, Derek could see how badly the man's hands shook as he took aim. The woman clapped a hand to her face and shrieked once more, then stumbled. The man sighted down the barrel and fired.

Blood and bone exploded through the air as the child flew free from the woman's grip. The tiny body rolled like a rag doll across the wet bitumen, coming to rest face down at his feet. Derek saw the handle of a kitchen knife sticking out of the woman's left eye. He fell back to his car, nerveless fingers pawing at the door. The woman fell to her knees, then onto her face, the knife handle forcing her head to one side. The pursuing child screamed, an animal ululation that sent goose flesh racing across Derek's skin. Fingers contorted into talons, she turned on the sobbing gunman and leaped. Moaning, the man clubbed the child to the ground with the stock of the gun, breaking her neck with a sound like snapping sticks.

After the carnage, the silence was shocking. Looking at the bodies, Derek struggled to keep a grip on his sanity. He staggered towards the gunman, who had slumped to the ground, shotgun cradled in his arms. His slack, pale face twitched and a thin line of drool fell from his mouth.

"Jesus Christ, what the fuck have you DONE?"

Derek stopped in the middle of the street, gagging at the sharp stink of blood and shit. Slowly, he grew aware of a knocking sound from behind. Shaking, he turned, and had to clamp a hand over his mouth to stop from screaming.

Pressed against the office window stood a little boy. His orange overalls were stained black, and gore clotted his blonde curls. The smile of maniacal glee plastered across his face sent Derek stumbling to his car. Tiny fists pounding on the window matched the frantic beating of his heart. Reaching the car, he tore the door open then heard the ratchet of the shotgun's action. He slowly turned.

"They attacked us. All of them. Oh god, oh god oh god oh god oh-" With one swift movement, the gunman tucked the twin barrels under his quivering chin and pulled the trigger. His head fountained into the air. The shotgun clattered to the ground as the body slumped beside it.

Derek vomited down the side of his car. Wiping his mouth on his sleeve, he climbed inside and shut the door. With a calm born of shock, he slid his seat belt across his chest and buckled it home, then reached for the key. The engine gave an ineffectual little whine. Derek twisted the key again, the jangle of metal like clashing cymbals. Nothing. Slowly, his head tracked around until he saw the toddler again, its mouth wide open with delight, eyes blazing with a demon fire. Derek felt the world shift on its axis, and a premonition of the future sent a tear tracking down his face. The radio's steady whine erupted into a cacophony of voices.

"Reports...thousands of deaths...keep away...don't trust." Static obliterated the rest, but Derek was sure he heard the voice sobbing with despair. The sudden crash of shattered glass sent him reeling into the street.

The noise acted as a signal. Suddenly, the road was full of screaming adults and laughing children. Armed with implements of every type, packs of children hunted adults with maniac glee, bringing men and women down in screaming, bloody heaps. A woman ran shrieking through the tumult, the legs of a child gripped tightly around her neck, its pudgy fists buried deep in her eye sockets. An elderly man held off a boy of ten with a rake, only to be hamstrung from behind by a cackling six year old wielding a sickle, who then buried it in the man's throat. Dipping his fingers in the blood pooling from the wound, the boy ran them down his cheeks, leaving tracks like war paint.

Farther down the street a house exploded, showering the road with brick and glass as a gout of flame filled the air. Body parts fell from the sky like a sign of the apocalypse. A child stood in the ruined front room, hair scorched away, skin peeled like an orange. Its bloody mouth gaped open in a joyous grin. Then Derek noticed a young girl staring at him with avid eyes from the opposite footpath, her fingers tightening on a golf club. He bolted.

Ignoring pleas for help, Derek shouldered through the press of bodies. Distantly, he noticed that all the adults wore the same expression; a combination of naked terror and utter confusion. Here were children, almost certainly their own, maiming and killing without compunction. It was like watching cattle being slaughtered. He saw one sobbing man refuse to even lift his arms to defend himself as a boy, likely his son, clumsily buried an axe in his face.

Derek felt a terrible realization blossom. He felt no shame in fleeing, about leaving these people to die. Something, everything, had changed. No one was here to tell him what to do, not his parents, or his wife, his boss, or even God, who Derek reckoned had abandoned his creations in one searing thought. All he had to worry about now was himself. Elbowing a woman in the face, he fought on, sparing a thought for his daughter *and good luck to her mother's new boyfriend*, he decided with a malicious burst of glee.

All he cared about now was the chaos of murderous children with evil stamped deep into their faces. Survival had replaced sales targets. A great weight lifted from his shoulders and he felt a smile spread his lips wide. Everything was so much simpler now.

Kicking and punching children aside, he fled up the street. A boy, draped in intestines, stepped from between two parked cars and swung at him with a cleaver. Swaying aside, Derek flung his hand out, gripped the boy by the face and slung him into the side of a car. The crunch of bone and buckling metal sent a thrill of ecstasy through him. What was left of his sanity quailed at the scream of triumph

211

that tore from his throat.

At the top of the street, Derek skidded to a halt. Panting like an animal at bay, his lungs burned white hot. All the adults were dead, or dying. All the children had turned towards him and he saw written in their feral faces an uncaring universe devoid of any rules.

A strange, savage exultation swept through him. All that he had known to be right and true, to love and care and walk the narrow road, fell away, leaving a core that screamed savagely for blood. Reaching down, he picked up a discarded axe. Testing its weight, he smiled.

"Come on, you little fuckers!" he screamed, insolently beckoning them forward. "If you're hard enough, have a fucking go!"

Their screams rose into the sky, and they charged up the hill to the echo of his savage, delirious chanting.

# Braindead

### by
### Sean Douglas

Braindead
by
Sean Douglas

I T'S NOT like you see in the movies.
The walking dead aren't all slow and shambly and half-rotten and hungry for flesh. It's more of a braindead thing. Like the dysfunctional robots of *Westworld*.

Not that I mind. I've seen a lot of movies and from what I can tell from watching movies, a real zombie apocalypse would suck. Hordes of festering gore-spattered corpses with their entrails hanging down like coat-tails or dress-trains. Fast zombies, slow zombies, who cares when there are hundreds of them sniffing you out? Chasing you down. Keeping you up at night with their insistent moaning and shambling and clawing and banging on the walls.

Maybe I'm skipping ahead here.

It all came from drinking the water. But I wasn't drinking the water. You see, I was on an energy drink kick. I was playing a lot of video games and I wanted to stay up all day and night, so I started buying energy drinks when I'd go to the store for cigarettes. I figured I'd get all jazzed up on caffeine and taurine and guanine and I'd lose weight while playing video games. So I tried out different brands and flavors. My favorite was Sobe Gold which is kind of citrusy. Nos is also kind of citrusy but not as good. Rockstar Punched tastes like spiked fruit punch. Full Throttle Fury tastes like orange soda. Most everything else tastes like dog piss. Not that I've done the Pepsi challenge, but you get the point.

So I was playing a lot of video games and I wasn't watching the news. We were on threat level orange or whatever, but I didn't give a fuck, because what are they going to do? There's no way that those pissed-off Middle-Eastern countries have the capability to lob inter-continental-ballistic-missiles at our asses. With the way we've got the world wired? No fucking way? We'd know about those bitches the second they left the ground. We'd know about them before they even got made. We were watching the air, but no one was watching the water.

Some asshole figured out how to make a nerve agent with shit you can buy at the supermarket, and terrorist cells all across America mixed up batches in their basements and dumped them into all of the reservoirs at the same time, then went home and hugged the Quran and shot themselves in the mouths without leaving notes.

At least that's what I figured. I'm still around and I wasn't drinking the water and I'm not going to. All of the fish went belly up but no one noticed until it was too late. Which meant that no one noticed at all because everyone woke up and made their morning coffee or brushed their teeth or had a nice cold glass of water or whatever and, bang, there it was. This shit was like acid, it was so strong that a millionth of a part of it would do the job. I didn't get hit because I was too busy smoking and drinking energy drinks and playing video games to brush my teeth or drink a nice cold glass of water.

One of the last times I went out to the convenience store at the end of my street to get more smokes and Hostess cherry fruit pies, the place was wide open with no one around. I grabbed my drinks and stood there, waiting like a dick for, like, five minutes. Eventually, I yelled "Hello!" and looked around. When no one came out I went around the counter to see if the guy was sleeping or lying on the floor with his head half off from being shot in the face during a robbery. But there was no one fucking there. No cameras either, so I grabbed a couple packs of cigarettes and some Sobes and stuffed them in a bag and backed out of the store. I felt a little guilty, like I was being watched, but it wasn't like I never stole anything before, and if I got caught I figured I'd just say that I fully intended on paying for what I took and talk my way out of it, all smooth like.

On the walk back home there were some old folks standing around in their yard but I didn't pay them any attention because there are always old folks standing around in their yards, looking up into the sky or down at their lawns or whatever.

So I went back to the video gaming and smoking and drinking of energy drinks and all was well with the world.

The next time I went out for more smokes and energy drinks there were some more people out and about and I figured something was up. I think maybe I stayed up for too long or I spent too many hours playing *Dead Rising* or whatever, because there were people sort of all over the place, but it wasn't like they were all fucked up and moaning and staggering towards me, arms outstretched with a hungry look in their eyes. They were just sort of slack-jawed and half-dressed and taking baby steps to no particular destination. Just sort of drifting in whatever direction the wind blew them, with a blank unfocused look in their eyes. It wasn't like they were bumping into shit or causing havoc. It was like the whole world had become an Alzheimer's unit. They were in the streets and in the yards and on the sidewalks but not like they were all mobbed up or something.

Every half a block or so I'd see someone staring up into the sun or down at the ground or off into the distance. And I'm no idiot. I know what happened. It's the zombie apocalypse and I expect that pretty soon they're going to figure out that I'm not dead and it'll be running buffet time. But like I said, they're not all fucked up and bitey. It's more of a brain-dead thing.

At first it was a little disconcerting and I gave them a wide berth when I passed. But after safely passing two or three, I figured they didn't want to eat my brains and I just made my merry way to the convenience store and got a bag full of Sobe Golds and four cartons of cigarettes and went back home, figuring I'd hole up and play games and wait until the proper authorities came around, canvassing the neighborhood for survivors.

Then it occurred to me. Maybe I'd better flip the TV on and see what the news has to say about the matter. Maybe there are some important advisories or whatever. Flip the cable box on. Nothing. Not that the cable was out. There was just nothing on. Well, not nothing. The TV GUIDE channel kept scrolling upwards into infinity, but half the channels were black or color bars or static. There were no grim-faced reporters reading off teleprompters.

That was when I realized there was something seriously fucked up going on. But what wa I gonna do, save the world? I barely got out of high school and I was supposed to come up with some big fucking plan?

I instantly gave up and crashed down in bed, fired up the X-Box and got ready to kill some zombies and then I had a revelation. Maybe the best and biggest idea I've ever had.

I went out the back door into the bright sunshine and looked over the backyard fence into the yard next door. The old cunt next door was out there in her housedress staring at the wind chimes hanging from her back door awning. I hated those wind chimes and I hated her. This old bitch was always peeking out the blinds and spying on the neighborhood like it was her job and she'd always call the cops whenever I had a few people over and we had a few beers and someone ended up passed out in the backyard. Or when I played my bass through my kick-ass half cab after 9:00 p.m. Like it was any of her business. And those wind chimes and the birds chirping always kept me up when I was trying to sleep during the day. Not like I could do anything about the birds chirping.

I walked around and undid the gate and walked over to her and said, "Hey, you old bitch!" and her head sort of lolled around in my direction but there was no real recognition. She was still all slack-jawed and dead-eyed and whatever.

I yelled into her left ear, "Fuck you! You desiccated old bag of horse shit!" and still nothing. I smiled, satisfied at my experiment and walked over to her backyard garden shed.

The shovel had a nice long wooden handle and I swung it like a baseball bat. "WHANG!" Right into her fucking face. Her face made a squishy cracking sound and she fell over. She laid there for a second making gurgly sounds and then rolled over onto her hands and knees like she was trying to get up. I wound up and kicked her in her ribs with all I had and she went down again. She tried to get back up and I used the shovel to pound her head into pudding. If it was anyone I cared about I'd have felt sick, but I hated this bitch and doing what I did just felt right. Now that's justice!

I stabbed the head of the shovel into the earth and reached into my pocket and took out a cigarette and lit it and that first pull felt better than most. I exhaled into the sunlit air and realized I had some work to do.

I made a list. You know how most people say, "You made my shit list."? Well now I actually had one. I went online. Facebook was still working. So was YellowPages.com. I looked up the names of everyone I could ever think of that ever pissed me off or did me wrong. It took the better part of a day. Maybe I've got a longer list than most people, but fuck it.

Then I made another list.

- Guns
- Bullets
- Shotguns
- Shells
- Booze
- Smokes

I went out and got into my car. Driving was kind of a pain in the ass in the suburbs and the city, what with people wandering around all brain-dead and all. It's not as awesome as you might expect. You might think it would be cool to run people over all day long but I'm a little smarter than that. Once I hit a deer with a friend's car I was driving and it fucked up his front end, so I figured if I wanted to keep moving I'd have to not hit anyone. At least not hard. All I had to do was drive at a moderate speed around the human obstacles. At least the highways were pretty clear because no one had enough time to get into their cars and onto the highways before the shit hit the fan.

I stopped at the gun store, the liquor store and then followed the GPS directions to the first house on the list.

Kicking in the front door was kind of a pain in the ass, but it was so worth it. Shooting the kid who used to be my friend, but ended up stealing my girlfriend in high school, right in the side of the head was incredibly cathartic. It was all up close and there was the smell of burnt hair and skin in the air and he dropped like a duffel bag full of bowling balls. Satisfying. She was the first girl I ever loved and I never forgave either of them for that. I mean, she was just as guilty, but I blamed him. I took out a black Sharpie and crossed him off the list. It felt great to have that weight off of my shoulders.

Got back into the car and sipped off the nearest bottle from the case of Johnny Walker Gold Label in the passenger seat. It was free. Why cheat myself?

I made a detour to the big box store and got a twenty-five pound sledgehammer and a crossbow and a sickle and an aluminum baseball bat and a golf club. Everything in the aisles took on a different light when I was trying to gather up some cool shit to kill people with.

Minutes later I was at the next address on the list. Hit the door near the latch with the sledge and it popped open. Fat fuck was still at the kitchen table in his pajama pants. Who even fucking wears pajama pants? Hauled back and nailed him in the back of the head with the sledgehammer. "Whammo!" Then I kicked him over and shattered every last bone in his body to splinters with the aluminum baseball bat.

And so on and so on.

Ex-roomate who ripped me off and sold my stuff to buy heroin? Shot two crossbow bolts into his head. One into each eye. Then cut his hands off at the wrists with a machete and watched him spurt blood from the stumps until he fell over and stopped moving, then pissed on him.

I've always believed that variety was the spice of life so I tried to keep things original.

High school bully that was now a cop? Filled his bathtub with him in it and dropped a television in with him.

Skinny smart-ass who got me fired because he ratted me out to the boss? Dragged him out into his own backyard and poured gasoline all over him, flipped a match and burned him alive.

That guy who I thought was my friend, but I later found out that he used to talk shit about me when I wasn't around? Stabbed him in the throat and watched him choke on his own blood. It was glorious.

That bitch that fired me for no apparent reason which made my then-girlfriend break up with me because she thought I was useless? Knocked her over and put a shotgun in her crotch and pulled the trigger and watched the blood pour out from the hole where her precious little cunt used to be and watched the color drain from her face and the lights in her eyes go out.

That high school teacher that used to yell in my face with the whole class watching and made me feel stupid and told me that reading comic books and playing video games was no way to live my life? Disemboweled him with the sickle and watched him die writhing around in his own entrails on his kitchen floor.

My step-father who always told me I was worthless and I'd never amount to anything? My shoulders were sore the nest day from stabbing him in the face and torso about a hundred times.

I'd like to say it was a busy day. But really it was a busy week.

Well maybe a couple of weeks. It's not like I really had to keep track of what day it was and I have to admit that I was pretty fucking wasted for most of it. Driving around drunk and just killing the fuck out of people then crossing them off the list.

Believe it or not, eventually I ran out of people. I didn't want to kill random strangers. They hadn't done anything to me and it's not like I was some kill-crazy asshole. I just had some axes to grind and bones to pick and it was the end of the world and the final judgment was at hand and I was judge, jury, and executioner.

When I crossed off the last name on my shit list I got to thinking about all of those girls that I never got to fuck. High school. Co-workers. That hot girl at the video game store. I made another list.

Going through that list was a little bit different. It took a little longer. It was really fascinating to find out about each and every one. Check out their CD and DVD collections. Try to figure out what their lives were like by the stuff they had around their homes. It's not like we could really have a conversation and catch up or get to know each other. After a while it almost got boring. The women weren't exactly responsive. Kind of gives new meaning to the expression *dead fuck*. And once you got their clothes off it was a pain in the ass to get them into anything else, so it's not like I got to play fancy lingerie dress-up party or whatever. And with a lot of them, finally getting what I'd always wanted was sort of sad and disappointing. I could do whatever I wanted to them but this serving of revenge was definitely not best served cold. I hadn't made a habit of taking advantage of chicks when they got drunk and passed out and this felt a lot like that, but I went ahead anyway and spent about a half a day with each of them kind of hanging out and getting it out of my system.

After a while people started dying from dehydration and exposure and whatever. Like the old and senile, these folks weren't feeding or watering themselves and eventually they just fell over and died. Nobody got back up to shamble around and to be honest it was a little disappointing. I guess I had seen too many movies.

But now I've got all the time in the world to watch all of the movies I always wanted to watch and play all of the video games I wanted to play and drink and smoke as much as I want. The whole world is mine, or at least that's how it feels. It's a little boring sometimes and a little lonely and it's kind of freaky watching the crows peck at the eyes of the people all dead in the streets and in their yards and on the sidewalks, but it's not like I have to go out much. I've got everything I need right here.

And if you happen to be reading this, then chances are I'm already dead. Maybe from old age and maybe from boredom.

Maybe some astronauts or an exploratory expedition from Canada or whatever.

I don't know how to work those big fancy international radios. Hell, I probably wouldn't even know one if I saw one. And my cell phone doesn't have international calling and I don't know how to go about setting that up either. And I don't know that if I did if I'd even want to try to get ahold of anyone because I'm doing just fine.

So if you're reading this, fuck you, I apologize for nothing.

# Desensitized

## by
## Kerry G.S. Lipp

Desensitized
by
Kerry G.S. Lipp

W HEN I finally finished watching every single video about serial killers or
mass murderers on Youtube, I decided to do something original. I hate
to take anything away from these guys, well, mostly guys with a few murderous
chicks mixed in, but they were all pretty evil in their own way.

Sure they had their differences. Some just killed, some raped then killed.
Some raped and then killed and then raped again. Some shot up schools, some
shot up churches.

But does any of that really shock anyone anymore?

No.

Well, maybe. The level of shock one of these garners depends on their media
coverage more than their methods. However, I'm sure that sometimes the two
serve each other.

I looked at all of them; interviews and documentaries, these cleverly disguised
tributes, and I learned. And after all that, I decided I wanted to do something
different.

And wait till you see what I came up with.

The idea came to me in 2013 when I saw that they were releasing a movie
about the Iceman, Richard Kuklinski, in theatres across the country.

HBO interviews with Kuklinski painted him as an angry, sociopathic youth
turned hit man later in life. He killed in lots of different ways, did all kinds of
experiments and avoided capture for most of his life. He showed little remorse
and openly talked about his crimes. He wasn't proud and he wasn't ashamed. He
cracked a lot of awkward jokes. The awkwardness came from not being able to
tell whether he was joking or simply speaking matter of factly. Truly fascinating.

The Iceman never admitted to rape. Despite that, or maybe because of it, he's
become a kind of folk hero in America. Perhaps even across the world.

I don't know.

We Americans are a paradox. We are oversensitive to things that are meaningless but desensitized to things that are so much worse. If you say a woman is hot

you become part of 'rape culture' but if you say "I'm gonna kill you." you don't become a part of 'murder culture.'

'Murder culture' doesn't exist, at least not yet. But it probably will after I'm through.

I put both those terms in quotes because it's all horseshit.

But that's not what this is about. It's about the instantaneous availability for anyone with an internet connection to access a near infinite number of documentaries and interviews with serial killers and mass murderers. You can even read details about their escapades and look at pictures of their victims.

And that's not even the bad part. There's value to a candid interview with a monster. Such a thing can reach a lot of people, and I think that the majority of people who seek these interviews out have a genuine interest in exploring the deepest and darkest parts of the humanity at its worst.

But when you turn that killer into a story and put it in the box office alongside The Hangover, what are you really saying? Are you glorifying the actions of that individual?

I think so, but that's just my opinion. But then, my opinion and my actions; well, that's what this is all about is it not? This is my blog. And thanks for reading, by the way.

At the very least, filmmakers and book writers and so many others profit from the actions of that individual. The most cynical part of me wonders if those monsters get a cut. They deserve it, after all. They're the ones that did the hard work, took all the risks. You know?

Consider the contribution of Ed Gein to popular culture. Without his homemade, human-skin decorations, Psycho, The Texas Chainsaw Massacre, and The Silence of the Lambs wouldn't exist. At least not as we know them. Gein only killed a few people and I think I'm in the majority when I say that I don't give a shit about his victims. His contribution to pop culture was well worth the defilement of their corpses.

The apprehension of Gein and the wide reports of his twisted crimes occurred in the 1950s. Psycho followed very shortly after. Movies about Gein or inspired by him have been constant ever since. One even swept the Academy Awards in the early 90s. Look it up.

Give it a few more years and there will be a Columbine movie. Yeah, I know there are a couple derivatives already–looking at you Zero Day and Elephant–but I'm talking a legit Hollywood movie where Harris and Klebold are characters. It hasn't happened yet, but it's coming. There will probably be some cool industrial music in the background, maybe even that song "Invisible Empire" by the Electric Hellfire Club that opens with the famous 911 call from the library, when the shooters kick in the front doors with guns blazing. Haven't heard it? Go give it a listen. It's hard to find, but I got you: https://myspace.com/electrichellfireclub/music/song/invisible-empire. It will give you chills.

It's been almost fifteen years. I'm kind of shocked that the diaries aren't on sale at the bookstore already. Doesn't matter; a quick Google search will take you straight to them.

I wonder if the diary would outsell the number of books about Cassie, the girl who said she believed in god. Come to think about it, I wonder how many people bought Cassie's book just to get the details of that shooting on April 20, 1999 rehashed to them yet another way.

This will probably happen with Sandy Hook, as well. Yeah, I went there. But just like Lanza, the box office doesn't discriminate and people will pay to see that shit. It might not make millions, but it'll make enough to cover the budget. There are already a bunch of documentaries about that terrible morning for free on yep, you guessed it, Youtube.

I know because I watched them all. They didn't even have commercials! I don't buy into any of the conspiracy theories, but just like everyone else, eager for a different perspective or some nasty detail that I'd missed, I devoured them all.

I don't believe that violence causes violence but I do believe in desensitization. And I believe in evolution. I think they are intertwined.

Christ, look at the evolution (if you can call it that) of sex in America.

Yeah.

We've got second grade blowjobs going on during movie day. The first thing a kid does with their brand new birthday present smart phone is send a picture of their dick or their pussy to their current flavor of the week. We've got kids creating their own brand of child pornography and then being shocked when it gets spread around the school. And the most fucked up part is that adults are probably too scared to report it when they find it. If they did, this country could easily and unapologetically transform them from a caring parent to a permanent red 'X' on the sex offender map.

So a lot of adults probably let that shit go. And a lot of them probably hoard it for themselves because there's nothing hotter out there than a sex tape. Even shot jerky and grainy from a cell phone. Especially if young'uns are involved.

Yeah, I'd say the chains are loosening a tad, at least on our children.

I don't care. I'm too old and too righteous to enjoy it and too hateful to procreate. I'd probably kill my own children rather than trying to raise them with this country the way it is. A few mothers have done that already. And it seems their preferred method is drowning.

Swing it all back.

It's hard to be original.

We've got sex slave mansions in Cleveland, Ohio, and prison guards looking the other way when sex slave mansion owners from Cleveland take the coward's way out with a bed sheet. But not too many people got the story of that guy's suicide, since it happened right around the time Miley Cyrus and her foam finger got a little freaky on MTV. Hell, after all that twerking, even the ones that did hear about Ariel Castro's suicide were too distracted to ask any questions.

We've got elementary school and movie theatre massacres. We've got bitches microwaving babies and we've got guys trying to grab infants away from angry wives and scalping the poor kid in the process. The last two happened in fucking Dayton, Ohio.

A forgettable big city and if things so terrible happened there and you didn't hear about them, just what else do you think is going out in the world? What about those towns that don't even have a newspaper? Or electricity? There a lot of places like that within the United States and a lot more outside of them. But if we don't know about something, it doesn't exist right?

So.

Since fiction can't possibly compete with all the wild shit out there in the world, please remind me why I'm supposed to be sensitive or even the slightest bit apologetic when my entertainment is a little edgy?

Oh, you frown on scenes that glorify sex or violence? Ok, good. Don't read anything or watch anything ever again. Have a nice, boring life. Enjoy living with nothing challenging your paradigms.

Most entertainers use this shit but they don't glorify it. They use it to explore the human condition. Who are we anyway and why do we do what we do?

How is it that the way we see ourselves, our reflections, isn't the way that others see us? We're all a lot worse than we appear. We don't match up.

We're all hiding some serious shit on the inside.

From the content I've consumed, I've come up with a few answers.

We do it because we can. We do it, well, because we do it. It's that simple. A lot of writers and artists and movie makers out there try to analyze exactly what "because we can" means. And they use real world examples to jumpstart their creative process. But I don't think they'd pick their subjects or their targets without the media planting the seeds.

Leave the entertainers alone.

If you want to go at anyone for glorification, go at the media. And to prove my point, just wait and see what they do with me.

Take a look at what dominates the headlines. I know this is a clich, but if our stupid ass society didn't eat it up, what we know as news would radically redefine itself.

But we're stupid, and it won't, and I can go to bed tonight with my laptop sitting on my chest telling me in intricate and vivid detail exactly what the Green

River Killer did to his victims.

Green River Killer. Man, that's cool name. I hope they come up with one like that for me. The Manifesto Massicress or something. Yeah, I like that.

I'm also a big fan of Jack the Ripper and the D.C. Sniper. Those names still induce dread up there with The Manson Family or The Zodiac or The Black Dahlia or BTK.

BTK.

I think that's the one that bothers me the most.

BTK.

You see those three letters and you ask what they stand for. Then you're told and you craft your own mental image of what those words mean. Even worse, what they mean in consecutive order. Your brain makes it as bad as it's capable of making it. And you know how awful it would be. And then you find out that this guy was worse. He choked his victims until they passed out, and then woke them up. And then he did it again. And again.

Bind.

Torture.

Kill.

Doesn't that just make a chill flutter up your fucking spine?

Absolutely.

And is that news? Should that make headlines? It's interesting, for sure. But with a country at war and in so much debt its governing body decided to shut down and facing a ton of problems that easily wipe out well over ten people a day, does BTK or any of this other sensationalist horseshit deserve the front page?

No.

And when you argue that publicly, and say that in the grand scheme of things, Dennis Rader, known by his superhero alter-ego, BTK, only actually killed like 10 people, you get dirty looks from the ladies heading home to watch Nancy Grace.

What this country thinks it is, and what it actually is, are asymmetrical. You can hold the mirror up, but if you look close, you won't see the same thing on both sides.

And I won't dare bring politics into this mess.

I don't know what to do with it anymore.

Actually I do. And I'm about to make my point. And that's why you're reading this. I hope you'll stick around for the video portion. And if you're coming to this after the video portion, I'm sure you'll understand.

Alright, almost time to post this. I'm not carrying out the live feed for several more hours. You've got plenty of time to get onboard and be a part of all this as it happens.

Just click this link - www.manifestomassicress.com - and be patient.

Please feel free to share with all of your friends. I hope I live long enough to see what the media nicknames me. I hope this post goes viral before I begin, but even if it doesn't, I bet it will in the aftermath. I'm taking my phone, I'll live tweet when I can.

I'm doing this for glory, but more importantly I'm doing it to bring awareness about glorification. Can't wait to see what happens. Thank you for taking this journey with me.

Love always,

Manifesto Massicress

Start Live Stream at www.manifestomassicress.com

I walk into the shopping mall with my gun raised. The camera on my head is rolling, filming, sending it straight to the net. I wish it could live stream my thoughts too!

Even though I stole this idea from a movie, Scream 4, I'll bet the screen looks a lot like Call of Duty, or Doom. And much like the seemingly superhuman protagonists that play those roles, I don't plan on missing many shots. My camera better not, either.

Once the media gets a hold of the websites I've got streaming this feed, the sensationalist dumbfucks will probably glamorize it and broadcast it live.

I hope they do. I hope they do it before they read the blog that I posted.

I hope they prove my point.

My first stop is the bathroom. It's crowded. I kill everyone inside with shots to the head. Blood sprays over the white tile walls, the white tile floor, the white tile ceiling. A couple of people try to run, and slip in the blood. Easy targets.

I'm not worried. I've chained several of the sets of the doors at this end of the mall. It's amazing how few people ask questions when you wear the right clothing and act with authority and tell them it's a 'drill.'

I've got plenty of time.

I plan on surrendering at the end, so I can live through all of my glorification or, please forgive the oh-so-American pun, goreification of what I'm doing.

I guess the difference between me and a lot of the monsters the media glorifies is that I know exactly why I'm doing this. It's not because I'm sick or mentally ill. I'm doing this as satire, a tongue-in-cheek response to the country and the culture I've spent my life in.

Over the top books and movies and video games do this all the time: Grand Theft Auto, God Bless America, American Psycho, and tons of others. But no one has done it the way I'm doing it. I just hope people understand.

I'm the South Park of mass murder.

The Manifesto Massicress.

I stare at myself in the bathroom mirror through a few splats of blood. I'm like a movie poster, a book cover, a video game box. The only thing that's missing is an explosion in the background.

"Damn. I look fucking cool," I say. Blood streaks my blonde hair and a twisted grin takes shape on my lips. Bleeding bodies slump up against the wall behind me. Through the mirror, I see the view I'm giving all the voyeurs watching live.

It's sexy.

I can't help it. I lower my head at a sinister angle, raise the gun, and pull out my phone. I take a picture, caption it with "do you think I look cool?" and tweet it.

@manifestormassicress

Then I shoot the mirror. It shatters. None of the shards properly reflect me or my actions. Each casts a different reflection in a different direction, and in each one, I twinkle, glow, look like one bad bitch.

But now it's time to move on.

I head to the food court. People scream and scatter. I spray a few bullets into the crowd.

The screams and gunshots are annoying and loud, and I pause for a second to jam my earbuds in and crank the industrial music as loud as it will go.

Marilyn Manson screams about not being a slave to a God that doesn't exist. I laugh knowing the media will probably get a hold of my iPod and try to drag down a few innocent musicians with me. It's not my fault that it's a good fucking song.

Anyway.

Fuck it.

People scatter in perfect time with the music. It's just like a movie, or a game. And a crazy thought hits me. Maybe instead of making a movie based on me, they'll make a game. That would be another first.

And I'm aiming, pun 666

I aim and shoot, aim and shoot. I'm not myself anymore. I'm not even a reflection of myself.

I'm myself on a quest. I'm a personification of the word focus.

I'm on a mission of murder and mayhem, to bring awareness to the glorification of both. And since I'm a pioneer, I'm doing it my way.

I stalk my way through the food court shooting at the biggest targets. Age, race, sex, hat backwards, hat forwards; I don't discriminate. A little girl's head is bigger than a skinny guy's knee.

I reload as needed and I toss a few more grenades. No one tries to stop me. A few people hold their phones up. Some are calling for help, but others are recording this.

Perfect.

To some degree, even the victims think this is cool.

I wonder if the news channels have picked this up yet. How many folks around the world are taking this journey with me through their screen?

I smile.

I've only been through the bathroom and the food court, and I've already taken the crown. The biggest mass murder in American history.

And I'm female.

And I'm hot.

And I'm just getting started.

There are several shoppers hiding under a table. I feel nothing as the grenade I throw into them explodes. Blood sprays as thick as the smoke. I just hope the viewers at home don't look away.

That they watch every kill. That they live this with me. And they understand. That is the most important part. That they get it.

Even though the rising death toll is already more than Sandy Hook and Columbine put together, I'm not done. Not even close.

I have another stop to make.

Just outside of the food court is the video game store.

My perfect timing is by design. I'd entered the mall right after the shop opened and on the same day that a premier release comes out. One that glorifies a lot of killing. The gamers, all "experts" in first person perspective murder, cower away from my pistol.

"Hang on a second. I just leveled up," I say. I pocket the pistol and pull out my shotgun.

Not a single one of them comes at me. I guess they all think I'll skip them and go at someone else.

They are wrong.

Virtual baddasses; real life cowards.

They don't do anything but pop like piatas. Pathetic. When I leave, no one is even quivering.

Maybe thirty minutes have passed.

Body count? I don't know for sure–the grenades make it hard–but I'd guess at least seventy. Wounded? Maybe triple that. Pretty good, but I can do better.

I'd done what I set out to, but you've always got to have a contingency plan.

I figured I'd have surrendered by now, but I haven't. Instead, I carry out the fourth act. I head into the department store at the north end of the food court.

The sales floor is empty. The dressing rooms are not. They are packed in. Hiding. Crying. Begging.

I slaughter them like cattle.

There is no sport to it.

I trade shotgun for pistol and I go down the line.

Bullet, head, dead, repeat.

I make it to my fifth dressing room, the last one in the line, before I hear the cops. They approach, and I realize they've got me cornered.

I stand on a few bleeding bodies behind the dressing room door. A mirror hangs facing me and I have a few seconds to study myself. I am beautiful and blood covered, glorious, determined. I think about the camera on my head and all the people staring at me as I stare at myself. No words exist for a moment like this.

I hear the cops coming. They take their time as they search every room. They get closer, and I can hear them swearing, disgusted at the massacre I've left in my wake. They've guessed I'm in the last dressing room–but they can't be sure.

They are just outside now.

I'm standing on bodies. They can't see my feet. But I can see their feet.

I fire through the door, the mirror. Glass explodes turning my reflection into puzzle pieces.

I hope America can put them back together.

They return fire. A couple of bullets graze me and I collapse onto the bodies. Grin on my face, I know it's time to surrender. I toss my gun.

An officer opens the door. With my hands raised, I see that my bullets hit two members of his team through the dressing room door.

Through the mirror.

The world is watching. Some watching my stream, some from a different perspective. Some probably both.

Wondering what the cops will do. What I'll do.

But it's over. I surrender.

They take me alive.

I know myself, and what I've done and why I did it. I just hope all the people watching from all their different angles see it the same way.

# The Uniform

### by
### John Grey

The Uniform
by
John Grey

S HERIFF DOOLEY WATSON screeched his Buick into the driveway and clambered out of it quickly. He was desperate to strip off that grey uniform, toss it out of sight in a closet or throw it down the cellar steps in the general direction of the washing machine. The grubby feel of it on his skin was sickening his stomach. He needed to shower, put on some civilian clothes, to cleanse himself of everything that uniform represented.

What a horrific day it had been. He thought he had seen everything the netherworld had to offer. But that was before he came in contact with Albert Winter and that house on Duseberry Road. He didn't want to think about it, had to rip away every reminder of his job before... before he didn't know what.

Why had he been the one to take that call? Why was it his job to burst in on this most hideous, gut-wrenching of crime scenes?

The family dog Elmer suddenly leapt out from under the porch steps, yapping madly, climbed all over Dooley, happily licking the long blue studded stripe that bisected grey trouser legs. For a moment, Dooley bathed in the attention from this affectionate pet but, as he was about to kneel down to pat the mutt's head, he suddenly gave it a swift kick in the ribs. The dog yelped, tottered backward and then looked up quizzically at its master. Its eyes, though round and undeniably innocent, jarred his mind back to what happened four weeks before that visit to the Carter house.

Mahorn had taken the call but he'd immediately turned the information over to Sheriff Watson.

"It's Louise Carter. She kept screaming 'My baby! My baby!'"

"What the hell's the matter with her baby?" Dooley had snapped back.

"She was hysterical. She didn't give any details. She just kept hollering 'My baby! My baby!'"

"You stay here, Mahorn. I'll go over, calm that dumb broad down."

On arrival at the Carter house, Sheriff Watson knew something was wrong. The screams had not subsided. The shrieks of "My baby! My baby!" went beyond motherly concern. Those cries were awash with the familiar numbing chords of death... horrible death.

The front door was open and Dooley ran inside, fumbling for his gun as he did so, through the kitchen and into the child's bedroom. His hand rose up to cover his mouth in reaction to the sight before him. Mrs Carter was standing in the middle of the room, clutching the mangled body of her baby in her arms. In the far corner, a large German Shepherd whimpered in sorrow at its own madness, traces of foam puffing round the edges of its snout. It looked like half the baby's face had been eaten away by that dog's sharp ivory teeth. Dooley, fighting back his own vomit, tried to pry the baby away from Mrs Carter but his efforts were useless. She clung to that piece of herself as if it was a life raft, ignoring the blood that siphoned down her cheap cotton dress.

Dooley had kicked the shepherd away just as he did with his own dog. It ran off, half-yelping, half-crying, not understanding what it had done wrong.


"Dammit," he muttered to himself as he unlocked his front door. "Why did I have to get into this business? Shit. I can't even go near my own dog and it reminds me of that...that baby."

From the parlor, he could hear the excited cheer of "Daddy's home! Daddy's home."

Twelve-year-old Kim and her brother, Mark, two years younger, raced out to greet their father. Instinctively, he reached out his arms to swallow them in his broad, muscular chest when something about their cheery, artless faces set him thinking about the Cunningham case.

Missy and George Cunningham, what a pair. Who would have thought that two children could be so wicked?

How old was the Thomas boy? Six? Or maybe seven? His walk home from school was a mere five blocks. Unfortunately for him, that journey took him by the Cunningham house, the lair of those two monsters. They invited him inside. What could he do? His mother had warned him about strange men but she'd said nothing about other children. She was not to know there were creatures like that out there, a boy and girl, not yet in high school, tying a small child to a chair in the cellar, taking their father's ax from the garage and then...

God, he didn't want to think about it. Dooley was the first outsider who went down into that dark pit of a basement. There was no age group, no specific family background, for this sort of horror. It was the devil's own work and it could strike anywhere.

"Too much TV," the judge had said, as if it were that simple.

Kim and Mark had been watching television when he arrived home. Just cartoons probably. Or maybe even soap operas. No, it was too late for soap operas. Instead of embracing the children, he pushed them aside roughly with a curt, *'Get out of my hair.'*

The job was really getting to him. Even their tears at this brisk dismissal couldn't stop him storming upstairs to the bedroom.

"What's wrong with the kids?" his wife Judy asked as he hurriedly unbuttoned his coat. She had just finished another load of laundry and was folding up the results on the bed and squeezing them into the dresser drawers.

"I can't take any more of this. I've got to quit. You won't believe what I saw today out on Duseberry Road.'

She had heard him threaten to quit many times before and her reply was always off-hand, "But it pays good money, darling. And, in another fifteen years, you can retire."

"If I live that long," he said loudly, his anxious fingers struggling with the belt buckle.

"Oh Dooley, you do exaggerate."

Exaggerate? How could a cop exaggerate? Every day, he saw the extremes of what human beings were capable of. There was no way to exaggerate that.

A dog eating a baby.

Two children slicing up a third.

And today - yes, that very day - Albert Winter. The ghoul to end all ghouls. An entire family slaughtered this time. Seeing that sort of sickness in the line of duty didn't trigger bursts of exaggeration. In fact, it did the opposite. A cop had to bite down hard on the grimness, make believe dismembered bodies and slime-hearted killers were just routine. You learned to laugh at the seamy side, the murders, the drugs, the scum-bags. But there were some crimes that took you over the edge. Like the dog and the baby. And those hellish Cunningham kids. And now Winter. Was any name ever more appropriate?

How could Judy understand? She stayed home all week, did house-work, watched TV, prepared milk and cookies for Kim and Mark when they came home from school. She didn't have to spend her days and nights in that grisly hell where human life wasn't worth any more than a pinch of spit. Judy turned towards him, face smiling sympathetically.

"Why don't you get out of that uniform? Make yourself comfortable. Watch a little TV with the kids. I'll have your supper on the table in a little while."

He barely heard her words. He was struck by something in her face that he hadn't noticed before. It was the mouth, the way it tried to pacify, to get him to drop his guard. What was the name of that woman? The one who lived in the raised ranch in Colby Heights? Two years ago, it was. *Goddamit.* How could he ever forget? Esther Goodfellow. That was her name. Goodfellow! What a laugh.

She'd slit her husband's throat when he was sleeping peacefully, cuddled him for four nights in a bed of blood as if nothing had even happened.

It was Jake Mason, his employer down at the hardware store, who had raised the alarm.

"Dooley," he said over the phone, "Joe Goodfellow hasn't been to work for days. Hasn't called in either. I've telephoned up to the house but no one answers. I'm concerned."

The sheriff drove up in the patrol car to the old house on Ridge Road to investigate. He knocked on the door and Esther Goodfellow opened it, wearing a see-through nightgown, and nothing else.

"It's about... it's about Joe," stammered Dooley, struggling to ignore the breathy rise and fall of her delectable body. "Some folks are worried. They..."

"Let's not talk about Joe, Sheriff Watson," she said softly.

The smile that sugared her words quickly started breaking down his resolve. It was the same smile Dooley was seeing now in Judy. He didn't know how to fight it then. He tried to black out what came next: Esther reaching out her hand, wrapping her fingers in his, leading him into the darkened bedroom. He should have resisted but she was such an amazingly attractive woman. Moaning softly, she let go his hand, nudged his body toward the bed. But suddenly, moonlight split the clouds, sprayed silver through the window and lit up the scene. Dooley stared aghast at the body of Joe Goodfellow, half in, half out of the sheets, head cocked to one side and drenched in stale blood. The sheriff jumped to his feet in shock. Esther, body still heaving as if interrupted in sex, could only laugh and laugh and laugh.

He pushed at Judy and she tumbled to the floor.

"What the hell's wrong with you, Dooley Watson!" she screamed.

"Nothing!' he yelled back. "I just want to be left alone."

"Suit yourself."

Judy stormed out of the bedroom. Dooley sat back on the bed, his head finding some solace in the upturned palms of his hands.

"My God," he muttered. "What's happening to me? I have to quit this job. It's going to drive me crazy. The dog. The kids. Even my wife. I can't even bear to touch them anymore. Everything's been poisoned. It's this Albert Winter case. It's Duseberry road. The last straw. It's pushing me over the edge."

Tears seeped from his eyes, rolled down his cheeks, his fingers. And then Dooley howled. Like a wild beast, he howled. He felt more of a victim than these poor corpses, a wife and two children, who had been hacked to shreds by the crimson-bladed carving knife that rested a foot or two from Winter's bony hands like a leopard between kills. At least those poor souls were dead. Dooley Watson was alive. That was the worst of it.

Forgetting his badge, his duty, Sheriff Watson had run from that dreadful place, slid behind the wheel of the patrol car, skidded away as fast as he could. He sped back to the police station, didn't report in, just exchanged vehicles, and wouldn't let his foot up from the accelerator until he was in the supposedly safe haven of his own neighborhood. But Dooley was quickly finding out that he couldn't escape even there. His gruesome job was following him inside that sanctuary. It was yapping in his dog's mouth, grinning from his kids, sliming out of the soothing words of his wife.

Dooley finally wriggled his head free of his hands, began to fiddle with the buttons on his jacket once again. His eyes met his reflection in the bedroom mirror.

"That face," shrieked Dooley. "I know that face."

"It's a thin line, Dooley," whispered Albert Winter, his cancerous expression glaring at the sheriff with unfettered hate. I know why you ran off this afternoon. It wasn't me you were afraid of. You were afraid of that thin line. The one I crossed. The one you are so terrified of stepping over. I mean how different are we? A wife, two kids, even a dog. That was my problem. It's yours too, isn't it. They get to you, Dooley. After a while, they just get to you.'

"It's this job," sputtered Dooley. "It makes you crazy. If I could only get this uniform off. Put on some jeans. A t-shirt. I could be just plain old Dooley Watson. High school football star. College grad. Army veteran. Husband. Father."

"It's too late. You've already seen me. And you've already seen yourself. You know what I am capable of. And now you"

Dooley's fingers froze. They no longer plugged away at those pesky buttons. He reached into a dresser drawer, drew out his hunting knife, ran his fingers along the sharpened edge, stormed out of the bedroom door and hurried down the stairs.

# About the Authors

Neil Baker (editor) is a former fish-fryer, dinosaur builder and school teacher. After a spell as an award-winning filmmaker and traditional animator, he returned to his first love, writing, and within a year had sold stories that appeared in *Ugly Babies, Cellar Door II, World War Cthulhu, Atomic Age Cthulhu* and *Occult Detective Monster Hunter: A Grimoire of Eldritch Inquests.* He now runs April Moon Books and his first publication, The Dark Rites of Cthulhu, enjoyed a great critical reception. Neil is based on the outskirts of Toronto and he is married with two small children. You can reach him via the contacts page at www.AprilMoonBooks.com.

Rob E. Boley grew up in Enon, Ohio, a little town with a big Indian mound. He later earned a B.A. and M.A. in English from Wright State University in Dayton, Ohio. He's the author of THAT RISEN SNOW and THAT WICKED APPLE, the first in a series of dark fantasy novels published by StoneGate Ink featuring mash-ups of classic fairy tale characters and horror monsters. His fiction has appeared in several markets, including A cappella Zoo, Pseudopod, Clackamas Literary Review, and Best New Werewolf Tales. Each morning and most nights, he enjoys making blank pages darker. You can get to know him better by visiting his website at www.robboley.com.

Michael McGlade has had 37 short fiction stories appear in journals such as Spinetingler, Dark Lane Quarterly, Dead Harvest, and Found Fiction anthology by Pleasant Storm Entertainment. He holds a Master's degree in Creative Writing from Queen's University, Ireland. You can find out the latest news and views from him on McGladeWriting.com.

Glynn Barrass lives in the North of England and has been writing since late 2006. He has written over a hundred short stories and edits anthologies for Chaosium's Call of Cthulhu fiction line, also writing material for their flagship roleplaying game.

A busy father of four, John Hunt is a published author who started writing in late 2009. Most of his writing is done during his spare time.

He lives and works in the city of Guelph, Ontario, Canada with his wife, four children, a dog and two cats.

Amy Braun is a Canadian urban fantasy author who started writing when she was in middle school, and then never stopped. Her published work includes the short story Call From The Grave as part of Mocha Memoir Publishing Toil, Trouble, and Temptation series, and the novella Needfire, as well as the upcoming Charlatan Charade in Lost in the Witching Hour anthology from Breaking Fate Publishing, and Secret Suicide in Lincoln Crisler's dark ritual anthology. When Amy isn't writing, she's reading, watching movies, taking photos, and trying to overcome ice cream addiction and choco-holism. You can find Amy on the web by following her blog, literarybraun.blogspot.ca, following her on Twitter, @amybraunauthor, and liking her Facebook Page.

Born in Ipswich, Massachusetts, in the heart of H.P. Lovecraft country, David Longshore holds degrees from Amherst College and the Naval Postgraduate School. A veteran of the U.S. Navy, he is the author of the Encyclopedia of Hurricanes, Typhoons, and Cyclones, as well as other non-fiction works. Previous examples of his horror and dark fiction have appeared in The Horror Zine, SNM Horror, and numerous other anthologies.

Ellen is a freelance writer living in the Rocky Mountains with her husband and two demonic cats who wreak havoc and hell (the cats, not the husband).

Thomas has a variety of literary and pulp stories appearing in online and print publications and worked in various capacities for Fictional International and smaller journals. Most recently, he's served as Fiction Editor for Issue 6 of the Portland, Ore. literary journal The Grove Review and is proud of his membership in the Buntho SF Writers Group, which grew from an Ursula Le Guin class at PSU. Semi-reclusive and secretive, he'd prefer you not to know that he got his MFA in 2006, has lived and taught across the country, or that he often ends his sentences awkwardly.

DJ Tyrer is the person behind Atlantean Publishing and has been widely published in anthologies and magazines in the UK, USA and elsewhere, most recently in Steampunk Cthulhu (Chaosium), Tales of the Dark Arts (Hazardous Press), Cosmic Horror (Dark Hall Press) and Serial Killers Quattuor (JWK Fiction), as well as having a novella available on the Kindle, The Yellow House (Dynatox Ministries). DJ Tyrer's website is at djtyrer.blogspot.co.uk. The Atlantean Publishing website is at atlanteanpublishing.blogspot.co.uk.

Bryan Nickelberry is a life-long resident of the greater Seattle area, and has been soaking up the local weirdness for as long as he can remember. In addition he's made the collecting of stories and the search for nuggets of wisdom through philosophical discussion his hobby of choice. Bryan finally began committing some of his own stories to paper just a few years ago, and has been working with anyone and everyone he can, to polish his craft. Bryan hopes to continue improving his skills and publishing as he moves into the future.

Joseph Jude is a writer, filmmaker, and painter. He has a BFA from the University of the Arts in Philadelphia, and is winner of the Spokane Film Festival Drama Award for his short Lip Service. He also has had work appear in the Aphrodite Gallery, AngelCiti International Film and Music Market, published in magazines and E-zines such as Death's Head Grin, Nth Degree, Wink, Aphelion, Down in the Dirt, and Short-Story.Me! and in collections such as Strangely Funny, and Time After Time.

Mere Joyce holds a Bachelor's degree in English and a Master's in Library and Information Science. A librarian and a writer, she knows the importance a good book, and the lifelong impact the right story can have. When she's not reading, writing, or recommending books, she is usually found at home, hoping she'll never have to deal with the Ghostpocalypse. She can be found online at merejoyce.blogspot.com.

**Jonathan D. Nichols**   *A Really Big Kitchen Knife*

Jonathan D. Nichols is a writer of horror, fantasy, science fiction, and suspense. In 2008 he was stationed in South Korea during his time serving active duty in the United States Air Force. During this time separated from his family he discovered he had a love for writing. He completed his first novel in less than a year and has been writing ever since. He currently has three unpublished novels and a large number of short stories. His works have been featured in the online horror magazines Blood Moon Rising and Deadman's Tome, as well as stories in multiple anthologies, to include Death Awaits by Harren Press, Dark Light 3 by Crushing Hearts and Black Butterfly Publishing, Grave Robbers by James Ward Kirk Press, When Red Snow Melts by Horror Novel Reviews Publishing, and others. Jonathan works in process management at a leading aviation company and holds two Master's degrees from Embry Riddle Aeronautical University. When is not writing, he spends time with his wife and three children in Bedford, TX. More about Jonathan D. Nichols can be found on his website at www.jonathandnichols.com.

**Jake Elliot**   *Joy Ride*

Having left fabulous Las Vegas, fantasy author Jake Elliot and his wife chose the Pacific Northwest as a great place to have new adventures. Without kids, they are guardians over a sometimes hostile cat by the name of Samson. Jake's current published works include four short stories in print, one story under a different name, and two more shorts scheduled out before the end of 2014. Out of two novels originally published by Damnation Books, the first book is temporarily out of print but a second edition is expected out by early 2015. There is also one short film he has credits for co-writing. You can find him at jakeelliotfiction.com.

**Herika R. Raymer**   *Swallet*

Herika R. Raymer grew up consuming books - first by eating them, later by reading them. Her mother taught her the value of focus and hard work while her father encouraged her love literature and art; so she has been writing and doodling off and on for over 30 years. After much encouragement, Mrs. Raymer finally published a few short stories and has developed a taste for it. She continues to send submissions, sometimes with success, and currently has a collection of stories in the works. She was the Assistant Editor for a science fiction magazine and Lead Editor for a horror magazine, so has a healthy respect for proofing and editing. A participant of the voluntary writer/artist/musician cooperative known as Imagicopter, Herika R. Raymer is married with two children and a dog in West Tennessee, USA. herikarraymer.webs.com.

David Kernot is an Australian author living in the Mid North of South Australia and when he's not writing, he's riding his Harley Davidson through the wheat, wine, and wool farming lands. He writes contemporary fantasy, science fiction, and horror, and is the author of around fifty published short stories in a variety of anthologies, magazines, and eZines in Australia and the US (and now Canada), including the Year's Best Australian Fantasy and Horror, and Award Winning Australian Writing. More information can be found at www.davidkernot.com.

Steve is British, living in Entebbe, Uganda, with his wife and two kids, and currently works as a security contractor in the bad places of the world. As a freelance writer he has been published in several UK and African magazines, including BBC Wildlife magazine, Soldier magazine, Combat and Survival magazine, SCUBA magazine, Church of England Newspaper, African Travel Review magazine, Land Rover World magazine, Your Dog magazine, Travel News and Lifestyle magazine (Kenya), What's Happening in Dar (Tanzania), The Dar Guide (Tanzania), Daily Mail newspaper (UK), and others. He has four books published by Gypsy Shadow Publishing: Trips to the Dark Side, Beneath the Surface, Surviving your African Safaris, Worm.

Matthew Wilson, 31, has had over 150 appearances in such places as Horror Zine, Star*Line, Spellbound, Illumen, Apokrupha Press, Hazardous Press, Gaslight Press, Sorcerers Signal and many more. He is currently editing his first novel and can be contacted on twitter @matthew94544267.

Konstantine Paradias is a jeweler by profession and a writer by choice. His short stories have been published in Third FlatIron's Master Minds anthology, World War Cthulhuand the BATTLE ROYALE Slambook by Haikasoru. His short story, "How You Ruined Everything" has been included in Tangent Online's 2013 recommended SF reading list and his short story "The Grim" has been nominated for a Pushcart Prize.

M. Lori Motley strives to suspend reality whenever possible. Her goal is to transport the reader outside the box or at least into a new box: a spider-webbed casket, a crystal coffer with a long-lost key, a cardboard box full of snakes, or even the small, dark center of a troubled mind. Learn more at www.MLoriMotley.com.

D. Ceder lives and works in London. He has an anthology out on Amazon called *One in a Hundred and Other Stories*, all of which were published or broadcast in the mid-90s, 3 of which received Honorary Mentions in Ellen Datlow's and Terri Windling's Year's Best Fantasy and Horror 1994-5.

M.J. Pack is a marketing professional by day and a horror aficionado by night. After years of selling everything from moonshine to fine jewelry she's decided to pursue a lifelong love of writing and start selling terror instead. She lives in St. Louis with her husband, her dog, and her dreams of becoming the next Stephen King. You can follow her on Twitter under the username @megslice.

Robert has always wanted to write, but only recently started doing so. Raised on a diet of King, Donaldson and Lewis (which explains a lot) Robert has been published in Midnight Echo, Ill at Ease 2, Darker Minds anthology, the Big Book of New Short Horror, Pseudopod, the BFS Winter Journal and Doctor Who Magazine. When he isn't writing, Robert can be found wrestling with Triffids, err, weeds, in the garden.

Sean Douglas does not want to get to know you and isn't interested if you want to get to know him. Sean Douglas is interested in smoking cigarettes and drinking coffee and not sleeping. Sean Douglas does not have any distinguishing scars or marks and where he lives is none of your fucking business.

Kerry teaches English at a community college by evening and writes horrible things by night. He hates the sun. His parents started reading his stories and now he's out of the will. Kerry's work appears in several anthologies including DOA2 from Blood Bound Books and Attack of the B-Movie Monsters from Grinning Skull Press. His story *Smoke* pioneered The Wicked Library podcast's explicit content warning. KGSL blogs at HorrorTree.com and will launch his own website newworldhorror.com sometime before he dies.

Australian short story writer and poet, US resident, with work in many publications from the Christian Science Monitor, Weird Tales, Journal Of The American Medical Association to the likes of the South Carolina Review and Southern California Review.

# Future releases from April Moon Books

## Soon

**Short Sharp Shocks Vol. 2:**
**Stomping Grounds**
Multiple monsters cause mayhem and misery!

## 2015

**Flesh Like Smoke - edited by Brian M. Sammons**
Shapechangers galore from today's best authors!

**Short Sharp Shocks Vol. 3:**
**Ill-considered Expeditions**
Pith helmets at the ready for some unfriendly welcomes!

**Short Sharp Shocks Vol. 4:**
**Spawn of the Ripper**
Our homage to Hammer, bosoms and blood!

**Short Sharp Shocks Vol. 5:**
**The Stars at my Door**
Optimistic sci-fi to cleanse the palate!

# www.AprilMoonBooks.com